A day for greeting cards and intimate dinners...
A day for red roses and chocolate hearts...
A day for lovers.

For those in love, no day is grander than Valentine's Day. And nowhere is love celebrated better than in this romantic collection of four original short stories, written by four favorite Harlequin authors.

my
Valentine

1993

ABOUT THE AUTHORS

ANNE STUART—Called a "genre great" and "everybody's favorite author" by *Romantic Times,* Anne has received every major award, including Romance Writers of America's prestigious RITA award. She has written forty-five novels, nineteen of them for Harlequin American Romance. With her husband and two children, she lives in Vermont.

JUDITH ARNOLD—The author of twenty-five American Romance novels and three Superromance titles, Judith is a two-time *Romantic Times* Reviewers Choice winner and a two-time RITA finalist. The recipient of an NEA fellowship, she has also had several plays produced. She lives in Massachusetts, with her husband and two sons.

ANNE MCALLISTER—One of American Romance's best-loved authors, Anne has won a Silver Certificate, several Reviewers Choice awards, and has been a RITA finalist. Three of her novels have been Waldenbooks bestselling titles. Anne also writes for Harlequin Presents. She makes her home in the Midwest with her husband and family.

LINDA RANDALL WISDOM—With fourteen American Romance novels to her credit, Linda has won a large, loyal audience with her trademark sexy, humorous romances. She is a four-time Waldenbooks bestselling author and a three-time Reviewers Choice finalist. She and her husband call Southern California home.

my Valentine 1993

Anne Stuart
Judith Arnold
Anne McAllister
Linda Randall Wisdom

Harlequin Books

TORONTO • NEW YORK • LONDON
AMSTERDAM • PARIS • SYDNEY • HAMBURG
STOCKHOLM • ATHENS • TOKYO • MILAN

MY VALENTINE 1993

Copyright © 1993 by Harlequin Enterprises Limited

ISBN 0-373-83257-5

MY VALENTINE 1993 first printing February 1993

The publisher acknowledges the copyright holders of the individual works as follows:

SAINTS ALIVE
Copyright © 1993 by Anne Kristine Stuart Ohlrogge

CHOCOLATE KISSES
Copyright © 1993 by Barbara Keiler

SIMPLE CHARMS
Copyright © 1993 by Barbara Schenck

MS. SCROOGE MEETS CUPID
Copyright © 1993 by Linda Randall Wisdom

Contents

SAINTS ALIVE

Anne Stuart

A Note from Anne Stuart

Valentine's Day always seemed like one of those odd, made-up sort of holidays, like Mother's Day or Secretary's Day, something created by the greeting-card companies to make money. So I wondered how old Saint Valentine would feel about all the commercial fuss. And how he'd feel about being associated with a pagan creature like Cupid.

And then, of course, Cupid can either be a chubby little toddler with a bow and arrow, or he can be Eros, a golden, winged young man. Obviously I preferred the latter, and the two disparate celestials seemed a perfect starting point.

Like most romance writers, I have an absolutely splendid husband, and after seventeen years of marriage we still try to make every day a Valentine's Day. Richie is warm and sweet, unlike every single one of my heroes, but he's also smart and sexy. I hope you all end up with someone as wonderful.

Cheers,

Chapter One

"I TELL YOU, I'm sick and tired of it," the old man grumbled. "Saint Nicholas gets all the attention, all the credit. Even Saint Patrick gets respect, and what did he ever do to deserve it, apart from getting rid of a few snakes? A good exterminator could have done the same. At least their holidays have some tenuous connection with their lives. What in God's name does Valentine's Day have to do with a Roman priest from the third century?"

Eros glanced idly at his compatriot. Saint Valentine was a grumpy old cleric, ascetic, demanding and irascible, but he'd grown rather fond of the old man after all these centuries. "Well, they beheaded you," he pointed out. "Maybe it's because people lose their heads when they fall in love."

"I'm not amused."

"You seldom are," Eros said with a sigh, stretching out his perfect, white gold body and wrapping his wings around him lazily. "Let's face it, Christmas is a lot more fun for most people than Valentine's Day. They get presents, everyone's nice to everyone else. It's no wonder Saint Nicholas is so popular. All they get from Saint Valentine is a lot of trouble."

"The trouble comes from you," Val snapped. "If it was up to me the couples we bring together would live in perfect harmony."

"Perfect celibate harmony," Eros said. "It's not that I don't agree with you. Sex does cause a great many problems. But think what life would be without it."

"A great deal more peaceful," Val said with a disapproving sniff.

Eros sighed. It was a long-running battle, sixteen centuries old, to be exact, and neither of them gave an inch. "We were paired for a reason, old man. If love was of your definition, the human race would have died out in the third century along with you and your fellow martyrs."

"And if it was up to you, life would be one long bacchanal, lust and licentiousness running rampant in the streets."

"It does sound wonderful," Eros said wistfully. "I miss those days."

"I miss my life of peaceful contemplation," Val snapped.

"But think of all the good we do," Eros begged, knowing he was driving the old man to distraction. "Think of all the happy couples we bring together."

"Think of all the angry couples who split apart."

"Think of the weddings."

"Think of the divorces."

"Think of the lovemaking," Eros said with a lip-smacking sigh.

"Think of all the animal lust," Val returned.

"I am, old boy, I am," Eros said with a soulful smirk. "Let's face it, if it weren't for me there'd be no romance, no marriage, no..."

"No rutting," Val said. "If it weren't for me there'd be no romance, no soul sharing, no tenderness or peace."

"I won't deny you're important," Eros said, wishing he could deny just that. "But give me good old-fashioned sex any day of the week if you want to get a couple together.''

"Their souls need to mesh first."

"Souls, schmouls," Eros said. "I'll prove it to you."

"How do you intend to do that?" Val inquired in his stiffest voice. Eros wasn't fooled. Saint Valentine might be a righteous old buzzard but he had a definite weakness for games of chance.

"A simple wager. We take the two most incompatible people we can find and put them together."

"We've done that before. Too often, if you ask me. It's no longer much of a challenge."

"Yes, but this time we'll see what works. Your hearts and flowers romance. Or my straight old-fashioned sex," Eros said, stretching a wing out negligently.

"Sounds ridiculous."

"Afraid to lose, old man?"

"The day I'm afraid to lose to an overgrown fairy like you will be a cold day in . . . in purgatory," Val fumed.

"Fairy?" Eros was more amused than incensed. "I'll have you know that when I was allowed to roam earth I was always passionately heterosexual."

"I'm talking about your looks, not your proclivities. You must be six feet tall, your wings are almost as long, your golden curls are ridiculous, and you ought to wear more than that white diaper."

"I have a perfect body," Eros said. "Why not flaunt it? Stop trying to change the subject. Do we have a wager or don't we?"

"What are the terms?"

"We already know the woman—we've discussed it in the past. Shannon Donnelly is past due to meet her fate. We decide on the man, and set a date. I'll humor you—we get them together by Valentine's Day next."

"Get them together? With your abilities you could get anyone into bed. What I want is a commitment," Val said.

"Of course. True love, forever and ever and all that crap. Are you on?"

"What are the stakes?"

"If I win, you give me a free hand. If I lose, we'll have those poor mortals embarking on a new round of celibacy."

"Sounds excellent to me. I agree. We've got Shannon. A sweet girl, about as close to a virgin as one can get nowadays."

"Poor thing," Eros murmured.

"We simply have to find the right man . . ."

"The wrong man," Eros interrupted. "We're going to make this difficult, remember? A true test of our abilities. We've got Shannon Donnelly, age twenty-nine, warm, loyal, innocent, optimistic. With an unfortunate predilection for wimps."

"Gentle men are not wimps," Val fumed.

"The ones she picks are. It's because she's so damned maternal. She's been so busy mothering her sisters and brothers that she's only attracted to men she can mother. We need someone who doesn't need mothering."

"We need someone she can respect."

"We need someone she despises," Eros said. "And I know just the man." He chuckled to himself. "I can't wait to see the sparks fly."

OF ALL THE PLACES in the all the world, Shannon Donnelly's current destination had to rank on the top of the list of least favorite. For one thing, she never liked Manhattan. Everyone was mean and crazy, the taxis tried to run you down, and the sun never penetrated the canyoned streets.

And while she liked to think of herself as a friendly, tolerant sort of woman, there was one breed of human being that she found completely insupportable. She considered lawyers to be among nature's least necessary species, and the man whose offices she was about to visit had little to justify his existence.

She could have refused, of course. But in order to do that she would have had to explain to her sister Moira exactly why she didn't want to risk running into her ex-brother-in-law's divorce lawyer, and she wasn't prepared to do that.

It was understandable that Moira couldn't go herself. The swine had made her cry on the witness stand, and that crime alone had Shannon ready to commit cold-blooded murder. Anyway, the transfer of disputed property was better made between third parties. Harold Rasmussen's lawyer and Moira Donnelly Rasmussen's sister were the obvious choices.

Except that Shannon Donnelly hated Harold Rasmussen's lawyer, and for what she considered to be very good reasons, even if they bordered on the irrational. Patrick Lockwood was just the kind of man she heartily disliked, a cool, manipulating yuppie who was too damned good-looking for his own or anybody else's good. Particularly her own dubious peace of mind.

If only she'd known who he was, that first day in court. She'd come, of course, holding Moira's hand, moral support for the first divorce in the Donnelly family in recorded history. Moira had been red-eyed but adamant, and Shannon was there, loyal as ever. If she'd simply stayed by her side she would have known who that tall, dark-haired man in the impeccable Italian suit was.

But she'd gone outside in the chilly autumn air to sneak one of the cigarettes that she'd almost managed to give up entirely, and he was standing out there, jacket pulled up to shield him from the wind, leaning against the old brick courthouse, his own cigarette cupped in his hand.

He gave her that look that fellow smokers give each other, one of guilty camaraderie, and she'd smiled at him, shrugging. He was appallingly attractive, with the kind of tall, lean body that she always found devastating. So devastating that she made an effort to date short, burly men. He had longish dark hair that was shot with silver, a narrow, clever face with high cheekbones, satanic eyebrows and a wide, dangerously sexy mouth.

"Can't give up these damned things," he said, and his voice was cool and beguiling in the crisp autumn air.

"I've almost done it," she said, fascinated with the sound of his voice. He was probably ten or fifteen years older than she was, and she always dated younger men.

"Almost's not good enough."

"Thank God I'm not a perfectionist," Shannon said with a sigh.

"Unfortunately I am." He stared down at his cigarette with active dislike, his dark eyes narrowing. He must have felt her watching him, for he glanced up at her, and he smiled.

She smiled back, and then the expression froze on her face. As it did on his. There was no explanation for it. Just a sudden awareness, something shockingly physical, and she wanted to reach out and touch him, to brush her fingers against his dark, lean face.

His eyes were green. The color of the sea in winter, and he stared at her with silent intensity, and his hand lifted, catching a strand of her wind-tossed auburn hair, running it through his long, elegant fingers.

Supposedly hair has no nerve endings. She could feel his touch through every fiber of her being. She held herself completely still, the cigarette forgotten in her hand, staring up at him in a stupid, mindless trance, until one of the court officers had appeared at the door, breaking the magic of the moment, and he'd stepped away, dropping his cigarette and crushing it out beneath his custom leather shoes. He smiled at her, the rueful smile of a man who shared a vice and something more profound. "See you at the next cigarette break," he said in his deep, beguiling voice.

It had taken her a moment to gather her scattered self together. It was ridiculous, the result of too much stress, too much worrying about her sister and this sudden, completely unexpected divorce.

Things like this didn't happen. It was a fluke, an aberration. The next time she sneaked out here for a smoke she was going to be reasonable, matter-of-fact, and chatty. There'd be no magic. No ridiculous sense of destiny that a less sensible person might be tempted to term instant attraction and an utter fool would call love at first sight.

She slipped beside her sister in the courtroom, squeezing her hand. "What kept you?" Moira whispered, her blue eyes, a match to Shannon's own, searched her face.

"Falling in love," she said flippantly.

"I don't recommend it. It'll end badly," Moira said, casting a bitter glance across the room at her soon to be ex-husband. Shannon followed her gaze, and felt a sudden chill.

"Who's that with him?" she asked, her voice no more than a hushed whisper.

"The tall, gorgeous one? His lawyer, of course. Patrick Lockwood. My lawyer warned me he's ruthless."

He must have felt her gaze. He looked across the courtroom at her, his sea green eyes narrowed as Harold whispered something in his ear.

He shrugged, flashing her that heartbreaking smile, before turning back to Harold. Dismissing her, dismissing that momentary, magical attraction as he concentrated on the business at hand.

And Shannon decided to give up cigarettes for good.

That was probably part of her problem, she decided one month later as the express elevator took her up to the forty-seventh floor of Patrick Lockwood's law offices at a speed far too fast for her peace of mind. If she hadn't given up nicotine entirely she would have been far more rational about facing Patrick Lockwood once more.

Not that it had ever made any sense to her; her instant attraction to the good-looking bastard who had made her sister cry. The man who managed to convince a judge that Harold Rasmussen was the proper legal owner of the Valentine Puzzle. The intricately carved Chinese puzzle had been a Donnelly family heirloom since time immemorial, and only members of the family knew how to unlock its convoluted secrets. It was carved of teak, made of a dozen pieces that fit together with fiendish delicacy. The one time Shannon had dismantled it she'd developed a blinding headache trying to put it back together, before she finally gave up and handed it back to Moira in defeat.

And then Moira had been besotted enough to give it to Harold on their wedding day. But the first married of all the Donnelly offspring had always done that, and since divorce, or even mildly unhappy marriages were unheard of in the Donnelly family, there'd never been any problem.

And who would have thought Harold and Moira would break the tradition? If any two people had been made for each other, these two seemed to be. The separation and divorce had blown up out of nowhere, the two of them were clearly miserable, but no one was listening to reason.

And Harold was insisting on the Valentine Puzzle, a fact that made no sense whatsoever. He could have taken a lot more from Moira. Instead, he'd handed over the house they'd bought together, the BMW, even the contents of the joint checking account without a murmur. All he'd wanted was the Valentine Puzzle, and the response to such a modest demand was a foregone conclusion.

Shannon had her own theory, of course, one she was wise enough not to share. Moira assumed Harold had insisted on the Valentine Puzzle simply to hurt her. Shannon thought he might still harbor some hope.

Which was why Shannon was riding in an elevator to the heights of Manhattan, to deliver the family heirloom into the enemy's hands. Things were currently at a stalemate, the divorce five months from being final, and as far as she could see, only the Valentine Puzzle had any chance at resolving a situation that had gone too far.

She still wasn't pleased at being the sacrificial lamb. Only two things had managed to convince her that she could do it. One, her sister's misery. She hadn't stopped crying since the divorce, and if Shannon could do anything to cheer Moira up she would have done so gladly.

The other was the certainty that the cold-hearted turkey who'd mopped the floor with her sister's tender feelings wouldn't be bothered with something as menial as the handing over of disputed property. He was doubtless in some other courtroom, destroying some other poor woman's life.

God, she wanted a cigarette!

The offices of Lockwood and Gebbie were just as she'd imagined. Chrome and steel and glass, soulless and heartless and cold. As cold as Patrick Lockwood's heart, as sterile as his sense of humanity. The receptionist guarding the door was in keeping, a blue-haired dragon who surveyed her coolly.

Shannon Donnelly had her pride. She plastered a totally fake smile on her face. "Delivery for Mr. Lockwood."

The woman just stared. "One moment, I'll see if he's busy."

Shannon could feel her face pale. "I don't need to see him," she said hastily. "If you'll just sign for this I'll be on my way."

"This is the Rasmussen property, isn't it?" the woman said. "Mr. Lockwood wished to be informed."

"It's the Donnelly property," Shannon said, her temper getting in the way of her need to make a speedy exit. "Something that your employer managed to steal from my family..."

"He'll see you now," the woman interrupted her.

Shannon stopped midspate. "How do you know?" she asked naively.

"He said if a red-haired, angry Donnelly brought the property I should show her into his office immediately. He's waiting for you."

For a moment Shannon didn't move. "What if I don't want to see him?"

She'd managed to surprise the very proper secretary. "Why ever not?"

It wasn't a question Shannon could easily answer. She was still clutching the Valentine Puzzle, wrapped in its red velvet bag that was worn and shiny with age. Maybe there was a remote chance that Harold had changed his mind. Moira would have gladly handed over anything else in exchange for it.

"Where's his office?" Shannon asked resignedly.

PATRICK LOCKWOOD was forty-one years old, old enough to know better. He prided himself on his realistic view of life, of people and the trouble they could get into, and his specialty of divorces suited his cynical nature perfectly. Perhaps if he'd gone into corporate law he might not be completely burned out.

Perhaps not. His profession had been very good to him. He'd made an obscene amount of money in a relatively short period of time, and the price hadn't been that high. He'd never had illusions to lose. It was his job to help couples dissolve their mistaken unions as equitably as possible, and he was damned good at it. He'd just gotten bored.

He didn't know when it started, his need to get out. Long before he'd had that strange encounter with Moira Rasmussen's sister outside the Queens County Courthouse. She didn't have anything to do with it— there was just something about her that had disturbed him, added to his growing feeling of discontent.

He'd taken it out on Harold Rasmussen's wife, unfortunately. He didn't usually feel guilty about his job, but Moira Rasmussen's tear-filled eyes could make a saint feel guilty.

He was far from a saint. And it wasn't guilt that was eating away at him, and it wasn't Moira Donnelly Rasmussen. It was her sister, Shannon.

He hadn't known for certain that she'd be the one who'd deliver the stupid box that Rasmussen had insisted on, but he'd thought the chances fairly good. Shannon Donnelly was at her sister's side throughout the brief hearing, flashing furious looks at him, patting her sister's hand, being maternal and devoted and fiercely loyal. According to Rasmussen, Shannon would do anything for anybody, and spent a great deal of her energies taking care of everybody else.

Harold hadn't even known he was being grilled. At this point Patrick knew everything Harold knew about Shannon, including her childhood scrapes, her respectable education, and her romantic history, which seemed to consist of dorks as far as Harold was concerned. Rasmussen had always liked his sister-in-law. And Shannon had obviously been fond of him as well. All in all, a happy extended family.

Patrick had never been quite sure why Harold and Moira were divorcing, and he hadn't bothered to find out. As far as he was concerned, marriages were doomed to end in either divorce or stalemate, and it was none of his business what prompted it. He couldn't quite rid himself of the suspicion that Harold was still in love with his wife. Oddly enough, Moira Rasmussen still seemed enamored of Harold. It was typical of the crazy state of modern marriages, and none of his concern.

Hester opened the door, giving him a knowing glance, and ushered Shannon Donnelly into his office. He rose, wondering why he was feeling nervous. Why he wanted to see a woman who despised him with all her passionate young heart. Why he'd gone to all this trouble.

She strode into the room, all long arms and legs and coltish grace. She looked younger than the twenty-nine years he knew her to be, innocent in a way he'd never been. Her long auburn hair was pulled away from her oval face, her blue eyes were cold and angry. She had a soft mouth. He'd been drawn to that mouth the first time he'd seen her, wondering what it would taste like. It had been the first time he'd been troubled by an erotic fantasy in what seemed like years. He'd been troubled ever since.

If he'd had any doubts about whether she hated him or not, the rage in her wonderful blue eyes dispelled them. In more than ten years of handling divorces he'd had more than his share of women hating him. He couldn't understand why he'd find her dislike so disturbing. And so stimulating.

"Miss Donnelly," he said, crossing the room to her.

She backed away from him, against the door that Hester had been discreet enough to close, and he realized she was more than angry, more than uncomfortable in his presence. She was afraid of him.

It was an odd realization for him. She had that stupid talisman clutched to her chest, and he wondered if he took it from her hands whether he might manage to touch her breasts.

Lord, what an adolescent fantasy! It was a good thing he was getting out of New York. If he was ten years older he'd be thinking his midlife crisis was getting to unmanageable proportions.

"Harold didn't change his mind?" she asked abruptly, and the sound of her husky voice was like a jolt to his nervous system. He hadn't heard her speak since those stolen minutes outside the courthouse, had only seen her glare at him, but he remembered the sound. The unmistakable appeal of that sexy, throaty quality. He wanted to put his mouth against her skin, to feel her voice vibrate against his lips. He controlled himself with an effort.

"About the Valentine Puzzle? Not likely. It was the only thing he insisted on. I told him he could get a lot more..."

"I'm sure you did," she said bitterly.

"Listen, your sister made out like a bandit," he said. "I could have gotten half of everything she owned. This is a community property state, and I'm very good at what I do. She's lucky she still has everything."

"She would have traded anything for the Valentine Puzzle," Shannon shot back, her nervousness vanishing.

"I can't imagine why. The piece doesn't have any verified value. It seems purely sentimental . . ."

"And that's why Harold wanted it. Though I wouldn't have thought he'd be the type for a cheap shot like that. It must have been your idea."

"My idea? Don't be ridiculous, Miss Donnelly. I don't give a damn what my clients want, as long as I get my fees."

"Which are substantial, no doubt."

"Very substantial," he agreed. "You know, I'm not really a bad guy. I was just doing my job."

"Isn't that what they said in Nazi Germany?"

He laughed. "Your temper matches your hair."

"Don't give me that," she shot back. "I can't stand stupid clichés like redheads being bad-tempered."

"Pardon me. You do have red hair and a bad temper."

"I have auburn hair and a righteous indignation. You broke my sister's heart, Mr. Lockwood."

"If anyone broke your sister's heart, which I take leave to doubt, it was Harold Rasmussen," he pointed out calmly.

"You don't think her heart was broken?" Shannon demanded in a dangerous voice.

"I don't think hearts ever get broken. We don't need to argue about it. Harold and Moira Rasmussen's troubles have been resolved."

"Fat lot you know," Shannon muttered.

"Have lunch with me."

She stared at him in disbelief. "What?"

"I asked you to have lunch with me," he said with deceptive calm.

"Why?"

He smiled wryly. "Damned if I know. Maybe I eat better when someone's glaring at me." He took the velvet bag from her, careful not to touch her breasts, and she let it go. The glare had faded in her surprise, and he wondered why she hadn't noticed the attraction between them. Or maybe she'd been too busy fighting it to notice.

"Well, eating with the enemy destroys my appetite," she said flatly.

"What about sleeping with the enemy?" He hadn't meant to say it, the words shocking him almost as much as they shocked her, but her reaction was almost worth it. Her soft mouth was open with shock, her blue eyes wide.

"You have the absolute gall to ask me to go to bed with you?" she gasped. "You don't even know me."

He smiled wryly. "I was planning to work my way around to it in a more leisurely manner, but you don't look like you're going to give me the chance to be subtle."

"I don't like you, Mr. Lockwood. I think you're cold and manipulative and wicked, and I can't imagine why you'd like me."

"I don't like you," he said frankly. "What's liking got to do with it? I happen to be profoundly attracted to you, and while I don't pretend to understand why, I know myself well enough to know that I want to go to bed with you. Since you're obviously about to bolt, I just thought I'd mention it."

"You know what they call one hundred lawyers at the bottom of the sea?" she asked in a dangerous voice.

"I expect you're going to tell me," he said wearily.

"They call it a good beginning. Let's hope you make the next round. Goodbye, Mr. Lockwood." She wheeled around, starting for the door, when he put out his hand to stop her.

She froze, he froze. The feel of her skin beneath his hand was hot, pulsing with life. She stared up at him, and her blue eyes were huge and luminous, her soft mouth parted in unwilling astonishment.

In retrospect he never knew what made him do it. He leaned forward and kissed her, putting his mouth against hers, putting his body against hers, pressing her up against the closed door as his arms cradled her head.

He'd never expected her to kiss him back. He'd been right about her mouth, it was soft, and damp, and the sweetest thing he'd ever tasted in a long, jaded life. Her arms slid around his waist, and her body welcomed his, and he wondered for one brief, mad moment whether he could reach behind her and lock the door, whether he could draw her down onto the carpet and strip her clothes off before she realized she was consorting with the enemy.

And then he stopped thinking about sex, too busy with the wonder of her mouth. He deepened the kiss, slanting his lips over hers, his tongue thrusting, and he heard her moan, a quiet little sound of surrender and despair.

The despair stopped him. He lifted his head to stare down at her, breathing heavily, wondering if she could feel how hard he was, knowing there was no way she could miss it.

"Damn," he said, his voice shaken.

Her eyes were closed, her face was pale, shaken. At the sound of his voice her eyes flew open, and she stared up at him in shock and belated fury. "Damn *you*," she said distinctly.

She shoved him away from her, and he was too astonished by what had just happened to hold on. A moment later she was gone, slamming the glass door behind her, obviously hoping it would break.

The offices of Lockwood and Gebbie were made of sterner stuff than that. He watched her go with mixed emotions. He didn't know where that kiss had come from. He wasn't an impulsive man, or one prey to his hormones. He'd half hoped to scare her off. There was no room in his life, in his plans, for a redheaded fury like Shannon Donnelly. He'd known it, even though he couldn't resist trying. She'd remember him with fury.

And he'd remember her, if he had to, as the one who got away. And made his life a great deal more comfortable by doing so.

Not that he felt particularly comfortable at the moment. He moved back to his desk, dumping the Valentine Puzzle on the glass top, his fingers lingering for a moment on the soft, worn velvet. Maybe if he'd met Shannon Donnelly fifteen years ago... But she would have been a teenager back then, and he was already a cynic. Life wasn't a question of meeting the right person at the right time. He'd seen enough to know that.

But life could be made a great deal more pleasant. He'd never been involved with someone like Shannon, someone fierce and loyal and surprisingly innocent. He'd gone for women as cynical and jaded as he was.

But he found himself remembering the taste of her, the shock of her response. The sweetness of her. And he thanked God he was getting out in time. Before he started believing in fairy tales.

Chapter Two

"WELL, YOU screwed that one up," Eros said.

"I don't like your choice of language," Val said primly. "Besides, you're the one who screwed up. If you hadn't tossed in all that heavy breathing they might have found they like each other."

"Like each other? He made her sister cry in divorce court. He took the one thing that mattered more than money to the Donnelly family. She's never going to like him. Not at this point, anyway."

"If he hadn't started putting moves on her..."

"'Putting moves on her'?" Eros echoed, much amused. "I think you've been around me too long, old man."

"That's for certain. This collaboration wore thin after the fourth century."

"Besides, if it weren't for the sexual tension there'd be nothing at all between them. Shannon would hate Patrick, Patrick would forget about her existence. It's the driving animal lust that's keeping this relationship going."

"It's not a relationship, it's one of the seven deadly sins."

"Give me a break, Val. It'll be sanctified by marriage, sooner or later. They'll have lots of children and live happily ever after."

"If you say so," Val said grumpily. "I'm beginning to feel this one is beyond either of us."

"Listen, have we ever been known to fail once we set our considerable talents to the task? It's the poor humans who fall in love without our help that get into trouble, get divorced.''

"Explain Harold and Moira Rasmussen then. We were responsible for them," Val said sternly.

Eros was abashed. "I still don't understand that one. They should have lived happily ever after."

"Maybe we've lost our touch."

"Speak for yourself, Val," Eros said, putting his long, elegant fingers together in a contemplative gesture. "I'm merely getting started. We'll simply have to up the ante. Got any ideas?"

Saint Valentine grimaced. "I suppose we could use the puzzle again. It worked once in getting the two of them together."

"A brilliant tactic on your part, I grant you that," Eros said generously. "I would have preferred if it were an erotic painting or something, but the puzzle was inspired. What did you have in mind?"

Valentine relaxed his customarily stiff posture. "Well, I rather thought we might see what we can do about her sister and brother-in-law while we're at it. After all, their union's already been sanctified . . ."

"Unsanctified, you mean. What do you think Patrick Lockwood was doing?"

"I don't pay any heed to that sort of thing. What God has joined together no man may put asunder," Saint Valentine said in a voice that brooked no opposition. "I intend to see both the Donnelly sisters happily married."

Eros scratched himself lazily beneath his left wing. "I just want to see them happy."

"You're getting sentimental in your old age."

"Not me," Eros protested. "Just voyeuristic."

"That's nothing new."

"Val, old friend, after all these years together I don't think we're going to be in for many surprises. And I know beneath your cranky exterior you have a heart of gold, no matter how much you try to deny it." Eros leaned back and adjusted his linen loincloth.

"Harrumph," Val said, trying not to look pleased. "I still don't think you have any business watching."

"Just enough to make sure things are going all right," Eros said in a wheedling tone.

"Don't try to convince me your motives are pure," Val said. "You and purity have only a passing acquaintance."

"True," Eros agreed. "But at least I'm easily entertained."

"I HAVE TO WHAT?" Shannon screeched. It was several months later, and Moira had come to her sister's apartment in the little town outside of Boston that had been home for the multitude of Donnellys since time immemorial. Moira had moved back in with her parents since the divorce, her protective brothers still hovered around, and Shannon had done her best to take care of everyone. This time, however, she had reached her limit.

Moira's red-rimmed eyes squinted in sudden pain. "You have to go pick up the Valentine Puzzle for me," she repeated.

"I won't do it," she said flatly. "Wild horses couldn't drag me there."

"Don't be stubborn, Shannon. If...Harold's willing to give it up we can't refuse to accept it. I suppose he's found someone new," Moira said in a sad little voice. "He no longer needs to hold on to the box."

Shannon's customary guilt swamped her at the sound of her sister's forlorn voice, but she fought it. "Harold is a fool," she said, "and so are you, for not fighting for your marriage."

"So you've told me," Moira said. "It just got out of hand, and neither of us was willing to bend. Let that be a lesson to you. Not that you'll run into any problem like that. The men you choose wouldn't dare stand up to you."

"Will you cut it out? Just because I'm not interested in macho bullies . . ."

"Harold isn't a macho bully!" Moira shot back, instantly defensive.

"So why did you divorce him?"

"Let's not argue about it. Do you want the Valentine Puzzle or not? Harold's willing to give it back—we'd be foolish to let anything get in our way."

"Why should I care one way or the other?" Shannon said, still fighting it. "It's yours—you're the first one married. Give it to your next husband."

"Shannon!" Moira protested. "I can't ever imagine marrying again. The first Donnelly to fail in memory—I wouldn't be likely to try again. The Valentine Puzzle will be yours when you marry."

"What makes you think I'll be the next one to marry? Jamie and Sally seem ready to take the step, and Sean's not far behind."

"What about that wimp you were seeing? I was sure I was going to have to stand up for you while you ruin your life like I ruined mine."

"Ted and I aren't seeing each other any more," Shannon said in a repressive voice. "Besides, you didn't ruin your life by marrying, you ruined it by divorcing."

Moira ignored the provocation. "Since when did you and Ted break up?"

"Since your divorce hearing." The words were out before Shannon could think twice.

"Too much for you," Moira said, clearly obsessed by the dissolution of her marriage.

"You could say so," Shannon said, thinking of Patrick Lockwood. For some reason Ted's gentle whine had grated on her nerves. In the three months since Moira's divorce she hadn't been interested in anyone. Anyone but the occasional, disturbing dreams about Patrick Lockwood and his kiss. "If you want the Valentine Puzzle why don't you go get it?"

"I couldn't face that lawyer. Not after what he did to me in court."

"Why doesn't Harold send it to you?"

"It's too important to trust to the mail, and you know it. It has to go through his lawyer anyway—there are releases to be signed and stuff like that."

"Releases you'd have to sign...." Shannon tried one more time.

"You're my representative. Please, Shannon. It's the last thing I'll ever ask of you."

Not for one moment did Shannon believe that. She was the oldest of her motley crew of six siblings, and she'd taken care of them most of her life. They'd come to depend on her too much, she knew, and that was partly her fault. There were times when she wanted to run away to an island, away from family and telephones and demands.

But life didn't offer such peaceful answers to her deep-seated longings. "All right," she said wearily. "I'll do it. But I don't like it. If it weren't for the Valentine Puzzle..."

Moira threw her arms around Shannon's body. "I knew I could count on you. Once we get the box back I can finally put Harold out of my life and get on with things."

"Maybe," Shannon said wryly. "I'm not sure if it's going to be that easy. I won't be able to leave for New York for a couple of days. I have to finish up at the Camerons and then . . ."

"Uh, Shannon," Moira said, and her nervousness simply increased Shannon's sense of impending disaster. "Patrick Lockwood's not in New York."

"His offices must still be there."

"He's dissolved his partnership."

"In two months?" Shannon said in patent disbelief.

"Apparently it had been in the works for awhile. The good news is that he's closer to us."

"That might be good news for you—I'm not sure the state of Massachusetts is improved any," Shannon said wryly.

"He's not here in Massachusetts. He's living on the coast of Maine. It shouldn't be more than a four- or five-hour drive. You could go this weekend."

Shannon shut her eyes briefly. "Couldn't someone else go?" she asked faintly, knowing the answer already.

"There's no one else I trust. Besides, you're the only one who's self-employed right now, who can take the time off."

"Lucky me," Shannon said faintly. "Maybe I'll get a job at Burger King."

"I knew I could count on you, Shannon," Moira said, her misty blue eyes never far from tears. "At least you don't have a problem with Patrick Lockwood. My lawyer actually said he was an awfully nice guy, but you know the boys. If I sent one of them they'd probably beat the hell out of Lockwood."

"And we certainly couldn't have that," Shannon said, ignoring her own bloodthirsty urges. "You're right, Moira. I have no problem with him. No problem at all."

AND SO three days later Shannon found herself driving up the coast of Maine, the chilly February sun bright overhead, a sense of something in her heart that she told herself was dread and felt dangerously like anticipation. Maybe Moira was right. There needed to be a sense of closure for Moira and Harold and their ill-fated marriage.

And maybe for Shannon. She needed to face Patrick Lockwood and see that he was just a man, after all. An attractive man, admittedly, but everything she despised in men. Overbearing, sure of himself, arrogant, and too damned sexy. Besides, she hated lawyers.

That kiss in his office had been a fluke, a strange aberration on both their parts. She didn't make the mistake of thinking he made a habit of kissing strange women. He wouldn't need to.

It had been a whim, a spur of the moment urge, and she'd been surprised enough and needy enough to respond, and it was no wonder that such uncharacteristic behavior on her part would haunt her. Once she saw him again, realized he was simply an arrogant, attractive man, she'd put things in perspective.

She should have known things wouldn't be that easy. Barkhaven, Maine wasn't exactly a small coastal town. It was on the coast, all right. Its own coast.

Patrick Lockwood had the unmitigated gall to live on his own private island, one devoid of telephone service or public transport.

I've come this far, she thought furiously. *I'm not about to give up now, no matter how much I want to. I've got to find a way to get out to his island and get the Valentine Puzzle, then the Donnellys will never have to think about either Patrick Lockwood or Harold Rasmussen again.*

In the end, it was astonishingly easy. Almost suspiciously so, but Shannon wasn't the suspicious type. "Hear you're needing a ride out to Barkhaven." The weather-beaten man sidled up to her as she stood on the dock, looking out over the dark green ocean. "M'name's Fred Rogers. I'm headed out that way, myself. I could drop you off, pick you up a couple of hours later on my way back, if you've a mind to."

She didn't hesitate. "That would be wonderful," she said, not sure if she believed it. She didn't bother questioning his miraculous appearance, she simply accepted it. Fate had conspired to get her out to Patrick Lockwood's island, and she'd be foolish to fight it. Within an hour they were under way, Shannon freezing to death in her down parka as they rode the increasingly choppy seas into the horizon.

"Lockwood doesn't get many visitors," Fred said, eyeing her curiously. "He know you're coming?"

"He hasn't been here that long to get visitors, has he?"

"He's been here close to ten years. Oh, not full-time, like recent, but he's pretty well-known around these parts. Minds his own business, does his job. People like him."

"It must be hard to be a lawyer when you don't have a telephone," Shannon said.

"He ain't a lawyer up here, missy," Fred said.

"Then what does he do for a living?"

"This and that. Why don't you ask him?"

"This isn't going to be a social visit," Shannon said primly. "I simply need to pick up something and then I'll be on my way. As a matter of fact, if you'd consider waiting for me it won't take but a minute."

Fred shook his head. "I've got to make it out to Moncouth Island and back before sunset. It's a fine day, but February's a nasty month, and I don't like to take chances. Besides, you can sit on the dock at Barkhaven, enjoy a bit of sunshine. Better than being cooped up on this old boat."

She much preferred the old boat to the thought of Patrick Lockwood's company, but she was too stubborn to admit it. "I'll be waiting for you."

Barkhaven Island was small, compact and hilly, with dark green conifers dotting the landscape, trailing down to the gray-green sea. She could see the house in the distance as Fred pulled the boat alongside the dock—it looked like an old summer cottage from a more gracious time. There were various barns and outbuildings, including a large hangarlike structure at the edge of the water. "Not expecting you, is he?" Fred said with a bark of a laugh. "You'll probably find him at the boathouse."

"That barnlike thing is a boathouse?" Shannon said. "What does he have in there, ocean liners?"

"You might say so. I'll be back in a couple of hours. Less, if the weather holds." He glanced up at the bright blue sky.

Sudden panic sluiced through Shannon. "There's not supposed to be any storm, is there?"

"Not according to the weather report. February's a tricky month, though. It pays to keep your eyes peeled."

She stood on the dock, shivering in her old jeans and down parka, and watched the sturdy little boat chug away from the island. She was foolish to feel nervous—there wasn't a sign of a cloud in the sky, and she knew as well as Fred did that the weather was supposed to stay clear and cool. She still couldn't rid herself of a feeling of impending doom.

It was the thought of facing Patrick Lockwood again that had got her down, she told herself. All that arrogant, elegant charm had a demoralizing effect on her, one she needed all her strength to fight.

I'm not going to react to him again. I need to confront him once more, and know that he is just a man, a little more ruthless, a little more gorgeous than the men she usually spent time with, but a human being nonetheless.

And the sooner she faced him, the better.

PATRICK LOCKWOOD was in an officially foul mood. That was one of the things he liked best about his retirement and new career—he could be as sour-tempered as he wanted to and no one noticed. Mainly because there was no one around. After forty-one years of living surrounded by an absolute mass of humanity, the peace and quiet of Barkhaven Island was a balm to his soul.

As the weeks had passed the quiet had sometimes become an irritant, but he wouldn't have traded it for all the pleasures of Manhattan. He took a certain pleasure in his hermitlike existence, and he had no intention of letting anyone intrude on it.

If he needed companionship he'd sail over to the mainland and spend some time with Fred Rogers and his cronies. If he needed something a little more physically satisfying he could always fly back to New York for a visit with Morgana. They'd parted on good terms, a few months before he'd left New York, and he knew perfectly well she'd welcome him back with no strings attached. She was as wary of commitment as he was, and they'd been perfectly suited.

But his relationship with Morgana had felt as hollow as the other pleasures of his existence. And he didn't think he'd go back, even to scratch a temporary itch.

He hunkered down, staring at the hull of the cabin cruiser. It was a real beauty—built for an industrialist in the early nineteen thirties, and even decades of neglect hadn't rotted the beautiful teak. The hull, however, needed to be completely redone, and the interior was a mess. He still hadn't found anyone capable of doing the inside work, and he hadn't made much of an effort. He preferred his boat salvage operation to be a one-man deal for as long as possible. Even knowing his own limitations, he wasn't quite ready to do anything about it.

Besides, at the prices he charged the clients who owned such venerable beauties, he could afford to be choosy. The owner of the boat he was working on was the CEO of a large drug company. Patrick had handled his second and third divorces for him, and Charlie would forever be in his debt. He could wait.

He heard the noise in the back of his brain, and he told himself he had to be imagining it. No one would be on his island, his private domain, opening the door to his boathouse-workshop. Not if they valued their skin.

He looked up, and saw her silhouetted in the sunlight streaming through the door. Tall, coltish, long legs encased in jeans, a parka disguising her shape. In the shadows he couldn't see her red hair, but he knew who she was, knew with a sudden sense of absolute doom. Nemesis, come to disrupt the even tenor of his wonderful solitude.

She stepped inside, closing the door behind her, closing the cold behind her, and squinted into the shadowy interior. "Excuse me?" she asked, in that husky, sexy voice he'd tried so hard to forget. "I'm looking for Patrick Lockwood. Do you have any idea where I might find him?"

He rose slowly, careful to keep his expression blank, as mixed emotions warred for control. He didn't want her there. She was part of his old life, a temporary attraction that would have gotten badly out of hand if he'd had the chance to pursue it.

On the other hand, she was staring at him with a complete lack of recognition, and he could read the tension in her body, knowing she'd steeled herself to face her enemy and not recognizing him when she came face-to-face with him.

Not that he could blame her. He knew perfectly well what she was seeing out of those magnificent blue eyes of hers, so like her sister Moira's, and yet so different, so much deeper, full of anger and passion and fierce loyalty.

She'd see a man who was six foot two, of course, but not much else was the same. He was wearing ancient jeans, ripped at the knees. An old denim shirt, a shearling-lined suede vest, sneakers that had no pretensions to running shoes, and a pair of leather work gloves were a far cry from his Armani suits.

She wouldn't recognize the face, either. He hadn't shaved in several days, and his hair had grown so long he ended up tying it back. It was more heavily streaked with gray now, a fact that afforded him some amusement. The woman looking at him so fixedly would think she was seeing the elegant Patrick Lockwood's handyman.

He'd underestimated her. As he stepped closer into the light from the overhead window, she drew in her breath. "Oh," she said flatly. "I didn't know it was you."

"What the hell are you doing here?" He'd meant to sound unwelcoming. He didn't want her disturbing the tranquility of his new life. He didn't want to see her, hear her voice, smell the faint trace of flowery scent that warred with the rich smell of the sea.

"If you think I want to be here you're crazy," she shot back.

"If you didn't want to be here you wouldn't be," he pointed out. "I don't recall inviting you."

"I came for the Valentine Puzzle."

"You mean that stupid box? Why should I have it?" he said, not moving. He didn't want to get any closer to her. It was an unfortunate, unavoidable fact that he still wanted her, wanted her quite badly, and his only defense was to keep his distance.

"What do you mean, why should you have it? You're Harold's lawyer. In case you've forgotten, I brought it to you."

"I haven't forgotten a thing."

She blinked at the sound of his voice, and she took her own step backward, away from him. "Harold's changed his mind, said we could come fetch the box, after all. Moira asked me to do it . . ."

"And, of course, you said yes. You know, Miss Donnelly, if you were a little less ready to bail your sister out she might have made a go of her marriage."

He'd managed to enrage her, something he'd been trying to do. "I didn't come all this way for amateur psychology," she snapped. "Just the Valentine Puzzle."

"Haven't got it," he said flatly. "By the way, how did you manage to get out here? I can't see you rowing all the way. I'd like to know who I have to thank for having my privacy breached."

"I wouldn't have breached your damned privacy if you had a telephone."

"Too far out."

"There are such things as cellular phones."

"Not for me. I suppose it was old Fred," he said. "He never could resist a damsel in distress. Is he waiting for you?"

"He's stopping for me on his way back."

Patrick swore then, in pungent, colorful terms. "He must have gone to Moncouth. I suppose I'm stuck with you for the next hour or so."

"You needn't suppose any such thing. I'll wait for him on the dock."

"Lady," he said wearily, "it's about fifteen degrees out there. Add to that a breeze off the ocean, and you've got a windchill factor of about forty below zero. I don't want him picking up a frozen corpse."

She was cold already, he could see that in the faint, bloodless color of her lips, in the stray shivers that racked her body. And no wonder—Fred's boat was serviceable but not equipped with much in the way of comfort, and the stubborn woman probably stayed out on deck, getting blasted by the wind all the way out here. ''I'll get you some coffee,'' he said testily.

''I'd rather die.''

''You might. You look like you're on the verge of pneumonia already,'' he said, wheeling away from her and heading for the workbench and his thermos, stripping off his leather workgloves as he went. ''There's a wood stove over here. If it won't offend your dignity too much to warm yourself.''

''I'm not cold,'' she said, her voice shivering.

''Like hell.'' He poured coffee in the cleanest mug he had, turned and waited for her approach. ''You're stuck here for at least another hour, Miss Donnelly. You might as well make the best of it.''

She was a reasonable woman. She stalked across the workshop, took the mug of coffee from his hand, and settled herself by the wood stove. ''I don't suppose you know where the Valentine Puzzle is?'' she said in a carefully neutral voice.

''I can think of two places. One, Rasmussen might have sent it to my ex-partner. Gebbie is taking care of my old clients—he might have it. But I don't think so.''

''What's the other place?''

''I think Rasmussen has it himself. I think he's expecting Moira to come get it, and he's hoping for a reconciliation.'' He poured himself some coffee into the thermos top, wishing to hell he hadn't given up cigarettes. Wondering if Shannon still smoked. He would have killed for a cigarette right then.

''What makes you think that? I know for certain that Moira didn't want this divorce.''

Patrick shrugged. "As far as I could tell, Rasmussen didn't want it, either."

Shannon drew in her breath with a shocked sound. "Didn't you do anything about it?" she demanded. "Suggest they could work it out, maybe with counseling?"

"My dear Miss Donnelly, that was none of my concern. I made a great deal of money handling divorces. It was hardly in my best interests to arrange tender reconciliations."

"Now I recognize you," she said, her voice sharp with dislike. "You may be wearing different clothes, but you've still got the same cruddy soul."

He lifted the thermos cup in a mocking toast. "Feel free to comment on the state of my soul any time," he offered. "I'm not exactly worried about eternity."

"You probably don't believe in it."

"You mean life after death? No. But then, I don't believe in much at all. I'm a very cynical man, Miss Donnelly. I've found I survive best believing in no one and nothing but myself."

"An interesting faith. I'm glad you feel you're worthy of it."

"I know my limitations." He set the coffee down, fighting the treacherous feeling that was flooding him. Damn, but he was feeling more alive than he had in the two months he'd been immured on the island. More alive than he'd had in years and years, with the exception of a few brief moments in his office, when he'd held this ridiculous woman in his arms. "And I know my strengths," he added.

"I'm sure you do. Do you feel any guilt about it? About the lives you destroy?"

"I don't destroy lives. People take care of that for themselves. I do my best to keep things neat and impersonal."

"Life isn't neat and impersonal," she shot back, outraged. "It's messy and passionate and nothing but trouble."

"Are we talking about life?" he inquired coolly. "Or what some people define as love?"

"I suppose you don't believe in that, either."

"Not particularly." The cavernous workshop had grown darker, eerily so, and a sudden foreboding filled him. "But you didn't come all the way out here to listen to my theories on the meaning of life."

"I certainly didn't. But now that you've mentioned it, why don't you enlighten me? What do you consider the meaning of life?"

"There is none," he said, crossing the workshop to look out the high window, out to sea. "Hell and damnation," he said in a vicious voice.

Shannon slid off the stool, coming up behind him, too close, disturbingly close. "What's wrong?" she demanded, rising on her toes to peer out the window. "Oh, no," she moaned. "Where did that come from?"

That was nothing less than a blizzard. The bright blue sky had turned black, the snow was coming down at a furious, pelting rate, and the wind was whipping it against the windows. "From a cruel and malicious fate," he said bitterly. "Fred's not going to make it back here any time soon."

"Will he be all right?" she asked anxiously, more concerned for a stranger than her own discomfort. That was one of the things he found most disturbing about her.

"Fred could sail through anything. However, he's smart enough not to. He'll hole up at Moncouth until this passes."

"How long will it take?" There was no mistaking the dread in her voice. His was just as unhappy.

"I have no idea. Maybe hours," he said. "More likely a day or two."

"And I'm stuck here?" Her voice rose to a panicked, undignified shriek.

He looked down at her. She was too close to him, her eyes wide with horror, her soft mouth trembling.

"We're stuck with each other," he drawled. "Welcome to Barkhaven Island, Miss Donnelly."

"Welcome to my nightmare," she countered.

"Exactly," he said. And he wondered how he was going to resist her. And if he was even going to try.

Chapter Three

"A CRUEL AND malicious fate?" Saint Valentine echoed. "I like that! Here I am, doing my best to give that cynical malcontent a purpose in life, and he calls me names."

"He wasn't pleased with the snowstorm," Eros said. "Personally, I thought it was a bit heavy-handed myself. You could have simply screwed up the old man's boat, stranded him on that other island."

"But then Lockwood would probably bundle Shannon up and sail her back to the mainland himself. He'd probably swim with her there if he had to, he's that desperate to get rid of her. I can't quite understand why. I thought she was the one who didn't like him, not vice versa."

"Val, Val," Eros chided. "Haven't you learned much about human nature by now? Patrick Lockwood is a hard case. He doesn't want to fall in love, and he's smart enough to know that in Shannon Donelly he's met his comeuppance. His only defense is to try to get rid of her. Otherwise he's going to have to come to the realization that all his carefully conceived cynicism is wrong. That there is such a thing as true love, and happy ever after."

"Do my ears deceive me?" Valentine said. "I thought you were more concerned with sex."

"First things first," Eros replied. "We just differ about our priorities. We both want the same thing. I think great sex is the path to true love. You think true love is the path to great sex. It's all a matter of attitude."

"I'm not interested in great sex," Val said haughtily.

"I know you aren't, but what about our couples? You wouldn't really want to condemn them to a life of celibacy, would you?"

"They'd be a lot more peaceful."

"Peace isn't everything. How long do you intend to keep this storm raging?"

Valentine scowled beneath his heavy white eyebrows. "As long as it takes," he said darkly. "These people belong together, and I intend to make certain they end up that way. With or without your help."

Eros grinned. "Then I'd best get my loincloth in gear. We don't want the entire East Coast buried under a blizzard. It's my turn."

"Be creative," Valentine begged, sounding suddenly vulnerable. And Eros realized, for not the first time, what a soft-hearted soul Valentine was beneath his crusty exterior.

"I'll do my best," he promised. And he set to work.

SHANNON WONDERED absently whether she was getting pneumonia. That was all she needed, on top of the other miserable complications in her life. She'd been freezing to death ever since she stepped on board Fred Rogers's rusty old boat. The cold was reaching deep into her bones, despite her down parka, and she hadn't thought anything short of a forest fire would warm her.

Now she was burning up. The wood stove had been hot enough, but standing dangerously close to Patrick Lockwood was even worse. She felt hot, her skin prickling, her face flushed, and it was either pneumonia or love. On the whole, she preferred pneumonia.

She controlled her urge to back away from him, tilting her head back to stare at him. He was so different, and yet still the same. Despite the worn denim, the long hair, the stubbled chin, he still had those same sea green eyes, eyes that watched her with an unsettling expression she couldn't begin to define.

"We might as well go up to the house," he said finally.

"Why?"

"So I can get down to the business of ravishing you," he drawled. "What else?"

She was not amused. "I think I'll stay here."

"Suit yourself. But I sure as hell can't work with someone watching, and I don't intend to keep stoking this fire. Besides, there's no food, no bathroom, and the generator isn't enough to power both buildings. When I'm up at the main house the power goes off here."

"You're such a gracious host," she said in her sweetest voice.

For a moment a grin lit his dour face. "You might as well accept it, Shannon. We're stuck here, and we don't have any choice but to make the best of it. You look like you could use a hot meal, and I could use a drink."

"I think I prefer 'Miss Donnelly,'" she said primly.

"I'm sure you do, Shannon."

She bit back her instinctive retort. "Is your cooking anything like your coffee?"

"They have a lot in common."

"Then I'll take care of my own meals," she said sternly. "One can die of poison as well as frostbite."

She watched as he damped down the stove, turned off the overhead lights, all with a graceful economy of effort. "Is this your boat?" she asked, waiting by the door.

He shook his head. "It belongs to a client. That's what I do nowadays—refurbish classic boats."

"Quite an upscale hobby."

He raised an eyebrow. "It's upscale all right. But it's not a hobby."

"I wouldn't think anyone who owns his own island would need to support himself."

"If you're being rude enough to ask how much money I have, I can tell you it's more than enough. And I didn't buy the island—it belonged to my grandparents, and I have to share it with my sister and her kids every summer. Apart from that, being a divorce lawyer was a very effective way to earn a living. There's an endless need for one's services. I no longer have to work for the money. I work for the satisfaction of working."

"Very noble."

"Not particularly," he said, pulling on a dark green jacket that had seen better days, following it with a blue knit seaman's cap. "I do it to please myself. Unlike you, I don't feel the need to take care of anyone else."

"What about your sister's divorce?"

"She hasn't got one yet. I figure it's just a matter of time. Most marriages don't work, and the Lockwoods beat the national statistics. There hasn't been a happy marriage in my family since they came over on the Mayflower."

"Your family should have waited for a safer boat," Shannon said. "Moira was the first known divorce in the Donnelly family, and if Harold had had a decent lawyer, it wouldn't have happened."

He didn't bother to respond to the provocation; he simply pushed the door open into the howling storm. "Keep your head down," he shouted over the noise of the wind, "and follow me. I don't want you landing in the ocean."

She didn't want to do it. Didn't want to leave the dubious safety of the cavernous workshop, didn't want to follow him through the storm like something out of "Good King Wenceslas." She didn't really have any choice. She didn't want to be abandoned in a dark, cold warehouse either, and she believed Patrick when he said he'd do just that.

The storm was unlike anything she'd ever endured. The snow whipped against her face, plastering her hair against her head, blinding her. She wasn't wearing boots, and her sneakered feet slipped in the ankle-deep slush. She could make out Patrick's tall figure just ahead of her, and she kept her eyes on him as she struggled through the storm, thinking dark thoughts.

She fell, landing on her knees hard, but a moment later Patrick was beside her, hauling her upright. "Keep going," he shouted through the raging storm, holding her hand. He was wearing heavy leather gloves, she was wearing lined ones, and she could feel the heat of his flesh all the way down to her bones.

The house was dark when they stumbled inside, dark but blessedly warm. Patrick shoved her into a chair, muttered something rude under his breath, and a moment later he was kneeling at her feet, stripping off her snow-caked shoes. She tried to kick him away.

"I can take care of it," she muttered, her voice trembling with the chill.

"Fine." He stood up, towering over her in the darkness, and she hoped he couldn't see how her chill-numbed hands fumbled with the fastenings of her parka. "I'll see what I can do about the generator. I switched it over when we left the workshop, but it seems to have quit on me."

"There's no power?" She couldn't disguise the panic in her voice.

"Not at the moment. The stove and refrigerator are gas-powered, the heat is wood, so I imagine we'll survive the storm. I suggest you get out of those wet things before you freeze to death."

"And slip into something more comfortable?" she said wryly. "I'm afraid I'm unprepared."

"Listen, lady, I'm too cold and too grumpy to be interested in seduction. I don't have a hell of a lot in common with the lawyer who kissed you in his office a few months ago, but I'm just as cynical. You can run around stark naked for all I care. I promise I can manage to keep my hands off you. Right now, all I'm concerned with is finding out whether the generator is working."

"You concentrate on the generator. I can take care of myself."

"Sure you can," he drawled, and she didn't need to see his expression in the dark room to recognize mockery. In a moment he was gone, leaving her alone, without a candle or a flashlight to pierce the unnatural gloom of the freak storm.

She stripped off her wet socks and parka, shook the snow from her hair, and rolled up the damp hem of her jeans. The floor was wet and cold beneath her bare feet, but she moved unerringly in the direction of heat, almost colliding with an old potbellied stove.

She could make out shapes in the darkness, and she stumbled toward a sofa. There was some sort of throw on it, and she wrapped it around her shivering body. It was soft, warm and wonderful, and for the first time in hours she felt completely safe. Until the lights came on with shocking suddenness, and she found she'd wrapped herself in what could only be Patrick Lockwood's bathrobe.

She stripped it off. Not even for the warmth the soft flannel offered was she willing to be caught wrapped in a piece of his clothing. She looked around her, curious. She'd stumbled into what must be the living room. It wasn't what she would have imagined Patrick Lockwood living in. In New York he must have had an apartment like his office, all glass and chrome and steel. This place was shabby and country and casual, with overstuffed furniture, bookshelves lined with both books and clutter, newspapers and magazines all over the place. The rug on the floor was Oriental, priceless, but faded. The wood stove was state of the art, the dirty dishes on the harvest table were Royal Doulton china. The place was full of untidy elegance, and it suited the man Patrick Lockwood seemed to have become. It was certainly a lot more comforting, welcoming, than he was.

She waited patiently for him to make his reappearance. He'd been absolutely right, she was starving, and she wasn't averse to cooking something for him as well. She just wasn't ready to tackle the kitchen without his permission. He'd gotten astonishingly sour-tempered since New York, a fact that she welcomed. She much preferred grouchiness to that sinuous charm that was far too effective. She could resist a grump. Couldn't she?

Part of the problem, she had to admit it, was the way he looked. She was usually immune to such shallow issues as a person's appearance. The old Patrick Lockwood had been a devastating combination of charm and elegance, from his tailored suit to his handmade shoes. He was smooth, impeccable, and practically awe-inspiring for a woman who considered spring cleaning to be emptying out her wastebaskets.

The new Patrick Lockwood was scruffy, unshaven, with ancient clothes that belonged more to the Salvation Army than Saville Row. Even so, he still possessed an innate elegance, one that left her feeling more than a little rumpled herself. Or maybe it was just wishful thinking on her part.

She got tired of waiting. The floors were cold beneath her bare feet as she started exploring. They'd come in through the kitchen, and the gas-powered appliances, though old, looked in working order. The shelves were well stocked, and a row of foul weather gear hung on wooden pegs by the door. She peered outside, but all she could see was a cloud of swirling white.

"Where the hell are you, Lockwood?" she muttered underneath her breath. And then her eyes narrowed, as she detected a shadowy movement a few feet away from the house. Something low to the ground, crawling.

"Hell and damnation," she muttered, flinging open the door and letting the howling storm inside. Without hesitation she waded out through the deep snow, barefoot, oblivious to the cold as she reached Lockwood's side. She knelt down beside him, barely able to see him through the heavy snow.

"What happened?" she yelled.

"Stop asking stupid questions and help me inside," he shot back, his voice tight with pain. She tried to haul him upright, but he was too heavy for her, simply tumbling her down into the snow beneath him, soaking her already damp clothes. She tried again, bracing her bare feet in the slush, and this time she managed to support him, half dragging him into the kitchen before he collapsed on the floor.

Snow had already piled inside the kitchen door, and the wind fought her as she forced it shut before turning to look at Lockwood. He was lying on the kitchen floor, his clothes caked with snow, his face white with pain, his eyes closed.

And then they opened, focusing on her. "Are you out of your mind?" he demanded in a harsh voice. "Couldn't you have at least put on your boots?"

She looked down at her feet, for the first time realizing how cold she was. There wasn't much she could do about it, short of leaving Lockwood lying there while she went into the living room to warm up, and while he deserved to be abandoned, she didn't really consider it an option. Instead, she sank to her knees beside him and began unfastening his jacket.

He tried to bat her hands away, but she ignored his clumsy efforts. "What happened?" she asked again, with all the patience she'd learned to display with her recalcitrant younger siblings.

"I twisted my ankle," he said in a sour voice. "It'll be fine—I just need to put some ice on it."

She shoved the jacket off his shoulders. "I'd think it would have had enough ice on it during your crawl to the house. What makes you think it's not broken?"

"It hurts too damned much. Listen, get your hands off me and go dry off. I don't need anyone to play Florence Nightingale . . . ouch!"

She'd begun to unlace the snow-soaked running shoes. "Which ankle?"

"The one you're mauling." He sat up, wavering slightly, and pushed her hands out of the way. "I can get the damned shoe off. Why don't you make yourself useful and get me a drink? Whiskey, two fingers, neat. The bottle's in the cupboard to the left of the stove."

"I think you need coffee. Something to warm you up." She sat back on her heels.

He glared at her. "Whiskey will warm me up just fine, thank you. If you've got some strange religious convictions against spirits then go lock yourself in the bathroom."

She rose haughtily and stalked over to the cupboard, ignoring his muffled groan of pain as he worked the snow-soaked running shoe off his foot. The bottle was where he said it was, three quarters full, and she poured them both stiff drinks. By the time she'd turned around he'd managed to pull himself upright. He was very tall, and even in the dimly lit kitchen, she could see the lines of pain around his grim mouth.

She handed him his drink, and he drained it in one gulp. "You'd better find yourself something warm and dry to wear," he said. "I don't want pneumonia to keep you here any longer than the storm will. You'll find some of my sister's clothes in the dresser upstairs. They won't fit very well, but help yourself."

"What about you?"

He hesitated, obviously loath to ask her for help. "You might get me some clothes, as well, from the bedroom upstairs. I'm not sure if I can make it up there at the moment, and I'm freezing."

"Aha," Shannon said. "A sign of weakness. And do I hear a please?"

He closed his eyes in exasperation, obviously wanting to tell her to go to hell. "Please," he said.

"Certainly. Do you need any help getting into the living room?"

"I can manage on my own."

"Very self-sufficient," she said in a biting voice. "If that's the way all Lockwoods are, it's no wonder they never stay married. It's a shame you try in the first place. At least you might do mankind a favor and stop reproducing."

"Marriage is not a requirement for reproducing," Patrick said in a tight voice. "And I've managed to avoid both."

"Bully for you. I'll leave you alone so that you can crawl into the living room without an audience."

HE WATCHED HER GO, and he found, despite the agonizing pain in his right ankle, that he was smiling. She certainly was a feisty soul. From the top of her dark auburn hair to the soles of her bare, frozen feet, she was pure, dangerously idealistic dynamite. He couldn't imagine anyone less suited to a man like him. And he couldn't imagine wanting anyone more.

He'd managed to disguise it fairly well. He'd been sour-tempered, unwelcoming, and all he had to do was keep it up until this freak storm abated, and then she'd be on her way, in search of her damned box and family harmony.

It shouldn't be that great a task for him. His damned ankle hurt like hell, and her very presence set his nerves on edge. It wouldn't take much to keep him terminally grumpy.

It also wouldn't take much for him to put his hands on her again. She looked up at him out of those wonderful blue eyes, filled with distrust, disdain, and confusion. And he knew, without arrogance, that if he touched her, her confusion would vanish.

The pull between them was both powerful and completely irrational. He realized it, she didn't. As long as he fought it they'd make it through, and he'd consider himself well rid of a dangerous threat to his self-contained life-style. As long as he ignored her soft mouth, as long as he stopped thinking about how her long, beautiful hair would feel beneath his hands, as long as he didn't fantasize about that coltish body with those endless legs, and how they might wrap around him...

He took a deliberate step, the pain in his ankle almost wiping away his involuntary erotic fantasy. It was a damned good thing she had disappeared. In his current pain-dazed state of mind he didn't quite trust his sense of self-preservation. If she helped him to the ancient, overstuffed sofa in the living room, he might not be able to stop from pulling her down with him. And then God only knew what would happen.

God knew, and anybody with an ounce of brainpower knew. He hopped on one foot, each bounce jarring his swollen ankle unmercifully, and he welcomed the pain with savage pleasure. Stop thinking about her, he ordered himself sternly. She's too young for you, too idealistic for you, too unselfish and too damned passionate. Passionate about life. She probably carried that same fierce passion into bed with her, and while he had no objections to sexual passion, he'd managed to infuse his life with a certain distance, a certain barrier. She was the sort to bring those barriers crashing down.

He dropped onto the sofa, closing his eyes for a moment. What cruel, vicious twist of fate had sent her to his island, to invade his privacy, his life, his soul? He needed to get rid of her, and fast. Before he couldn't let her go.

He must have dozed off. When he opened his eyes again her hands were on his shirt, unfastening it.

He stopped her, catching her smaller hands in his, and his eyes blazed up into hers. She was wearing some old clothes of his sister's, baggy and much too big for her, but at least she looked warm and dry. It was more than he could say for himself. He was cold, damp and clammy, despite the warmth of the wood stove.

"You really want to undress me, Shannon?" he drawled.

She tried to pull her hands away, but for some reason he was loath to release her. "I don't want you to get pneumonia, either," she snapped. "I want to get off this island as soon as I can, but I'm not about to leave a sick man."

"Trust me, if I was on my deathbed I'd still want you to go," he said wryly. Her hands were still and warm beneath his cold fingers.

"Why?"

He hadn't expected her to ask. But then, she'd been singularly obtuse about the undercurrents between them, and while it might be dangerous to point them out to her, ignorance was no defense. She didn't want to get involved with him any more than he wanted to get involved with her.

"Why?" he echoed. He levered himself up, still holding her hands captive so she couldn't back away. He put his free hand behind her head, underneath her thick fall of still-damp hair, and brought her closer, closer, putting his mouth against her soft one, tasting her breath, tasting the whiskey and coffee and startled, involuntary desire of her. He did it on purpose, to make a point. He could offer her sex. But romance had no part in his cynical life.

It took all his control not to deepen the kiss. He pulled back, mere inches, and his eyes stared into hers. "That's why," he said flatly.

She had a dazed look in her eyes. "What's wrong with that?" she said finally.

He released her hands, swinging his legs over the side of the sofa with a pained grimace. "What do you mean, what's wrong with that? You're a woman who believes in true love, marriage and happy ever after. I'm a man who believes in nothing at all."

She sat back on her heels, staring up at him. "You don't believe in love?"

"Not one bit. I think there are two possibilities between men and women. Friendship, and sex. And the two are mutually exclusive. Marriage is simply part of the financial infrastructure of society, and divorce the logical culmination. Now in case you've missed the point, I want to go to bed with you. Quite badly, as a matter of fact, and have since I first saw you. The problem is, I happen to like you. You're smart, you're loyal, you're funny. I don't think you'd fare too well with what little I have to offer someone like you. I'm too old for you, Shannon. Too old in years, and far too old in the ways of the world."

He couldn't tell what she was thinking. She simply stared at him for a moment out of those wonderful blue eyes. "That's quite a speech, councillor," she said finally. "You been working on it long? Or have you tried it on other women to see whether it would work?"

"What do you mean by that crack?"

"No woman can resist a challenge. They probably all thought they could be the one who would teach you how to love. Show you that there is such a thing as happy ever after."

"Are you offering to give it a try?"

"Not me. I know a lost cause when I see one."

"That's good. Because I've never slept with a woman who hasn't known exactly what she was getting into, and I'm not about to start. Tempting as you are, I'm keeping my hands off you, Shannon Donnelly. And if I were you, I'd keep my distance."

"Afraid you might change your mind?" she asked in an even tone of voice.

"No," he said. "I'm older and wiser than you. I'm afraid you might change yours."

She smiled then, a wry grin that lit her face and hit him in the gut with a force that made the pain in his ankle seem a mere inconvenience. "Not likely, Grandpa," she said, rising from the floor with unconscious grace. "I ran you a hot bath. Take it while I see what I can find to feed us."

"I can take care of myself..."

"Give it a rest, Lockwood," she said. "I have to cook for myself, and I don't want you hobbling around in the kitchen, getting in my way. Accept help for a change. It's not going to compromise your honor."

She turned away from him and headed into the kitchen, not bothering to see whether he needed any help. Which was just as well. It took him three tries to get to his feet and stay there, and by the time he reached the bathroom door he was afraid he might throw up. The room was steamy from the bath, and he could smell the faint trace of her perfume lingering in the air.

He hobbled over to the window, staring out into the raging storm that continued unabated. "God, how could you do this to me?" he murmured out loud.

And there was no answer but the howling wind.

Chapter Four

"HE CERTAINLY is a stubborn one," Eros said.

"I rather like him."

"You just like him because he thinks you're God."

"Blasphemy," Saint Valentine said, without any real intensity. After sixteen hundred years he'd grown used to Eros's attempts to bait him. "I happen to like him because he has a certain code of honor, even if he doesn't recognize it himself. He refuses to take advantage of Shannon, even though he knows she'd succumb to the lure of the flesh if given half a chance."

"Only the lure of his flesh," Eros corrected lazily. "You know as well as I do her sexual experience is just about nil. This is the first time she's really been tempted."

"Patrick knows it. And he thinks he can't give her what she needs, so he's nobly denying himself."

"An absolute saint," Eros said wryly. "Actually, he can give her exactly what she needs, and I mean to see that he does so as soon as possible. Nobility is all well and good, but we don't have that much time."

Val looked startled. "What do you mean?"

"It's February thirteenth. We decided we had till February fourteenth to take care of these two lovebirds, and a deal is a deal. Speaking of which, why did you sprain his ankle? If you think that's going to keep him from getting beneath her skirts, you don't know my man."

"She's not wearing skirts," Val said, giving him a disapproving glare. "I just thought it might move things along a bit. She's the kind of girl who likes to take care of people, so I thought I'd let her take care of him. Give her time to realize her own feelings."

"Valentine, you are so out of touch with reality," Eros said with a weary sigh. "For one thing, she's a woman, not a girl. For another, she's spent too much of her life taking care of men. She needs a man to take care of her in return, not some wimp she can mother."

"Let me do this my way..."

"The hell I will. Your efforts at tender courtship are failing miserably. It's time for hormones to come into play. I'm getting them in bed together, tonight."

"It's too soon!" Valentine protested. "They barely know each other."

"It's almost too late. Come on, Val, lighten up. With us playing our parts, we've got love at first sight, forever and ever, amen. They're made for each other."

"They're complete opposites!"

"Made for each other," Eros repeated firmly. "And I intend to make certain they realize it to the fullest extent. We've had enough of your pussyfooting. It's time for action."

HE COULD SMELL the coffee. Smell something wondrously like steak. He could hear her, humming underneath her breath as he lay in the warm, deep tub, thinking about her, allowing his mind to drift along sensual byways, ignoring the danger. And he could hear her curse, loud and long, when the power went off again, plunging the house into darkness once more.

He cursed, too, as he dressed in the dark bathroom, listening to the wind howl outside. He almost pitched headfirst through the window as he attempted to pull on his jeans, and he had to lean against the wall, panting, as he yanked a T-shirt over his head.

Shannon was still cursing when he limped out of the bathroom, but she'd managed to find some candles. He could see the faint glow from the kitchen, feel the heat from the replenished wood stove. She was surprisingly self-sufficient in his less than convenience-equipped household. He found that disturbing.

"Do you need any help?" he called to her, balancing on one foot.

"Not unless you feel like crawling back out into the snow to work on the generator again," she said, appearing in the kitchen door, a candle illuminating her flushed face.

"Not particularly." He sank down on the sofa. "Is there any chance it'll turn back on by itself?"

"Afraid not. We're in the dark till I can get out there and do something about it. Maybe if the wind dies down . . ."

"Maybe not. I don't feel like chasing around in a blizzard, looking for you. You've got plenty of candles around. You'll just have to put up with the romantic atmosphere."

He could see the faint trace of amusement in her eyes, and the thought irked him. He'd been deliberately bad-tempered, hoping to convince the woman that he could resist her. It was safer that way, but for a moment he was sorely tempted to show her just how much effort it was costing him. If she thought she could get away with mocking him, daring him not to react to her, he might have to . . .

No, he didn't have to do anything. As much as he wanted her upstairs in that old-fashioned bed that had held unhappy couples throughout his family history, he wasn't going to do anything about it. If he did, she might not want to leave when Fred reappeared. And he might not want to let her go.

It would end badly. These things always did. The more intense the attraction, the more in love people fancied themselves to be, the more painful the inevitable crash. Not that he was naive enough to think love had a damned thing to do with it. But an innocent like Shannon Donnelly would doubtless convince herself it was love once they shared incredible sex. Women, particularly romantic, passionate young women like Shannon Donnelly, tended to make that mistake.

And there was no doubt in his mind that the sex would be incredible. He had only to touch her and she was ready to go up in flames. Just as he was.

Which was why he needed to get her the hell off this island. If he had to row her to the mainland himself, through a blizzard, he might just do that. A man was capable of a great deal when his entire peace of mind was at stake.

"So why did you come here?" he made himself ask, his voice deliberate. He knew how to put someone on the defensive—he'd spent a professional lifetime doing just that.

She leaned against the doorway, watching him out of her still, beautiful eyes. "You know that as well as I do. To pick up the Valentine Puzzle. Harold said he was willing to hand it over and—"

"That's not what I mean. Why you? Why not your sister, if she's the one so hot to own it? You sound like you couldn't care less about the stupid thing. Why not those strapping brothers of yours, or even your parents? Why you?''

"Are you conceited enough to think I jumped at the chance to see you again?" she countered hotly.

"Not at all. I imagine you fought it tooth and nail," he said, and watched her flush at the accuracy of his random guess. "I want to know why you got saddled with this particular task."

"I'm the only one who's self-employed..."

"Not good enough. It's a weekend."

"I'm the only one in my family who won't punch you in the nose?" she offered.

"Nope. I think you'd probably love to punch me."

"Not really," she said, and her voice was low and troubled.

Not the direction he wanted things to go in, he thought. The more he tried to fight with her, the more he was drawn to her despite his best, or was it his worst, efforts. "Try again," he suggested coolly. "Why are you here?"

"If you're so smart, Mr. Lockwood, why don't you tell me?" She was trying to sound just as cool as he was, but she wasn't nearly his match in schooling emotions. She was standing in the doorway, soft and vulnerable, and he wondered just how badly he'd have to hurt her to drive her away.

"You came because you spend all your time taking care of everyone's problems, letting them use you, no matter how much it's going to cost you personally. You live your life through them, ignoring your own needs."

"My own needs are none of your damned business," she shot back.

"You're right. And let's keep it that way."

Suddenly the anger left her, and that wry, devastating smile danced around her mobile mouth, lit her wonderful eyes. "Why are you trying so hard to scare me away, Lockwood? Afraid I might get too close? What about your needs? Don't you have any?"

"I can take care of my own needs, thank you."

"If you prefer it that way," she said with a shrug. "Does that mean you don't want steak?"

It hadn't worked. He felt the frustration rising within him, and he knew at least half its cause was purely sexual. "You're supposed to hate me, Shannon," he said wearily.

"Honestly, Lockwood, I'm trying. You're just not doing a good enough job convincing me." And she disappeared back into the kitchen.

If only she couldn't cook, he thought several hours later, feeling full, lazy, and half-seduced by a combination of the candlelight, the bottle of red wine she'd unearthed from one of the cupboards and the coffee that made his stuff taste like toxic waste. If only she didn't make him laugh, with her wry, self-deprecating humor that carried just enough barbs to keep him alert. If only she wasn't so damned luscious.

"You know," she said, leaning back in the chair, warming her cup of coffee with her long, beautiful hands, "I'm afraid I like you after all."

He was stretched out on the sofa, his ankle propped up on the armrest, watching her. "Bad mistake," he observed, still wanting a cigarette. "I may have charm, but deep down I'm not a very likable person."

She laughed, and the soft sound was like a fist in his stomach. "I haven't seen much evidence of your famous charm, Lockwood," she said. "All you've done is growl at me since I showed up here."

"There's a very good reason for that," he said.

"Oh, yeah? What's that?"

"I like you, too."

She should have looked properly terrified. Instead she looked pleased. "What's the problem with that?"

"I thought I already explained it to you in great detail. I can either like you, or sleep with you. You're the kind of woman who'd think it was possible to do both, and I'm the kind of man who knows it's not."

If he'd hoped to daunt her, he'd failed. She reacted to his bald statement with detached, clinical interest not quite masking that damned humor. "Once you sleep with a woman you don't like her any more, Lockwood? Sounds pretty twisted to me. You must have really terrible self-esteem problems, to think that someone who might fall in love with you has got to be unlikable."

He didn't rise to the bait. "I didn't say that," he said, taking a sip of his coffee. "I think the women I've been involved with have all been wonderful women. There just hasn't been any room for friendship between us, once sex comes into the picture."

"So you start out as friends and end up as... enemies? Lovers? Strangers? Which is it, Lockwood?"

"Depends on the woman," he said. "As a matter of fact, I don't usually make the mistake of trying to seduce my friends. It's much better to keep the two relationships separate."

"What happened the last time you turned a friendship into a romance?" She couldn't disguise her curiosity.

He hooted with laughter. "I've never had a romance, Shannon. If you're asking me what happened the last time I made the mistake of sleeping with a friend, then I..." The words trailed off. Patrick Lockwood, a man who had made his reputation and a solid fortune based on his glibness, was lost for words. He looked at Shannon, watching him so intently, and he could say nothing but the truth. "I don't think I ever have."

He wondered how she was going to react to that. Whether she might foolishly suggest there was always a first time for everything.

She didn't. She simply nodded. "It's probably just as well. You've already done your part on behalf of unhappy couples in this world through your career. You don't need to add to their number."

"It makes sense," he agreed, watching her in the wavering candlelight. The wind and storm still whipped against the house, and in the distance he could hear the crash of the ocean. Inside it was warm and safe, dangerously, seductively so. "I just don't know how interested I am in being sensible."

She glanced up at him, and he could read the wary expression in her blue eyes. Could read the wariness in her soul. "Lawyers are always sensible."

"I'm not a lawyer any more. I'm a boat restorer."

"That's a step in the right direction," she acknowledged, rising with an unconscious grace that had him clenching his teeth. "Can I get you more coffee?"

"No. I don't like being waited on."

"You know, I would have thought that's exactly what you liked," she said. "Keeping women in their place and all that."

"You know, you can be very irritating," he said.

"I'm trying my best, Lockwood," she said with a dulcet smile.

"I know you are. You're trying your best to make me into someone like Ted Jensen or Paul Miller."

She sank back down abruptly, her face pale with shock. "How do you know about them?"

"Harold Rasmussen likes to talk," he replied, setting his coffee cup down on the cluttered table. "He was married to your sister for five years, and in that time he got to know you pretty well. He passed that information along."

She was no longer pale, she was charmingly pink with emotion. "Harold isn't a gossip," she said in a stony tone of voice.

"No, he's not. But he's no match for a lawyer who knows how to ask the right questions."

That startled her even more. "You asked him about me? Why?"

He shrugged. "Curiosity, I suppose. Coupled with an irrational lust. I wanted to find out whether you were the kind of woman who'd be interested in a brief, no-commitment fling."

"And what did you find out?"

"That I was out of luck. You pick spineless men who need mothering, according to Harold, and then you don't sleep with them. You let them and your family drain you, emotionally, financially, and you keep making the same mistake over and over again."

There was no longer any glint of humor in her blue eyes. Patrick told himself he should be glad. Instead, he felt like the bastard she thought him to be. "Fairly accurate," she said in a cool, tight voice. "So you decided you wouldn't get anywhere with me?"

"Not exactly. I'm not a man to admit defeat. I decided you needed a hero, a man who could stand up to you, a man who didn't need a mother to whine to. But I'm not the man you need."

"Amen to that."

It was his turn to be amused. "I could always change my mind," he said. "I could always change your mind."

"Forget it. I've already told you, I like you, even though my common sense is giving me hell for it. You've made your position perfectly clear—it's sex or friendship. When it comes right down to it, there are very few men I actually like. And I could find some-one interested in a fling quite easily."

"I imagine you could."

"So we'll keep it this way," she said briskly, rising again, clearing the dishes off the table with madden-ing efficiency.

He watched her move, his eyes settling on her curves. "Very wise," he said, trying to convince him-self. Wondering if he was going to have to resort to a cold shower on such a miserably cold night.

"HELL AND DAMNATION!" Eros was hopping up and down with rage.

"Stop that blasphemy," Valentine said, unable to hide his smug smile. "Didn't I tell you sex wasn't the answer to everything? The two of them have too much sense to go frolicking around . . ."

"If you hadn't sprained his ankle he might be feel-ing more energetic," Eros snapped. "I can't believe a man with Lockwood's history could suddenly wimp out like this."

"He isn't wimping out, he's showing decent re-straint," Val said sternly.

"If he shows any more restraint then we've both lost our bet."

"I can live with that," Val said, but he didn't sound the slightest bit convincing.

"And Lockwood and Shannon will part company, probably never to see each other again. When we've already done enough to ensure that they're made for each other. You know what that means, Val? It means they'll be unhappy the rest of their lives. They'll probably marry someone else, and they'll make their spouses unhappy, and their children unhappy, and their grandchildren..."

"Forget it, Cupid," Val grumbled. "We're not responsible for the well-being of the world."

"Sometimes the well-being of the world can all boil down to two people who are right for each other, even if neither one of them wants to admit it."

"You're being a romantic again, Eros. You're taking this loss too much to heart."

Eros growled low in his throat. "You mealy-mouthed old saint. We're not going to lose this one."

Val shook his head. "I think I've lost my touch. I don't trust my own judgment any more, after Shannon's sister got divorced."

"I know what you mean," Eros said in a softer voice. "It took the heart out of me, too. But we can't give up. Maybe we gave up on Moira and Harold too quickly. Maybe we have more work to do."

"But what...?"

"I don't know. I do know that Patrick Lockwood is going to take Shannon Donnelly to bed tonight."

"Animal lust isn't the problem," Val said with a depressed sniff.

"No," said Eros. "But it might be the answer. Out of the way, old man. I have work to do."

SHANNON LEANED her forehead against the kitchen wall, taking a deep, shaky breath once she was alone. Patrick Lockwood had the most astonishing effect on her. She'd never been so vulnerable to a man as she'd been to him, from the very moment she'd seen him, outside the courthouse.

The emotions she'd gone through had left her crazy, there was no other excuse for it. First she'd been attracted, then charmed by him. Followed by fury, when he'd humiliated her sister, rage at his arrogance, and undeniable desire when he'd kissed her. Fear had followed closely, a logical reaction to her own illogical response to a man she should hate.

She'd thought she could fetch the Valentine Puzzle and keep hating him. His bad-tempered scruffiness ought to have made it easier. Instead it made him more human, more accessible, and impossibly enough, more attractive.

Being housebound in the midst of a freak storm only made it worse. The intensity of the elements stirred the intensity inside the house, and the glass of wine she'd allowed herself hadn't done a thing to calm her. Being around Patrick Lockwood was just about the most dangerous thing she'd ever done.

She wanted to hide in the kitchen. She wanted to crawl under the table and keep away from him. Never in her life had she been so overwhelmed with feelings, ranging from tenderness, annoyance and outright longing. She wanted Patrick Lockwood as she'd never wanted anyone before, and that yearning was completely irrational. And yet she couldn't deny it.

A little voice echoed in her head. A man's voice, soft, charming, telling her to go to him. She could almost imagine another voice, probably the voice of her conscience, telling her to watch out and behave herself. Her conscience sounded like a grumpy old man.

She shook her head, trying to clear away the ridiculous fancies. Maybe even the one glass of wine had been a bad idea. She was not going to go to bed with Patrick Lockwood. Her sexual history had been short and not very sweet, and she wasn't the sort of person who gave in to biological urges, no matter how overpowering. Particularly when she wasn't even sure if she liked the man.

But she was in love with him. There was that stupid voice, echoing in the back of her head, and this time she wasn't sure if it was her conscience or that weaker, lustier self. She couldn't be in love with him. It made no sense—she couldn't fall in love with someone like Patrick Lockwood. Could she?

Don't listen to that voice, she told herself. Listen to your conscience. You are not giving in to your basic urges, urges you've never even noticed before. You are going to help Lockwood up to bed and then you are going to lock your door, lock your hormones away. You are not going to go to bed with him.

YOU ARE NOT going to go to bed with her, Patrick told himself sternly, sitting upright on the comfortable old sofa. It doesn't matter how much you want to—that very intensity of wanting is the greatest danger sign of all. Listen to your conscience, that wise old man who's telling you to be a decent human being for once in your life. You don't believe in happy ever after, and she does. You'll break her heart, and if you really care about her you won't want to do that.

But why should he really care about her? He scarcely knew her, and he wasn't the kind of man who tended to care about anything or anybody. He'd lived his life that way on purpose, allowing no one to get close to him, with the single exception of his sister and her motley crew of children.

They were hellions, the three of them, invading the island every summer, and driving him crazy. Crazy enough to regret that he was never going to have any of his own.

That's what Shannon needed, of course. Children to mother, so she wouldn't keep picking men who depended on her. She needed to find a real man, one who could stand on his own two feet without trampling on hers, someone to love her and give her babies and he wasn't that man, damn it! Why did he keep wishing he was?

He wasn't going to bed with her. He was going to hobble upstairs, lock the door behind him, and just hope she'd have the sense to keep her distance. Because if she didn't, he might listen to that seductive little voice that kept telling him to take her, and ignore the stern voice of his conscience.

He wasn't going to bed with her. Was he?

She appeared in the kitchen door, her dark auburn hair tousled, her eyes wide and wary. Understandably so. "What should I do about the fires?"

"I've loaded this one," he said. "Just make sure the candles are out, and then we can go up. There's a guest room upstairs, unless you'd rather sleep on the couch."

There was no missing the relief on her face. "Either one sounds fine. Do you need some help navigating the stairs?"

"No," he said sharply, frustrated desire eating a hole in his already frayed temper. He hobbled toward the stairway, silently cursing his ankle. If it wasn't for that ridiculous accident he'd be more in control. He'd have the power on, not this damned seductive candlelight. He wouldn't be tempted to pull her into his arms and wrap that long, thick hair around his wrists.

He made it halfway up the stairs. There was no reason for him to stumble, no reason at all, and yet he did, banging his knee against the step, hitting his head, cursing a blue streak when she raced up behind him, her beautiful hands on his arm, helping him upright.

He wanted to push her away, but such a churlish action might have sent her hurtling back down the narrow stairs, so he told himself he had no choice but to lean on her, breathing in the sweet flowery fragrance of her, accepting the fact that his ankle was far from the stiffest, most painful part of his body.

They stumbled into the bedroom, and she fell back against the door, his body pressed up against hers. And those two damned voices in his head began to babble, and the only way he could silence them was to bend down and kiss her.

She tasted like coffee, and wine and heaven on earth. The moment his mouth touched hers he was lost, and he knew it. Nothing, short of her pulling away, could stop him, not common sense, not self-preservation, not the control he'd always valued. Her mouth opened to his, her arms slid around his waist and she tilted her head back beneath his, returning the kiss.

He threaded his hands through her thick auburn hair, as he'd fantasized doing, and it felt like silk running through his fingers. He stroked her cheekbones with his thumbs, kissed her nose and eyelids and the tiny little mole by her upper lip, and she made a soft sound in the back of her throat, one of despair, one of surrender. He lifted his head to look down at her, and the only light in the room was from the oil lamp in the hallway.

"This is crazy," he said, his fingers entwined in her hair.

"Crazy," she echoed, her arms around his waist.

"I didn't want to hurt you, Shannon," he murmured against her skin. "And I'm afraid I'll have to."

"I'm willing to take the chance," she said, and leaning up, she kissed him again, her mouth soft, damp, and open for his.

The pain in his ankle seemed to have disappeared as he moved her across the room to the high old bed. He lifted her up, settling her on the pile of old quilts, following her down with his body, and he couldn't get enough of her mouth, her sweet, hungry mouth.

Her hands were shaking, clumsy as they slid up under his T-shirt, and it took him a moment to remember that she hadn't had much experience. And what she'd had, she hadn't enjoyed. She was nervous, fevered, tugging at him, and he knew she expected him to make it fast.

He had no intention of granting that particular desire. He took her wrists and pushed them back against the bed, stilling her squirming body with his hips pressing down against hers. It took her a moment to quiet, and in the dimly lit room her eyes were huge and wary.

"Did you change your mind?" she asked, her voice a mere whisper of sound.

He rocked his hips against her. "Does it feel like it?"

Even in the dim light he could see the color flood her cheeks. Lord, she was an innocent! He felt like the worst sort of lecher—if he was a decent human being he'd climb off her and let her go.

But he wasn't about to be a decent human being. He didn't want to listen to that voice in his head—he wanted to listen to the voice that drummed in his blood. And so did she.

"Then why did you stop?" she asked, holding very still beneath him. She was wearing an old shirt of his sister's, one that had once belonged to him, and it buttoned all the way up the front. He was going to enjoy taking it off her. Slowly.

"We have plenty of time," he said. "There's no need to be in such a rush. Is there?"

She didn't answer, but he could see the uncertainty in her eyes. Lecher, he called himself. But he didn't move. "Is there?" he asked again, leaning forward to touch the corner of her mouth with the tip of his tongue.

She shivered in his arms, a tremor of pure reaction. "No," she said, her voice a mere breath of a sigh. But she spread her legs, cradling him against the heat of her, in silent supplication.

He groaned, deep in his throat, controlling the urgent need to thrust against her. "We're going to take our time," he said, and his voice sounded rough in the darkness. "We both know this isn't a good idea, but we're going to do it anyway. We might as well at least do it right."

"I don't understand."

He smiled then, abandoning second thoughts, principles and regrets in one moment. "I'll show you," he said. And he put his mouth against her throat.

Chapter Five

SHANNON WAS AFRAID. She shouldn't have been. It wasn't as if she were totally inexperienced, it wasn't as if she thought Patrick would hurt her, or do anything weird. She wasn't frightened of him. She was frightened of herself, alone in the darkness. Afraid she'd disappoint him. Afraid he'd disappoint her. Afraid that what was supposed to be so overwhelming, so stupendous, would be ordinary and messy. If it failed to be extraordinary with Patrick, then she was plumb out of luck, because her reaction to him was miles beyond anything she'd ever even begun to experience.

But she was also afraid that it would be exactly what she'd dreamed. Exactly what people made such a fuss about. That she would love this man, and make love with this man, and he would be exactly what he said he was. Cold and cynical and distant. And she'd be lost.

But she was already lost. His mouth on her throat was slow, warm, sliding down the column of her neck. He'd released her wrists to work on the tiny buttons of the baggy shirt she was wearing, and his mouth followed where his hands had bared, tasting her skin.

She slid her hands under his T-shirt, and his skin was hot, smooth, strongly muscled beneath her hands. His long hair was loose, flowing over her, and she buried her face against it as the cool night air touched her skin. He pushed the shirt off her, and his mouth closed over the lacy scrap of a bra that she scarcely needed. Outside the wind howled, the windows rattled; inside it was dark and warm and dangerous.

He pulled his shirt over his head and sent it sailing across the room. He unfastened her jeans, pulling them down her long legs, and she let him do it, wanting to feel him pressed against her, wanting all that hot, hard flesh against hers.

"Tell me what you like," he said, his voice soft and seductive in the shadows. "Do you like this?" He covered her breasts with his hands, his long fingers skilled and arousing. "Or this?" He followed with his mouth, touching her slowly, languorously, taking the peak of her breast and rolling it against his tongue. She arched off the bed in instinctive reaction, and her hands reached up to clutch his shoulders.

"Yes," she gasped. Her voice rose in a strangled cry as he moved to the other breast. "Yes."

"That's good," he murmured against her skin. "I like doing it." His hands moved down her sides, deft, artist's hands, cradling her hips, his thumbs tracing her pelvic bones as his mouth moved down her torso, kissing, licking, tasting.

She shivered in his arms, moving restlessly. She was more aroused than she had ever been in her life, and she was afraid it was going to disappear if it took too long, afraid that she'd lose it, that white hot burn of desire that lashed through her body.

He'd stripped off his own jeans, she wasn't certain when, and she could feel him against her thigh, hot and hard and ready. She reached down to touch him, and he groaned, a sound of longing and desire that burned an answer within her. He was damp, more than ready, and she didn't know what was holding him back.

"I want you," she said, sliding her hands up to clutch at his arms.

"Do you?" he murmured in response, ignoring her efforts. "I think you could want me more." His lips brushed against the sensitive skin of her stomach, and a ripple of reaction ran through her body.

"I need you," she said desperately, her body shifting back and forth in frustration.

"I know you do," he agreed, cupping her hips in his hands. "You just don't know how much." And he put his mouth against her.

She arched off the bed with a muffled shriek, her fingers and toes digging into the quilt that lay beneath her. She didn't want this. It was too intimate, it felt too good, it was too much, too much....

The first spasm hit her, a ripple of reaction that shook her, frightened her, a reaction she quickly tried to halt.

He lifted his head to look at her, and in the candle-lit darkness she could see his wry expression. "You're not supposed to fight it," he said.

"Now," she said in a tight voice, yanking at his shoulders, pulling him up, toward her.

"You're a demanding woman, Shannon Donnelly," he murmured, kneeling between her thighs, and she could feel him, hot and pulsing against her. "But we're not going to do this all your way."

She braced herself for his entry, knowing he was large, but he pushed, slowly, steadily, and there was no discomfort, just a glorious filling when she had seemed so empty. She wrapped her arms and legs around him, prepared to force him to completion, but he pushed her down against the mattress, impaling her, holding her still with his hips as his hands cupped her face with surpassing gentleness.

"There's no hurry," he said again, and his voice shook with laughter and desire. "It's a lot more fun if we take our time."

He kissed her then, his mouth open and slanted across hers. He kissed her with his lips, his tongue, his teeth, kissed her so thoroughly that all her sensations seemed to center in her mouth, center in her heart, center in her loins.

He began to move, pushing into her, pulling back with a steady, rocking motion, and she clawed at him, trying to hurry him, but he kept on, slow, sensual, completely in control, taking her to a place only he knew, taking her there on his timetable, at his pace.

She couldn't force him to the quick finish that had seemed to offer her only chance of fulfillment. She couldn't do anything more than follow his lead, mindlessly, their bodies rocking together in an ancient rhythm that was timeless and overwhelming.

She gave up thinking. She gave up rushing. She kissed him back, slowly, lazily, her hips arching to meet him, in no hurry. The night was dark, velvet, endless; there was no one around to know, no one around to hear. It was warm and wet and magic, and now she wanted it to last forever, for the darkness to close around them like a soft old quilt, keeping them safe.

She had no warning. When it hit this time she was lost, and she couldn't pull back. Her body convulsed in his arms, totally out of control, and she screamed something, she wasn't sure what, as she dug her hands in Patrick's sweat-slicked shoulders.

His body went rigid in her arms as he followed her down that dark pathway, his own control vanished, and she cried out again, shivering and shaking in his arms.

It was a long time before she could release him. Her arms felt weak and rubbery, her whole body trembled with belated shivers of reaction. He recovered sooner, marginally so, and his lips brushed against her damp eyelids, her trembling mouth.

"It's much better when you don't rush it, isn't it?" he said with a soft, shaky note of laughter in his voice.

"Much better," she agreed, and her own voice wasn't much more than a thread of sound.

"And much better if you don't try to control it." He kissed the side of her mouth, and she turned her head to meet his lips. Her own felt swollen, sensitive and incredibly hungry.

"Much better," she echoed.

"I like the way you scream."

She didn't think she could still blush. But she could, hiding her warm face against his shoulder. "At least no one could hear me."

"No one who wouldn't appreciate it," he temporized, his hands smoothing the hair back from her flushed face. "Are you always so noisy?"

"I don't know."

"Let's find out, shall we?" And he began to move again, slowly, and she realized with shock, quickly followed by pleasure, that he was hard again. And she was ready for him.

"Noisy, isn't she?" Saint Valentine observed with a disapproving sniff.

"Isn't she?" Eros smacked his lips. "If only you'd let me watch..."

"They don't need an audience. I don't imagine things have changed much in the last sixteen hundred years. Mankind has pretty well explored all the biological options available. I'm certain they didn't do anything you haven't already seen."

"That doesn't mean I didn't want to see it," Eros shot back. "There are certain things that always retain their freshness. The first time people who are meant for each other make love..."

"They're already on their second time," Val announced. "And she looked like such a demure young thing. It's your man that's having such a lustful effect on her, Eros."

"I certainly hope so. Can I at least listen?"

"No. I wouldn't be feeling too cocky if I were you. Haven't you been listening to what Lockwood's been saying?"

"I've been trying. You keep stopping me," Eros said, greatly aggrieved.

"I mean before you pushed them into bed together? He doesn't believe in love. He doesn't even believe men and women can be friends, once they make love. If he continues to believe that, then he's just destroyed their relationship."

Eros ran a hand through his shoulder-length blond curls. "Isn't that where you come in? Show him the error of his ways, point out that true love isn't just a question of bodies. It's hearts and minds and souls."

"I never thought to hear you admit it."

Eros stuck his tongue out at the old saint. "I'm not a fool, Val. We've got them enraptured with each other. Shannon's in love, and he managed to break through her inhibitions, no thanks to you and your sprained ankle. We just have to get Patrick to realize he can't live without her."

"And how do you expect us to do that? The bet ends at midnight tonight. We don't have much time."

"If you'd just let me take a little peek..." Eros said, attempting a winning smile.

It got nowhere with a judgmental old sourpuss like Saint Valentine. "You don't need to look. You need to think. We can't fail again. I don't care what works, your way or mine. Just so long as it works."

Eros could just imagine another one of Shannon's delicious little screams. He shook his wings, forcing his mind back to more practical matters. "We can't fail," he said. And it was more a prayer than a statement of faith.

THE BEDROOM was flooded with bright early morning light. Shannon opened her eyes warily, not certain she really wanted to. She felt achy, sticky, and tired. And better than she'd ever felt in her entire life.

She was wrapped in Patrick Lockwood's arms, her body still entwined with his. The last thing in the world she wanted to do was wake him up. For now, while he slept, tucked up against her, he was hers. From everything he'd ever told her, that state of affairs wouldn't last for long.

How could she have done it? How could she have fallen completely, hopelessly in love with a cynical stranger, a man who said he didn't even believe in love?

She tried to tell herself it was infatuation. Midlife crisis, postadolescent crush, mindless lust, or even PMS. But it wasn't. She knew, as well as she knew the

Valentine Puzzle was the talisman of the Donnellys, that in Patrick Lockwood she'd met her destiny. And if he didn't realize it, she was going to spend the rest of her life one very unhappy lady.

He was a stubborn man, as well as a cynic. And she didn't have any delusions about her powerful beauty, overwhelming charm, astonishing brilliance or devastating charisma. She was just an ordinary woman who happened to fall in love with the wrong man.

But the kind of woman who knew how to fight for what she wanted. And she wasn't going to give up without one royal battle. She didn't want to live her life without a grumpy snake like Patrick Lockwood. And she wasn't going to.

He had to be asleep. His breathing, his heartbeat was regular, even. But his arms held her tight against his body, and his hands threaded through her hair. In his sleep he knew how right they were together. How would it be when he woke up?

She wasn't ready to face that moment. Even with the bright sunlight warming the bedroom, she wanted to hide away from the new day. And the broken heart it just might bring.

She took in the details of the bedroom without moving her head, details that had been lost in the dark last night. The bed was an old spool bed, high above the yellow pine floor, and the rag rugs were faded and cozy. The flowered wallpaper, the multipaned windows, the warm quilt wrapped around them were all remnants of a simpler time. She wanted to live in that time, with Patrick. Wanted to live in this bedroom, paint her pictures by the clear bright light of the island. And she was horribly afraid she was going to end up back in the post-industrial dankness of Massachu-setts.

Alone.

HE WAITED UNTIL he was certain she was asleep again. He had no idea what time it was—he'd forgotten to wind the grandfather clock downstairs, and the rest of his seldom-used timepieces were electric. The sun was already warming the house, and he knew he should get up and load the wood stove, then see about coaxing the generator back into a semblance of working or-der. He didn't want to go anywhere.

He didn't remember when he'd last slept with a woman. He and Morgana had had an unwritten rule—neither of them had wanted the commitment of wak-ing up in the morning with another human being. He wanted to wake up with Shannon. He wanted to kiss her awake, slowly, lazily, wrapping her elegant body around his before she even realized what he was do-ing. He wanted the damned storm to continue, lock-ing them together on the island, so that he had no choice but to keep her with him.

The bright sun mocked that desire. He slid out of bed, careful not to disturb her, and she flopped over on her stomach with a muffled grunt, her long au-burn hair spread out across her narrow back. It was no wonder she'd fallen back asleep. Neither of them had that much rest during the long, energetic night.

He winced when he put his weight on his ankle, but the pain was surprisingly minor. He hadn't even no-ticed it during the night, another surprise, given the various things he'd tried with Shannon. It couldn't have been as bad as it had appeared to be. Either that, or rampant lovemaking was an unknown cure for sprained ankles.

He needed a shower, he needed coffee, he needed his sanity. He needed to remember who and what he was, what he believed in. Last night had been an aberration, brought about by nothing more than an intense case of desire. It was a physical hunger, easily satisfied. He'd be crazy to start thinking he wanted anything more.

But then, this morning he was just a little bit crazy, he thought later, leaning against the old wooden counter in his kitchen and sipping at the freshly perked coffee. He'd fixed the generator, stoked the fires, reset all the clocks and brewed the coffee, all while Sleeping Beauty upstairs slept on. He kept glancing out at the bright blue sky, half hoping another freak storm would blow up, one like the day before. There'd been no warning—the sky had been just this brilliant blue. But he had the depressing feeling his luck wasn't going to hold a second time.

Not that Shannon Donnelly's enforced stay on the island was good luck, he reminded himself. Bad luck was more like it, disastrous. It had upset everything he'd worked for, everything he'd believed in. When he looked into her wonderful blue eyes he forgot that love was just a euphemism, that till death do you part was a joke. When he looked at her he started to dream. And he thought he'd rid his life of useless dreams.

"Is there any of that for me?" Her voice was husky, shy from the kitchen door. He glanced up in surprise, for one unguarded moment drinking in the sight of her.

She'd taken a shower, and her hair was wet and curling slightly around her face. She was wearing the clothes she'd come in, the baggy cotton sweater and faded jeans, and her feet were bare. He hadn't gotten around to properly appreciating her toes during the long night that had been far too short. Surely she couldn't leave before he dealt with her toes?

"Sure." He turned from her, deliberately busying himself pouring her a mug of coffee. She'd looked so damned luscious, and so uncertain, staring at him from the doorway, that he'd wanted to cross the room and pull her into his arms, to kiss away the doubt and worry in her fine blue eyes.

By the time he'd turned back to her, mug of coffee in hand, he'd forestalled that particular disaster. He was careful not to touch her when he handed her the coffee, careful to step back away from her with no appearance of haste.

"Stay with me," he wanted to say, and it was no little voice in his head this time, it was coming from his heart. "I suppose you have work you have to get back to," is what his mouth said, and it came out all wrong.

The wariness in her eyes disappeared, replaced by blank acceptance. "Yes," she said carefully.

"Harold said you were an artist."

She shook her head with a wry, self-deprecating smile. "Sometimes I'm an artist. Usually I'm a painter."

"What do you paint?" He wanted to somehow retrieve the situation. If she was going to leave, and she had to, for her sake and his, then at least he wanted her to leave on friendly terms.

"Walls," she said flatly. "I freelance for a small decorating firm. I'm an absolute whiz at trim."

"I imagine you are."

"How's your ankle?"

"Much better." He almost countered her politeness by asking her whether she slept well. He was in a better position to know exactly how she slept. "Stay with me," he wanted to say, but he couldn't. "I imagine Fred will show up before long," he said out loud.

She drained her coffee, setting it down with a nervous little thump. "Then I'd better get myself organized," she said brightly, and left him alone once more.

The way he wanted to be, he reminded himself. Even if he asked her to stay, she'd be a fool to agree. For all that she spent her life taking care of the rest of her family, she certainly ought to know when she was better off out of a situation. There was no future for them, and if she couldn't see it, at least he could. He wasn't about to leave the island unless he had to. It was remote and wildly beautiful, but too isolated for someone like her.

No, she wouldn't want to stay, and he was saving them both a great deal of embarrassment by not asking her to. Especially since he wasn't ready to share his solitude with anyone. Was he?

And if he wasn't, why did the future stretch out with such unaccustomed bleakness?

He glanced out the window, down to the dock and the gray-green sea beyond. The snow was already melting in the bright sun, and in the distance he could see Fred's boat, chugging closer and closer, and he cursed, something low and vicious and unexpected.

"What's wrong?" She was back again, her voice bright and cheerful, her eyes red.

"Nothing. Fred's here."

"Oh," she said.

"Let me find you some boots so your sneakers don't get soaked when you walk down to the dock. Fred will probably have some food on board, or I could ask him to wait while you eat something."

"No need," she said. "I'm not very hungry."

He shrugged. "Suit yourself. I'll just dig up some boots..."

"Don't bother," she said, pulling on her parka. She'd already found her still-damp sneakers, and if he didn't know her better he'd assume she was cool, efficient, glad to be going. But even though he'd been around her less than twenty-four hours, he knew her almost better than he knew himself. He knew he was breaking her heart. And there was always the remote possibility that he was breaking his own as well.

He wanted to go to her, but his feet were rooted to the floor. "I'll walk you down to the dock...."

"Don't bother," she said again. She started for the door, stopped, and turned back to look at him. "You'll be sorry," she said suddenly.

"Sorry? About what?"

"Sorry you let me go," she said, walking back to him, tall and graceful and determined. "I'm the best thing that ever happened to you, Patrick Lockwood, and if you're too stubborn and cynical to realize it, then you're a fool." She put her hands up to his shoulders and pulled his face down to hers, kissing him on the mouth, and he could taste the salt of her tears.

She moved out of reach before he could put his arms around her, moved out of reach before he could respond. "You know where to find me," she said, pulling on her gloves, trying to blink away her tears. And then she was gone, out into the snowy morning without a backward glance.

He didn't move for a moment. This was what he wanted, this was what he needed. His solitude, his self-contained life. There was no room in it for a stubborn redhead.

She was halfway to the dock before he found his boots. She was climbing into the boat when he raced down the slush-covered hill, half limping, half running, wearing an old sweatshirt. She saw him coming, but she made no move to stop Fred. She merely stood in the bow of the boat and watched as he skidded to a halt at the end of the dock.

"I don't," he said.

"Don't what?"

"Know where to find you," he said irritably.

"You could find out," she said, not moving. Beneath her, the boat was rocking on the rough sea. Fred was watching the two of them with unabashed fascination. "That is, if you cared. But you don't care about anything, do you? You already warned me about that."

"You didn't listen."

"I listened."

He took a deep breath, fury and frustration and something he didn't recognize warring for control. And then he knew what that third emotion was, something he wasn't familiar with. It was hope.

"I'm too old for you."

"Yes," she said.

"You'll go crazy out here, with no one for company."

"Yes," she said.

"Get off the damned boat."

"Yes," she said.

She took a flying leap into his arms, and he caught her, holding her tight against him. He kissed her, once, a dozen times, and she was kissing him back, oblivious to the weather, the audience, and common sense.

"Danged if this ain't better than a soap opera," Fred announced cheerfully.

Patrick lifted his head. "We're getting married, Fred. You want to be my best man?"

"Married, eh? I knew it would come to this. You'd better wait for your sister. She knew you'd fall, sooner or later," Fred said with a chuckle.

"I want children," Shannon warned when she could catch her breath.

"Lots of them," Patrick agreed.

"And I'll paint the insides of the boats you fix. When I'm not painting sunsets."

"You can paint anything you damned please," he said, pulling her tight against him, where she belonged.

"Guess I've got a wedding present for you," Fred said, delving into a canvas sack and coming up with a familiar-looking red velvet bag. "This arrived this morning, before I set out to pick up your bride-to-be."

"It's mine," Shannon said, reaching for it.

"No, it ain't," Fred said. "It was sent to Lockwood there, with a message. Might make sense to you—it didn't to me." He tossed the velvet bag across the water, and Patrick caught it effortlessly.

"What's the message?"

"Comes from someone named Harold. Says he and Moira are back together again, and they won't need you or this box again. It's your turn."

Patrick looked down at Shannon. "I don't know if we need magic charms, either," he said.

"Look at it this way, Lockwood," she said, taking it from him and then sliding her arms around his waist. "We need all the luck we can get."

"Just like a soap opera," Fred said again. "Which reminds me, you two."

"What?" Patrick said, moments before he set his mouth against Shannon's.

"Happy Valentine's Day."

"IF IT HADN'T BEEN for me, they'd be going their separate ways," Eros said hotly.

"Don't be ridiculous. They were all set to go their separate ways despite all that voluptuous sex. It was the power of true love, pure, sanctified true love that made the difference," Saint Valentine intoned.

"Sex."

"Love."

"Well," said Eros, "maybe a judicious combination of both. It does tend to work better that way."

"I never thought I'd hear you admit it."

Eros smiled sweetly. "Of course I admit it. Considering that I won the bet."

"Don't be absurd! You almost wrecked everything!"

"I won," Eros repeated. "With your help. Maybe we'll call it a draw this time."

"Voyeur!" Saint Valentine thundered.

"Fascist," Eros shot back. "Don't try to fool me, Val. You aren't nearly as hard-hearted as you'd have me believe. You're just as pleased things worked out as I am."

Saint Valentine glanced toward the tiny island of Barkhaven, Maine, a tentative smile wreathing his lined, austere face. "Do you suppose they'll live happily ever after?" he questioned in a softer tone of voice.

"With the two of us on their side? Absolutely, old man. Absolutely."

CHOCOLATE KISSES

Judith Arnold

A Note from Judith Arnold

I hate February. I've lived nearly my entire life in the Northeast, where February is generally bitter cold, overcast and wretched. By the time it arrives we've already had two months of blustery weather, and the "Winter Wonderland" novelty has worn thin. The snow is dirty, the heating bills are appalling, the driveway is permanently locked in ice, a season's worth of sooty ashes has spilled out of the fireplace onto the rug, the kids have cabin fever and everyone's skin is so dry we begin to resemble a family of lizards.

The reason February is the shortest month of the year is that no one could possibly stand thirty days of it. Most people don't even bother to pronounce the month correctly; they call it Feb-yoo-ary. February is as painful to say as it is to endure.

Except for Valentine's.

I'm sure there's some religious/historical/mythical reason that Valentine's Day falls exactly at the middle of the month, but I've got my own theory: After two weeks of February, people are desperate. They need something so wonderful, so thrilling, so magnificent it motivates them to slog through those first fourteen days—and its afterglow keeps them warm for the rest of the month.

For me, that wonderful, thrilling, magnificent thing—the epitome of Valentine's Day—is chocolate.

My husband understands. Every year on Valentine's Day he brings me an adequate supply of the stuff. I've learned to pace myself so a two-pound box of chocolates can last me until March 1, and then I'm home free.

This is what true love is all about: not empty words and gestures, not flowery sentiments, but a recognition of what your soul mate needs to get through the worst month of the year, and a willingness to provide it. My husband isn't a chocolate fanatic, but he has his own needs in February. Without going into detail, I can report that those needs include a roaring fire in that ash-filled fireplace, some strategically lacy apparel and children who are extremely sound sleepers.

Actually, it works out quite well. He gives me chocolate and I'm happy. I give him what he wants—and I'm happy.

This year marks our eighteenth Valentine's Day together, twelve of them as husband and wife, nine of them as Dad and Mom to the two greatest boys in the world. We've somehow managed to get through all those miserable Februaries with smiles on our faces and love in our hearts. A little chocolate goes a long way!

Judith

Chapter One

"YOU BROKE MY HEARTS!"

Ned Wyatt dusted the snow off his black denim dungarees and glanced toward the road. He'd been accused of breaking a few hearts in his day, but what did that have to do with anything? She'd been the one driving the minivan, after all; he'd been riding a bicycle. If anything had broken it would have been his bones, not her heart.

Then again, she'd said *hearts*. If she had more than one heart, anything was possible.

He heaved himself to his feet and looked around. His eighteen-speed bike lay on its side several yards down the road, apparently undamaged. He recalled the way it had lurched under him like a wild bronco, spitting pebbles and slush in all directions until he'd deliberately jumped clear of it.

Closing his eyes, he replayed the near-collision in his mind: the van cruising down the road toward him as he coasted out through the wrought-iron gates in the stone wall surrounding Wyatt Hall. The whine of the van's tires losing traction on the slippery road as the driver slammed on the brakes. The violent spin. The van's rear bumper bouncing off the stone wall, sending the vehicle teetering on two tires, tilting precariously for the longest, ghastliest split second Ned had ever endured before it finally dropped back onto all four tires with a jarring thump.

As he pulled himself out of the snowbank, he heard the driver's high-pitched cry: "My hearts! You broke my hearts!"

"Now, wait a minute," he said with what he considered admirable poise. He stalked down the slope to the van. "I didn't break anything. I'm not at fault here."

"Of course you are! What kind of maniac rides a bicycle in the middle of February?"

The kind of maniac who'd grown restless from too many days of slate skies and frozen precipitation, he almost retorted. When he'd awakened that morning to a clear, sunny day, he'd decided to treat himself to some fresh air and exercise. He'd bundled up and gone out for a morning jaunt in the brisk, biting cold. He'd balanced a huge red valentine-shaped box of candy across the handlebars of his bike, figuring he'd ride north along the winding rural lanes he'd known as a child and then circle back to town and deliver his gift.

He wasn't sure what impulse had compelled him to detour through Wyatt Hall's austere iron gates. He hadn't thought of the estate as home in twelve years, and he'd felt like a visitor as he pedaled around the circular driveway to the stately pillared entrance of the mansion. It was a grand house, three stories of Georgian brick with a slate hip roof and four towering stone chimneys. It would make a majestic setting for Melanie's silly shindig.

He didn't think much of the pretentious party his sister had organized for that night at the family estate. Debutante cotillions were absurd, even when they were scheduled in honor of Valentine's Day and even when his niece was one of the debutantes. He would attend because Melanie had begged him to. But he still found the entire notion of a society debut laughable.

"It's a disaster," the van driver was moaning. "Everything is ruined. My hearts, my buns—oh, God, my kisses!"

Ned paused. From where he stood, her buns looked terrific, packed tightly into a pair of snug blue jeans. She stood on tiptoe with her back to him, leaning into the rear of the van. Her shoulder-length brown hair caught the early morning sunlight and shimmered with red highlights. Her puffy down vest hid her torso, but her legs were long and slim and enticing.

Her hearts, her buns and, oh, God, her kisses. What an intriguing combination.

He sternly reminded himself that she was talking about food. The side of her van featured the painting of a huge gold cornucopia, along with the words, "Fantasy Feasts—Let Us Cater to You."

"You're catering the cotillion?" he guessed, approaching the rear of the van.

The driver groaned and turned to him. She had wide blue eyes, sweet pink lips and a surprisingly angular chin. Ned would definitely like to pursue the subject of her kisses with her. And her buns and her hearts, too—however many she had.

Her beauty couldn't disguise the sheer panic illuminating those crystalline blue eyes and darkening the natural blush along her cheekbones. "This is an absolute disaster!" she wailed. "Why didn't you watch where you were going?"

"Are you all right?" he asked, recalling once more the horrid sight of her van spinning like a top on the icy road.

"How can I be all right?" She glanced over her shoulder at the van and shuddered. "I'm about to lose the biggest job of my life, thanks to you and your idiotic bicycle tricks. And you want to know if I'm all right?"

"I wasn't doing tricks," he protested. "I was just riding."

"In the middle of snow and ice."

"I didn't know I had to get permission from the weatherman to take a ride."

"And you had to ride here, of all places. This is private property. It isn't a bike trail. How the hell was I supposed to know some maniac on a bike would be speeding out from this private driveway—"

"This is *my* driveway," he told her, growing tired of her ranting, even though he couldn't imagine ever tiring of her stunning blue eyes.

"Don't be ridiculous. It's Wyatt Hall."

"I'm Ned Wyatt."

She stopped in mid-tirade. "You're who?" she asked in a tiny voice.

"Ned Wyatt." He extended his right hand. "And you're...?"

"Claudia Mulcahey," she said in an even smaller voice. She lowered her gaze and slipped her hand into his. Her fingers were pale and slim; he detected a slight tremor in them. "I guess—I mean—you must be related to Mrs. Steele."

"Melanie Steele is my sister," Ned said. He clasped Claudia Mulcahey's hand without bothering to shake it. It felt delicate in his, graceful and cool and feminine. The trembling indicated how much her driving mishap must have frightened her.

He didn't want to let go, but she withdrew her hand before he could think of an excuse to keep holding her. "Well," she said with a tortured sigh, "not only is this job completely ruined, but I've just called my customer's brother a maniac. I may as well crawl in a hole and die."

Ned nudged her aside so he could survey the interior of her van. "You may as well assess the damage and see what can be salvaged. Melanie has her heart set on this stupid cotillion. She's not going to take it well if her caterer crawls into a hole and dies."

Claudia grimaced. "What can I do? Everything's ruined. My cakes..." She pulled two overturned metal trays toward her. They held large chunks and smaller crumbs of golden and devil's food cake, along with dislodged sheets of plastic wrap. "The layers for two triple-tiered heart-shaped cakes. I was going to assemble them here at Wyatt Hall, but they're all broken. And my kisses..." Her voice threatened to crack and she swallowed. Lifting an overturned bowl, she shook her head. "Homemade chocolate kisses. Not the candy-store kind. There they are, under the seat with the strawberries. And the cheese biscuits and the date-nut buns and the braided loaves. Oh, no—did the yogurt dip spill? This is a disaster!"

Ned scrutinized the mess. A puddle of viscous white—the yogurt dip, he presumed—stained the floor near the sliding side door. Strawberries lay scattered about. Trays leaned at dire angles, spilling food items across every surface.

"Yeah," he concurred. "It's a disaster."

"What am I going to do? I can't possibly make everything all over again. I have so much prep work, and without the cakes . . ." Tears welled in her eyes.

"Hey," he said in a soothing voice. He wanted to envelop her in a hug and comfort her—and then, if she responded at all positively, he wanted to discuss her kisses and her buns. She was a fine-looking woman, and it had been six long months since he'd left Manhattan and the lively social life he'd enjoyed there. He wondered if Claudia had a date for Valentine's Day.

Of course she had a date: Glenwood, Connecticut's first annual Valentine's Day cotillion, masterminded by Melanie Wyatt Steele. If Ned knew what was good for him, he would send the charming Ms. Mulcahey on her way so she could bake some more heart-shaped chocolate and vanilla layers before sundown.

"Surely you and your partners can whip up another cake."

"What partners?"

He leaned around the open door to view the side of the van. "It says, 'Let *us* cater to you.'"

"I'm us," Claudia admitted. "I'm all there is to Fantasy Feasts. 'Let *me* cater to you' sounded obscene, so I told the guy to paint *us* instead."

Ned contemplated the potential pleasure of letting her cater to him. "I'll help you bake a cake."

"You?"

"Why not?"

"You're a Wyatt."

"Cripes, you're right," he agreed, smacking his forehead with mock dismay. "Forget it, then. Wyatts never help. It goes against everything we stand for."

"That's not what I meant." She sighed, evidently struggling to compose herself. "Your sister hired me to cater her Valentine's Day cotillion. She's paying me a lot of money. I can't let you do any of the work."

"Why not? Two minutes ago you were blaming this whole fiasco on me."

"But you're..." She glanced away, her cheeks growing apple red. "I mean, you're a *Wyatt*."

"What exactly is the problem? Should I change my name?"

Squaring her shoulders, she confronted him. "You are a Wyatt. I am an employee of a Wyatt. Okay?"

"You," he argued, "are a snob. You think just because I grew up in Wyatt Hall I don't know how to peel carrots?"

"I'm sure you know how to peel whatever you want," she snapped. Her eyes grew flinty as she stared up at him. "Wyatts can do anything, can't they? They can stage debutante balls and write out humongous checks and go bicycle riding in the middle of February. I have no doubt they can peel carrots, too." She took a deep breath and reined in her temper. "If you'll excuse me, I have a job to do." She slammed the rear doors shut.

"Wait a minute." He chased after her as she marched to the driver's door. "Do you think I'm not good enough to help you?"

"I don't want your charity, Mr. Wyatt."

"This isn't charity." Far from it. He wasn't offering his assistance out of the goodness of his heart. He was offering it because he wanted to practice his peeling technique on her vest, for starters. He wanted to find out if her skin felt as soft as it looked, and if her hair revealed its fiery highlights in indoor lighting. He wanted to get friendly with her.

He also wanted to make sure the cotillion proceeded without a hitch. He knew his sister. He knew how much work she'd put into organizing the party. If the food wasn't perfect, she would throw a tantrum powerful enough to hit seven on the Richter scale.

He gripped Claudia's arm and turned her to face him. "Listen to me, Ms. Mulcahey. If being a Wyatt makes me so special, I'm going to exercise my high-and-mighty prerogative. Either you can be reasonable and accept my help or I'll call my sister and tell her you're about to ruin her party."

Claudia gazed up into his eyes, no doubt trying to decide how serious his threat was. To his surprise, a smile spread slowly across her luscious lips and her eyes sparkled with a blend of amusement and audacity. So much for intimidating her.

Of course, if she were all that easy to intimidate, he wouldn't be anywhere near as interested in her.

"You want to help me, Mr. Wyatt?" she asked, challenging him with her gaze. "You can start by cleaning my van."

CLAUDIA WAS QUESTIONING the wisdom of accepting his offer of help when she noticed the red satin candy box crushed under her right front tire. By the time he'd returned to the van after stashing his bicycle on the other side of the massive stone wall surrounding Wyatt Hall she was overcome with remorse.

"I've destroyed your candy."

He stared down at the flattened box and shrugged. "I can buy another box."

"It's Sunday morning. The stores won't be open." Bad enough she'd almost killed Ned Wyatt. But even worse, she'd destroyed some woman's Valentine's Day present.

Lucky woman, she added as she shot him a quick, surreptitious glance. Not only was Ned Wyatt rich but he was gorgeous.

Now that her heart had stopped pounding and her brain had stopped reeling, Claudia made a careful study of the bike rider she'd nearly run over. She absorbed his athletic legs, his rugged chest, his broad shoulders and finally his face: long, straight nose, thin lips, hazel eyes outlined by short black lashes, golden complexion. His hair was thick, dark and unfashionably long. The wind had tossed and tangled it into the kind of adorably unruly mess that made a woman's fingers itch to fix it.

Men like Ned Wyatt never brought her two-pound boxes of chocolates on Valentine's Day, she thought glumly. In Claudia's life February 14 had always been a day for hard work, not romantic frivolity. Ever since she'd been old enough to help out at her parents' diner, she'd spent Valentine's Day serving meals to loving couples, smearing pink frosting on cupcakes, twisting caps off cheap bottles of domestic wine and smiling politely as young swains toasted their ladies. To Claudia, the day had traditionally meant generous tips, nothing more.

Now she was independent, running her own company. She had no time or energy for falling in love. When Jimmy McNeill broke up with her last fall, he'd said it was because she was more devoted to Fantasy Feasts than to him—and she hadn't bothered to refute the accusation.

Not that she regretted her hard work and dedication. In truth, she didn't regret losing Jimmy McNeill, either. Last year on Valentine's Day he'd been tasteless enough to send her a card that read, "Happy V.D."

Even if she hadn't noticed the elegant candy box, she would have assumed that Ned Wyatt was a romantic man. His sister was certainly romantic enough, scheduling the town's first debutante cotillion in a generation on this most romantic of days and personally designing the menu to reflect the rich, sweet sentiments of the holiday. "On one special day a year, the heart isn't just a muscular pump in our circulatory system," Melanie Steele had declared. "It's the symbol of love and romance."

And Claudia had planned a rich, sweet menu: Champagne-boiled shrimp, mushrooms stuffed with bacon and herbs, veal marsala, chicken kiev, creamed asparagus. There were even crudités and yogurt dip for health-conscious guests. The pièce de résistance was a dessert table laden with heart-shaped cookies and twin heart-shaped cakes, one white and one devil's food, both slathered in peppermint pink Valentine's Day frosting.

A menu that had looked divine on paper looked positively nauseating spilled and strewn across the interior of her van. Yet when she glimpsed Ned Wyatt in the seat next to her, she lost track of the chaos behind her. She smelled not the rich aroma of chocolate but his wintry, minty male fragrance. His hands rested on his knees, his fingers too blunt to be patrician, his knuckles thicker than a blue-blooded man's were supposed to be. His chin was shaded by a trace of beard. His eyes were clear, blessed with so many colors she couldn't begin to name them.

"You really don't have to do this," she said.

"I really *want* to."

She eyed him speculatively, then ignited the engine and accelerated down the road. Ned Wyatt was nobody's fool. He must have some underlying reason for accompanying her back to her house on the south side of town. He'd called the cotillion "stupid;" maybe he wanted to sabotage his sister's party by adding chili peppers to the cake batter.

"I just want to warn you," she said. "It's not going to be fun."

Even with his eyes forward she felt the power of his gaze, the allure of his smile. "Fun is where you find it," he said in a low, dark voice.

A shiver of dread—or was it expectation?—rippled down her spine. He has a girlfriend, she reminded herself. He'd been on his way to see her that morning, armed with that great big box of chocolates.

"I'm sorry I ran over your candy," she said. "I'll replace it with a basket of homemade cookies."

"That won't be necessary."

"But I want to do it. Who was the candy for, anyway?" It was a nosy question, but she figured that if Ned could make her food problems his business, she could make his love life her business.

"My mother."

"Your mother?"

"Isn't that what I just said?"

Did that mean he didn't have a girlfriend? "I thought your mother lived in Wyatt Hall."

"If she lived there, I wouldn't have had her candy with me. I would have given it to her."

"Then who lives there?"

"At the moment, no one."

"That great big house is empty?"

"We're still debating what to do with it. My mother decided she was sick of rattling around all alone in the house. Ever since my father died, she's been saying she wanted to move out. Six months ago, she finally bought herself a condo."

"Is she going to sell the house?" Claudia didn't think there would be many people who could afford to buy it.

Ned shrugged. "I think she'd like to give it to the historical society or something. Melanie thinks my mother's going batty. When my mother bought the condo, Melanie went into a major panic and demanded that I come to Glenwood and deal with the situation."

"Have you dealt with it?"

"It isn't a situation. My mother's happy where she is. Melanie will just have to get used to it."

"Is that why you're in Glenwood?"

"Originally." He leaned over to pluck something from the floor at his feet. "But since I've been here I've discovered that I like being out of New York. I've had it with all the crowds and noise. I'm enjoying myself here. I have a temporary office in town and I can accomplish just about anything with a phone, a fax and a modem."

"What kind of work do you do?" she asked, trying to glimpse the object in his hand.

"Investment consulting. I specialize in financing for start-up companies, new technologies." He rubbed the small, round item with his thumb to clean it, then lifted it to smell. "Wow."

She shot him a swift look in time to see him pop an errant chocolate kiss into his mouth. "Don't! It was on the floor!"

"It wasn't dirty," he said thickly, his mouth filled with gooey chocolate. "Wow, that's incredible! I've never tasted a chocolate kiss like this before."

She smiled. "It's my specialty."

"What's the secret ingredient?"

"If I told you, it wouldn't be a secret."

"Are we going to make more of these?"

She chuckled and shook her head. "If we do, you'll probably eat all of them."

"Three-quarters. We'd set aside a few for the cotillion."

She steered onto the driveway of her modest ranch house, sending arcs of slush in all directions. "For the last time, Mr. Wyatt, you really don't have to do this."

"Call me Ned," he said, gazing at her with a hunger she could interpret in more than one way if she dared. "As for helping you with your kisses, Ms. Mulcahey... I think that's something I really *do* have to do."

Chapter Two

CLAUDIA WAS STIRRING the chocolate and corn syrup she'd just melted in the microwave when the dreaded phone call came. "Hello?"

"Claudia! Where the heck are you?"

It was Melanie Steele. And she sounded frenzied. Claudia glanced over at Melanie's far from frenzied brother, who stood at the sink, rinsing out the bowl that had once contained yogurt dip.

Over the past half hour he'd made himself indispensable, helping her to clear the van of any salvageable food. While she made the cake batter, he'd cleaned the van. Now the cakes were baking in their valentine-shaped pans in Claudia's industrial double oven.

Claudia still faced a ton of work. She had no time to explain everything to Melanie. If she had a spare minute, she would have preferred to spend it gazing appreciatively at Ned's lanky, virile physique, at his disheveled mane of hair, his snug-fitting black jeans, his surprisingly competent hands and his sexy hazel eyes.

"You know where I am," she said to Melanie. "You've just called me."

"I am at Wyatt Hall." Melanie's tone was edged with hysteria. "There's no food here. You said you would start bringing the food over at nine. It's now almost ten o'clock and there's no food here."

"I—uh—I had to revise my schedule," said Claudia. From across the room she saw Ned grinning at her, openly eavesdropping.

The eavesdropping she didn't mind. His grin, however, stroked her nerves into an overheated state of awareness. One corner of his mouth was skewed slightly higher than the other, lending his smile a predatory quality.

Why had she let him inside her house? Why had she trusted him—and herself? The brightly lit kitchen was as unromantic a setting as she could imagine, yet whenever she glimpsed Ned Wyatt she felt soft and syrupy inside. She could focus only so much on the numerous tasks that awaited her. Part of her mind— the warmest, most womanly part—clung to him like sweet, sticky honey and refused to let go.

She turned to stare at the yellow ceramic tiles lining the wall. "Mrs. Steele, everything is just fine. I'm very busy right now, so—"

"When are you going to start bringing the food over?" Melanie continued. "I told my friends they'd get to see the cakes if they come here at twelve."

"The cakes aren't going to be ready at twelve," Claudia informed her.

Melanie shrieked. "I'm paying you a good dollar for those cakes."

"And they'll be worth it," Claudia assured her. "I'll bring them over as soon as they're ready."

"What do you think, we can sit around all day waiting?" Melanie sounded as if she were speaking through clenched teeth. "If you don't have the cakes here by noon—"

"You can see them this evening," Claudia insisted, struggling to keep her exasperation out of her voice.

This was the most important job Fantasy Feasts had ever had. Melanie Steele was her most influential client. "I promise you, the cakes are going to look magnificent. Why don't you wait and be surprised?"

"I wanted a preview," Melanie said petulantly.

"I wish I could give you one, but I can't. Trust me, everything's going to be wonderful." Unless you keep me on the phone all morning, she added silently, glancing toward the cooling chocolate in the bowl on the butcher-block island. "I really have to get back to work, Mrs. Steele. Just relax. The cakes are going to be great."

Melanie mumbled something and hung up. Claudia hung up, too. She rested her head against the cool, smooth tiles and let out a weary sigh.

"She certainly has a way with people," Ned remarked, sounding much too close. Claudia flinched and spun around to find him directly behind her, leaning against the work island and regarding her with a wry smile.

"Your sister is very nice."

"My sister is a shrew. What did she do to you?"

Claudia pressed her lips together to keep from blurting out her true sentiments. "What she did was hire me to feed one hundred-fifty people at Wyatt Hall this evening. It's an opportunity I can't afford to blow." She pushed past Ned and reached for the bowl of chocolate.

Ned rested his elbows on the island, propping his head in his hands and watching her. "Are those the kisses?"

"They will be."

"When do I get to eat them?"

"Tonight. Can you pass me those candy molds near the sink?"

While Ned went to get them, she pulled a bottle of bourbon out of a nearby cabinet. Ned turned back in time to see her pour several generous splashes into the chocolate. "Ah, so that's the secret ingredient?"

"One of them." She added a few more ingredients, then poured the chocolate into the molds.

"How did you learn to do this?" he asked.

"How did you learn to finance new technologies? This is my job, Ned. It's what I do."

He gazed around the room, silently appraising her work space, a modest suburban kitchen which had been completely remodeled with industrial appliances to accommodate her business.

Claudia dreamed of someday moving Fantasy Feasts out of her home and into a commercial building with space that she could design from scratch. But she would have to land quite a few more jobs like the Valentine's Day cotillion before that could happen.

She also hoped she would be able to hire an assistant or two. She desperately wanted an *us,* as in "Let us cater to you." She wanted to reclaim her weekends, to be able to share the burdens as well as the pleasures of her work.

It would be nice to have company while she worked, too, she thought as she glanced up from the candy molds and found Ned observing her intently. An odd ripple of heat coursed through her, and she decided that if she ever did have the chance to hire an assistant she'd make sure it wasn't a man with bedroom eyes.

She filled the last molded indentation. Ned reached out and caught a drip of chocolate on the rim of the bowl. He licked his finger and moaned. "This is fantastic."

"It's just candy," she said with a laugh.

"I can't believe I'm doing this." He ran his finger around the bowl. "I don't even like chocolate."

"Everybody likes chocolate," she argued, sliding the trays into the refrigerator.

"Not me." He belied his claim by pulling the bowl closer to him and scooping another bit of the candy onto his finger. "Chocolate's too complicated. I like vanilla better."

"Vanilla's too virginal," Claudia said, then bit her lip and cringed. Merely uttering the word "virginal" in Ned Wyatt's presence seemed like a fatal mistake.

His silence convinced her of it. She risked a fleeting glance his way. He was once again regarding her with inscrutable intensity, his gaze penetrating, his smile enigmatic. A tiny drop of chocolate clung to the corner of his mouth and Claudia found herself wondering what it would be like to capture it with a kiss.

Forget it. Even if the only woman in his life at the moment was his mother, Claudia couldn't allow herself to entertain any notions about kissing Ned. He was out of her class, in every definition of the word. The scion of the richest family in town, the brother of the most powerful shrew in town . . .

Forget it.

She headed toward the oven to check the baking cake layers. To her surprise, Ned blocked her path. "You like chocolate better than vanilla?" he asked.

"No," she lied.

"But you think complicated is better than virginal."

She felt her cheeks grow warm. "I'm sorry I said that."

"I'm not." He skimmed his finger along the side of the bowl once more. "This is the most complicated chocolate I've ever tasted. Maybe that's why I like it so much."

"Well, enjoy yourself," she said, moving to step around him.

Before she could stop him, he poked his chocolate-covered finger into her mouth. Her eyes widened with shock, but her tongue reflexively lapped the rich bittersweet flavor from his skin. His sensual grin caused her cheeks to grow hotter. A feverish flush spread through her body.

She opened her mouth and backed away. "Mr. Wyatt—"

"Uh-oh," he said, still grinning. "That's an extremely vanilla reaction."

"I'd just as soon keep things vanilla between us," she mumbled, trying to forget the erotic sensation of his finger between her lips, trying to convince herself she'd responded not to the smooth, hard texture of his fingertip but to the chocolate blanketing it. "I don't even know you."

"I don't know you, either," he conceded, "but I think I'm beginning to understand what a fantasy feast is all about." He traced a writhing line through the thickening vestiges of chocolate in the bowl. "Come on—share it with me." He extended his finger toward her.

"Really, Ned—"

He brushed his fingertip along the curve of her lower lip. Her muscles grew suddenly, treacherously tense as he smoothed the warm, fluid chocolate across her lip. Her breathing grew shallow, her hips taut as his gaze bore down on her, his eyes glittering with green and gray and amber as he ran his finger slowly over her mouth.

She sucked on her lower lip, removing the chocolate with her teeth and then her tongue. His smile faded and he leaned toward her. He was going to kiss her, and for a crazed moment she wanted him to.

With a small, helpless moan, she spun away. "You'd better leave," she whispered.

She heard him exhale. He drummed his fingers against the counter. A faint laugh escaped him. "I left my bike at Wyatt Hall."

She didn't dare to look at him. She knew that if she did she would once again succumb to that aching expectation, that yearning for his kiss. "I'll drive you there."

"You've got cakes in the oven."

"I'll drive you when they're done."

"You're the most beautiful woman I've ever seen."

That got a guffaw from her. "If you want to sweet-talk me, you're going to have to do better than that."

"Would my efforts be worth it?"

Grinning, she shook her head. "I have a lot of work to do. I didn't invite you here so I could listen to blarney."

"*Blarney?*" he echoed, incredulous. "*Blarney?* St. Patrick's Day is next month, sweetheart."

She sidled past him and opened an oven door. "When your last name is Mulcahey, you're allowed to say 'blarney' whenever you want."

"Is that a fact?"

"On the other hand," she continued, testing one of the cake layers, "when your last name is Wyatt, you're never allowed to say 'blarney' at all."

"We WASPs use a much cruder term," he said. "Something to do with bovine digestive systems."

"Your word will do as well as mine. They both describe the line you just handed me."

"It wasn't a line," he declared, cupping his hand over her shoulder and urging her around to face him. "You're a beautiful woman."

He sounded much too sincere. And for a few mindless minutes, she could believe that he thought she was beautiful.

"Do you really want to keep things vanilla between us?" he asked, his voice low and husky.

No, she wanted to cry out. No, she wanted to make things as complicated as chocolate. But while she could allow herself a brief, reckless daydream, she wasn't stupid enough to follow through on it. "Did it ever occur to you that I could be married?"

"Are you?"

She lowered her eyes to his jaw, to the smoky shadow of his overnight growth of beard. "No," she confessed. "But I'm not interested in an affair, Mr. Wyatt. I'm not looking for a romp. If that's what you came here for, you're wasting your time."

"Well." He released her shoulder and she drew in a long breath. "That was blunt."

"Blarney isn't my long suit."

"Do you believe in Valentine's Day?"

"As a profitable day for Fantasy Feasts? Sure."

"Where's your spirit of romance?"

She shot him a scathing look. "I'm a poor kid from the wrong side of the tracks. Romance is a luxury I can't afford."

That silenced him. And broke the spell between them. He turned and carried the bowl to the sink. "Do you want me to wash this?"

What she wanted was to stop feeling so attracted to him, to stop responding to his intriguing eyes and his provocative smile and the strong, hard heat of his hand on her shoulder, his finger on her lip. Given the impossibility of that, she wanted him to keep his distance from her.

"If it makes you happy, go right ahead."

He sent her a short, meaningful look, one that told her exactly what would make him happy.

It was the most un-vanilla look she'd ever seen.

Chapter Three

10:27 a.m.

NED EXAMINED THE wicker basket on his lap. Although small, it held an alpine heap of homemade cookies which were held in place by a square of artfully wrapped red cellophane and a white satin ribbon. He had watched Claudia prepare the basket, awed by her efficiency and her casual grace.

This was a woman who knew what she was doing.

He thought about the women he used to date in New York. They were invariably professionals like himself, intelligent, articulate, well read and up to date. He couldn't picture any of them baking a cake.

It wasn't as if Claudia Mulcahey were old-fashioned or unliberated. She wasn't plump and maternal; she didn't seem particularly nurturing. What she was was ... competent. Efficient. In charge of her world.

That she was willing to get behind the wheel of her van after her calamity earlier that morning was more evidence of her courage. He recalled the way her hands had trembled within his, right after the skid. She wasn't the sort to fall apart, though. She permitted herself a moment's terror, then squared her shoulders and forged ahead. She was brave and talented and ...

Damn, so sexy. He relived the arousing sensation of her tongue curling around his finger when he'd poked it into her mouth. He recalled the way her breath had grown shallow and her breasts had risen and fallen under her sweater. He recalled his own body's response, a craving for something much sweeter and more complicated than chocolate.

He hadn't even known he liked chocolate. He suspected that Claudia Mulcahey could introduce him to plenty of other hungers he'd never known before.

They were nearing Wyatt Hall and he assessed his options. He could keep pursuing her in the hope that sooner or later he'd get to satisfy those hungers. Or he could thank her for the cookies, hop onto his bicycle and ride to his mother's town house.

No contest. As she turned onto the circular driveway leading up to the house, he didn't bother to glance at his abandoned bicycle.

She drove around to the kitchen entrance at the rear of the house. Several other cars and trucks were parked there, among them his sister's black Mercedes. He smothered a scowl. He wasn't in the mood to see Melanie, but he couldn't very well hide in the van.

"You really don't have to help," Claudia said as she turned off the engine.

"Why do you keep saying that? I *want* to help."

She eyed him dubiously. "It's a beautiful day. The warmest day in two weeks—you said so yourself. You don't want to spend it lugging trays into the kitchen."

"And why don't I want to do that?" he asked with artificial patience.

"Because guys don't like kitchens. They think it's a hazardous environment. Bad for their machismo."

"You're speaking from experience, I take it."

She nodded.

"Past lovers?"

Her cheeks darkened with that now familiar lovely flush for a moment, but that was the only evidence he'd flustered her. "My father," she told him.

"One of those old-fashioned machismo types, huh?" Ned guessed.

"My father owned a restaurant in Norwalk. A diner, actually. He was the boss and he never set foot in the kitchen. His idea of running a restaurant was to greet the customers when they were on their way in and take their money when they were on their way out. My mother was the head cook, I worked as a waitress and did some of the cooking, too. My father claimed he was running the place, but did he ever lend a hand in the kitchen?" She answered her own question with a snort.

"I'm not your father."

"You're also not a diner employee. You're a man who grew up in this palace—" she waved at the massive brick edifice before them "—and if you keep wanting to help me, I'm going to suspect you of ulterior motives."

"You know my motives," he said, deciding he could be as forthright as she was. "There's nothing ulterior about them."

She lowered her eyes. He regretted losing sight of them, as beautiful as blue topaz, but he satisfied himself by admiring her long, tawny lashes. "The only fantasy feast you're going to get from me is food," she warned.

"What are you afraid of?" He tucked his thumb under her chin and lifted her face to his.

She appeared on the verge of answering. Her lips moved as she mulled over her words, then moved again. The temptation was unbearable.

Leaning across the console between their seats, he touched his mouth to hers. Just a light, tantalizing brush, scarcely a kiss. Just enough to let her know how thrilling a longer, deeper kiss would be.

She pulled back slightly and gazed at him, her eyes clouded with doubt. "I don't even know you," she whispered, a plea filtering through the words.

"And what little you know you invented. I grew up in this palace, so I shouldn't help you in the kitchen. Men are bosses, women cook. It's a sunny day, so I shouldn't want to be with you. Well, here's a news flash, Claudia, I'm not what you think."

"I don't know what I think!" She sounded frustrated.

The light kiss had left him pretty damned frustrated, too. He could tell her what to think: that some of his happiest memories of growing up at Wyatt Hall had involved sneaking into the kitchen and keeping Edie, the cook, company while she whipped up meals. That while his own culinary skills rose no higher than punching buttons on the microwave, he was a willing learner. That by running her own company, Claudia displayed a boldness and a commitment that turned him on as much as her eyes and her lips and her sleek, feminine proportions.

Rather than tell her with words, he slid his hand into her hair and guided her back to him. Their lips met and he sensed hesitation in her—but no real resistance. He moved his mouth gently, coaxing, skimming, teasing. When she didn't withdraw, he let his tongue slide between her lips.

She tasted like candy, like those fatefully delicious chocolate kisses of hers. He felt overwhelmed by the need to devour her, to absorb every morsel of her, to consume her until he himself was consumed by the passion exploding to life inside them both.

He felt a shudder of pleasure seize her. He heard her shaky sigh. Abruptly she turned away and stared out the side window. She wrestled with her breath for a moment, then reached for the door handle. "Don't do that again," she whispered before shoving the door open and getting out.

Sure, he thought sardonically. He wouldn't do that again. Why give in to the desire that blazed between them? Why do anything as logical as admitting that they wanted each other?

He met her at the rear doors. Before he could speak, let alone gather her into his arms for another kiss, she preempted him by placing into his outstretched hands a large aluminum tray.

With a wry nod, he headed for the porch. Peeking through the window next to the door, he spotted a woman with a moon-round face framed in frizzy silver hair inside the kitchen. He grinned.

Edie saw him the instant he saw her. Bursting into a smile, she hastened to the door and swung it open. "Ned! What are you doing here?"

"I should ask you that," he said, easing past Edie's short, bulky body and setting the tray on a counter. "Don't tell me my sister dragged you out of retirement for this wingding of hers."

"She didn't have to drag me," Edie protested. "When she told me she was opening the house for a debutante ball, I insisted on overseeing the cleaning service. Somebody has to make sure they don't break anything."

"Can't Melanie handle that?"

"Your sister," Edie confided, sotto voce, "is behaving like a she-devil. You'd think it was *her* debut instead of her daughter's."

"Poor Amy," Ned murmured. He wondered whether his niece had any interest at all in debuting or was simply fulfilling her mother's ostentatious dreams.

"Don't worry about Amy," Edie assured him. "She's never done anything she didn't want to do."

A knock on the kitchen door interrupted Edie. Ned turned to see Claudia balancing a tray of meat and watching them through the window. "Let's prop the door open," he said, hurrying over to let Claudia in. "We've got more trays to unload."

"We?" Edie asked before scowling at Claudia. "You're the cook Melanie hired, I take it."

"I'm the caterer," Claudia introduced herself. She set down the tray and extended her hand. "Claudia Mulcahey."

"I'm Edie Mueller," Edie said haughtily. "Head cook at Wyatt Hall for thirty-two years." She sized Claudia up with a deprecating look, then eyed the trays disdainfully. "I don't know why Melanie felt it necessary to go outside for a cook."

"She hired Claudia because you're retired," Ned said gently. "She wasn't going to ask you to put together a feast for hundreds of people."

"One hundred fifty-two," Edie argued. "And just because I'm retired doesn't mean I couldn't have done it."

"You're one of the family, Edie. Why don't you re-relax and let Claudia and me do the work?"

"You're one of the family, too, Ned," Claudia remarked, putting a frost on the words. "Why don't you both relax?" Pivoting on her heel, she stalked out of the kitchen.

"Feisty little snip, isn't she?" Edie muttered.

Ned gazed after Claudia. "Yeah," he sighed, picturing the flash of ire in her eyes. She could act as aloof as she wanted; her eyes gave her away. They seethed with emotion: sometimes anger, sometimes amusement and sometimes irrepressible longing.

"Your sister really should have let me handle this party," Edie groused. "Letting a stranger take over my kitchen ... She should have let me do it."

Ned could have argued that, for all her skill as a cook, Edie had never concocted anything quite as exciting as Claudia's chocolate kisses. But that would only have made Edie angrier.

"My sister," he said with a genial smile, "obviously wanted you to be in charge of monitoring the cleaning crew. You can't do everything, so Melanie asked you to help out where she needs you most."

"Well, I suppose," Edie conceded, puffing up a bit at the magnitude of her responsibility.

"In fact, you'd better go see what they're doing," he urged her. "And check their pockets. You never know what they might steal."

As Edie scurried off to guard the cleaning crew, Ned went back outside to the van. He found Claudia trying to balance two trays of shrimp and took one from her. "Edie's been with my family for ages," he explained.

"How lucky for you all," Claudia said archly.

"It's just that she doesn't like the thought of being replaced."

"You can assure her that I'm not replacing her," said Claudia. "I'm a caterer. She's a servant. That may be putting a pretty fine point on it, but—"

"Claudia." His temper was unraveling and he clung tightly to the platter of shrimp to keep himself from grabbing her by the shoulders and giving her a hard shake. "What are you getting at?"

Claudia gave him a deceptively innocent look, her eyes round and innocent. "Nothing, Ned. I think it's just lovely that your family has servants. I think you and Edie ought to go somewhere and watch reruns of 'Upstairs, Downstairs.' I'll take care of this." She lifted her tray and stormed toward the house.

Ned ground his teeth and chased after her. "I'm going to help you."

"If you keep swinging that tray back and forth, you're going to spill those shrimp. And if you do that, I swear, Ned, I'll dump the new batch of yogurt dip on your head." She stomped into the kitchen and let the screen door slam shut behind her.

He took a deep breath and another, until his irritation began to wane. All right. He'd been a rich kid and he'd made it all the way to rich adulthood without ever having had to sling hash at a greasy spoon. That was a fact. He couldn't change it. He was a Wyatt.

And she was a Mulcahey. And she was working for his sister.

It was a professional arrangement, just as his parents' employment of Edie Mueller had been a professional arrangement. Just as certain business people's employment of Ned was a professional arrangement. He billed them for his services and they paid him handsomely for his talents. Did that make him a servant?

When you were a Wyatt, he supposed, you were born into a certain social class and it didn't matter what you did—that class always remained with you.

Ned would just have to prove to Claudia Mulcahey that class could mean many different things.

"THERE YOU ARE!" Melanie squawked.

After leaving her tray of shrimp on the counter, Claudia had walked down the hall to the dining room to see how the buffet was going to be set up. The room was large, with cherry wainscoting and hunter green walls, a Queen Anne's table polished as bright as a mirror and long enough to seat thirty comfortably, and three crystal chandeliers. While regal, the room was oddly oppressive. Claudia couldn't imagine eating in it.

The room transformed to stultifying when Melanie Wyatt Steele swept in from the Great Room. Almost at once Claudia noticed the resemblance between Melanie and her younger brother. She and Ned both had handsome features, but on Ned they looked, well, *handsome*.

At the moment, Melanie was clad in an expensive-looking velvet warm-up suit and appeared frantic. "Have you brought the cakes?"

"I'm afraid not," Claudia said with uncharacteristic diffidence. For all she knew, this could cause Melanie Steele to blackball her all over town.

"I want everything perfect tonight," Melanie went on, fussing with the pile of neatly folded lace napery that lay waiting on the sideboard. "My daughter and her friends have been looking forward to this moment all their lives."

I doubt that, Claudia thought.

"And the cakes—when you described those valentine-shaped cakes, well, that was what finally won the day, Claudia. Everything has to be perfect, especially the cakes."

"Everything will be perfect," Claudia promised.

"Because there will be *tears* if something goes wrong. *Tears*." The way she stressed the word implied that if one girl shed one tear that night, Claudia would be sentenced to death.

"My, my," came a deep, husky voice from just beyond the doorway. "You're certainly on today, Mel."

"Ned! What the heck are you doing here?"

Ned sauntered into the room. His gaze flickered toward Claudia before coming to rest on his sister. "I'm helping Ms. Mulcahey," he said, turning to Claudia. She might have just imagined it, but she thought she saw him wink. "Should the meat be refrigerated or does it go in the oven?"

"I'll take care of it," she mumbled.

"Wait a minute," Melanie interjected as Claudia neared the doorway. "What's going on, Ned?"

Ned's smile grew roguish, one corner of his mouth rising higher than the other, the way it had earlier that day. "Nothing's going on with me. What's going on with you?"

"So help me, if you're trying to interfere with Ms. Mulcahey's work—"

"Interfere? Me?"

"I'm warning you, Ned. Tonight's too important for you to be getting in Ms. Mulcahey's way. Run along now, Claudia," Melanie imperiously dismissed her. "You take care of the meat. I'd like to talk to my brother."

Run along now, Claudia repeated silently, doing her best to stifle her rage. Pressing her lips together, she headed for the door. Ned stepped aside to let her pass, but he discreetly reached out and gave her hand a squeeze.

Her palm burned where his thumb had pressed into it. Her fingers tingled. She loathed him as much for having such an effect on her as she loathed his sister for behaving so condescendingly toward her.

Halfway down the hall she paused to compose herself. God knew whether that gorgon of a cook would be lying in wait for her in the kitchen. She closed her eyes and inhaled deeply.

"Dear Lord, Ned!" Melanie's voice was muted, but Claudia was able to make out the words. "Don't you have enough to do today? You shouldn't be fooling around with that girl. You were supposed to go to Mother's and keep her happy until I could get over there and help her with her dress."

"It amazes me that you can run everybody's life so well," Ned said caustically. "Mellow out, sis. You take care of you and I'll take care of me. And I'll take care of Mom, too, although you know as well as I do that she doesn't want anyone taking care of her."

"And for heaven's sake, stay away from the caterer. I know she's cute in an unrefined sort of way, but really, Ned—don't waste your time."

"I'll decide what's worth my time and what isn't."

"Trust me, Neddy—*she* isn't. If you're looking for sport, go back to New York. Here in Glenwood people take these things seriously. I won't have you tarnishing your reputation—"

"My reputation? If I have a reputation, I'm sure it's already tarnished beyond redemption. At least, I hope it is."

"Don't joke about it, Ned. You're thirty-four years old and you're still single. People are going to start wondering."

"Wondering what? That I'm gay or that I'm a sleazy womanizer?"

"Both, probably."

"Wow. That's a lot to live up to."

"I'm serious."

"Indeed you are, Melanie. You're beyond serious. You're critical."

Hearing footsteps approaching the doorway, Claudia turned and raced down the hall to the kitchen. To her great relief, the room was empty.

Her temper remained white-hot as she slid the platters of meat into the refrigerator. The hell with all of them, she fumed. Melanie, Ned—and Edie.

She felt hands on her waist and flinched, jerking the tray in her hands. A half dozen shrimp tumbled onto the floor, looking like succulent pink-and-white parentheses.

"Damn it!" She'd seen more food spilled in the past two hours than she had in her entire career.

"No swearing," Ned whispered, his hands still spanning her waist and his lips close to her ear. "If anything makes Melanie mad, it's naughty language."

"Maybe I should expose her to my complete vocabulary."

"Let her be mad at me, not you," he advised. His fingers felt strong, his thumbs digging into the cramped muscles of her lower back, his palms molding to the curves of her hips.

It took all her willpower not to lean into him, to draw his arms fully around her. His breath ruffled her hair, warming the nape of her neck while the refrigerator continued to throw cold air in her face. "I'm mad at you, too," she muttered, easing out of his grip. "Do you know what shrimp costs?"

He scooped up the shrimp nearest his feet. "Edie always said her floors were clean enough to eat off."

"You seem to have quite a habit of eating off floors."

"These are edible," he said, collecting the last of the shrimp. "We'll rinse them off in the sink. It'll be our little secret."

"They've been steamed in champagne," she argued. "If you rinse them off, they'll lose the flavor."

"Steamed in champagne?" He appeared intrigued. "You actually boiled champagne?"

"Cheap stuff," she assured him.

He ran the shrimp under the water. Then he shook them off and took a bite of one. "It tastes great."

"Can you taste the champagne?"

"I don't know what I'm tasting. All I know is, I like it." He held the end of one curling pink shrimp and jabbed the other end between her teeth. She remembered the way his chocolate-covered finger had felt in her mouth. The shrimp made a poor substitute.

She mustn't think that way. She mustn't keep eating out of his hand. The symbolism of it was as alarming as the act itself.

Ned seemed unnaturally fascinated by the motions of her mouth as she chewed. She turned away and forced herself to replay his sister's ugly words.

One thing Melanie had said was true: Claudia wasn't going to be Ned's sport.

"I'm done here," she said quietly, closing the refrigerator door. "I have more food to bring over. Why don't you get the cookie basket out of the van and go on to your mother's?"

He contemplated her for a minute, his eyes filled with questions. "I can't ride my bicycle with that basket," he finally said. "It was hard enough balancing the candy box on the handlebars."

For her own well-being, she knew she should get away from Ned before he had the chance to stick anything else in her mouth. She should tell him getting the cookies to his mother was his problem, he'd just have to find a way. Instead, when she opened her mouth, what came out was: "I'll drop you off at your mother's on my way home."

Seeing the way his face lit up made her regret the offer...and then made her not regret it quite so much.

She liked Ned Wyatt. More than she should. More than was safe or wise. She liked the way his hands had felt on her, the way his mouth had mirrored hers, opening as he slid the shrimp between her teeth and closing as she bit down on it. She liked the way his eyes danced with color and emotion, with challenges and all those questions she couldn't begin to interpret, let alone answer. She liked the way he smelled, the way he'd sounded when he'd told her she was beautiful. She liked the way he'd kissed her.

Maybe it was sport to him. Maybe he was as phony as his supercilious sister. He was a Wyatt, after all.

But no matter what she told herself, no matter how much she wanted to protect herself and avoid unnecessary risks, she wasn't ready to say goodbye to Ned. Not yet.

Chapter Four

"WHAT A PLEASURE! Come in, come in!" Standing in the open front doorway, Ned's mother clasped her hands together and beamed at Claudia.

She had never met Mrs. Wyatt before, although she'd certainly heard enough about her. The Glenwood weekly newspaper ran a story about her in practically every edition. But the photographs didn't do her justice. Like her son and daughter she was handsome, with strong, decisive features and piercing hazel eyes. She had an easy smile and a down-to-earth manner that Claudia found refreshing after her encounter with Melanie.

"I'm afraid I can't stay," she demurred. "I'm just here to drop off Ned and his bicycle." After introducing Claudia and handing his mother the basket of cookies, he had returned to the parking lot to unload his bike from the rear of the van.

"Nonsense," said Mrs. Wyatt, taking Claudia's arm and practically dragging her into the condominium.

The living room was small, decorated with spare pieces which Claudia knew must have cost a fortune. Fresh flowers stood in vases in the foyer and on the polished coffee table. The place looked warm and inviting, elegant yet lacking the aristocratic stuffiness of Wyatt Hall.

"Now," said Mrs. Wyatt, gleefully eyeing her reluctant guest, "let me fix some tea and then we'll have some of these scrumptious-looking cookies."

"Mrs. Wyatt—"

"I want to know all about you," Mrs. Wyatt continued, waltzing into the kitchen with the basket. "Ned never introduces me to his girlfriends. This must mean something."

"I'm not his girlfriend," Claudia corrected her, following her down the hallway to a cozy, sunny kitchen. "I'm a caterer. Mrs. Steele hired me to do the food for the Valentine's Day cotillion tonight."

"Be that as it may," Mrs. Wyatt responded vaguely. She placed the basket on the breakfast table and started to prepare tea. Claudia had to remind herself that this tall silver-haired dynamo in jeans and a baggy old sweater was in fact the town matriarch, a woman who had once presided over Wyatt Hall with an army of servants at her beck and call.

Sending Claudia another beaming smile, she said, "Ned is in love with you, isn't he?"

Claudia blanched. "No. We only met this morning."

"Please sit." Mrs. Wyatt pushed her, with surprising force, into a chair. "So, you met this morning and it was love at first sight."

"No. It was an accident. I nearly ran him over."

"I suppose we should all be grateful that you didn't." She patted Claudia's shoulder. "He's a good man, Claudia—may I call you Claudia? A little frisky, but that's part of the fun. Have you set a date yet?"

No wonder Melanie had been worried when Mrs. Wyatt had moved away from the family estate, Claudia thought. Someone had to keep an eye on her.

"Ned and I are not getting married, Mrs. Wyatt," she said carefully.

"Nonsense. The pendulum's swinging back, my dear. Ten years ago, eighteen-year-old girls like my granddaughter wouldn't have sat still for a debutante cotillion. Now we're seeing the old traditions return, the old rituals being embraced. Living in sin is passé."

"I'm trying to tell you, Mrs. Wyatt—your son and I met when my van skidded on some ice and he fell off his bike. We're not living in sin. We're not getting married."

Mrs. Wyatt poured water into the teapot. "Why not? You don't love Ned?"

"I hardly know him."

"But what you know, you love," she said with conviction.

"Well . . . he's very nice," Claudia conceded, trying not to think of all the other things he was: Forward. Mischievous. Virile. Gorgeous. Tantalizing.

Wealthy. Upper crust. Patrician.

"Ned and I come from very different backgrounds," she attempted, wishing he would get himself into the kitchen and set his mother straight.

"Where you come from isn't as important as where you're going. Who cares about backgrounds? You haven't got a criminal record, have you?"

"No, but—"

"Well, then, it hardly matters." With a flourish she untied the white ribbon atop the basket of cookies, then paused at the sound of Ned's footsteps in the hallway. "We're in the kitchen, Neddy!" she called, folding back the red cellophane and inhaling deeply. When Ned entered, she gave him a buoyant hug. "These cookies smell splendid! I'm so glad you didn't bring me one of those heart-shaped boxes of chocolates this year. That's so clichéd."

"Oh. Well—" he exchanged an amused glance with Claudia "—I thought you might prefer cookies. Claudia baked them."

"What a marvelous talent to have! Ned, she's perfect."

Ned exchanged another look at Claudia. If he noticed her puzzlement he chose to ignore it. "She's very talented, Mom. Go ahead, dig in." He offered the basket to his mother, then helped himself to a cookie, took a bite and groaned contentedly. "What is this?"

"Butterscotch and rum," Claudia told him.

"I thought it was going to be vanilla." A lazy smile traced his mouth as he gazed at her. "I should have known to expect something more complicated. Try one of these, Mom." He searched the mound of cookies for another butterscotch-rum one and handed it to his mother.

Claudia pushed back her chair. "I've really got to go. I have so much to do—"

"Oh, please, have a cup of tea, first," Ned's mother said. "It's nearly lunchtime, and I'll bet you're planning to skip lunch. Am I right?"

"I usually do eat lunch," Claudia protested, feeling the need to defend herself. "But the cotillion begins in just a few hours, and I have a lot of preparation—"

"So, fuel up. Have a cookie." The telephone rang and Mrs. Wyatt sighed and rolled her eyes. "It's been like this all morning. You'd think this party was the biggest event of the season. Then again, I suppose it is." The phone rang a second time and Mrs. Wyatt put down the teapot. "If you will excuse me..." With a blithe smile, she left the kitchen.

Claudia turned to Ned. "Your mother thinks we're getting married!"

Ned didn't appear at all concerned. "She's always about ten steps ahead of the rest of us."

"Ned! Would you please tell her we're not ten steps behind her? I tried to explain that I was the caterer, but she wouldn't listen to me."

"She knows who you are. I introduced you and now she's eating your homemade cookies. They're almost as good as your chocolate kisses, by the way," he added, helping himself to a second cookie. "But I don't think my mother could handle a treat as intense as those kisses."

"Forgive me if I sound harsh, Ned, but I don't think your mother can handle reality. She thinks I'm your girlfriend!"

"My mother is very realistic," he argued mildly. "Take a look around you, Claudia. This is the way she is. No muss, no fuss. She likes to keep things simple."

"Sure. And when she gets sick of the simple life she can buy herself a penthouse in Trump Tower or forty beachfront acres in Greenwich."

"That's not her style," Ned insisted. "Wyatt Hall was my father's home. My mother loved him, so she moved in and made a happy life for herself there. And now she's happy here—in a five-room condo, with a lady who comes in once a week to dust and vacuum. She drives a six-year-old car and buys most of her clothing through a catalog."

"Maybe that just proves that she's off her rocker," Claudia muttered.

"Or else it proves," Ned argued, "that she's a working-class woman who feels most comfortable living modestly."

"Your mother? The queen of the Glenwood Historical Society—a working-class woman?"

"Her father was a union man—he worked on the Bridgeport docks. She won a full scholarship to Pembroke. John Edward Wyatt III happened to be captain of the crew team at Brown. It was love at first sight."

So, you met this morning and it was love at first sight.... His mother's words reverberated inside her. *Where you come from isn't as important as where you're going....* Well, just because things had worked out that way for Ned's mother and father didn't mean they would work out that way for Claudia and—

"You aren't John Edward Wyatt IV, are you?"

Ned grimaced. "My dirty secret is out. Promise you won't hold it against me."

"I really have to go." She stood and crossed to the door, feeling the urgent need to clear out before Ned's mother's bizarre perspective started to make sense to her. She didn't care if Mrs. Wyatt was the daughter of a union man. She'd gone on to give birth to a son with a multimillion-dollar name.

And with the most mesmerizing eyes and the most wicked smile. And the most arousing kisses.

"I've really got to go," she repeated, feeling strangely as if she were pleading for her life.

He rose, too. His gaze softened, as if he recognized her apprehension and understood it. Taking her elbow, he ushered her out of the kitchen.

His mother was descending the stairs. "Was I that long on the phone?" she asked apologetically.

"Claudia has to leave," Ned explained. "She's got a lot to prepare for the party tonight. For some reason, she thinks if everything isn't perfect Melanie will give her a hard time."

"Melanie *will* give her a hard time," Mrs. Wyatt said with a long-suffering smile. "Giving people a hard time is what Melanie does best. Claudia, dear, I'm so glad we had this chance to meet. I assume I'll be seeing you tonight."

"Yes," said Claudia, adding under her breath, "I'll be the one who's working."

"I'll be right back," Ned told his mother before escorting Claudia outside.

She assured herself he was only showing good manners by walking her to her van. In a matter of minutes she would be rid of him. He was going to stay and visit with his mother and she would be free.

Free to return to her house alone, to bustle around her kitchen by herself, without any interference from a man who thought there was nothing unseemly about glazing his finger with chocolate and stroking it across her tongue.

Merely thinking about the time she'd spent with Ned in her kitchen sent a ripple of heat through her. She didn't want to go home alone. She wanted him to come with her, to help her make more kisses, to taste and nibble and share the devilishly complicated flavor of them with her. She wanted to gaze into his eyes and feel his arms around her and his mouth on hers again. She wanted to believe in love at first sight.

But she didn't. And when Ned drew to a halt beside her van and dipped his head to hers she turned her face.

Denied her lips, he nipped the sensitive edge of her earlobe. Fresh shivers of arousal filtered through her, gathering in the cradle of her hips. "Your hair is the prettiest color," he whispered.

"Only when the sun hits it," she mumbled weakly, wishing she had the willpower to pull away.

He grazed the skin below her ear and she reflexively tilted her head so he could kiss her throat. "Are you going to be working all afternoon? I could stop by later."

To help her? she wondered. Or for something else? "I'll be working," she informed him, wondering if he heard the breathless wavering in her voice. "I mean, *really* working, Ned. Maybe it would be better if you didn't stop by."

"Better for whom?" He slid his lips up to her chin, then higher, to her mouth. Her pulse roared in her ears as he thrust his tongue past her teeth, as he tightened his arms around her exactly as she'd hoped he would, as he pulled her slender body to himself and let her feel his response to her. His hips surged, pressed, rocked against her in a way that left her giddy and gasping, eager for more.

"Don't," she moaned, hiding her face in the hollow of his neck.

Sighing, he loosened his hold slightly but refused to let go. "I want you."

She knew that without his having to say it. "But you scare me."

He chuckled. "Why? Because I'm John Edward Wyatt IV? Because you think my mother's off her rocker? Because you think I'll get in the way of your catering the perfect cotillion?"

"All of the above," she admitted with a faint smile.

"Or maybe you're scared because you know damned well we make better kisses together than you can make by yourself."

"Don't talk like that."

He traced the angular edge of her jaw with his fingertips. She imagined his touch elsewhere, on her arms, her belly, her breasts. She imagined making kisses with him in every possible way and her pulse grew even louder, faster, sending its throbbing heat through her body.

"You want me, too," he guessed.

Of course she wanted him, more than she'd ever wanted a man before. And that scared her most of all.

"Tell your mother this isn't love at first sight," she muttered, easing out of his embrace and opening the door of the van. "Desire isn't the same thing as love. Anyway, I don't have time for love. I have to focus all my energies on Fantasy Feasts right now. I'm barely treading water. If I don't do a perfect job with this cotillion, my company might go under. I don't even have time to stand here talking to you."

His fingers reached her temple and twirled through the silky hair there. "It's hard to believe a woman can't find a little time for love on Valentine's Day."

Ned was more polite than Jimmy McNeill had been, but the message was the same: if Claudia put her professional survival ahead of her love life, she had something wrong with her. When Jimmy had left her she'd been sad but not devastated. If Ned left her—

Left her? What was she thinking? They'd known each other less than three hours. For her to climb into her van and drive home would hardly constitute the end of a torrid romance.

Yet as long as he kept weaving his fingers through her hair, as long as he kept gazing at her with his hypnotic, jewel-like eyes, as long as she remembered the heat and texture of his mouth on hers, his tongue dueling with hers, his body pressed to hers . . .

Torrid certainly seemed like the right word.

"I'm going," she said with as much firmness as she could muster.

Ned kept his hand on her arm until she was settled behind the wheel. "I'll be by," he promised.

"I'll be working."

"I don't doubt it." He took a step back and started to close the door. "We've had kisses and cookies and we've had shrimp—the sweets and the hors d'oeuvres." A sly smile curved his mouth. "It won't be long, Claudia, before you and I have the main course."

Chapter Five

NED BIKED HOME from his mother's place, enjoying the sunshine and the hint of spring's fragrance released into the air by the thawing earth. At his mother's insistence, he'd eaten half a sandwich before he'd left. At his insistence, his mother had refrained from interrogating him about Claudia.

He wasn't sure he subscribed to her faith in love at first sight. However, he couldn't deny that throughout his twelve lively years of postgraduate bachelorhood he had never felt anything like the imperative craving he experienced every time he thought of Claudia Mulcahey.

There was something tough and determined about her, something strong and self-aware and extremely appealing to a strong, self-aware man like Ned. Claudia knew what she wanted and she went after it, and she wasn't looking for anyone to make things easy for her.

He could make things easier. Along with the sensual pleasure of their final kiss, he was haunted by her words, her concern that if the Valentine's Day cotillion was a flop Fantasy Feasts might go out of business.

He didn't want her business to fail. He couldn't bear the notion that Claudia would have to fold up her tent and go back to working in a diner—not when she had genuine talent. He'd tasted her chocolate kisses; he knew what a culinary genius she was.

And to think the fate of her business rested in the hands of his cantankerous older sister....

Ned prayed that the cotillion would be a success and that Melanie would sing the praises of Claudia's catering to all her snooty, snobby friends, and that Claudia would find herself besieged with contracts for her services.

But even a success tonight wouldn't be enough.

She needed a larger work space, assistants, storage facilities.... She needed the proper capital. Ned could put together a suitable package of financing for her if she let him.

He headed down the stairs to the den. His condo was in a complex across town from his mother's. It was a nice enough place, and his one-year lease included an option to buy. It would be a bit small for two people, though.

"Cripes," he said aloud, then laughed. He wasn't about to invite Claudia to move in with him, was he?

The light on his answering machine was flashing. He punched the button and listened.

"Neddy?" Melanie's voice squawked out of the speaker. "I was just wondering if you could do me a great big favor and bring Ramona Warner to the cotillion with you tonight. Since she isn't related to any of the debutantes, she can attend only as someone's guest. Could you please bring her as your guest? It would be so much fun for both of you. I know it's last-minute, but she really would love to come and she's very fond of you."

Melanie did matchmaking the way she did everything else—without subtlety. Her attempt to hook Ned up with Ramona Warner was last-minute because she'd only just seen him with Claudia that morning. Evidently Melanie was prepared to do whatever was necessary to keep him from fraternizing with the lower classes.

Shaking his head, he pulled out the telephone directory and looked up Fantasy Feasts. The phone rang four times and then Claudia's machine clicked on: *Hi, you've reached Fantasy Feasts. Please leave your name and number and let us cater to you.*

"Claudia?" he shouted over the tape. "It's Ned. If you're there, pick up!" *Cater to me!* he almost demanded, but he figured that might frighten her.

A minute passed and then, to his delight, he heard Claudia say, "Hello, Ned."

He wanted to discuss ways of raising capital for her company. He wanted to tell her that he missed her, that kissing her outside his mother's condo had been a prelude, not a finale, and that she had nothing to be afraid of. He wanted to describe his own fantasy feast, starting with her lips and working his way down to her luscious hot buns.

"How are your hearts?" he asked.

"My hearts? The cake layers, you mean?"

"Yes."

"They came out well. I was just about to start making the frosting."

Frosting. He'd already painted her lips with molten chocolate. Now he was assailed by visions of her with cold, sugary white stuff on her lips.

"I'll be right over," he said.

"Ned—"

"What I was thinking," he hastened to explain, "is that if I drive over we can use your van and my car to transport the food. It would cut down the number of trips you have to make.''

She didn't speak for a minute; evidently she was assessing his offer, weighing the possible hazards in accepting his help. ''All right,'' she finally said. He wondered whether that meant she was no longer afraid of him or she missed him as much as he missed her—or quite simply that she didn't want to have to make so many trips to Wyatt Hall.

What it meant to him, he acknowledged after saying goodbye, was that they would be traveling to Wyatt Hall in separate vehicles. He wouldn't be able to glance to his left and see her clean, sharp profile. He wouldn't be able to lean across the console and steal a kiss the instant she turned off the engine.

But before they left for Wyatt Hall they would be at her house, in her kitchen, surrounded by hearts and frosting.

The possibilities made him smile.

OVER THE WHIR of her hand-held mixer she almost didn't hear the tapping on the door connecting the kitchen to the garage. She turned off the appliance and opened the door.

She had known it would be Ned, yet seeing him, having him so close, feeling his presence fill her kitchen... Well, there was no adequate way Claudia could have prepared herself.

''I do have a front door,'' she pointed out. ''You don't have to come in through the garage.''

He grinned. ''I came to help out, not to act like a guest.'' He shrugged out of his jacket and gazed around the kitchen. Spotting the bowl of fluffy pink frosting, he headed directly to the island, finger poised for dipping.

"Behave yourself," she scolded, shoving him away before he could poke his finger into the frosting.

"Oh, come on. Just a teeny, tiny little taste?"

He looked so imploring, so irresistibly boyish, she relented with a sigh. He dabbed his finger into the soft pink confection, licked it off and started with surprise. "It's peppermint."

"What did you expect?"

"Strawberry, I guess. It's awfully pink."

"Of course it's pink. Today's Valentine's Day," she reminded him.

His smile grew deeper. "You're catching on," he murmured in a disturbingly husky voice.

Aware of how close he was to kissing her—and how much she longed for another of his kisses—she quickly turned away, grabbing the mixer and turning it on, clinging to its handle as if it were a weapon. "If you came here to romance me," she shouted over the drone of the motor, "you can leave."

"I came to help you," he said, then shook his head. "Not true. I came because I couldn't stay away." He said it so frankly, so bluntly, she had to accept his words as the truth.

If she matched his honesty she would have to admit that ever since she'd driven away from his mother's condo she had been thinking of him, reliving his kiss, obsessed with him. Wishing he would come to her.

She could scarcely admit it to herself. She wasn't about to admit it to him. "Well, if you're here to help, you may as well help," she said, guiding the spinning beaters deeper into the frosting. "There's a roll of plastic wrap on the counter by the phone. Could you bring it over?''

He located the box and carried it to her, then moved behind her and planted a kiss on the crown of her head. Her scalp tingled, sending a flutter of sensation down her spine. She shivered and clicked the motor speed higher, whipping the fluffy pink frosting against the sides of the bowl.

Ned slid his hands to her waist and pulled her back against him. "Turn the machine off," he murmured.

She felt him through her jeans and his, felt the hardness of him against the small of her back. She swallowed, shivered . . . and turned the machine off. "Please, Ned." Her voice emerged small and breathless. "Don't play games with me."

He slid his hands forward, flattening them across her belly. "I'm not playing games," he swore, his lips close to her ear. "Watching you cook turns me on."

"I'm not cooking," she argued inanely, wishing her legs didn't feel so weak, wishing her hips didn't want to nestle back against him. "I'm whipping up the frosting."

"Whipping it up," he reiterated, putting an erotic emphasis on each syllable. "Indeed."

"Ned . . ."

He spun her in his arms, then pressed into her again, this time seeking the warmth between her legs. "After you whip it up," he asked, his eyes sparkling with an odd blend of amusement and blatant arousal, "what do you do?"

"I spread it—" Blushing furiously, she cut herself off.

"You spread it," he echoed, insinuating his knee between her legs and nudging them farther apart. "It sounds delicious."

"Coming from you, it sounds X-rated."

"It sounds wonderfully gooey." He bowed and brushed a light, searing kiss across her lips.

"Actually it can get kind of crumb-y," she punned, finding the courage to meet his bold gaze.

"I suppose that would happen if you don't spread it properly."

"Or if the cake is too warm," she said, swallowing the tremor in her throat as his thigh moved between hers. "The layers have to cool down."

"I'll bet they do." He flexed the muscles of his thigh slowly, subtly against her. She closed her eyes and suppressed a moan. "I like my layers warm, though."

"Then you can't frost them," she argued, her tone rasping. If he didn't kiss her soon, really kiss her, kiss her the way he had outside his mother's house...she didn't know what she would do.

He rocked against her in a deliberate rhythm. "Can't the layers be warm and firm at the same time?"

"Not when it comes to cake."

Reaching around her, he scooped a dollop of frosting onto his finger. "Taste it," he whispered, presenting his pink-glazed fingertip to her.

This was insane. She had work to do, tons of work, the most important work in her life. Yet, as if under a spell, she opened her mouth and ran the tip of her tongue over his finger.

Simultaneously his tongue darted out to lick the frosting. Their tongues touched, sweet and sticky with peppermint, and she sank against the butcher-block island, buffeted by the deluge of hot sensation that seared her.

"Make love with me," he said, half a plea, half a demand. His gaze burned through her, expressing desire and need, lust and something more.

"I can't," she groaned, even as her thighs tensed around his leg, as her tongue tingled with the flavors of confectioners' sugar and butter, peppermint extract and passion. "I can't, Ned."

"Because of the cotillion?"

She nodded. Let him believe her professional pressures and deadlines were what was preventing them from finishing what they'd so recklessly begun with a finger full of frosting. Let him believe that Fantasy Feasts was her only reason for saying no.

There would be time later, after she'd composed herself, to remind him that he was a Wyatt with a Roman-numeral name, pampered and privileged, a citizen of a community where she would always be an outsider—an employee.

If Ned was looking for a quick fling, she wasn't interested. And if he was looking for anything more than that, it wouldn't work out. She would never belong in his world.

When his hands relaxed at her waist, however, and he eased back from her, she found herself wondering whether a quick fling with Ned Wyatt might be worth all the heartache and regret she would feel afterward, after he'd had his sport and returned to his proper place among the ranks of the elite.

No man had ever excited her the way he could. No man had ever made her want so much. Not that she believed in love at first sight, not that she believed any of the blarney his mother had dished out, but... Lord, wouldn't it be nice if Ned wanted the same things Claudia did?

What he wanted, she acknowledged with a doleful sigh, was to have his cake and eat it, too. She acknowledged that cake and chocolate kisses, while delectable treats, would never be enough to satisfy her.

Chapter Six

"FINANCING?" she asked.

They were in the kitchen of Wyatt Hall. Seated on a stool, Ned observed as Claudia arranged her cake materials on the counter. This time everything had survived the trip across town in her van.

Following in his car, his back seat filled with heaping trays, Ned had felt her absence keenly. He had wanted to be with her, smelling her clean fragrance, admiring her stunning blue eyes.

Of course, if he'd been seated beside her in her van, he might have been unable to resist the temptation to reach out and grab her. And then she would have lost control of the van and it would have skidded on an icy patch of road and all the food would have been ruined again.

And then they would have had to start all over. Which might have been kind of fun.

For him, anyway. For her it would have been tragic. As soon as he'd stopped trying to seduce her at her house, she'd become compulsively businesslike, trooping around the room like a marine sergeant, barking orders as if she viewed the cotillion as a military campaign—with Melanie serving as the commanding officer of the opposing forces.

Fortunately Melanie wasn't at Wyatt Hall when they arrived. Edie was, but after huffing and puffing about Claudia's invasion of her precious kitchen, she let Ned convince her that the florist needed her invaluable advice regarding the flower arrangements in the ballroom. Once he'd dispatched Edie, Claudia got to work assembling her cakes.

It seemed like a good time to broach the subject. "Nothing complicated," he told her. "I'm only thinking of what you could accomplish with the proper capitalization."

She flashed him a sharp, blue-eyed glance. "Proper capitalization, huh," she repeated dubiously. "Pretty fancy language."

"All it means is having enough money to get Fantasy Feasts to the next level."

"The next level of what?"

He watched as she smoothed the pink frosting over the largest chocolate cake layer, which sat on a doily-lined silver tray. With a deft flick of the pan, she dropped the second layer on top of the first.

"Imagine what your life would be like if you could work in a kitchen like this all the time, in a shop downtown in the business district. If you had a clerk, and an assistant and an eye-catching sign out front."

"Yeah, right," she snorted. "That sounds like a lot more fantasy than feast."

"Not if your company had an infusion of cash. That's where I could help you out."

She shot him another look, this one decidedly suspicious. "What am I, the newest Wyatt charity?"

He shook his head and chuckled. "No one's going to *give* you a penny. However, I can put together funding—"

"A loan? Forget it." She cut him off. "I'm already paying off my van, a mortgage and the refrigerator in the cellar. I'm not taking any more loans."

"I'm not talking about a loan, either," he explained patiently, trying not to let the graceful gliding motions of her fingers distract him. "I'm talking about an investment. I could find you a silent partner, someone looking for a promising business to sink his money into, in return for a portion of your profits."

"Profits?" She laughed. "I'm just barely breaking even."

"Most new businesses don't start breaking even for years. If you're not in the red, you're doing great."

"Who's going to invest in my company?" she asked, flipping the smallest chocolate layer onto the cake. "Who in his right mind would invest in my rickety little catering company when they could buy something safe and sound, like municipal bonds?"

"You've got a better chance of avoiding bankruptcy than some municipalities I know," he argued, smiling. She dragged over a bowl of chocolate kisses and used them to create a decorative border around each layer. "And if my clients wanted to buy municipal bonds they wouldn't come to me."

She eyed him warily. "And by getting these clients to invest in Fantasy Feasts you pick up a whopping commission."

There was that, sure. But more was at stake than simply Ned's commission. He wanted Claudia to succeed because it meant so much to her. Because she was entitled to it. Because if she didn't succeed she would leave Glenwood with her spirit broken in two.

It was her spirit that excited him, more than her reddish-brown hair and her pure blue eyes, more than her prowess with shrimp and sweets. He wanted her nearby and he wanted her happy.

"I can think of at least two clients who might be interested in parking some money with you. I'd need to examine your profit-loss records, your debt service and so on. But—"

"You think I'm going to let you see my private financial records?"

"I'd have to see them, in order to persuade my clients to invest in Fantasy Feasts."

She set down her knife and gripped the tray. "Here's what you'd learn from my records, Ned, I'm your basic hand-to-mouth model. My bank balance resembles what you probably spend during an average night out with a woman."

If she'd been meaning to discourage him, she'd made a mistake. "Now, there's an idea. Why don't you and I spend an average night together tomorrow and see if it resembles your bank account?"

Claudia bit her lip. Maybe he was pushing too hard. But after the way she'd responded to him barely an hour ago, the way her body had arched and surged against his and her hips had moved with his and her eyes had closed in near surrender . . .

Why shouldn't he push a little? Why shouldn't he bring this relationship to the next level? No matter how anxiously she was avoiding his gaze right now, he knew she was as interested as he was in taking things further.

"I don't want you spending your money on me," she muttered, lifting the tray carefully.

"All right. We'll keep it cheap. I'll rent the video, you make the popcorn." At her skeptical glare, he shrugged. "Hey, I can do a low-rent date just like you."

"Right. And you can also peel carrots." In a huff, she handed him a bag of them, and holding her head high she carried her magnificent cake out of the kitchen.

Ned was lost in reverie. A bowl of popcorn, his toasty wool afghan spread over them, a 1950s thriller about mutated insects on the TV in the background... and afterward, they could discuss making a formal announcement and setting a date.

An average night with the most extraordinary woman he'd ever met, he thought with a smile. It could be the most exciting night in his life....

He heard a scream, and another, and a loud thump. This might be the most exciting night, after all, he thought as he bolted from the kitchen. But he was no longer smiling.

"WELL, IT WAS TOO *PINK!*" Edie ranted. "The color startled me! In all my days, I've never seen a cake that color pink!"

It wasn't a cake any more. It was a mess of smeared frosting and crumbs strewn across the marble floor of the ballroom.

Claudia wanted to weep. She sat on the hard, shiny floor, less than an inch from where she'd been standing when Edie had noticed the cake, shrieked and dropped her dry mop at Claudia's feet where she would trip over it. Two stories above her loomed the ornately corniced ceiling of the ballroom. Chairs and settees stood along the room's perimeter, along with tables festooned with flowers and the elegant dessert table where the cakes were supposed to be displayed. An arching stairway that looked as if it had been designed for debutantes soared to a balcony along the inner wall.

It was all so opulent, Claudia thought, wondering what kind of picture she made seated Indian-style on the polished floor with frosting spattered on her jeans.

"It's all right," Ned was saying. She tilted her head only enough to see him ushering Edie away. A good idea, too. Claudia was ready to strangle the old hag. There had been something suspiciously deliberate in the way Edie had tossed down her dry mop in front of Claudia's foot. "Everything's going to be all right."

"Everything's *not* going to be all right," Claudia snapped. "We're down one cake."

"So you'll make another. Look, Edie will oversee the cleanup. We can get whatever you need from your house and you can bake the cake here. I'll be right by your side, doing whatever has to be done. Come on, Claudia—we can do it."

"You're not going to let her make another cake like that, are you?" Edie sputtered. "It looked horrible. Repulsive! Much too pink."

"Edie, please," Ned silenced her, evidently aware of the homicidal turn Claudia's thoughts were once again taking. "Just clean the floor, all right? Come on, Claudia," he said brightly, extending his hands to her and hoisting her to her feet. "If we work really fast—"

Claudia yanked her hands from his. If he touched her, they wouldn't work really fast. They'd get sidetracked. He'd dip his fingers into the new batch of cake batter and he'd slide his arm around her...and they'd be lost.

"Don't help me," she grumbled. "Just keep the official Wyatt cook away from me. She tripped me on purpose, Ned."

"Of course she didn't." He turned to Edie, seeking corroboration.

The plump white-haired witch shrugged innocently. "I couldn't help myself. It was a ghastly looking cake. I finally understand what shocking pink means. I would never serve a cake like that."

"Well, I've got news for you," Claudia declared pugnaciously. "I'm going to serve *two* cakes like that. Out of my way," she commanded, brushing past Ned. If she'd been disconsolate a minute ago, she was fired up now. Nobody, not Ned with his seductive hazel eyes and incandescent smile, not Edie with her territorial testiness, not Melanie Steele with her haughty affectations—*nobody* was going to keep Claudia from catering this cotillion successfully. If it meant working nonstop for the next ten hours, running the kitchen in jeans and a ponytail, frosting the cake at the very moment Glenwood's finest young ladies were being presented to society, she would do it. If it meant locking Ned out of the kitchen, out of her thoughts, out of her heart, she would do it.

This party was going to be Claudia's personal triumph. She refused to consider any other outcome.

She was swinging through the kitchen door when she felt Ned's hand on her shoulder. "I've got a lot to do," she said in a flinty voice, ordering her body not to respond to the sensual strength of his fingers.

"I know," he said. She heard no suggestive undertone in his voice, only quiet concern. "Listen, Claudia. Bring everything you'll need for tonight. Everything. You'll have a room upstairs, your own private bathroom. We've got towels, bath salts, easy chairs...whatever you need. The house is yours.''

She opened her mouth to object. She had a perfectly fine shower at home. She had towels. She had a bed—which she hadn't had time to make that morning.

She could imagine what the upstairs of Ned's childhood home would be like: the sumptuous bedrooms furnished with antiques, the private baths with their brass fixtures, the hallways as wide as Claudia's entire house. The elegance. The class.

Contrary to Ned's claim, the house wasn't hers and never would be. But given how hard she was going to have to slave during the next few hours to make this party come out right...

She deserved the run of Wyatt Hall. She deserved to pretend the house was hers. And all these troublemakers—Melanie, Edie, and most of all Ned with his alluring lips and his mesmerizing touch—had better stay out of her way.

Chapter Seven

CLAUDIA RESTED HER HEAD against the high lip of the claw-foot tub and sighed. The air in the bathroom was steamy with the tart scent of apple blossoms. The water swirling around her tired body was thick with fragrant bubbles.

Downstairs, the third batch of chocolate cake layers was chilling in the refrigerator. She didn't trust Edie not to sabotage her cake yet again, but Ned had promised to protect it with his life. He had a way with Edie.

He had a way with Claudia, too, she admitted dolefully. More than the lavish decor of this bathroom, more than his generosity in opening a bedroom suite for her, more than his insistence on guarding her chocolate cake... Oh, yes, Ned had a way with her.

The scented bubbles of her bath caressed her flesh and made her think of him. The warmth of the water melted her tension the way his hands had when he'd rubbed the small of her back. The rising vapor whispered across her skin the way his breath had an instant before he'd kissed her.

And kissed her. And kissed her.

She forced her eyes open and looked around once more, taking note of every expensive detail in the room. *This* was what John Edward Wyatt IV was all about. She mustn't let herself forget that.

Pandemonium reigned downstairs, but tucked away in her cozy second-floor retreat she was completely shut off from the musicians setting up on the balcony, the bartenders in the solarium, the waiters, the grounds crew stringing spotlights along the driveway. She couldn't hear anything but an occasional bubble breaking against her chin.

So much still to do. The cake to frost, the entrées to heat, the appetizers to arrange on trays. But all she wanted to do was luxuriate in the tub, imagining what her life could have been like if what Ned's mother had said about love at first sight were true. She closed her eyes again and fantasized that the warm, lulling water was Ned's fingertips, stroking her, enveloping her breasts and rippling between her thighs. She moaned out loud.

"Claudia? Are you all right?"

Oh, God!

She pushed herself up to sit, causing the water to splash against the sides of the tub. The frothy suds parted to reveal her breasts and she quickly sank below the water again and stared in panic at the narrow space where the bathroom door stood ajar. "Ned?"

"Are you okay? I heard you—" He pulled the door open, saw that she was perfectly okay, as well as very wet and naked, and slammed the door shut. His eyes burned an afterimage into her mind, wide and surprised . . . and unmistakably appreciative.

"Sorry," he mumbled from the other side of the door, sounding not the least bit sorry. "I came up to tell you Edie thinks she should start heating the ovens. I wanted to check with you. And I heard—well, it sounded like you were in pain."

She recalled the tortured moan that had escaped her—and the tortured thoughts that had prompted it. She supposed there was a kind of pain involved in what she'd been feeling. And she wasn't about to share her feelings with Ned.

"I'm just a little tired," she called through the closed door. "What time is it?"

"Quarter to five."

That gave her an hour and fifteen minutes till the first guest arrived. "Tell Edie she can start the ovens at five-thirty." She had plenty of time to heat the canapés, then the entrées for a seven-thirty dinner.

"All right." He hesitated. "I'm going to have to go home soon. I have to change into a monkey suit for this gig."

Claudia conjured a mental picture of Ned in a tuxedo, his long legs flattered by crisp black trousers, his broad shoulders filling an elegant evening jacket, his collar accented by a bow tie. Not one of those big foppish bow ties, she hoped, but something sleek and sexy.

"You'd better go," she called to him, partly in self-defense. Picturing him in his evening clothes—or more accurately picturing him tugging loose whatever tie he had on and then undoing the collar of his dress shirt, kicking off his shoes . . . it was all she could do to keep from moaning again.

She had to put him out of her mind. She had to focus on the cotillion and nothing else. That was what mattered: catering a great party and bolstering her company's reputation. Ned was a diversion, an infatuation. Their lives had intersected today, but tomorrow they would go their separate ways.

Unless he'd been serious about finding her a silent partner. In which case, she amended, they might have a few professional dealings. Nothing more.

"I'll see you later," he shouted through the door. She had to strain to hear his footsteps crossing the bedroom to the hall. For a crazed moment she'd wanted to call him back, to invite him into the bathroom, into the tub with her. If tomorrow they were doomed to become business acquaintances, they could still have tonight.

No, they couldn't. Tonight she had to do her job so wonderfully Ned would have no trouble finding financial backers for her. And then she could set up shop downtown, as he'd suggested, and put up a big bright sign in front and hire an assistant.

That was what she should be dreaming about, she decided. Fantasy Feasts. Not a fantasy man.

THE SMELL OF CHOCOLATE cake lingered in the kitchen. Claudia's valentine-shaped pans lay scoured and sparkling in the drying rack beside the double-basin sink. Edie was seated in her armchair near the window, thumbing through a magazine, her face set in a grim frown.

"The ovens go on at five-thirty," Ned said, surveying the orderly room on his way to the back door.

Edie nodded without looking up.

"Claudia will be down in a while."

Again, a surly nod.

"Edie." Ned hunkered down next to her chair and pulled the magazine out of her hands, forcing her attention to him. "Why are you being so grouchy?"

"I'm not being grouchy," Edie retorted. "Just because she came in here and took over my kitchen and then she went parading around the ballroom with that ridiculous cake—"

"It was a beautiful cake. Melanie special-ordered it. And Claudia's just doing her job."

"I don't like her job," Edie blurted out. "It used to be *my* job. No one ever asked me to make cakes like that."

"Oh, Edie..." He clasped her hands within his. "No one can replace you, you know that. But you're retired. You've earned the right to take it easy. I just want you to kick back and enjoy yourself."

"I see that girl working in my kitchen," Edie complained, "and she's doing everything different from the way I did it."

"She's a different person. She does things her own way."

Edie's eyes narrowed on him. "You've got the hots for her."

He grinned unapologetically. "Is it that obvious?"

"I'll grant you, she's young and pretty. But she's got a chip on her shoulder, Ned. She doesn't understand the Wyatt way of doing things."

"Neither do I, sometimes," Ned confessed. "Frankly, I'm kind of interested in the Mulcahey way of doing things."

"You should find a girl from your own class."

"I should find a woman I admire—and love," he said, half to himself. Straightening up, he walked to the refrigerator, opened it and snuck two chocolate kisses out of the bowl. He gave one to Edie. "Taste that," he ordered her, "and see if you still don't like Claudia."

Eyeing him suspiciously, Edie bit into the chocolate. Her eyes grew round, her jaw grew slack and she popped the rest of the candy into her mouth and sucked on her fingers. "Oh, my," she said weakly. "That's something."

"It's something, all right."

"What did she put in there?"

He would never reveal Claudia's secret ingredients. "Magic," he joked.

"I can see why you're in love," Edie said, reaching for the candy in his hand. "Give me another."

Ned shook his head. "This one's for me. Treat her nicely, Edie, and maybe she'll give you a few herself."

"Well...I suppose I can tolerate her for an evening," Edie conceded gruffly, although her smile remained, along with a trace of chocolate on her teeth. "Go home and get dressed. I'll make sure her cakes stay in one piece."

"Thanks." Ned winked and headed for the door. Not until he was outside did he eat the chocolate kiss he'd taken for himself. He bit into it and was reminded of his brief glimpse of Claudia's body beneath the rainbow-flecked bubbles in the tub, her hair pinned up and glistening with drops of water, her face dewy, her throat pale and her eyes as blue as heaven.

His body grew hard as he swallowed the kiss, hungry for more kisses, *her* kisses. If Claudia's chocolate could win Edie's grudging respect, it was no wonder it won Ned's respect—to say nothing of his limitless lust.

Tomorrow, he promised himself. They'd get through this ludicrous party tonight and tomorrow he and Claudia could really get down to business.

THE OVEN WASN'T ON.

Claudia had entered the kitchen dressed in her black

wool sheath—with a full-length apron over it—her comfortable low-heeled black pumps and plain gold earrings. She was ready to frost her chocolate cake.

She was also ready to forge a truce with Edie Mueller. But Edie wasn't there.

Claudia checked the wall clock. The ovens should have begun preheating by now. She twisted the dial on one, listening for the click and the *woof* of the gas vents igniting.

Nothing.

She twisted the dial again, off and then on, off and on. Nothing.

No, she gasped under her breath. Enough things had gone wrong for one job—for one lifetime. She had had a near-accident, smashed two cakes, and fallen in love.

And now this.

The oven had been working earlier. What happened?

She raced down the hall in search of help and spotted Edie near the open front door. "Edie!" Claudia cried, discarding her pride. "Edie! The main oven isn't working."

"Don't be silly," Edie clucked. "You obviously don't know how it works."

Claudia held her tongue. "I was hoping you could turn it on for me."

"It's that accursed pilot light," came a familiar voice from outside the front door. "I'll take care of it." In swept Ned's mother, dressed in an elegant burgundy velvet gown spangled with seed pearls. She tossed her mink cape to one of the doormen and sent

Claudia a smile of sheer delight. "Don't you look lovely!"

Claudia glanced down at her pinafore apron and her plain black dress. If anyone looked lovely, it was Mrs. Wyatt.

The sight of Ned's mother in a dress that probably cost an amount equal to Fantasy Feasts' catering bill for the cotillion took Claudia aback. She struggled to recall the robust, energetic woman she and Ned had visited earlier. The statuesque woman who stood before Claudia now was every inch the town matriarch, her makeup impeccable, each strand of hair meticulously placed. Diamond-encrusted mabe pearls clung to her earlobes and her wrist was encircled by a tennis bracelet so thick it probably weighed more than a tennis racquet.

"If it's just a pilot light," Claudia said deferentially, "I'm sure I can relight it."

"Nonsense," Mrs. Wyatt refuted her. "Even Edie can't relight it. My dear, departed husband couldn't relight it. I am the only person who knows how to relight it."

Claudia shot Edie a quizzical look. Edie confirmed Mrs. Wyatt's remark with a nod.

"Now, if you want to serve hot food, let's get the thing done," Mrs. Wyatt declared, striding across the entry to the hall.

"Are you sure you want to do this, Mrs. Wyatt?" Claudia asked, hurrying to catch up with her.

"I've been blessed with a certain talent for repairing recalcitrant ovens," Mrs. Wyatt explained. "It would be as wasteful for me to deny my talent as it would be for you to deny yours."

"Mine?"

"Those cookies. They were superb, my dear. I hope Ned paid you a fortune for them."

Claudia didn't bother to set Mrs. Wyatt straight. Ned's mother was pushing up her sleeves with the gusto of someone about to join a bar brawl. "Here, hold these for me," she said, removing her tennis bracelet and a pearl-and-platinum ring. Before Claudia could stop her, she had pulled the wire shelves out of the top oven and leaned into the oven chamber.

"Mrs. Wyatt—"

A loud clanking noise emerged from the back of the oven.

"Mrs. Wyatt, I think—"

"Stubborn little valve," Mrs. Wyatt growled, pulling her head and shoulders out of the oven. Her hair was mussed, her eyes aglow with purpose. "I'll need a screwdriver."

"Mrs. Wyatt, you shouldn't be doing this. It's such a special night—"

"I am *not* going to eat raw veal," Mrs. Wyatt declared, yanking open a drawer and removing a screwdriver.

"Couldn't we call a repairman?"

"At five-thirty on a Sunday night? He'd charge an arm and a leg." She climbed back into the oven and tackled the broken valve.

Claudia gazed at the jewelry in her hand. It had probably cost enough arms and legs to fund an Olympic swim team.

"Mother!" Melanie Steele screeched as she bounded into the room. Her dress, a bright pink brocade gown, was less regal but probably more expensive than Mrs. Wyatt's. Her hair was a frightful array of curls. Her throat was strung with so many gold necklaces she looked like a pampered dog who'd broken free of its leash. "Mother, get out of the oven right now!"

"I'll get out when I'm ready to get out," Mrs. Wyatt said, her voice emerging in a distorted echo. "Claudia, dear, I need a different screwdriver. In that drawer. An adjustable wrench, too, if it's in there."

Claudia glanced at Melanie, who was wringing her hands. "Why is my mother in the oven?"

"She's trying to get the pilot light started."

"And why is there only one cake on display in the ballroom? We're supposed to have two!"

"The other one isn't frosted yet," Claudia explained.

"Mother, you're going to ruin your coiffure," Melanie carped as Claudia placed tools in Mrs. Wyatt's outstretched hand.

"You can fix it for me," Mrs. Wyatt explained. "How is Amy? Excited to death?"

"Amy and her friends are upstairs listening to some wretched rap singer on a portable CD player. I don't know where she picked up such abominable taste in music. We should never have let her go to Bennington." No response from Mrs. Wyatt. Melanie turned her sharp hazel eyes on Claudia. "Well? Frost the cake!"

Not knowing what else to do, Claudia tucked Mrs. Wyatt's bracelet and ring into the pocket of her apron and tackled the cake. Fortunately she'd made extra frosting. As long as Ned didn't show up and start stealing tastes from the bowl, what she had would cover all three layers.

Melanie's eyes shuttled from Claudia's efficient labor to her mother's visible bottom, shifting and twitching as she plied her tools inside the oven. "I swear," she muttered, "that woman is the most humiliating mother a person could have."

Claudia doubted Melanie's daughter would agree, but she kept her opinion to herself.

"Aha!" Mrs. Wyatt crowed, at last wriggling out of the oven. "All set. Where are the matches?" The pilot light ignited without an explosion and Mrs. Wyatt dusted off her hands and smiled smugly.

"You're a mess," Melanie announced, grabbing her mother by the elbow and hauling her out of the kitchen.

Claudia finished frosting the cake, then slid her trays of stuffed mushrooms into the oven to heat. As she dappled the cake with chocolate kisses, she felt her pulse rate return to normal. Everything was going to be fine. The party was going to go well. She was going to survive—to triumph.

She lifted the cake and started for the door to the hall—and discovered Ned filling it, clad in a gray silk double-breasted tuxedo. His shirt was white, fastened with onyx studs. His bow tie was a muted red, thin, underlining his thin lips. His hair was barely tamed, curling down over his collar in back, and his eyes danced with pleasure as he regarded her.

"You look good," she let slip.

"You look almost as good as you looked in the bathtub," he told her. She blushed, partly from embarrassment and partly from arousal. "Don't drop the cake," he said, hurrying into the room and taking the tray from her.

"Thanks," she whispered as he set the tray on the counter. "I don't think I can handle another calamity."

"You," he murmured, "can handle anything. That's one of the most exciting things about you." He took her hands in his and drew her toward him, lowering his mouth to hers.

She held her breath, waiting for his kiss, needing it. Just as his lips were a whisper away from hers, his sister's voice blasted into the room, preceding the rest of her by a good couple of seconds. "Where are they? All right, I want them now. Where are they?"

Claudia sprang back and jerked her hands away from Ned's. "Where's what?"

"My mother's jewels."

"Oh—right here," Claudia said, pulling the ring and bracelet from her apron pocket.

"Thief!" Melanie howled. "She's a thief! Arrest that woman!"

Chapter Eight

MORE THAN TWO HOURS had passed since Melanie Steele had accused Claudia of stealing her mother's jewels, but the accusation still smarted.

The kitchen was redolent with the aromas of hot cholesterol-laden entrées. A battalion of waiters conveyed trays of food from the kitchen to the dining room. The chocolate and vanilla valentine cakes stood in proud display in the ballroom, where a chamber orchestra played to a rapidly dwindling throng. The presentation of the town's richest young ladies was fine, dancing was amusing, checking out one another's ball gowns was important—but Claudia's gourmet catering was currently the major attraction for the first annual Glenwood debutante cotillion's ravenous guests. Claudia ought to have taken satisfaction in that.

Edie was treating Claudia with surprising courtesy. In fact, it was she who had suggested that Claudia step outside for a breath of air. "I'll make sure everything stays hot until it's served," Edie assured her. "You go out and clear your head."

She stood outside the kitchen door, trying not to shiver in the frigid night air. Everything was going smoothly. She had endured disaster after catastrophe after debacle and somehow she'd pulled this thing off.

So why did she feel miserable?

Surely it had nothing to do with the fact that once Ned had chewed out his sister and ordered her to apologize to Claudia he'd vanished into the glamorous swarm of guests. The party had begun and Ned had transformed into a full-blooded Wyatt. Flirting benignly with the giggling debutantes, ushering blue-haired dowagers to chairs, he was the proper Wyatt host. Claudia could almost see the Roman-numeral IV in his posture, his demeanor.

Who was she kidding? All day he'd been nothing more than a man on the prowl, trying his luck with the lady caterer. But he knew his place—in the ballroom with the guests. And she knew hers.

The orchestra played gamely on; she heard the strains of music coming from the ballroom.

"Care to dance?"

Claudia flinched and spun around to see Ned stepping out the kitchen door. She suffered the same acute reaction to him as she had earlier: he was as suited to suave gray silk tailoring as he was to black denim. He looked as wonderful shaved and barbered as he did scruffy and windswept. Dressed up or dressed down, he was irresistible.

She resisted, anyway.

"You ought to go back to the party," she said quietly, turning back to gaze at the cars parked beyond the tiny porch.

Ned sidled up next to her and slung his arm around her shoulders. "I'd rather party with you."

"Ned." She didn't hide her exasperation. "I'm working."

"Edie's holding down the fort. Dinner is a major success, by the way. They're scarfing it up like there's no tomorrow."

"Why don't you go back inside and scarf it up, too?"

"Because there *is* a tomorrow," he said, urging her around to face him. "I've done my duty to my niece, danced with my mother, made chitchat with the garden-club ladies—and now I'm on my own time. I want to spend it with you."

His eyes were luminous in the silvery light. His smile was earnest yet surprisingly seductive. She had to force herself to remember that, just as he'd said, there *was* a tomorrow. Whatever silly dreams she'd entertained about a romance with him would vanish as soon as the moon set on Valentine's Day.

"Come upstairs with me," he murmured.

Her bones melted in the heat of his gaze, in the palpable aura of his passion. She couldn't give this man her heart, and she couldn't give him anything else without giving him her heart as well.

Who was she kidding? Her heart was already his. She was going to wind up despondent whether she went upstairs with him or not.

He leaned toward her, brushed her lips with his...and she resigned herself to the inevitable, to her own imperative yearning. She loved him. She couldn't stop this from happening.

There was a back stairway—the servants' stairway, she thought ironically, wondering whether Ned had ever had a reason to use these stairs before now. He held her hand tightly as he led her along the second-floor hallway to the room in which she'd washed up and dressed for the party a few hours ago. He locked the door, then gathered her into his arms. "I almost dove into the tub with you this afternoon," he confessed, unclasping her barrette and fluffing her hair loose about her shoulders.

"I almost invited you to dive in," she admitted.

He smiled, his teeth gleaming in the moonlight that filtered through the curtains by the bed. "We should have done it," he said, tugging his bow tie until it hung in two narrow red ribbons. "We should have forgotten all about the cotillion and spent the rest of our lives in the tub."

"No. In fact, I should be down there right now—"

"Edie's taking care of everything," he swore, sliding his jacket from his shoulders. He removed the onyx links pinning his cuffs and then the matching studs adorning the front of his shirt. Claudia recalled her little fantasy of him stripping off his tuxedo. The reality was much more enthralling.

"Are you sure? I don't want anything to go wrong. And Edie doesn't like me."

"As long as she's in charge of the kitchen, she loves you," he reassured her. "Running the kitchen is all she ever wanted to do."

"She wanted to destroy my cakes," Claudia muttered, her gaze fixed on the crisp white front of Ned's shirt as he removed the last stud. "I don't know why she suddenly turned nice."

"I gave her a kiss," he explained. At Claudia's startled look, he grinned and tugged his shirttails free of his trousers. "One of your chocolate kisses. A single bite and she understood why I'm crazy about you."

"My kisses, huh," Claudia said, aware of the tightness in her voice as her vision filled with the magnificent sight of his naked chest, a plane of streamlined muscle accented with a dart of black hair. "You want me for my kisses."

"For starters." He tossed his shirt aside, then reached for her. She automatically lifted her hands to his chest, combing her fingers through the manly mat of hair and tracing the warm, responsive skin underneath. His deep sigh caused his chest to vibrate against her fingertips.

He took the kiss he wanted, sliding his tongue deep, filling her mouth as he sought and found the zipper at the back of her dress. She felt a brief chill as he drew it down to her waist, then a flash of heat as he returned to undo the clasp of her bra. If there was a cotillion going on downstairs she didn't know about it. If the future of her company was at stake she didn't care. All that mattered was Ned's hands on her back, his mouth on hers, his kisses sweeter and more complicated than anything she'd ever concocted in her kitchen.

Her dress tumbled to the floor at her feet, and then her bra, her slip, her stockings. Ned guided her hands to his trousers and she opened them, refusing to think beyond the moment, the power of his hardness bulging against the smooth gray fabric, the ragged tempo of his breath as she eased his briefs over his hips and down his long, well-toned legs.

Ned scooped her into his arms and carried her to the grand four-poster with its elegant bedding. Then he joined her on the crisp linen sheets, stretching out on his side and gazing lovingly at her body as it lay shimmering in the spill of moonlight. "You're beautiful," he whispered before setting his hand loose on her skin, exploring the lines of her collarbone and then the hollow between her breasts, the concave stretch of her abdomen.

Her hips shifted uncomfortably; her nipples grew taut in anticipation of his touch. "You're beautiful, too," she said, skimming her hand along the ridge of his shoulder and then roaming forward into the wiry hair that darkened his upper chest.

"Oh, God." It was half a groan, half a growl. "I've been wanting this all day. I don't know how much longer I can wait."

With a mischievous smile, she moved her hand down across his abdomen, curious to see if his condition bore out his words. At her glancing touch he groaned again. She did, too.

He grabbed her hand and pulled it away. Rising above her, he pressed her arms to the mattress and bowed to kiss her breasts. "Everything about you tastes so good," he murmured, swirling his tongue over the beaded tip of one breast, then shifting and teasing the other with his teeth. "Peppermint pink frosting doesn't come close."

"What a relief," she joked, although she was feeling far from relieved. Her body surged under him, ached for him, felt uncomfortably empty and feverish. She arched her hips and he rubbed against her, hot and heavy. They gasped in unison.

"Claudia . . ." He let go of her wrists and slid down her body, nibbling her belly, stroking her navel with his tongue, grazing down farther until he pressed a fierce, hungry kiss between her legs. When she was sure she couldn't hold back any longer, he kissed his way back up.

Her body rose to meet his conquering thrust. She gripped his shoulders, clinging to him as he withdrew and thrust again. She felt as if her heart had split in two, her soul, her spirit, her very essence, all of it opening to let him in, to let him take possession of her. She was his.

His surges were deep, hard, shuddering. The muscles in his back flexed and stretched; he wove the fingers of one hand into her hair while the other cupped her bottom, lifting her to maximize every plunge, every sensation. The tension inside her built to a wild, almost agonizing pitch—and then burst, releasing her into ecstasy.

She felt him hover in her arms, suspended at the peak, and then he let go, sinking down on her, relaxing his hands, his lips. ''Claudia,'' he sighed, a hushed, prayerlike sound.

He closed his eyes and let his head sink onto her shoulder. She stroked his sweat-damp hair back from his face, feeling oddly protective of him. At that one instant, as passion receded and left a sensuous languor in its place, Claudia felt she and Ned were truly equals. She wasn't the poor girl from the local diner. He wasn't the lord of Wyatt Hall. They were simply lovers.

Ned's breathing grew more regular, his head heavier as he dozed. Through the stillness she heard the faint, distant sounds of the party.

Claudia cuddled Ned to herself, aware of how transient this moment was. Soon reality would return.

Tears welled up in her eyes but she swiftly batted them away. She loved Ned, but as he'd said, there *was* a tomorrow. And when it came, she would be a blue-collar Mulcahey and he would be John Edward Wyatt IV.

The gap was too wide; not even love could bridge it.

Chapter Nine

"WHAT DO YOU MEAN, this is your room?"

Ned loitered in the doorway of the bedroom, watching as Claudia gathered her clothing and assorted toiletries. "I mean," he said calmly, "this room was mine when I was growing up."

She didn't know why she should care that the room he'd let her use—the room in which he'd made love to her—was *his* room and not just some anonymous guest room. But she *did* care. And it bothered her.

She was tired, edgy and anxious to get home. Downstairs, the party was over and the guests had been replaced with a maintenance crew.

Claudia's hands trembled as she folded her jeans and stuffed them into her tote bag. She couldn't look at the rumpled bed. Seeing it would only remind her of what had occurred there a few hours ago, what had occurred in her heart. What would never occur again.

The party was definitely over.

"Please, Claudia. Stay the night. Stay with me," he said.

She glanced at him and felt her refusal lodge in her throat. She could think of nothing she'd rather do than stay the night with him, stay the year, stay for all eternity with him. But she couldn't. Just as making love with him had been inevitable, leaving him was inevitable. She'd realized that truth when they'd emerged from the bedroom and headed downstairs.

Three waiters had assailed her with questions. One of the debutantes had flounced over to Ned, grabbed his arm and squealed, "Amy's so lucky to have such a foxy uncle. Come dance with me."

Claudia hadn't seen him again—until now. She'd packed up the leftover food to be delivered to a soup kitchen in Bridgeport, lugged her equipment out to the van and then trudged up the stairs to gather her personal things.

She had assumed Ned had left the house when all the other guests had, but now he was standing in the doorway, blocking her exit. His tie dangled from his open collar, a graphic reminder of the hasty, eager way he'd undressed earlier. His eyes, while reflecting the late hour, were as bright with longing as they'd been then.

They had been good in bed. Better than good. Claudia had given Ned everything. But she couldn't give it again, not when they would only be going their separate ways tomorrow.

"You have all your stuff here," he went on. "Why not stay?"

"If I didn't trust you," she muttered, "I'd think you told me to take a bath and change here at Wyatt Hall just so I'd have a change of clothes with me."

He didn't deny it. She glanced his way and found him smiling sheepishly. "So I was planning ahead," he admitted without remorse. "I brought a change of clothes for myself, too."

"Do you bring all your girlfriends to Wyatt Hall to seduce them?"

His smile faded. "No. I didn't seduce you, Claudia. I made love with you."

"Did you really?"

His gaze narrowed into a frown. "What would you call it?"

Love, she thought. She'd made love, given love, reveled in love. She wanted to say the word aloud, pledge it and hear him say he felt exactly as she did.

But she was afraid she wouldn't hear what she needed, so she said nothing at all.

He came up behind her, reached around her and stilled her trembling hands against the tote bag. "Here," he said, reaching into the pocket of his jacket and pulling out a small hinged box. "Take it. Don't say no. It's Valentine's Day."

Her heart stopped beating, then started again, accelerating to a crazy speed. Holding her breath, she opened the box. In a bed of velvet sat a beautiful round chocolate kiss.

"What?"

"Oops—wrong box," he said, shoving it aside and groping in another pocket for a second box.

The shiny gold ring inside featured a large ruby flanked by two smaller diamonds. "Oh, my God," Claudia gasped.

"Put it on."

"Ned—"

"Don't say no." He pulled the ring out of the box and slipped it onto the ring finger of her left hand. Then he turned her to face him. "Happy Valentine's Day."

"I can't accept this," she said, even as her gaze lingered on the ring. It fit perfectly.

"Why can't you accept it?"

"Well, it would imply..."

"That we're going to get married," he completed the thought. He slipped his thumb under her chin and tilted her face up so their eyes met. He looked solemn, and—if she dared to believe it—very much in love. "Is that a problem?"

She couldn't shake the fear that it *was* a problem, but she wasn't ready to face it yet. "You didn't steal this from your mother, did you?"

He smiled slightly. "No. You're the jewel thief, not me." When she stiffened indignantly, he hastened to add, "I bought it this afternoon. The jeweler down on Main Street was open for last-minute Valentine's Day business. He must have known someone might get notions of marriage at the eleventh hour."

"But your sister hates me," she reminded him, dredging up every possible argument.

"So don't marry her. Marry me."

No more evasion. He'd proposed and asked if she had a problem. It was time to confront the issue head-on. "I'm a Mulcahey, Ned."

"Do you want to keep your name? I can live with it if I have to."

"Ned, I'm being serious. The closest I've ever gotten to the world you live in is through the kitchen door."

"The world I live in is right here." He tapped his chest in the vicinity of his heart. "And it's right there—" he gestured toward the bed. "You're already in my world, Claudia, and I don't want to let you out. I want you to stay."

There was no sense hiding from her feelings. More than anything in the world, she wanted to stay in his world. "I love you," she told him.

"Then say yes."

"Yes."

He folded his arms around her and covered her mouth with his. His kiss spoke eloquently of love, of joy, of growing desire. Before things got out of control he pulled back and caught his breath. "You understand what this means," he warned.

Panic twinged inside her. Did it mean she would have to host pretentious galas like that evening's cotillion? To become a garden-club matron and a dues-paying member of the historical society?

"It means," he explained, "that I'll give Fantasy Feasts financial guidance for free, but you'll have to keep me supplied in chocolate kisses for free."

She grinned. "That sounds fair."

He reached for the box with the candy in it. "When I saw Edie hogging all the leftover chocolate kisses, I grabbed the last one. I put it in this box so it wouldn't melt all over the inside of my pocket."

"No," Claudia teased. "You put it in the box because my kisses are as precious as jewels."

He wedged the candy between her lips to silence her. "They are," he agreed, then angled his head and bit the other half of the candy into his mouth. Their lips touched, their mouths merged and their tongues shared the marvelously complicated flavor as Ned closed his arms around her.

If this was his world, Claudia thought, she would never leave. She belonged here, in his arms, in his heart . . . and in his bed.

And as the final seconds of Valentine's Day ticked away, they sealed their promise of love—with the sweetest of chocolate kisses.

SIMPLE CHARMS

Anne McAllister

A Note from Anne McAllister

Whenever I think of Valentine's Day, my thoughts turn to elementary school—to the laboriously decorated white paper bags that we all made to serve as our Valentine "mailboxes," to the tedious printing of my own name twenty-three times and the deliberate selection of the absolutely perfect Valentine (out of a packet of "five each of five designs") for the one boy who mattered. And, of course, I hoped against hope that he would be as conscientious in his search for the perfect card for me.

It was probably this last vain hope that inspired this story. It seemed to me, even at the tender age of seven, that the height of romantic fantasy was to know a boy who actually thought about such things!

In real life, I learned, as Jane does in *Simple Charms,* that love goes beyond flowers and candy, cards and charms. They are but signs of what we would like our relationship to be, symbols of our hopes and dreams. They point the way toward, but they never replace, the passion and tenderness and generosity of spirit that exists in a day-to-day relationship based on love.

I wish for each of you a lifetime of that very special love.

Happy Valentine's Day.

Anne

Chapter One

"Look!" Jane heard the high-pitched, childish gasp the moment she started to write on the blackboard.

"It's gone!"

"Gone? Naw."

"Yes, it is. D'you suppose she lost it?"

"Duh. How could she lose it? It was on her finger, stupid."

"I'm smarter'n you, Jeremy Proctor. I bet she gave it back."

"Maybe he dumped her."

"Miss Kitto? *Dump Miss Kitto?* He wouldn't dare!"

Jane hesitated for an instant, then continued, her hand moving steadily across the blackboard printing in big square letters NEW YEAR'S RESOLUTIONS.

When she'd finished, she turned around and smiled determinedly into the sea of curious, upturned faces.

There were twenty-three of them, all belonging to the gap-toothed, grinning innocents who comprised half of the second grade at St. Philomena's Catholic School in hilly San Francisco. Jane's class.

Jane adored them, and they thought that their Miss Kitto was Betty Crocker, Wendy Darling and both Madonnas, the spiritual and the material, all rolled into one.

For the most part Jane tried not to disillusion them.

"I know you're all thrilled to be back after Christmas vacation," she said brightly.

There was a chorus of groans.

"And I know you're all ready to get a good start in the new year. That's why I've written three words on the board—New Year's Resolutions. Can anyone tell me what that means? Jeremy?"

Jane often called on Jeremy first, thereby—she hoped—taking the joy of interrupting away from him.

"How come you're not wearin' your ring?"

Jane had been afraid of that.

Her students had shown an avid interest in the progress of her engagement to Paul Crawford ever since school had begun. What was Paul like? How had Jane met him? When was the wedding going to be? How many bridesmaids was she going to have? Where were they going on their honeymoon?

And most important of all: were they all going to be invited to the wedding?

And now, where was her ring?

How was Jane, having previously assured both her students and herself that Paul Crawford was her idea of her perfect man, going to explain to them that the wedding was off?

"We're talking about resolutions, Jeremy," she said, hoping to deflect their interest through sheer willpower.

"Don't know nothin' 'bout them," Jeremy said flatly. "Where's your ring?"

There was a low murmur of assent from the group. Every one of Jane's students looked equally curious and expectant.

Leticia Morely raised her hand.

Jane smiled her relief. Leticia Morely, with her long, black braids and her patent leather Mary Janes, could always be counted on to stay on task and know the answer. She reminded Jane of herself at that age.

"Resolutions are decisions," she recited. "We make them to make ourselves better." A pause. "You gave your ring back, didn't you, Miss Kitto?"

Jane sighed. She wanted to run her fingers through her hair. She twisted the bracelet on her arm instead.

The children waited, just looking at her, not even squirming. There was no hope for it.

"Yes, Leticia, I'm afraid I did."

Jeremy folded his arms across his chest, scowling. "Well, he coulda dumped her."

"Why did you do it?" twenty-three voices demanded.

Where was it written, Jane wondered, that she had to explain her life to a horde of seven-year-olds?

Still, she knew she would try. It was the sort of relationship she'd had with them from the start.

"We...decided we wouldn't suit."

"Didn't you love him?" Leticia asked.

Jeremy made a gagging sound.

Jane gave him a reproving stare. The question was a fair one. Certainly she'd thought she had.

When handsome, successful, Bay City lawyer Paul Crawford had asked her to marry him last December, Jane had been thrilled. He was intelligent and refined, clever and well read, quiet and conservative, not to mention spit-and-polish handsome.

Now she tried to think how to explain her change of heart. "We didn't value the same things."

"Like what?"

She sighed. "My bracelet."

Twenty-three horrified faces stared at her. *"He didn't like your bracelet?"* they gasped in unison.

The entire second grade at St. Philomena's thought Jane Kitto's charm bracelet was close to magic.

She wore the bracelet every day. A simple silver chain with a variety of charms, it had been Jane's prize possession since she'd received it the Christmas she was seven.

Her grandmother had given her the chain and the first charm, a sterling silver ballerina. The nineteen others had appeared one after another, each succeeding Valentine's Day.

From whom Jane didn't know.

"Your Secret Admirer," her best friend, Kelly, had teased her for years.

And though Jane had laughed, she had hugged the thought close to her heart. Somewhere out there was a person who understood her, cared about her, loved her.

She'd dreamed about him for years.

Her students could have cared less about the man. It was the charms that intrigued them. One or another of the charms frequently became the starting point for many class discussions, provoking conversations about occupations or places, hopes or desires.

The notion that someone might not actually appreciate such a prize was unthinkable.

"It's just as good that you dumped him then," Jeremy said bluntly. "You need a better guy."

And Leticia added piously, "He wasn't worthy of you."

Jane smiled at them. "I appreciate your confidence in me. Now we really must get back to work. Who can think of a good New Year's resolution?"

Hands waved, voices shouted.

"Not to beat up my sister!"

"To eat my broccoli!"

"To say my prayers!"

"Whoa, one at a time." Jane wrote them on the board. "Everyone take out a piece of paper and make a list, too. So you can encourage each other along the way."

When at last there were twenty-three resolutions written and copied, Jane said, "Father Morrisey has suggested that we make a class resolution as well. Something that will really make a difference."

There was silence in the room. A little scuffling of feet.

"How about trying to have the whole class get *A*'s in spelling?"

There were grumbles and shaking heads.

"Or resolving to be quiet in line when Sister Clementia takes us down to the lunchroom? Or is that not just hard, but impossible?" Jane grinned at them, then glanced at the clock, "Well, you just think about it for a while. Let's get out our math books now. Then after recess we'll discuss it."

There was a bit more muttering as the children got out their math books. Jane refreshed their Christmas-fogged memories about the concept of borrowing from the tens column, then turned them loose on an assignment.

They settled down to work. She saw Jeremy mumbling something behind his fist and Leticia's foot sneak out to connect with his ankle. Jane ignored them. She sat behind her desk and stared out the window. She had enough to think about.

Paul.

Marriage.

Love.

What the future held.

All of the above.

Last year at this time everything had seemed so clear.

She'd come back from two years studying art history in London determined to get a teaching job, find a husband and begin a family.

When she'd met Paul, their immediate rapport had seemed preordained.

Their courtship had been quick and painless. And on Christmas a year ago, she had blithely accepted his ring.

Things were perfect, she'd thought. Everything was right on schedule.

And things had gone swimmingly.

Until Valentine's Day.

She'd looked forward to this Valentine's gift. And she'd felt a thrill of anticipation when she saw the small brown box awaiting her.

She'd hurried into her apartment, dumping everything else willy-nilly into the chair, while she'd fumbled open the box, smiling and eager to see what her Secret Admirer had come up with this year. She expected a wedding cake, a miniature engagement ring, a pair of turtle doves.

It was a tiny silver mask—the tragic one.

She had stared at it, stunned.

Her mind grappled with the implications of the tiny charm. What was he saying? That he disapproved of her engagement to Paul?

But that was foolish! What was there to disapprove of? Paul was perfect for her.

Her fingers had closed around the little charm, smothering it in her palm. She felt the cold silver bite into her flesh the way the sight of the tragic face bit into her heart.

She set her mind to groping for another significance for the charm, and finally she found one.

Right before Thanksgiving she had been in a small community production of *A Thousand Clowns*. He could have known. He might have even seen her in it. A play. A mask. A clown mask.

Yes. It made sense.

And when she showed the charm to Paul, that was the symbolism she gave it. Even so Paul hadn't been thrilled.

"One more charm on that heavy, clunky thing? You need something small and elegant, Janey."

But Jane was attached to this bracelet.

She had shrugged him off, busying herself with flower choices and china patterns, bridesmaid dresses and guest lists.

Until Christmas Eve.

They'd snuggled together on the sofa, kissing softly, touching. And then Paul had pulled back slightly. Still with his arm around her, he had reached into his pocket and pulled out a small, shiny, red package.

"Open it."

The shiny paper gave way to a black velvet jewelry box. Jane opened it and found a narrow gold chain bracelet with one charm. A tiny woman in flowing robes, a balance scale in her hand. The emblem of justice. The symbol of lawyers.

Paul was looking at her expectantly.

"It's . . . lovely."

"A new beginning," Paul said, his fingers fumbling with the bracelet already on her wrist. "To replace this one."

He worked the clasp loose and the bracelet fell into her lap. Her wrist felt barren, naked.

"B-but—" Jane began, but couldn't find the words. Her heart started hammering.

Abruptly she pulled back, clutching her wrist with her left hand. "I can't."

"What?"

She shook her head. "I appreciate the gesture. Really, I do, Paul. But I like this bracelet. It's a part of me! It's made me who I am."

He simply stared at her. "Oh, for heaven's sake, Jane. Don't be sappy." He drew himself together and looked right at her. "If you love me, Jane, you'll wear mine."

And Jane, looking back at him, felt her dreams crack and crumble, saw them begin to collapse.

"I'm afraid you're right." She slipped out of his arms, rose from the couch and went to stand by the window. His gaze followed her, a mixture of consternation and faint alarm.

"What are you saying, Jane? What sort of nonsense is this?"

She eased the ring off her finger, crossed the room and held it out to him. "It's not nonsense, Paul. It's true. You said it yourself."

He stared at her. "You said you loved me."

"I know. I thought I did."

The clock ticked. The tap dripped. The trolley clanged down on the corner, then started on up the hill.

Paul waited. Jane didn't speak, didn't look at him again.

She hadn't seen him since.

Math ended. Recess came and went. Jane stopped thinking about Paul, about dreams, about the future.

She pulled herself together and prepared to begin a unit on social studies.

The kids were squirming, chattering among themselves. She gave them a stern look. Most quieted.

Jeremy kicked Leticia. "Tell her!"

"No."

"Why not?" Jeremy rocked his chair onto its back legs. "She said she wants to know."

"It isn't tactful."

Jeremy sputtered. The chair came down with a crash. "Tactful? What's that?"

Leticia rolled her eyes.

"Then I'll tell her. We got you a resolution," he said to Jane, blue eyes flashing defiantly.

Jane had forgotten all about it. "Have you?" She smiled. "Wonderful," she said, even as she was surprised that it was Jeremy who'd been giving it so much thought. "What is it?"

"We're gonna find you a man."

"WHO DO THEY HAVE in mind?" Jane's friend Kelly wanted to know. She juggled eggs from the refrigerator to the stove, pausing to give Jane a speculative glance as she went.

"No one, I hope," Jane said firmly. The very thought made her shudder. "Can you imagine the mess twenty-three second-graders could make of my love life?"

"Not much worse than you've made," Kelly said cheerfully as she stirred the eggs into the cookie dough. Her sons, Devin and Garrett, sat on the floor watching her every move. "I couldn't believe it when you told me you'd dumped Paul. He was everything you ever wanted.'' She shook chocolate chips into the dough, then slanted Jane a glance. ''Wasn't he?''

Jane shrugged. She hadn't told Kelly about the bracelet yet. She did now. Kelly listened sympathetically, then sighed. ''You're really waiting for him?''

There was no use pretending she didn't know what Kelly meant. ''He understands me so well.''

''He might not even be a *he*, remember,'' Kelly said. ''You don't know. He might be your grandmother after all.''

''No.'' Jane was sure of that.

Kelly smiled. ''Probably not. But he hasn't been exactly forthcoming, has he? Sweeping you off your feet and galloping off into the sunset?''

''No, but—''

''And don't you think he should have by now if he were really interested?'' She put down the spoon and gave Jane's shoulders a squeeze. ''I don't mean to rain on your parade, Janey, but you've got to be realistic.''

''You're not telling me anything Jeremy Proctor and twenty-two other second-graders haven't already said.''

''You mean they've discussed your Secret Admirer, too?''

''After Jeremy dropped his bombshell, Leticia tried to salvage the situation by telling me they'd find me my Secret Admirer. She was roundly booed.''

Kelly's eyes widened. ''I thought they loved him.''

''They love his charms. But he's not tangible. For me they want a 'real man.' ''

''Not a bad idea.''

''He *is* a real man.''

''Dan Capoletti.''

"What?"

"It's probably Dan Capoletti."

Jane stared. "Dan Capoletti's going to be a priest!" Jane said when she could manage the words. "He's the deacon at St. Phil's this year."

"To keep an eye on you," Kelly predicted.

"I doubt if the diocesan office chose St. Phil's for that reason," Jane said drily.

"Think what you want. But he is tall, dark and gorgeous. He's probably in the seminary out of desperation, just sitting there waiting for you to come in and sweep him off his feet."

"Be serious, Kel."

"I am. Who else has been staring at you with those big dark goo-goo eyes since first grade? Who else kissed you and ran away? Who else sweated all over you in junior high square dancing and never said a word? He's just the type."

Jane found the thought intriguing. Strong, silent Dan Capoletti had, in fact, watched her for as long as she could remember. He'd even kissed her, back in second grade, though he'd kept away for months afterward.

And he was precisely the sort of intuitive, sensitive man who would spend hours each Valentine's Day trying to decide on the perfect symbolic charm.

"Why don't you ask him?" Kelly suggested.

"I couldn't!"

"Then I guess you'll have to count on your students' help."

"I don't need a man," Jane said firmly. "Marriage isn't everything."

"Nor, to misquote Vince Lombardi, is it the only thing," Kelly agreed. "But it's what you want, isn't it, Janey? What you've always wanted?"

Jane looked at her friend, glanced at the childishly scribbled pictures on the refrigerator, at the towheaded little boys sitting on the floor by her feet. She took in the pile of unfolded laundry on the dryer, the scattering of toys under the table. She heard the faint masculine murmur of Jeff's voice in the study as he talked on the phone.

She thought about her own apartment where nothing was out of place, where the countertops gleamed and the floors shone. She thought about the three-item shopping list on her refrigerator and the way she could sit for hours and hear only the drip of the tap and the tick of the clock.

She thought about her "office," which she never used in the spare bedroom, and the cool, wide bed where she slept each night by herself.

It wasn't that she was unhappy. It was that she was alone. So alone.

"You know it is," she said at last.

FIRST CAME Cathy Chang's uncle, Bennett, who got coerced into coming along on the field trip to the fire station because he was a fireman. The following Monday she was treated to Suzy Giannini extolling the virtues of her cousin Frank, and then Bobby Palermo singing the praises of Uncle Vito.

Two days later Patrick Driscoll's widowed father, Jed, had the misfortune of delivering his son's forgotten lunch and found himself under close inspection by the entire class.

"Do you date, Mr. Driscoll?" Leticia Morely asked him.

Jane wanted to crawl under the desk.

"You have to stop this," she told them in no uncertain terms when Jed had left, flustered. "You embarrassed him. And me."

"We're only trying to help," Cathy Chang said.

"I think a little less matchmaking and a little more subtraction drill would be a good idea," Jane suggested. She tapped the assignment she had written on the blackboard.

They groaned.

The door opened. "Ja—Miss Kitto?"

Jane glanced up to see Dan Capoletti looking in. Ever since Kelly had put the notion into her head, she hadn't been able to look at Dan without speculating. He was smiling at her.

"Father Jack would like you to drop by the rectory after school."

"Is something wrong?"

"Not a thing. Everything's peachy." He winked and shut the door.

Jane stared after him. Had Dan Capoletti actually winked at her?

Promptly at three-thirty, when the last of the stragglers had bundled up book bags and homework papers and departed, Jane presented herself on the doorstep of the rectory.

Father Jack Morrisey met her, grinning. "Ah, good. We've just been talking about you."

We? He and Dan? "Talking about me?"

"You know St. Phil's centennial is coming up?"

Jane felt herself sag. So it had nothing to do with the bracelet after all.

"Yes, of course. Everyone knows."

"Well, not yet." Father Jack was still grinning, rubbing his hands together. "But they soon will. We've just been handed the coup of the year. WZSF is going to cover us on Local Flavor!"

That was the highly rated San Francisco-oriented television show that aired nightly just after the news. It was indeed a coup.

"They want to cover the church and school, then and now," Father Jack went on. "Do some history. Sit in on the class, talk to the teacher, that sort of thing."

"What a good idea. Sister Clementia—"

"—thinks it's a good idea, too." Father Jack opened the door to the sitting room and held it for her. "We're lucky to have an alum of St. Phil's at WZSF. It was his idea, actually. He was before your time, of course, but I imagine you've heard of him?"

Father Jack gestured toward the man slowly rising from the chair, silhouetted against the afternoon sun streaming in the window. "Zack Stoner."

Jane stopped dead.

Zack Stoner?

The man's broad shoulders blotted out the sun as he moved across the room toward her. He held out his hand.

Father Jack gave Jane a little shove. "Jane, I'd like you to meet Zachary Stoner."

Jane felt her hand engulfed by hard, rough fingers. She tried to shut her mouth.

"Zack, this is the second-grade teacher I've been telling you about, Jane Kitto."

Jane's gaze flickered up long enough to encounter deep blue eyes and a wicked grin. "Miss Kitto." His voice was rough and slightly smoky. Sexy, Kelly would have said.

But if his voice was sexy, his grin was pure devilment—the sort of grin that had forever made the good sisters of St. Philomena wring their hands and check their chairs before they sat.

Jane tried to pull her hand away.

Zack held on. His gaze flicked briefly to meet Father Jack's. "We've met."

Chapter Two

"HAVEN'T WE?" Zack Stoner's amazingly blue eyes connected once more with hers.

"Er, yes."

He remembered? Jane was astonished. She couldn't imagine why he'd want to. Their encounter hadn't been one of his finer moments.

Father Jack looked at Zack, puzzled. "I thought you were older than Jane."

"Four or five years," Zack acknowledged. "She's not as young as she looks."

Jane glared at him. He grinned unrepentantly.

"Anyway," he went on with a wink at Jane, "I remember her. Well."

"That's wonderful. You're old friends, then." Father Jack beamed and rubbed his hands together.

"I wouldn't say that," Jane began hastily at the same time Zack said, "Yes."

Father Jack blinked at their contradictory responses, then shrugged amiably. "Whatever. I'm sure it will work out fine."

"What will?" Jane felt the walls beginning to press in on her.

"The filming for Local Flavor, my dear. Zack needs a liaison person here at school. And since it's your class Zack will be visiting, we decided on you."

"*Me?* My class? But . . . Sister Clementia . . . certainly she— She was here when we were students, you know," she reminded Zack.

"I remember."

"That's precisely the point, Jane," Father Morrisey said patiently. "Sister Clementia, for all that she can still hold her own with a classroom of third-graders, is no match for this fellow here." He winked at Zack, then turned twinkling eyes on her. "I know you can handle him."

And when Jane opened her mouth to protest, he went on, "And Sister Clementia agrees with me. I know I'm springing it on you rather suddenly, but the opportunity just came up. I was talking with Father Corey in the diocese office just yesterday, and he had been talking to Zack, and one thing led to another—" Father Jack shrugged "—and you know what I always say—"

"The Lord works in mysterious ways," he and Jane intoned together, then laughed. His was his usual strong, hearty laugh. Jane's was a faint, wobbly echo.

How often had she heard him say that? How often had she quoted those very words to her class, hoping to encourage them when they balked at some unwelcome request?

"You never know what good might come of it," she'd said to them just this morning when they'd been discussing their efforts to find pen pals in Japan. "The Lord works in mysterious ways."

But this mysterious?

Jane sighed.

Father Jack gave her an encouraging smile and clapped Zack on the shoulder. "Be good to our Miss Kitto," he instructed Zack. "She's the best."

"I'm sure she is," Zack said so piously that Jane stared at him.

He winked at her.

She felt a frisson of something—fear, awareness, primal panic?—slip down her spine.

Father Jack put his hand on the doorknob. "I'll just be off, then. I know you two can handle all the arrangements, and I have a basketball game to go to— the eighth-graders are playing St. Ad's. See you later."

Before Jane could open her mouth, the door opened, the door shut, and he was gone.

She stared after him, words of protest forming, then dying unspoken in her mouth.

She shot Zack a quick glance, annoyed to realize that maturity had done nothing to mitigate her reaction to him. He had always seemed to her larger than life, stronger, tougher, threatening.

There had never been anything civilized in him at all. She could see nothing in the adult Zack Stoner to deny that impression.

Their eyes met.

"You've grown up," he said. "And very nicely, I might add." His appraisal was thorough and frank. It made Jane distinctly uncomfortable.

"You haven't," she told him, "if you're still trying to disconcert people."

He grinned. "I wasn't trying."

She felt like an idiot. Not surprising. She often did around the male of the species. An only child, she'd never known the rough and tumble world of boys. Her shopkeeper father had been a quiet, courtly man, not the sort given to frogs and rocks and worms in his pockets.

Not at all the sort of boy that Zack had been.

Jane had been terrified of him. She was doing better now with her second-grade boys. Obviously she still hadn't made the transition to those over four feet tall.

Zack gestured to an armchair. "Sit down."

Jane sat gratefully, needing to disguise wobbling knees. But she didn't really breathe a sigh of relief until he moved around to the other side of the desk and took a chair as well. She hoped it would make him seem less formidable.

It didn't.

There was a lean, pantherlike grace to all Zack Stoner's movements, from the way he walked across a room to the way he had settled behind Father Jack's desk and absently brushed a hand through his unruly dark hair.

She was afraid that, like a panther, he might spring.

He grinned disarmingly and, as if he realized the train of her thoughts, said, "Don't worry, I've become civilized since we last met."

"Really?" She couldn't hide the amazement in her tone, nor her chagrin at how easily he seemed to read her thoughts. She pursed her lips. "I'm not worried."

"Of course you aren't."

The remarkable thing was he seemed to believe it.

The one time she had dared to challenge his belligerent, tough-guy facade had been more an act of desperation than of courage. She was surprised Zack didn't know that.

If she hadn't thought then—and didn't think now—that cowering or running away would have provoked an even worse reaction from him, she'd have lit out as fast as her feet could carry her!

He looked at her now, his posture as lazy as his expression was sharp. "So, Janey Kitto, tell me what you've been up to."

"Me?" She was startled that he was interested. "I've been teaching, doing some design work. Nothing very amazing. Not like you."

A corner of his mouth twitched. "I am pretty amazing."

"And modest."

The grin widened. "That, too. You don't think you had it in you to be a wide receiver?"

"I didn't like mud," Jane explained.

"I can see where that would have stopped you."

His solemn tone made her smile. "You really have done very well," she said earnestly. "No one ever would have thought—" she stopped, embarrassed.

Zack didn't seem to be. "You're right. No one would have."

During elementary school, if anyone had been voted least likely to succeed, let alone come to the aid of St. Philomena's, Jane knew it would have been Zack Stoner.

He'd been the despair of the entire faculty during his student years, putting hermit crabs in the holy water, smoking in the vestry, and beating up anyone who dared stare too long in his direction.

Certainly Sister Clementia and Sister Gertrudis and all the other holy sisters whose lives Zack Stoner had bedeviled throughout the years had wrung their hands and predicted what judgment would befall him.

And now here he was—back again—like the prodigal son.

No, Jane corrected herself. The prodigal son had come back destitute and begging forgiveness.

Zack had come back in power.

From a fame and fortune standpoint at least, Zack was the brightest star in St. Philomena's galaxy of successful graduates.

His salvation, despaired of in the convent, had been assured on the football field. He'd done well in high school, both as a quarterback and as a receiver. It was, Jane had heard said, the only thing that had kept him in.

But whatever had made him stay, it had been enough to get him a scholarship to Notre Dame, where he had blossomed. A Heisman Trophy candidate in both his junior and senior years, he had gone on to become one of the most highly acclaimed wide receivers in the pro game.

And his talents didn't lie only in athletics, as Jane had discovered not long ago. Now he was doing television work, as well.

According to Kelly's husband, Jeff, two years ago while recuperating from a broken leg, Zack had been invited to provide color commentary on Sunday-afternoon telecasts. He'd been a natural.

"And now he's doing other stuff. He's on most nights. You gotta see him," Kelly had insisted. "You won't believe it."

And Jane, seeing him for the first time on the tube at Kelly's last Thanksgiving weekend, had had to agree.

She'd stood and stared, fascinated by the lean, rugged-looking man on the screen, remembering the scruffy, hard-nosed boy he had been.

He'd developed charm somewhere along the way. He'd become articulate. He'd learned to smile.

He was still Zack Stoner, though. His dark hair was as unruly as ever. And his expression, when he wasn't smiling, was still hard and intense.

Looking at him on television that autumn afternoon, Jane had thought she wouldn't ever want to face him on a football field. Or anywhere else.

And now she was.

She swallowed carefully, crossed her legs and folded her hands in her lap and recalled what it was that had brought them face-to-face.

"What is it you'd like me to help with?" she said in her most businesslike tone.

Zack blinked, then shrugged and shoved a paper across the desk at her. "We've got a seven-minute spot to fill. I've been giving it some thought, and these are some of the ideas I've had for what we ought to cover."

Jane looked deliberately down at the paper he'd given her, reading every word carefully, taking her time. It was thorough and businesslike. Grudgingly she was impressed.

Zack sat quietly, waiting. She tried to pretend he wasn't there. But out of the corner of her eye she could see his hands, clasped loosely on the desktop. She could see strong forearms, lightly dusted with dark hair. She jerked her eyes back to the paper in her hand.

He'd thought of all the angles. Or someone had, she reminded herself. Perhaps Zack wasn't the brains, but only the glamour boy.

"Who wrote all this?" she asked him.

"I did. Father Morrisey says there're about five boxes full of old photos at the rectory," Zack told her. "And he thinks there're more over at the convent. I figured we could sort through them and pick out the best. Then we'll shoot them on film and we can do a commentary over the top. Sort of like that Civil War series.''

''With quotes from old-timers?''

He nodded. ''Yeah. I thought maybe we could find some old parishioners, maybe some old nuns—''

''Do you think they'll talk to you? You were such a wretch.''

He grinned. ''That's where 'Your Prissiness' comes in.''

''What?''

He feigned shock. ''Don't tell me you didn't know your nickname?''

Well, she did, of course. But she'd never admitted it, not to anyone. And she certainly wasn't acknowledging it now. ''I should think if you want my help, you'd try to be nicer.''

''Me? I haven't changed that much. What do you want...me to go down on bended knee and say, please, Your Prissiness, I need you desperately.''

Jane blushed. ''Oh, for heaven's sake!''

''Come on, Janey. Where's your sense of humor?''

''I'm looking for it,'' she said. ''I find you rather hard to deal with, you know.''

''I don't believe it.''

''Believe. Really, Zack, you can do this without me. They'll talk to you. Sister Clementia—''

''We've been through that,'' Zack said impatiently. ''You never used to be this slow, Janey. I want you. Father Jack assured me you'd do it. And—'' he looked right at her ''—I figured you wouldn't mind helping an old friend.''

''I—''

"You helped me out once before, didn't you?" His voice was soft, but his blue eyes challenged.

Jane hesitated.

It was true. She had.

That didn't mean she'd liked it, however. Nor that she wanted to do it now.

Zack Stoner made her nervous. She never knew quite what to expect. He wasn't an easy, predictable man like Paul had been. There was nothing sedate and polite about him. On the contrary, he was even now a very physical presence. One that she found decidedly unnerving.

But she knew he wasn't going to let her off easily. If she declined, he'd let everyone in the world know. And they would all want to know why.

And Jane wasn't sure she could tell them.

He was handsome. He was sexy. He was "dynamite," according to Kelly. She didn't need Kelly telling her she was chicken.

"All right," she said finally and less than graciously. "I'll do it. I'll intercede with the nuns for you. But that's it."

"What about helping me go through the photos, letting me film your class, giving me your views of St. Phil's, having dinner with me?"

"*What?*"

He looked at her hopefully. "Father Jack said you would." He made his tone almost plaintive.

Jane wasn't fooled. "Father Jack didn't say anything about dinner."

"Didn't he?" Zack managed to look surprised. A corner of his mouth quirked.

Jane scowled at him. He met her gaze steadily, his eyes teasing but challenging.

And he smiled. Jane had never seen a smile like it in her life, so full of life and eagerness and promise.

Paul had never looked at her like that!

She swallowed hard and opened her mouth to decline.

Zack shook his head. He lifted his hand and gently touched her chin, closing her lips. "Don't say no."

SHE HADN'T.

Score one for him, Zack thought as he drove up the narrow street where Jane lived. He'd been fully prepared for her to deny him. It wouldn't have surprised him in the least. Jane Kitto had disapproved of him years ago.

Until he convinced her otherwise, he suspected she still would.

He was a guy who liked a challenge. Jane Kitto was one for the books.

She looked remarkably like the little girl he remembered from their elementary school days.

She was taller now, but no curvier. She still looked like a waif.

A well-dressed waif, he thought wryly. Today's matching outfit was as neat and trim as her starched white uniform blouses and plaid skirts used to be.

Her eyes were the same—a wide, guileless green. She wasn't wearing glasses now. Contacts probably. An improvement. Her hair was better, too. She used to wear it skinned back with a center part and two long braids that hung halfway down her back. It was still long, but she wore it loose and it was, frankly, gorgeous. If her braids had made him want to yank them, these luxuriant tresses made him want to tangle his fingers in them, bury his face in them.

A guy could forget all about her prissiness if he concentrated on her hair.

Zack didn't think he'd better concentrate on her hair. At least not yet. All in good time.

Right now he had a job to do. And getting her to go to dinner with him was the first step.

SHE SHOULD have said no. No, no, a thousand times no!

It was foolish, insane and ridiculous to be going out with Zack Stoner. He wasn't her type at all.

But she could hardly tell him that!

He wasn't interested in her that way, and she would look like an idiot if she even faintly implied that he was. So when he'd challenged her, when he'd said in that soft, slightly gruff voice of his, "Not afraid, are you?" of course she'd acquiesced.

And why not? she asked herself irritably.

It wasn't a date. It was business. They were two adults working on a project, that was all.

And if he was a handsome, sexy man, so what? It didn't mean she would succumb to his charms.

Still, it wasn't every day a fast-lane marvel like Zack Stoner asked her out. And she had as much curiosity as the next woman. Why not satisfy it?

Determinedly putting all her rationalizations out of her mind, she scavenged through her closet for the umpteenth time, trying to find the perfect outfit, knowing full well she didn't own one.

At last she settled on a red wool dress. It was the brightest, most confident dress she owned. She would need that when she dealt with Zack Stoner, she told herself. One always did.

She sat down at her dressing table and began brushing out her hair. "The Lord works in mysterious ways," she told her reflection.

And while she brushed, she remembered her first encounter with Zack Stoner all those years ago....

IT HAD HAPPENED on a Thursday, art day, and, as such, Jane's favorite day of the week. She liked school, all of it. But more than anything, Jane liked art.

Especially drawing. The cut-and-paste collage assignments were fine, the clay pots were fun, the wire sculptures were interesting.

But Jane preferred a sharply pointed pencil, a wide white sheet. Whenever she could, she drew horses. Horses that ran like the wind, skimmed the mountaintops, flew across canyons. Horses that ran untethered, as wild and free as Jane's imagination, as different from her narrow, buttoned-down life as possible.

And that was exactly what she was doing that Thursday afternoon in January, shutting out the damp, foggy San Francisco afternoon, her mind racing free across the meadows and her pencil dashing across the page. It was easier than usual since her desk partner, Diane, was absent, and she could spread her papers across both their spaces.

She was just finishing the windblown mane when the door to the classroom banged open and a furious Sister Gertrudis stalked in, hauling with her a rigid, reluctant Zack Stoner.

Jane didn't know Zack Stoner—except by reputation. But that was enough.

He was a "bad boy," according to her mother who'd heard rumors. He was "a roughneck hooligan," according to her father, who'd chased Zack and his unholy friends out of his shop. He was "well on his way to perdition," according to ancient Father O'Driscoll who had discovered the hermit crabs and the cigarette smoke, and he was surely "the devil's spawn," according to Sister Gertrudis who had him in sixth grade and who held him up to the impressionable second-graders as an example of how not to behave.

Jane believed it. Every word.

She was a law-and-order girl, a do-gooder with more gold stars in her halo than Sister had check marks on the good deeds chart.

Jane had no use for fierce, aggressive ruffians like Zack Stoner. She crossed the street whenever she saw him two blocks down. He would, she was sure, take great pleasure in chewing up and spitting out a nice little girl like her.

She slid down in her seat now. But as terrified as she was, sitting there watching Sister Gertrudis grab him by his upper arms and shake him, she couldn't seem to look away.

His hard stubborn jaw fascinated her, his obstinate sneer amazed her. The silent screaming energy emanating from him reminded her of the strongest, swiftest horses she'd ever drawn.

"Zachary doesn't belong in sixth grade," Sister Gertrudis announced in stentorian tones. "He isn't mature enough. Are you, Zachary?"

Jane saw his lips tighten. She saw a pulse in his jaw tick.

"He is not," Sister Gertrudis repeated. "And his behavior this afternoon with the shoe polish proves it. Zachary will be joining your class today, children," she told the wide-eyed second-graders. "And I want you to keep a close eye on him to see if he's mature enough to be here. If not, Zachary," she said to the scowling boy, "tomorrow you will be joining the kindergarten."

Jane would have died if Sister Gertrudis had spoken that way to her. She would have melted right through the floor where she sat. But Zack Stoner stood right where he was, stubborn and defiant, until Sister Gertrudis delivered the final ignominy.

She turned him around and swatted his bottom, then said, "Go sit next to Jane."

Jane froze.

With Sister Gertrudis dogging his heels he moved slowly down the row until he stood next to Jane's desk. She watched his approach without lifting her eyes. She saw that all the nap on his cords was rubbed off at the knees. She saw that his laces were broken and knotted, that his shoes were scuffed.

"Sit down, Zachary," Sister Gertrudis commanded.

For an instant Jane thought that he wasn't going to do it. She envisioned those clenched fists, which she could see out of the corner of her eye, moving with lightning quickness to punch Sister Gertrudis right in the stomach. She saw herself jumping up and standing on her desk, trying to stop the inevitable bloodshed.

Fortunately he sat.

"Try not to act like a baby, Zachary," said Sister Gertrudis. Then, turning on her heel, she left.

As soon as she did so, Sister Clementia began scurrying about. "Back to work, children," she said, bustling up and down the rows.

Reluctantly, still tittering and snickering and shooting glances at the mutinous Zack, the children began to comply.

Only then did Jane venture a glance at the boy sitting next to her, and a fleeting glance it was intended to be—until she saw the unshed tears lining the lashes of his eyes.

Zack Stoner? *Cry?*

Well, he wasn't, really. Not yet.

But the very fact that he might astonished her. She wouldn't have believed it possible. If, as Sister Clementia claimed, angels were souls born without bodies, then it seemed reasonable to Jane that boys like Zack Stoner were born without tear ducts.

She swallowed a tiny gasp.

His eyes fastened on hers, fierce and furious and stubbornly unblinking. To be called a baby by Sister Gertrudis was bad enough. To cry would be a disaster. He would never live it down.

He glared at her. She reached into her desk and smuggled him a tissue.

At first she thought he wasn't going to take it. He continued to look daggers at her even as she reached over and stuffed it into his hand. But just then he did blink, and one of the tears fell, its telltale existence streaking down his cheek, betraying him.

The two of them stared at each other. Then Jane saw Wendy Dailey begin to turn and sneak a glance at Zack.

That was when Jane did something no little do-gooder ever does.

She leapt to her feet and blurted, "Sister! I need help! I can't make his hooves come out right." And she headed for the front of the room, her drawing paper in her hand.

Sister Clementia stared at her in shock. The class began muttering, giggling and tittering, astonished. Jane was astonished herself. It was completely out of character. First, little do-gooders do not jump out of the seats without permission; second, they do not speak out of turn; third, and this was what surprised Jane in retrospect more than anything else about her behavior that afternoon, little do-gooders *do not* lie!

Jane Kitto could draw a horse with her eyes closed and the pencil between her teeth. She had been born drawing hooves. And yet she persisted, spreading her paper out on the teacher's desk and suffering Sister Clementia's disapproval and instruction.

She wondered that Sister Clementia or God, Himself, did not call her to judgment at once.

But Sister Clementia, though she scolded Jane for jumping out of her seat, took her request absolutely seriously. She bent over the desk, sketching in a hoof, erasing it and putting in an altogether different one, this one more ridiculously inadequate than the last.

Jane watched. Or tried to. Mostly what she did was avoid looking back at Zack.

Finally Sister Clementia was finished. "There. I'm glad you asked for help, Jane. I'm always happy to give it. But you must remember to raise your hand."

"I will, Sister," Jane replied dutifully. She took her paper and headed back to her seat.

Zack Stoner was scowling at her. Dry-eyed.

She gave him a tiny smile. He ignored her.

Jane didn't care. She had done what needed to be done. She took her seat and started drawing again.

She had wasted precious moments and she had to make up for it. She bent over her desk, drawing like the wind. She quickly erased Sister's hooves and did her own far superior ones. Then she shaded the legs, made slashing marks to show the way the horse scattered the rocks beneath his feet as he ran.

And as she drew she imagined herself riding him, her long, dark hair no longer confined, but streaming out behind her in the wind as she and her horse flew down the mountains.

She drew, forgetting Sister Clementia, forgetting the smell of chalk dust and stale lunches, forgetting everything—even Zack Stoner—until the bell rang.

When it did, she looked up, slightly disoriented.

"That's not much good," Zack Stoner said.

Jane looked at him, then at the drawing, the fantasy fading as she looked at it dispassionately. "No," she said truthfully. "It's not."

He blinked as if her agreement startled him. Then he frowned at her.

"But I'm getting better." She reached into her desk and pulled out a stack of similar papers. "See. They look more like they're running now."

She steeled herself for a dismissive, hurtful remark. But he didn't say anything, just looked through them, one by one.

"How come you draw so many horses?"

Jane shrugged. "I like horses. They can take you on adventures."

He just looked at her blankly.

"Sometimes when I'm bored or tired of where I am, or sometimes when Father O'Driscoll is just talking on and on, I pretend I'm on a horse, flying over the hills. It's lots better than being here.''

"That's stupid."

"Is it?" She didn't think so. But then, she could hardly expect Zack Stoner to agree. They probably didn't have anything in common. It was just a few minutes ago she'd even begun to suspect he was human.

He was pushing her drawings around, looking at them again. He stopped when he came to the one of the big black stallion with the white blaze and fierce, indomitable expression. He looked mean.

"I like him," Zack said.

He would, Jane thought. That stallion was so big, so powerful, so scary that Jane had never drawn it again.

"You can have him."

Zack looked at the paper she held out. He hesitated, then his fingers closed on it.

He didn't say anything at all. And she realized suddenly that while she and Zack were talking, all the other children had picked up their books, put their chairs on the desks and left. Sister Clementia was standing by the door looking at them.

"I've got to go. Kelly's waiting," Jane said quickly. She gathered up her own books, put her chair on her desk and hurried out the door.

SHE HADN'T TALKED to Zack Stoner since.

Until today.

She spun around in front of the full-length mirror, letting the soft, red wool skirt swirl against her legs. She swept her long, dark brown hair up away from her face, using a clip to hold it, then letting it cascade down her back.

Too girlish, she decided, and did it swiftly up in a French twist. Better, she decided. Much better. Then she stood still to fasten a silver chain around her neck and stepped back to study the whole effect.

She looked, she thought, about as good as she could. The dress, by its very simplicity, was understated. But the chain brought it some sparkle. And the deep red color acted as a counterpoint, promising, perhaps, a bit of pizzazz.

She hadn't worn it with Paul. Paul had preferred deep, dark blues, hunter greens, basic gray. Quiet colors.

Jane was fond of them herself. But she knew what Zack would say if he saw her wearing one of them.

"Miss Mouse," he would call her. He'd called her it before, years ago, after their initial encounter. He'd been teasing, and she'd known it. But she hadn't known how to respond.

She still didn't know. But tonight she was wearing red. She knew she would need all the pizzazz she could muster if she had to hold her own for an entire evening with Zack.

She was just reaching into the closet for her shoes when the doorbell rang.

Instinctively her hand went to her bracelet. Her fingers sought the tiny pewter lion, the one she'd received the year her father had died. "Courage," she whispered to herself.

With Zack Stoner she would need plenty of that.

Chapter Three

HE WAS EARLY. Not very. But enough so that she was still in her stocking feet when the doorbell rang.

Jane's fingers sought the lion, giving him one last squeeze. Then, drawing a deep breath, she went to answer the door.

She should have stopped to put on her shoes, she thought. He seemed taller than he'd been that afternoon, more imposing than ever.

Deliberately Jane pasted on a smile. "Come in. I'll just be a minute. You found the address all right?"

"No problem," Zack said, just as if her comment hadn't been inane. He followed her in, and the room seemed suddenly to shrink.

It never felt like this when Paul had come in. She backed toward the door to her bedroom, still keeping her eyes on him.

His dark hair was as combed as Jane had ever seen it, but it still had an untamed look. He wore a pair of dark wool slacks, a pin-striped blue and white shirt and a muted-paisley burgundy and gray tie. Only his jacket hooked over his shoulder gave him a look slightly more daring than a banker.

Yet even in such civilized clothes—perhaps *because* of the civilized clothes—he still made Jane quiver, as if she were an unarmed lion tamer and he were an unknown cat.

He had been easier to deal with when he was younger, she thought. When she'd known exactly what to expect from him—a yank on her ponytail or a teasing "Miss Mouse."

Now she hadn't a clue.

"Just let me get my whi—shoes," she said quickly and fled, face flaming, in search of her highest heels.

He watched her go, bemused. She still reminded him of a mouse. If she had whiskers, they'd twitch, he thought with a grin.

He crossed the room to the window so that when she came back it would look as if he was just appreciating the view.

What he was doing was studying her apartment.

When he'd been a boy—after the day she'd given him that tissue, after the day she'd shocked him to the core—he'd spent a lot of time trying to figure her out.

He'd never noticed her until then. She'd had a habit of blending into walls and furniture. One second you saw her, the next you didn't. Like a mouse.

How did mice live? he'd wondered.

Sometimes out of curiosity he'd followed her home. Whenever she'd noticed him, she'd cut over to the other side of the street. He couldn't figure her out.

And now, here he was, almost twenty years later, in Miss Mouse's house.

It wasn't what he'd figured. He'd pictured chintz and doilies. Antimacassars and porcelain bric-a-brac. He saw spare sleek-lined teak furniture, Finnish wool rugs on highly polished floors. Stunning abstracts hung on the walls. Horror books, of all things, joined volumes of art history on her shelves. There wasn't a knickknack in sight.

"Is the ferry passing?"

He turned to see her standing in the doorway. She was about four inches taller all of a sudden. But just as stunning.

He couldn't keep the appreciation out of his eyes as they skimmed over her small breasts and willowy curves.

"Not at the moment," he managed, recalling she'd asked something about the ferry. "You're very pretty." A corner of his mouth lifted. "But then, you always were."

Her face flamed. "Don't be ridiculous," she said briskly.

"You don't like compliments?"

"Not obviously false ones." She opened the closet and plucked out her coat.

He cocked his head, watching her, curious at her response. "Are you accusing me of lying?" he asked softly.

She turned, holding her coat against her breasts. "I—oh—" She made a tiny irritated noise. "Why is it always my fault?"

He grinned. "Because I think you're pretty?"

"Stow it, Zack," she said gruffly.

His grin widened. "That's my Jane."

"I am not—"

"I like your apartment." He cut off her protest. "It's not fussy."

"There's no room to be fussy in a place this size," Jane said, startled at the change of subject. She moved to shrug into her coat. He took it from her and held it, allowing her to slip it on.

She glanced back at him. The smile he gave her made her take a deep breath. She'd hoped her moments in the bedroom had given her the panache to carry this off. She eased her arms into the sleeves. Zack's fingers brushed her shoulders, lifted her hair, made her shiver. Her mind spun. Her heart thumped. So much for panache.

"Would you be fussy if you had room?" His voice seemed to come from miles away and right inside her ear at the same time.

Jane jerked her mind away from her reaction to his touch, trying to focus on what he was asking.

"Fussy?" She frowned. "No, I wouldn't. I don't like fussy. I like—" she groped for words to explain how she felt and found only one "—space."

"Wide open spaces where you can ride and let your imagination take you on adventures."

She stared. "I can't believe you remember all that."

He shrugged. "It was a memorable day."

"I guess."

He grinned. "You were a memorable girl."

"That's why you called me Miss Mouse forever after."

"I called you that out of affection."

Jane snorted. "Sure. You adored me."

"Well, not right then. I appreciated you."

"I was terrified out of my mind."

"At me? You didn't act like it."

"Desperation."

"Are you terrified now?"

"Just a little."

One brow lifted. "A little terrified?"

"Mmm." She opened the door and went out into the hallway.

Zack followed. "Why?"

But she couldn't—*wouldn't*—go so far as to discuss that. Her terror now hadn't so much to do with childish fears as with adult ones.

Of course Zack was strong, tough and all the things that had intimidated Jane Kitto the child. But that wasn't what provoked her uneasiness now. Now it was sexual awareness. In spades.

How idiotic is that? she asked herself.

Every woman past the age of puberty in the entire San Francisco area was likely aware of the sheer masculine magnetism of Zachary Stoner. He probably expected it.

The trouble was *she* hadn't expected it.

He wasn't at all the sort of man she was normally attracted to. He was too blatantly, ruggedly masculine. Not at all like Paul. Or like Alistair, the Scot she'd met in the Victoria and Albert Museum, or Jonathan, who adored Gainsborough and who'd taken her punting on the Cam.

There was a sort of raw, elemental power to Zack Stoner that was all too apparent. Generally she preferred the more subtle male—the suave, debonair, quietly sensitive sort.

The sort of man who would have sent her almost twenty years' worth of charms.

Clearly her hormones didn't see that. Of course, Jane realized, they could hardly be blamed. They weren't dead, after all, just underutilized. Since she'd broken up with Paul, she hadn't looked at another man.

And she'd better stop looking at this one, she thought now. Unless she wanted a one-night fling— not marriage and family and all those things she'd admitted to Kelly that she wanted—she was wasting her time on Zack.

Even if she did only want a one-night fling, she'd most likely be wasting her time, Jane reminded herself ruthlessly.

A girl who, in elementary school, he'd called Miss Mouse, a woman whose most memorable feature was her prissiness, was hardly likely to tempt Zack Stoner.

It wasn't a date. It was business, pure and simple, and she intended to remember that.

"I'm not used to going out with men like you," she said to answer his question.

He cocked his head. "Men like me?"

"Wide receivers," Jane explained, deadpan.

Zack started to laugh.

Jane opened the front door. The January night was cool and clear, with the smell of the sea and a hint of hot oil from Mama Tom's Chinese Kitchen in the air. She took a deep breath and let it out slowly, trying to steady her galloping pulses.

The car he led her to was a dark gray late-model Audi, very conservative and eminently respectable. Zack noticed her surprise.

"You were hoping for a Ferrari?"

"Or a Lamborghini," Jane said as she settled against the cool leather seat. Zack shut her door, then came around and slid in next to her.

"I wouldn't have guessed you'd be a car buff."

"Before I started teaching, I wouldn't have known a Lamborghini if it had run me over. The boys in my class were appalled. It didn't take long before I found out that education is a two-way street. Now other classrooms at St. Phil's have farm animals and holy pictures on the walls. Mine have farm animals, holy pictures and fast-car posters.''

''Good for you. We'll feature them in the shoot.''

Jane grimaced. ''That'll go over big with the parish council.''

''Would it cause problems? Really?''

''Probably not. They've given me quite a bit of latitude. But I do try not to shock them deliberately.''

''Ah. It's like I thought all along—this prissy business is nothing but a facade.''

He was delighted to see her blush.

''So tell me,'' he said, pressing his advantage, ''deep down where it counts are you still the same? Do you still hanker after horses?''

''Horses? Oh, you mean like the ones I drew? You really do remember everything, don't you?''

He shrugged. He didn't tell her that for years he'd kept the one she'd given him in his wallet. That even now he'd put it in a frame and hung it in his house in the country.

''Yes,'' she said. ''I guess I do, now and then.''

''Never got one?''

''No.''

''I did. We'll have to go riding sometime.'' He said it casually, not wanting to push. She was as skittish as any mustang he'd ever seen.

''There aren't a lot of places to ride in the city.''

''I've got a place about an hour north along the coast. You'll like it.''

Jane didn't say anything to that. He saw her fingers clench and unclench around the wool of her skirt.

''You were right,'' he went on, ''about riding, I mean. It's like you said, it takes your mind off things and helps you focus on others. Sometimes you can just get out there and ride . . . and dream. And—"

Damn. He had to shut up. He was going too fast, saying too much, quoting her words. He flexed his fingers on the steering wheel.

"You do remember a lot," she said quietly. "I would have tried to forget it if I were you."

"No." Zack was certain about that. "There are some things a guy needs to remember."

He didn't say anything else. Nor did Jane. They drove in silence the rest of the way to the heart of the financial district, where Zack turned in to a multistory garage and parked in a reserved slot.

"Very impressive," Jane said when he came around and opened the door for her.

"The parking place? Yeah, it's one of the perks of the job. The studio's right across the way." He nodded toward the building across the street. He cupped her elbow with his fingers and started for the steps. "Come on."

Jane expected them to cross the street to get to the studio, figuring that there'd be a restaurant in the building. But Zack didn't cross. He kept walking.

"Where are we going?" she asked, when they crossed another street and turned another corner, leaving the studio behind.

"Here." He led her in.

"Here?" she echoed. *Here*, she suddenly realized, was the lobby of the skyscraping Bank of America Building, that deep red marble landmark with its famous Carnelian Room atop.

"Is there something wrong with it? If you'd rather not have drinks here . . ."

"No, of course not. I just . . . just thought we were going to . . . to work."

"We are."

Fifty-one floors later he led her out of the elevator and along the hall toward the lounge overlooking the Golden Gate. The city was spread below them. Sparkling with jewellike lights, Columbus Avenue angled away toward the wharf. The twin spires of Sts. Peter and Paul church drew her eye. The triangular tip of the Transamerica Building, below her for once, did the same. Coit Tower stood out like an artist's thumb. Jane stood and stared.

Jane had been to the Carnelian Room once before, with Paul. It was the first place he'd taken her after they'd become engaged. It had seemed an eminently romantic place then, with its paneled walls, dim lights and stunning views, the hushed voices, the soft music and the subtle clink of crystal.

It seemed exactly the same now.

And when Zack helped her remove her coat, then held her chair for her, she was acutely conscious of the brush of his fingers against her shoulders.

Even more disconcerting was the moment when he sat down across the tiny table from her and looked straight into her eyes. His were deep set and so dark a blue as to look almost black in the muted light. Jane had heard the expression *bedroom eyes* plenty of times. She'd never understood it until now.

"So," she said briskly, sitting up straight and folding her hands on the tabletop, "how can I help you with St. Phil's?"

"You really want to talk about St. Phil's?"

"That's what we're here for, isn't it?"

Zack smiled. "One reason. But not the only one—I hope. I think we have a bit of catching up to do."

"We weren't exactly soul mates back in school."

"Maybe not."

"Definitely not," Jane said firmly. "I told you, I was terrified. I used to cross the street when I saw you coming."

"I noticed that."

Her eyes widened. "You did?"

He nodded.

"Oh, hell."

He looked shocked.

"I do swear now and then," Jane said. "Or didn't you think I could?"

"I think you can do anything," Zack told her.

She stared. "You're crazy. I'm the original chicken."

"No," he said. "You aren't. You weren't." His eyes challenged her.

The waiter appeared and Jane felt an enormous relief at not having to meet it, whatever *it* was.

"I'll have a glass of Chardonnay," she said quickly.

"And you, sir?"

"Club soda." Zack smiled ironically at Jane's surprised look. "See? Nothing to be afraid of. How can you cross the street in fear of a man who drinks club soda?"

Jane looked at him suspiciously. "You don't drink?"

He grinned. "Alcohol is calories. Calories make pounds. Pounds slow me down. We're playing Atlanta Sunday. If we win, we'll go to the Super Bowl. I want to go. And I need every bit of speed I can muster if I don't want to get crushed."

Jane smiled.

He cocked his head. "You like the notion of somebody pounding me into the ground?"

"It has its moments," Jane admitted.

"Sadist."

She laughed. *"Moi?"*

The waiter returned with their drinks and Jane was glad to wrap her fingers around hers. It gave her something to hold on to. She took a long sip.

Zack leaned back in his chair and regarded her over the top of his glass. His expression was warm and there was—unless she was already under the influence of the Chardonnay—something decidedly hungry about it. Jane felt another shiver down her spine.

"It's always the sweet ones who're bloodthirsty."

Jane laughed. "Too right."

"Did you like England?"

Jane sat up straight. "How did you know I was in England?"

"Father Jack told me." Zack raised his glass and held it out toward her in a toast. "Said you were working on your Master's."

"In art history."

"Not drawing?"

"I'm not good enough. But I appreciate it."

"I appreciate you," Zack said.

Jane, halfway into a sip of wine, nearly choked. Gamely she swallowed, blinking rapidly, praying she wouldn't start coughing and not be able to stop.

"Are you all right?"

She cleared her throat desperately. "F-fine," she croaked.

"Take it slow," Zack said. "We've got all night."

We don't, Jane wanted to say. *I turn into a pumpkin at ten o'clock.* She didn't say it. She thought he might believe it.

He lifted his glass in a toast. Warily Jane lifted her own. Silently their glasses touched, their eyes met.

"To St. Philomena," she said quickly.

Zack looked at her a long moment, his dark gaze unreadable. Then he clinked his glass against hers. "To us."

Jane's eyes bugged.

"A successful partnership," Zack went on.

She almost choked again in her relief. Carefully she set her glass down on the table and looked out through the window toward the city. She watched a ship make its way slowly toward the bridge, then watched Zack's reflection as he sat opposite her.

To us, he'd said. *To a successful partnership.* Surely that was all he meant.

But, she realized later, they never talked about St. Philomena's again.

Zack pursued the subject of her studies in England, asking about her experiences. And he wasn't content with the once-over-slightly that she usually gave. He wanted to know more about why she had decided to go in the first place, what she'd seen, what she wanted to do with it now.

And Jane told him, haltingly at first, unsure that he wasn't just humoring her. But he seemed actually interested in her notions about making art accessible to children—more than most people she'd met in the year and a half she'd been home—and so she talked.

"I love art. It opened up the world for me. I want that for other people. So I always knew I would teach.

But I needed to see a bit more than what I'd seen in books first."

Zack nodded. "Makes sense."

He was a good listener. He sipped his club soda and cocked his head and listened intently, smiled encouragingly, nodded understandingly.

Before long Jane forgot her initial nervousness. What she couldn't seem to forget was her awareness of him as an attractive, sexy man.

But even though it remained in the back of her mind, it wasn't long before Zack's sexual attractiveness became a part of a greater whole. She was amazed.

They finished their drinks, and Zack suggested that they adjourn to a little Italian restaurant nearby. "It's cozier than this. A place where friends can get reacquainted." He looked at Jane hopefully.

She wasn't entirely sure about the wisdom of coziness or about getting reacquainted with Zack Stoner, but she couldn't think of a good reason to decline, especially since she'd already said she would have dinner with him.

The restaurant had heavy walnut wainscoting, dark burgundy wallpaper and small, intimate candle-lit tables. They were given a table in an alcove.

"So tell me," Jane said when they'd ordered, "how does it feel to be a great success?"

"Better than it felt to be a sixth-grader at St. Phil's."

She smiled. "You must be very pleased with yourself. And you must be getting a kick out of coming back and showing them up."

"Once I would have. Once I wanted to want to rub their noses in it."

"But not now?"

"Now I'm smarter." He looked at her from beneath hooded lids, his smile lopsided. "Now I think I learned something there." He shrugged. "So I guess I owe them."

He sounded almost mellow. Jane heard none of the chip-on-the-shoulder attitude that she remembered.

"I'm glad."

Zack smiled. "Me, too."

The awareness hit her again full force. What was it with her tonight? she thought irritably.

She remembered plenty of meals with Paul, where their gazes had met and she'd never felt anything like this.

Cool it, she cautioned herself. *Be calm. Relax. This is Zack Stoner you're panting about. There is no point. Remember that.*

And she tried.

All through their pasta primavera she tried. All the while he charmed her with a series of funny stories about his college days and his football career. All throughout the dinner they shared, and during the quiet ride back to her apartment afterward she made an effort to keep her distance.

But it was hard.

It was especially hard when he stood so close to her on her doorstep, touched his hand to her hair, loosening the strands from her twist.

"I like it down," he told her. Then he dropped the lightest of kisses on her nose.

"Er," Jane managed.

"Wear it down," he said softly. His breath touched her cheek. Jane's pulses were pounding and the blood was surging in her veins.

It was all she could do not to lift her hand and touch her fingers to the spot where his lips had touched!

He stepped back and took her hand. "I've got practice the rest of the week," Zack apologized. "I'll be tied up."

Jane cleared her throat. "O-of course you will." She sounded as if she'd swallowed a frog, she thought desperately.

"So I won't be able to get around for a few days. Next week maybe we can go over those photos? Do some of the interviews?"

"That'd be fine." She knew she should be pulling her hand away. His thumb was rubbing her knuckles. His fingers squeezed hers lightly. It felt so erotic she didn't dare wonder what his hands would feel like on her shoulders, on her breasts.

Then his fingers touched her bracelet.

Sanity came streaming back. She drew her hand away.

"Thank you for a lovely evening."

Zack just looked at her. A slow grin lit his face. "Very nice. Very well brought up. Sister Clementia would be proud."

Jane felt the blood rush to her cheeks.

"You match your dress," he told her. Then he leaned forward and kissed her again, this time on the lips.

It wasn't a long kiss or a passionate one. But there was something about it—some indefinable air of promise.

Or was it a threat?

"Night, Janey," he whispered.

Jane couldn't say a word. She watched him go down the steps, moving with easy athletic grace. Had Zack Stoner changed? Or hadn't he?

She knew one thing for sure: he could still make Jane Kitto quake in her shoes. His very gaze could still make her tremble—but for far, far different reasons.

Sister Clementia would be horrified to learn that it was now within Zack Stoner's power to make a good many of Jane Kitto's thoughts impure.

IN THE MORNING she was back to normal. Her wardrobe seemed perfectly adequate. Her lips no longer tingled. Her thoughts were her own.

She had survived. And all those fuzzy, fiffy feelings she'd had yesterday about Zack Stoner had melted into the past. It had been every bit the aberration she'd believed it was.

When the secretary came to the teachers' lounge to say she had a phone call, Jane wasn't even thinking about last night. All she could think was that it was her mother. She dropped everything and hurried to the office.

"What is it?" she demanded as she grabbed the receiver. "What's happened?"

"Nothing. Yet." The voice was sexy and decidedly male.

"Zack!" Jane swallowed her shock, tried desperately to modulate her tone. "Zack," she said again in a less astonished voice, "what is it?"

"I just called to tell you what a nice time I had last night."

"Er...I did, too," Jane said, nonplussed. Her fingers moved unwittingly to touch her lips. Realizing it, she jerked her hand away. "Thank you for dinner."

"You're very welcome." She could hear the smile in his voice, could imagine what it looked like. She gave herself a little shake.

"Everything all right, dear?" the secretary asked her.

"Fine." Jane cleared her throat. "Is there anything else you want?" she said to Zack briskly.

"To kiss you again."

"Zack!" Her cheeks burned. "I meant about the documentary."

"Just to set up a time when we can meet after I get back next week. I want something to look forward to," he added softly.

Jane took a careful breath. He was teasing her, that was all. He was the same Zack Stoner he'd always been, out to annoy. Only now he had a better weapon than ever: sex appeal. "I'm sure we can arrange something when you get back."

"Promise?"

"For heaven's sake!"

He laughed. "I'll see you, then. Sweet dreams, Janey." And he rang off, leaving Jane standing there, staring at the receiver in her hand.

"Something wrong, dear?" the secretary asked when Jane put down the phone.

"Oh, no," Jane said.

But she didn't know who she was trying to convince—the secretary or herself.

HE SHOULDN'T have done it, Zack told himself on the upthrust of a push-up, his body braced on his outstretched arms. Around him three dozen other bodies moved in unison to the rhythmic bark of the coach.

He'd had to, he admitted as he lowered his body back down. He'd needed to hear the sound of her voice.

But he'd made her nervous again, he thought, up once more, his arms working like pistons, sweat staining his cut-off shirt.

So what else was new? he thought, and again his body went down.

Jane. That's what was new. Jane and the way he was beginning to feel about her.

Ordinarily Zack found women amusing but expendable. He rarely put himself out for them. He'd never had to.

They'd always seemed pretty much interchangeable to him.

Except Jane.

It had been astonishment to begin with. Gratitude. Then his curiosity had been piqued. He'd watched her from afar, his Miss Mouse. He'd speculated. He'd guessed.

And now, after years and years, they'd come face-to-face. He'd been prepared to be disappointed.

He wasn't. He'd been charmed.

He was less certain how she felt about him.

SHE HAD MORE SENSE than to allow herself to become infatuated with Zack Stoner! He wasn't at all what she wanted—or needed.

But as the days went past, it seemed that he was invading her life.

He called three more times that week, leaving cheerful little messages on her answering machine.

The morning paper's sports section included an interview with a certain All-Pro wide receiver.

Saturday night, while she was sitting home grading papers, she inadvertently happened to watch the weekend show, "Scouting Report." It was just her bad luck that the commentator had chosen this week to talk about receivers, and further bad luck that he happened to interview Zack.

Why hadn't she remembered that Jeff had said Zack was going to be on it?

Well, she was too tired to get up and change the channel. The spelling tests she was grading were not particularly mesmerizing. So she actually couldn't help watching the interview. She leaned forward, looking more closely, found herself wishing she'd thought to put a tape in the VCR so she could have a copy of the interview.

But of course she wouldn't have done that since she had forgotten he was even on.

Of course.

Sunday afternoon she went to Kelly's for noon dinner. Afterward she helped Kelly do dishes while Jeff took the boys into the den to watch football.

"If you want to go watch, go watch," Kelly said.

"Me?" Jane looked at her, startled. "Watch football?"

"Not football. Zack Stoner."

"Don't be ridiculous."

But even as she spoke she was edging toward the door to the den. There was a silence, then a cheer. The announcer's voice babbled excitedly. "... Stoner—"

Jane hurried into the den to watch as a man in a white jersey dodged first one defender, then another, leaped over a third, then broke free, running ... running....

"Wooooweee!" Jeff, sitting bolt upright on the floor now, slapped his palms on the rug as Zack scored. "Man, can that guy run!"

And then Jane saw Zack being pounded by his teammates, hugged by the quarterback, all the while grinning his wicked grin and looking as handsome as the devil, even all sweaty and with his hair hanging in his face.

"Promising indeed," Kelly said with considerable approval. She slanted a glance in Jane's direction. "Is he a good kisser?"

"Ye—" Jane stopped short and blushed a brilliant red. "How would I know?"

Kelly just laughed.

"That's hardly the point," Jane said stiffly.

"I'd say it's precisely the point. You need someone to take your mind off Dan Capoletti."

"Who's Dan Capoletti?" Jeff asked.

"Janey's Secret Admirer."

"The deacon at St. Phil's," Jane corrected.

Jeff stared at her. "The deacon at St. Phil's has been giving you those charms?"

"No," said Jane.

"Yes," said Kelly.

Jeff shook his head. "Women," he muttered, then looked up at his wife. "What's Stoner got to do with it?"

"He took Jane out last Monday night."

"Our Janey? And *Zack Stoner?*"

"See?" Jane said. "Jeff knows how ridiculous it is."

"Jeff's just a man."

"So he knows exactly why a man like Zack would never be interested in a woman like me."

"Stoner would be interested," Jeff said, surprising Jane.

She stared at him.

Jeff shrugged. "They don't call him 'The NFL's Gift to Willing Women' for nothing."

Jane felt hot blood sear her cheeks.

"For heaven's sake, Jeff," Kelly protested, giving her husband a furious glare.

Jane looked away. The television camera was still on Zack. He was still grinning. He was still gorgeous. Of course women would be willing. And his seductive grins and soft words had doubtlessly charmed plenty of them.

As a child, he'd projected a tough-guy image. As an adult he projected a charming one.

Today's image was likely no more reliable than yesterday's had been.

Jane felt like an idiot for having been tempted, however briefly, to be taken in by it.

"I am not willing. We're doing a project together," she said firmly. "He was kind enough to invite me out to dinner. We were two professionals having a business meal."

"Then how do you know he's a good kisser?" Kelly asked.

Jane threw her hands in the air. "I give up! You deal with her," she said to Jeff. "She's obviously obsessed. I'm going home. I have to grade two sets of papers before tomorrow."

Kelly followed her to the door. "I'm sorry, Janey. I was only teasing."

Jane grimaced, recognizing her own short fuse for what it was. "That's okay."

"Did you like him? Really?"

"Oh, for heaven's sake!"

"I only wondered." Kelly looked at her, hurt in her wide blue eyes.

Jane relented. "He was very pleasant."

"And he did kiss you?" Kelly pressed.

Jane gritted her teeth. "I'm sure Zack Stoner kisses lots of women. After all, as Jeff pointed out—"

"Jeff's got a big mouth and a brain the size of a pea."

"You married him."

"Because I have a brain to match. We only want the best for you, Janey."

"Then help me keep my mind on the things that matter." She lifted her arm and jangled her bracelet in Kelly's face.

Kelly bit back a groan. "Zack's a real live man at least."

"But not my type."

EASY TO SAY. Easy to believe—unless you were face-to-face with the man.

But instead of a phone call sometime later in the week, which Jane had convinced herself she could handle with aplomb, Monday afternoon at one-thirty, right when she was in the middle of showing her second-graders how electricity worked, the door opened.

She looked up just as she was hooking the wire from one end of the battery to the other, preparatory to touching the light bulb to the wire.

Zack stood grinning at her.

"Wow! It works!" Jeremy Proctor yelped.

Jane looked down. The light bulb was glowing brightly.

Of course it is, Jane, you ninny, she admonished herself. It was the electricity that was turning on the light, for goodness' sake. It was just a matter of natural law.

But was it natural law for her throat to constrict, for her palms to perspire and her fingers to tingle?

Or was Zack Stoner's megawatt grin causing that?

"M-Mr. Stoner," she stammered.

"M-Miss Kitto," he mocked, grinning.

Jane's face flamed. The kids turned in their seats and began nudging each other, mumbling, muttering Zack's name.

Jeremy Proctor practically knocked Leticia right out of her chair.

She yelped. "What are you doing?"

"That's Zack Stoner! *Zack Stoner—*here!" Jeremy stared at Leticia's baffled face. "*You don't know who Zack Stoner is?* He's only the best wide receiver in the whole NFL."

"That's nice." She was staring speculatively at Zack. "But it doesn't matter," she added after a moment.

"Doesn't matter?" His tone betrayed his horror at this sacrilege.

"It doesn't. What's important is that it's him. You know," Leticia said impatiently. "*Miss Kitto's him. The one.*"

Chapter Four

CAREFULLY JANE set the light bulb on the table and wiped her palms on the sides of her skirt. "I'm in the middle of a class, Mr. Stoner."

He nodded. "Looks interesting."

"Yes. It is," Jane agreed with determined calm. "We are studying the principles of electricity."

It seemed to arc again between them even as she spoke. She hoped to heaven no one under the age of nine noticed.

"Good idea." A corner of Zack's mouth lifted. "Then you'll know when it hits."

"That's lightning, you mean," Jane said. "A natural manifestation of electricity."

"So it is."

Was this lightning striking, then? And where was her resolve when she needed it?

Go away, she urged silently. *Just go away.*

Zack didn't move. Jane licked parched lips. "What can I do for you, Mr. Stoner?" Her voice sounded to her reedy and a bit desperate.

"You said to come by. I thought we'd set up a date."

There was a collective juvenile gasp. Heads swiveled back and forth looking avidly from Zack at the back of the room to Jane at the front. Leticia rubbed her hands together, grinning.

"Not that kind of date," Jane said sharply. Then, to Zack she said, "I said 'call me.' I did not say come by. And I certainly didn't say come to my class! We are very busy now, Mr. Stoner. I will see you in the principal's office. After school."

"The principal's office?" Zack looked at her, dismayed.

"You do know where it is?"

"Have they moved it?"

She shook her head.

He sighed. "Then I know."

Jane didn't allow herself to breathe again until he'd actually gone out and shut the door. Then she placed both palms flat on the desk to support herself. Her knees were abominably weak.

"Wow," Jeremy said when Zack was gone. "Zack Stoner right here in this classroom." He looked around with such reverence that Jane wondered if he might find the room more inspiring in the future. "And he asked Miss Kitto for a date!"

"He was setting up an appointment."

"He said *date*," Leticia insisted.

"He misspoke."

"Would you go with him on a real date?"

She couldn't tell them she already had. But she wouldn't lie to them either. Still, there was no way. . . .

"Enough of this now, boys and girls. We have work to do."

Finally, with considerable prodding on her part and grumbling on theirs, Jane got them back on task. But she could hardly wait until it was time for their PE class.

She would have dealt with him then, but Sister Clementia came in, wanting to discuss the school assembly. And by the time she'd left, the children were banging and thumping in the hallway on their way back from gym.

Drawing a deep breath, Jane steeled herself in case they decided to take up the business about Zack again. Fortunately they had a new preoccupation.

"It's too hard," Cathy Chang complained.

"The rope's too fat."

"It's so high."

"We'll never be able to do it."

Jane looked at them as they straggled in and slumped in their seats. "What's this? You can't do something?"

"Mr. Deal says we gotta climb the rope," Jeremy told her. "To the top." He looked at the classroom ceiling which was about a third of the height of the gymnasium.

"But we can't," a dozen of them chorused.

"But that doesn't mean you won't ever be able to." They muttered darkly.

Jane jangled her bracelet in front of them. "See this? What's this?" She held up one of the charms.

"A skier," Bobby Palermo said promptly.

"Yes. And it's also a challenge."

"What d'you mean?" The muttering stopped. The kids leaned forward, listening.

"I am not much of a skier," Jane admitted. "I was terrified the first time I put them on. But I'd gone to Tahoe with a friend's family before Christmas, the year I was in fifth grade, and of course, what does one do in Tahoe in the winter but ski? I broke my wrist. I didn't intend ever to ski again. Then on Valentine's Day, I got this charm. I suppose it could have been his way of commemorating my disaster on the slopes—" Jane smiled wryly "—but somehow I didn't think it was.

"I saw it as a challenge. I thought to myself, 'He thinks I can do this.' He's challenging me to try—to face my fears and make the effort. Do you know what I mean?"

"The rope," Bobby said fatalistically.

Jane nodded. "The rope. You can run away or you can stay and try. It's the same way in life." Jane settled the skier back in among the other charms. She got up and smiled at her students. "Every day we have challenges thrown at us. Sometimes we even go looking for them. But most of the time they'll find us. Like the rope has. So, what are you going to do?"

The children looked at each other. Jeremy lifted his chin. "Face 'em."

Jane nodded. "Good for you."

Leticia raised her hand. "So if Mr. Stoner asks, you'll go out with him. Right, Miss Kitto?"

JANE KITTO KNEW a lot about the power of psychological intimidation, Zack had to give her that. He didn't know very many linebackers who could intimidate him the way Jane Kitto could.

Sent to the principal's office, for God's sake!

It had been years since he'd sat in a chair like this one and waited alone to meet his fate.

He sighed and stretched out his long legs, then shifted uncomfortably and hunched in the chair, resting his forearms on his thighs and knotting his fingers together. Three o'clock. The second hand moved with excruciating slowness. How well he remembered.

He should have left and come back when school ended. But he was afraid she would sneak away if he did, that she'd come in briefly, discover that he wasn't there yet and use it as an excuse to vanish.

She hadn't looked exactly glad to see him. She'd looked, in fact, horrified. Or had she been merely nervous? He wished he knew. But short of crossing the room and kissing her, he didn't know an accurate way of assessing her response.

He didn't think she would have thanked him if he'd done that!

He rubbed a hand around the back of his neck and tried to figure her out.

He'd never tried figuring out a woman before. He'd either liked them or he hadn't. He either bedded them or he didn't. If they weren't interested, he couldn't be bothered.

He knew that if any other woman had given him the sort of signals he was getting from Jane Kitto, he'd have been long gone.

But he wasn't leaving now. He wanted to talk to her, wanted to see her again, wanted to get under her skin the way she'd got under his.

Zack lifted his gaze and watched the movement beyond the frosted-glass window in the door, heard the cheerful voices of people who hadn't a care in the world and felt the same panicky, clammy feeling he used to feel sitting here.

Don't be ridiculous, he told himself. *This isn't the principal you're waiting for. It's Jane.*

But Jane was a bigger mystery than all the school principals in the world. He'd always known what his relationship was to them.

With Jane he hadn't a clue.

He ducked his head now as he heard, beyond the door, the secretary say something and laugh.

He heard Jane's cheerful reply.

Not surprising. She always had a kind word for everyone. Even roughnecks like him.

Was a kind word all he was ever going to get from her?

His fingers knotted together. He started to sweat.

JANE HESITATED only a second before she opened the door to the principal's office. Then she put on her biggest, bravest smile and went in. "Ah, good. You're here," she said, pleased at how brisk and efficient she sounded.

Zack hauled himself to his feet. He ran a hand through his hair. "Where else?" he said wryly.

Jane smiled. "Bring back old memories?"

"More than a few."

His tone made her look at him more closely. "You don't sound as if you enjoyed it."

He shrugged and she saw a hint of the tough-guy boy he had been. She was tempted to probe further. She didn't. The less she knew about Zack Stoner the better.

"I suppose you came today to find out what I've accomplished," she went on, determinedly. "I spoke to Sister Clementia and she'd be happy to talk to you. So would Sister Immaculata and Sister Lucy. Do you remember them?"

He winced. "Vividly."

"They remember you, too."

"I'll bet."

"They said they'd look forward to renewing the acquaintance. It's just down the street."

"Let's go now."

"You can if you want. You don't need me."

"I want you."

The words stopped her dead.

She felt as if flames were flickering up from the collar of her dress, scorching her neck. *He doesn't mean it the way it sounded, you idiot,* she chastised herself, embarrassed by her own initial interpretation of the words. She took solace in believing that it was what happened to a woman who spent too much time in the proximity of Zack Stoner.

Flustered, Jane glanced over at him, hoping he hadn't seen her misinterpretation.

His grin was open and teasing. He wasn't saying a word, letting his smile speak for itself.

Jane, still beet red, gave him a baleful look. "I keep hoping you'll grow up."

"I'm a big boy," he said, his tone still teasing.

"Mature," she corrected.

"I try. I'm just not always successful." He grinned and touched his chest with his fist. "Mea culpa. You can't blame a guy for trying, can you?"

She opened her mouth. He closed it again with his fingers. "Don't answer that. Come on, Jane. Live dangerously. Walk down to the convent with the Big Bad Wolf. You know you want to. You want to see what the nuns say when they see me again."

A reluctant grin touched her lips at the truth of this last statement. "It might be interesting."

"So let's go." He opened the door and hauled her out after him. "I always knew there was a bit of voyeur in you."

The secretary looked up, heard the words, saw Zack's hand on Jane's wrist and stared at them, open-mouthed.

"I'm abducting her," Zack said.

The secretary's jaw sagged even farther.

"Oh, heavens," Jane muttered, swept along by forces she didn't quite understand. "There goes my image."

Zack just laughed.

"You know," Jane said to his back, "you really haven't changed a bit."

"YOU JUST GET better and better." Sister Immaculata Murphy's bright blue eyes snapped with enthusiasm as she thumped her walker on the floor for emphasis and beamed up at Zack from the chair in which she sat.

Was Zack blushing? Jane looked closer, amazed.

Yes, he was. In fact, she realized, he had been to a greater or lesser degree ever since they'd arrived.

He was, for all that he had been a dreadful little boy, a current convent hero, and the sisters hadn't hesitated to tell him so.

Sister Mac's eyes had positively lit up when the two of them had walked through the door to her room an hour ago.

Jane had expected him to glance at his watch or grit his teeth, but he simply perched on the edge of the nun's bed, swinging his legs like a little kid, answering her questions and, whenever she faltered, picking up the story where she left off.

Of course, Jane told herself, it had to do with football.

But when the talk turned to St. Phil's and then to Sister Mac's own teaching experiences there and elsewhere, Zack's interest didn't flag. He called a halt only when it became clear that the elderly nun was tiring. "Can we come back again?" he asked Sister Mac.

"Of course! Anytime. I'm so glad you came. It's nice to see old students, and—" she beamed "—to know they're using what we've taught them to such good ends.''

"You think you taught Zack football?" Jane said, laughing.

Sister Mac lifted her chin. "Certainly. Best broken field runner St. Phil's ever had." She winked. "Learned it all trying to get away from Sister Gertrudis, didn't you?"

Zack didn't deny it.

Sister Mac laughed. "And he's polite, too. I taught him that." She turned her gaze on Jane. "I'm so happy to see you together," she went on. "The two of you make a lovely couple."

"Oh, we're not—"

"Don't we though?" Zack said smoothly. "Jane's always been good for me," Zack said, taking her hand. She tried surreptitiously to pull away. He held on tight.

Sister Mac chuckled. She shook her head at Jane. "And I'm equally sure he's good for you. Aren't you, Zachary?"

"I try," he said modestly, lowering his eyes.

Sister Mac patted Jane's hand. "She was always such a timid little thing," she said to Zack.

"You'd be surprised," he said to Sister Mac. "She's braver than she looks."

"You don't have to talk about me as if I'm not here," Jane complained.

"Don't worry so, dear," Sister Mac said. "You'll be fine. Have faith."

"What?" Jane said confused. "Have faith? I do, Sister. I do."

"In God, yes, I know." Sister Immaculata patted Jane's arm. "It's not enough."

"What?"

"Think of your life as a football game. God is like the coach, my lovely. Of course you have faith in Him. You'd better or there's not much use playing. But suppose you're the quarterback and you're fading back to pass. It's all very well and good to believe in your coach, but He's not catching the ball, is he?" She looked hopefully up at Jane with her bright blue eyes.

Jane swallowed, nonplussed.

"Think about it, sweetie." Sister Immaculata gave her a beatific smile. "It will come to you."

"HAVE FAITH in your wide receivers. An interesting theological construct," Zack said as they were walking toward the church parking lot. He was still holding her hand and he grinned.

Jane didn't. "Sister Immaculata is getting senile."

"Yeah, right," Zack scoffed. "So," he asked when they'd reached his car, "where do you want to go to dinner?" He lifted his arms above his head and stretched lazily.

Jane looked away, not wanting to see the stretch and flex of his muscles, or the inch of tanned flesh that appeared when his shirt rose above the waistband of his jeans. "I don't."

She kept on walking toward her own car.

A second later Zack had caught up with her. "You don't? Why? What's wrong?"

"Nothing's wrong. I just have other plans."

"Yeah? What?" His patently disbelieving tone was the last straw. She whirled on him, hugging her purse against her breasts as she glared up into his face.

"Work! I have work to do, Zack! I have papers to grade. Lesson plans to make. A job. Adult responsibilities. And trusting wide receivers won't get it done, I'm sorry to say. Besides, I don't remember being asked!"

He opened his mouth, then shut it. He stuffed his fists into his pockets and rocked back on his heels. "You're right. I didn't ask. I assumed. I'm sorry."

"Thank you," she muttered, his apology coming as a surprise, making her feel at an even greater disadvantage. She looked at the ground.

"So, will you? Have dinner with me?"

"No, thank you."

"But—"

"You asked, yes. But the reasons still apply. I can't." She wasn't giving in. Wasn't.

"Won't."

"What?"

"You can," he said flatly. "You don't want to. So you won't. Fine. I've got the picture. Goodbye."

He spun on his heel, strode to his car, got in and drove off without looking back.

HE DIDN'T KNOW why it hurt so much.

She was only a mousy little second-grade teacher. A woman who couldn't hold a candle to the bevy of beauties who were forever chasing him, calling him, desperate for a little of his attention.

He could call any one of a dozen women, and not one of them would choose to grade spelling tests over sharing a meal with him.

Fine, he thought, reaching for the phone, he'd call one.

He picked up the receiver and started to punch out a number. His fingers faltered. He slumped back in his chair. He put the receiver back on the hook and stared out across his plate glass view of the San Francisco Bay.

Who was he trying to kid?

"'IT'S NICE to see old students and know they're using what we've taught them,'" Jane said aloud in a crabby mocking tone as she slammed the kitchen cabinet door. "All well and good if what they've taught you is broken field running," she muttered, opening the refrigerator, peering inside, scowling, banging it shut again.

It wasn't what they'd taught her.

Eight years of Catholic grade school. Four years of Catholic high school. Five years of Catholic college. And what had she learned better than anything?

Guilt.

She'd hurt Zack's feelings.

"He's a big boy. He said so himself. He'll get over it," she told herself firmly, giving up on finding anything to eat and flinging herself onto the sofa to stare at her bare feet.

But she'd seen the hurt flicker in his eyes.

"Other women have turned him down," she said out loud. "At least they'd better have."

But other women probably hadn't been so irrationally obnoxious in doing so.

"Oh, hell," Jane muttered, because if she was ever going to assuage her guilt, she knew what she was going to have to do.

SHE DIDN'T KNOW his phone number. She didn't know where he lived. He was not, as she should have realized, in the phone book. Celebrities weren't.

It took her the rest of that evening and the following day to find out. That was the easy part. Now she had to do something with the information.

One phone call told her that she would be apologizing to his answering machine or leaving a message that would have him calling her. Maybe.

What if he didn't?

She screwed up her courage, picked up containers of Szechwan chicken with cashews, shrimp almond ding, stir-fried pork with straw mushrooms, rice and hot and sour soup, then caught the Powell-Hyde trolley over to Russian Hill and, without giving herself a chance to have second thoughts, marched up the steps to the double glass doors of Zack's high-rise building.

There she encountered the doorman. And if her second thoughts hadn't stopped her, he did.

"To whom are you delivering, miss?" He looked down his long, narrow nose at her, skewering her right there in the middle of the gleaming marble floor.

There was apparently no question that she was delivering rather than coming to see. Jane hoped it was because of the redolent bag she was carrying and not because she didn't look like the sort of woman who might otherwise belong here. Perhaps she should have dressed in something more elegant than canvas trousers and a jacket and sweater.

"I've come to see Mr. Stoner."

"One moment, please." He picked up a phone.

Zack probably wasn't even here, Jane thought desperately; then thought, perhaps even more desperately, that he might be. It had been a bad idea, coming with a peace offering, a meal he hadn't invited her to, a meal she hadn't told him she was bringing. She began to back toward the doors.

"Your name, miss?"

"Jane Kitto."

The doorman repeated her name. "Very well, sir." He put down the receiver and inclined his head toward the elevators. "You may go up. Eighteenth floor. Apartment three."

"Thank you."

Jane used the time in the elevator to pray. She invoked every saint she could think of and a few that she was sure had been labeled questionable by now. She still hadn't finished when the elevator slid to a silent stop and the doors opened.

Zack was standing there, barefoot, in a pair of faded jeans and a much-laundered forest-green polo shirt. He let out his breath when he saw her. "It is you."

"Believe me," Jane said fervently, "no one would impersonate me. It isn't worth the stress."

Zack laughed, but he sounded a bit uncertain. "Come on in."

At least, Jane thought, he didn't say, "What do you want?" and force her to apologize in the elevator.

He led her across the hallway to one of the four doors that opened off it, ushering her into his apartment.

He had told her he didn't live in the city for the most part, that he only kept a pied-à-terre where he could sleep and cook a quick meal. Jane had envisioned something like the tiny efficiency she'd lived in during her last year in college. She hadn't come close.

Zack's apartment was in the northwest corner of the building. The living area was glass on both exposures giving almost floor-to-ceiling views across the Bay toward Sausalito and Marin county, of Mount Tamalpais and the Golden Gate Bridge. There was a nubby, ivory-colored Berber carpet that ran from wall to wall, but scattered here and there were stunningly intricate Oriental rugs. Furniture was at a minimum—a dark brown, soft leather sofa and chair, a bookcase, one small end table. As Zack led her farther into the room she could see a dining alcove and kitchen area.

"I suppose that's where I should point you," he said, giving the bag an appreciative sniff.

"I... brought dinner," Jane said almost apologetically. "I mean, maybe you've eaten, and I know it's terribly presumptuous. And maybe you don't want it. I didn't ask, I know. But I was... I was rude yesterday and it bothered me, and I wanted to make up for it." She met his eyes frankly, grateful that she only saw surprise. "So...I'm sorry." She thrust the bag at him.

Zack took it, fumbled it, recovered quickly, then stood holding it almost gingerly in his hands, just looking at her. One corner of his mouth quirked. "And they say I've got the stickiest hands in the business." He shook his head wryly, still looking at her. "I'm... amazed."

Jane felt herself coloring furiously. She backed toward the door. "I'm sorry. I shouldn't have come."

"No! I mean, yes, you should have. Oh, not because you needed to or anything, but... I'm glad you came." He grinned. "You have the most incredibly scrupulous conscience. I never imagined." He shook his head.

"I didn't hurt your feelings?" Jane asked cautiously.

He opened his mouth, then closed it again. He set the sack on the table and began setting the small white containers out one by one. Finally when he had the last one out, he slanted her a glance.

"I should say no, shouldn't I? I mean, it'd be polite. And nobody wants to admit he was expecting anything, right? Nobody wants to say he's been shut down?" He rubbed a hand against the back of his neck. "But, yeah, I guess you did."

"I'm sorry. I didn't mean to hurt you," Jane said, feeling lighter in the face of his honest response.

He wasn't looking at her now. He was fishing through a drawer, coming up with chopsticks, setting them on the table, sticking serving spoons into each of the containers, then getting plates out of a cabinet. "Did you really grade papers? Were they better than...?"

"No, of course they weren't."

"Then why?"

The fact that he wasn't looking made it easier to be honest. "I was afraid to."

He looked over at her and scowled. "I thought you were over that."

"Not afraid like when I was seven," Jane said. He opened the refrigerator and pointed to beer or soda. She picked the latter. He opened two and handed her one. "This has more to do with the, uh, situation."

He held out a chair for her, then went around and sat down across from her. He filled a plate for her and another for himself.

"You felt pushed?"

"I don't know. It's...I need to understand the—the boundaries."

He looked confused.

"This was—is—supposed to be business. And you're...you're...very handsome." Her cheeks felt warm. She ducked her head.

He grimaced around a mouthful of chicken. "Thanks, I think. But I don't see how that makes a difference."

"People have, er, noticed. My students. The, uh, secretary. And the principal. Sister Mac. Other people, as well."

Zack glanced up. "Not you?"

Jane blushed. "Of course, me," she said irritably. She glared at him, saw a corner of his mouth twitch. "You scoundrel. You're making this as hard as you can, aren't you?"

"Yeah, kinda," he admitted. "Let me guess. They want you to jump my bones."

Jane glowered at his accuracy. "I'm sure this isn't surprising for you," she began testily, but Zack cut her off.

"Not entirely, no. But I'm not always as eager to go along with it."

Jane's eyes widened. She almost choked on her shrimp. "You're saying you...you *would?*"

"Sure." His gaze flickered toward the bedroom door. "You want to?"

"No!"

He sighed. "Hell." Then he went on eating without missing a bite.

Jane stared at him, perplexed. In the silence he lifted an eyelid and gave her a slow wink.

"Zack!" She couldn't help it. She started to laugh. "Oh, damn, but you're incorrigible."

"Am I?" He looked pleased. "I thought maybe I was slipping."

She was laughing now. "Not a bit. And you're enjoying this!"

"Doesn't happen often. I can't think of the last time a lady brought me dinner, told me I was handsome and in the next breath said she didn't want to go to bed with me."

"That's not the way it was," Jane protested, still laughing.

"No?" He eyed her hopefully.

She sighed and flipped a bamboo shoot at him. He grinned and made a tsking sound, shaking his head. "For shame, Janey. What would the nuns say?"

"I shudder to think."

They looked at each other and smiled.

Zack finished cleaning his plate, then settled back against his chair and folded his hands across his flat belly. "So, what you're saying is, you were rude to me because you didn't want to fulfill their expectations, right?"

"Umm, more or less. So I brought dinner to apologize."

"Apology accepted."

"Thank you."

"Now, the question is—" he gave her a level, speculative look "—where do we go from here?"

Chapter Five

JANE SWALLOWED, caught in the blue magic of his gaze, silently cursing the part of her that was affected by Zack's desirability, his compelling presence, teasing smile, sex appeal. It would be so much easier to deal with him if she weren't.

She drew a careful breath. "I guess we do the documentary."

"And then walk away?"

She shrugged, watching as a Navy carrier moved slowly past Alcatraz toward the ocean into the sunset, deliberately not looking at Zack. "Well, I'm sure we'll remain friends."

Out of the corner of her eye she saw a slight smile twist Zack's mouth. Irony perhaps.

She supposed she had been presumptuous. They didn't have much in common, other than a certain awareness. Or maybe she had the awareness, and he acted like this with every woman.

Maybe he was just being kind, saying what was expected of him. That was a mortifying thought. But she wasn't exactly the sort of girl she thought football players went for.

"Will you come up to my place this weekend?"

His sudden question jolted all her speculations right out of her head. "What?"

"If we're going to remain friends—" and, yes, there was a twist of irony in his tone "—I thought maybe you'd come see my house. And my horses. Come riding with me."

"Riding?" Jane said the word as if it were in a foreign tongue.

"Horses," Zack qualified with just enough emphasis to make her feel like an idiot.

Jane gave him a narrow look to see if he was teasing her again, but his expression seemed perfectly straightforward. She hesitated. She thought she ought to say no. Self-preservation seemed to require it. But if she did, she might hurt his feelings again.

And hadn't she just finished saying they could be friends?

"Thank you, yes. I'd like that."

Zack let out a pent-up breath. "Well, good." He grinned at her.

Jane didn't grin. She felt somehow as if she'd just agreed to go ten rounds with a tiger. She pushed back her chair. If she was going to do anything as foolish as that, she needed to go home now and start psyching herself up for it.

She began gathering up the empty containers.

"Want to hang around awhile? I was going to go through the pictures I got from Father Jack. Sure you wouldn't like to help?"

Jane hesitated.

"It'd be a friendly thing to do," he said guilelessly.

Jane gave him a dirty look. He laughed. "Come on, Jane. Dare."

She sighed. "All right."

Zack rinsed the plates and put them in the dishwasher. She wiped off the table. Then she waited while Zack brought the boxes of photos out from his bedroom.

At first they looked through the same box together, finding the most amazing old graduation photos.

There were lineups of nuns in habits that made them look as if a stiff wind would send them sailing across the Bay. There were other photos of girls in calf-length dresses standing beside bicycles, and boys with football jerseys, crouching and scowling at the camera.

"You come from an auspicious tradition," Jane said, reading the back of the photo. "These are the eighth-graders of the Class of '23. City parochial co-champs."

"Let me see." Zack took the photo from her, studying it, grinning, then setting it aside to be filmed.

They took ages over almost every photo, until finally Jane realized that it was getting late and they'd barely dented one box.

"I'll take a box in on the sofa. You stay here. And no stopping unless you come across something really super. Otherwise we'll be here all night."

"You can spend the night."

Jane rolled her eyes. "I bet you say that to all the girls."

"No," Zack said, giving her a steady stare.

"I thought you were the NFL's gift to willing women." She quoted Jeff's words and was immediately embarrassed.

Zack muttered something rude under his breath. "Don't believe everything you read in the papers."

"No?"

He gave her a hard, flat stare. "No."

Unnerved, Jane grabbed the biggest box and headed for the sofa. There she forced herself to ignore him, curling into the corner, tucking her feet under her and setting to work.

For the most part, with considerable effort, she kept her mind on her job. But periodically, when she heard

Zack stifle a snicker or mutter something to himself, she would look over at him.

His dark head was bent over the photos, and she could tell from the curve of his cheek that he was grinning. As she watched, he ran an idle hand through already tousled hair.

Her fingers itched to do the same. Deliberately she forced her attention back to the box, picking up another photo. And she'd committed herself to spending a weekend with him? Heaven help her.

"Want a cup of coffee?" Zack asked.

"No. I'm fine." She got to her feet, flexing her shoulders. "I need to go. I put the best of the photos on the end table for you to look at later. You might find a few you can use." She plucked her jacket off the back of the armchair and slipped it on.

"Thanks. I'll go to the convent tomorrow. With the photos and a tape recorder we ought to be able to get some pretty good stuff." Zack pulled on a black pile pullover.

"You don't have to see me home."

"Yes, I do."

One look told Jane it wasn't worth arguing over. She went ahead of him out the door. He took her arm when they were going down the steps of the apartment building and let his fingers slide down until they clasped hers. Jane swallowed, excruciatingly aware of the rough brush of his fingers, the hard calluses on his hand.

There was almost no one on the trolley. They sat side by side on one of the front benches, Jane's hand still in Zack's. She felt him touch her wrist, sensed his fingers playing with one of the charms on her bracelet.

"You wear this a lot, don't you?"

"All the time." She gave him a level look, daring him to make something of it, daring him to challenge her the way Paul had.

He just looked curious. "How come?"

"It's special." She held it out so he could see it better in the passing streetlights. "The bracelet and the first charm came from my grandmother. The others came from someone else."

"Someone else? Someone . . . special?"

"Yes. My—" she hesitated "—Secret Admirer, I guess." She gave a short self-conscious laugh. "Or maybe he's not an admirer, just the person who understands me better than anyone else in the world."

Zack looked startled. "You think so?"

"Yes, I do. He's thoughtful and sensitive, perceptive, kind. The greatest," she said simply.

Zack shook his head wryly. "He's human, isn't he?"

"I imagine so."

"Suppose you find out who it is and he's not all that great?"

Jane scowled. "Are you putting him down?"

Zack shook his head quickly. "No. Of course not. But it's a hell of a lot to live up to."

Jane nodded. "It is." She knew she said it in a challenging tone. And why not? Her Secret Admirer embodied what she wanted in a man. Zack, with all his flippant remarks, ought to know that.

"He is," she added to make the point even clearer.

Zack didn't reply. He stared straight ahead.

Jane hoped he was thinking about what she said. She hoped her steadfastness about the bracelet and the man who had given it to her had let Zack know she wasn't looking for a temporary fling.

They got off at the next corner and walked from there, unspeaking, until they reached Jane's door.

She wondered if he'd press to come up, but he stopped on the steps. "I won't see you upstairs."

Jane looked at him closely, hoping that, in making her point, she hadn't hurt his feelings again. But he looked simply thoughtful, not wounded.

She gave his hand a squeeze and smiled. "Thank you."

"For not coming up?" Zack's grin was rueful. "And there's another blow to the ol' ego."

"You're not going to make me feel sorry for you," Jane said, but she was smiling.

"I wouldn't dream of it." He leaned forward, bent his head and touched his lips to hers.

It wasn't a long kiss, and yet it seemed somehow to touch Jane's very core. Its impact startled her.

"Thank you for dinner, Janey. Thank you for apologizing. It was remarkably kind of you." He paused and cocked his head, considering her. "Do you feel shriven?"

She felt stunned. Her fingers went to her lips. Still she managed to nod. "Yes, I think I do."

And it was true.

In fact, once she went to bed, she only tossed and turned for an hour or so, remembering the blue of his gaze and the touch of his lips before she finally managed to sleep the sleep of the just.

JANE WASN'T QUITE as sanguine about her weekend trip as she pretended. In fact, she wouldn't have been Jane Kitto if she hadn't had second thoughts. She scarcely slept a wink on Friday night. Her stomach was queasy when she got up.

What if she got sick? What if she turned green in Zack's Audi? Threw up on his leather seats? Fainted in his arms?

She studied her face in the bathroom mirror, looking for signs of impending rash. She examined her tongue to see if it was coated. She practically gagged herself in an effort to see if her tonsils were enlarged.

She almost swallowed the tongue depressor when the doorbell rang.

Shutting her eyes, she said a brief, desperate prayer for the return of her sanity or a fatal heart attack.

Neither had occurred by the time she went to answer the door.

"Hi. All set?" Zack was leaning against the doorjamb grinning when she opened the door. He looked stunningly handsome, devilishly daring, decidedly male.

She didn't think she'd ever had a friend quite like him before. In fact the thought almost made her laugh.

Jane looked at him mutely, gathered what was left of her common sense, good manners and wits from the four winds, and managed to nod her head. "Almost. Come in."

The anticipation had been, as usual, worse than the event.

Zack went out of his way to be an entertaining conversationalist, a relaxing companion, and before they'd barely crossed the bridge into Marin county, Jane began to relax.

It was almost two hours to Zack's place. He owned forty acres along the coast with a split-level redwood house overlooking a grassy hillside facing the sea.

Jane was enchanted. "It's beautiful."

"I'll show you around the house, fix us some lunch, then we can ride."

Zack's house had a living area with one wall of glass overlooking the ocean and one wall of stone with a huge fireplace built in. The kitchen faced the woods. The bedrooms were on the upper level.

"Take your pick," Zack said.

The master bedroom faced the sea. There were two others, smaller ones, which had windows opening toward the woods. Zack stood holding her overnight bag, waiting.

"I'll take this one." She chose a small room that would get the morning sun.

He put her bag on the bed without a word. "If you want to clean up or anything, the bath's right through there. I'll make some lunch."

He seemed perfectly content with the choice she made. Of course he was, Jane thought. They were friends, colleagues.

They ate sandwiches and salad for lunch. Then Zack took Jane down to the barn, introduced her to his neighbor who came to do the stables every day and took her through to meet his horses.

There were four of them. One was a big black horse with a white blaze. "Spirit," Zack called him, and Jane could well believe it. He reminded her of the horse she'd drawn that she'd given Zack.

Zack spoke to him soothingly, stroking his neck. Spirit bent his head forward poking at Zack's shirt-front, nudging his pocket.

"He wants his treat," Zack said, and he looked almost embarrassed. Wryly he reached into his pocket and took out a piece of carrot. It disappeared in an instant. Spirit was back at once, looking for more.

"Enough," Zack said. He saddled a small chestnut gelding for Jane and after a shorter time than she believed possible, she was galloping through the meadow with Zack at her side, her childhood dreams becoming an adult reality as the sun touched her cheeks and the wind streamed through her long, dark hair.

She turned to Zack, laughing, and saw him smiling at her, an expression she'd never seen before on his handsome face. There was something of tenderness there, of joy, of the same kind of freedom and acceptance she felt.

It turned into a magical afternoon.

They rode all afternoon. Then Zack cooked steaks on the grill, and they ate in front of the window that overlooked the ocean.

They listened to records, reminisced, tossed a football on the lawn. Finally, in the dark, they walked for miles along the beach, then came back and sat on the rug in front of the fire.

Their bodies brushed, their hands touched, and once Zack's lips—Jane was almost sure—grazed fleetingly against her hair.

But when she climbed the stairs, she went alone to her own wide, cold bed.

It was what she wanted, she told herself.

It was lovely, but this was Zack. Rough-and-tumble, tough and terrible Zack. And even if there was a gentler side to him, he was still not in her league. Whatever her hormones felt, it wouldn't do to let herself want more than they already had.

So she went to bed and counted the charms on her bracelet, touched the tiny tragic face and told herself that perhaps this Valentine's Day, her perfect man would make himself known.

In her mind's eye, she tried to imagine him—her marvelous, mystical stranger.

Who was he, this perfect hero, this secret swain who was courtly, charming, suave, subtle, kind and sensitive, plus understanding of her need to hang on to the past?

She tried Dan Capoletti's face on him, but it didn't seem right. She tried to imagine others. But he slipped out of focus, faded in and out.

Jane sighed, frustrated. Why couldn't she imagine him?

Why did she keep thinking about Zack across the hall?

THE SMELL OF BACON and waffles woke her. Every muscle in her legs and rear end told Jane she'd spent far too long on a horse. Still, when they'd eaten and Zack asked if she wanted to ride again, Jane didn't demur.

They rode first through the woods, then down the hillside, along a bluff trail to the beach, then back north toward the house. The wind was colder than yesterday. Whitecaps scudded along the tops of the waves. Far out at sea Jane could see an oil tanker moving south. Just beyond the surf line several pelicans circled, swooped and dived.

Jane sat astride her horse and savored every moment of the brisk winter breeze and the sights and sounds of a wildness she'd only dreamed of.

She felt a wistful sort of melancholy when, at last, it was time to throw the bags in the car and head back to the city. And the closer she got, the more wistful she felt.

Zack, too, was quiet in the car on the way home. Now and then he glanced over at her, but he didn't speak.

Jane wondered if he was regretting having taken her. It must have seemed a very tame two days to a man like him.

"Did you finish going through all the photos?" she asked.

"Yeah, and the videographer went out Friday and shot a lot of background I can use for the voice-over. Also did some footage with Sister Immaculata and Father Jack." He glanced at her. "All that's left is you."

"Me?" Jane had almost forgotten that.

"A quick visit to a classroom. Yours naturally. I'm setting it up opposite some stills of former classes. You know, the stiff and proper bunch with the nuns decked out in their sails. I have to be in Berkeley most of the week doing some setup for an upcoming segment. How about if I come Thursday? Or Friday?"

There was obviously no point in declining—even if she did live in fear of what Jeremy or Bobby or, heaven help her, even Leticia, might say on camera.

"Thursday," Jane decided. "Friday will be the Valentine's party and they'll be crazy enough without you coming as well."

The city seemed more crowded and noisier than ever when at last they drove up Jane's street. At the corner the trolley braked and clanged. Mrs. Calcagno was shaking her dust mop and carrying on a shouted conversation with Mrs. Shin. The Liang boys were chasing the kids from Jackson street. The McCluskeys' dog was barking at the DiPalmas' cat.

Jane stopped on the porch. "Listen to the noise. I never hear it ordinarily. Now it's almost overwhelming."

"I think that every week. Someday I'm moving up there and never coming back."

And then I'll never see you again, Jane thought, and was startled when the thought made her feel so bereft.

She managed a smile. "Thanks for sharing it with me this time. It was lovely."

Zack smiled faintly, his eyes were dark, his expression unreadable. "I'm glad you enjoyed it."

They stood then, simply staring at each other. Jane felt an unaccountable urge to reach out and touch him, to run her hand down the hard length of his arm, to touch her fingers to his still-stubbled cheek. She clenched one hand over her wrist, twisting her bracelet instead.

"Well," she said brightly after an interminable moment, "I suppose I'd better get busy. Lots of papers to grade since I played hooky all weekend. Thanks again."

Then, with all the daring she could muster, she went up on tiptoe and brushed her lips across his cheek. Without even waiting to see his reaction, she turned and went inside, hurrying up the steps, never looking back.

BY THURSDAY AFTERNOON Jane had twenty-two second-graders who were, as Kelly's mother used to say, "shot from guns," and one she had to send home with chicken pox.

It didn't matter that Valentine's Day was still another day away. The kids were giggly and silly, bubbling about cards and parties and who loved whom.

Jane did her best to ignore it. She didn't tell them that Zack was coming. They would have got absolutely nothing done if she had.

After lunch, when the buzzing became more intense, Jane bowed to the inevitable, allowing them time to draw Valentines for each other, insisting only that they keep the socializing down to a reasonable level.

She sat down behind her desk and tried to compose herself for his arrival.

It wasn't that she was afraid of him anymore. Not at all. It was that she'd spent the entire week thinking about him, recalling their weekend together, remembering the sight of him early in the morning and late at night.

She didn't see him as Zack Stoner, enfant terrible, anymore. Nor did she see him as the fast-lane success story he'd become. He was Zack Stoner, her friend, her confidant, the man who had, quite insidiously, become a part of her life.

She would miss him when he was gone.

The door opened. Twenty-two heads swiveled. When they saw Zack, they let out a cheer.

"I knew it! He's come for her," Leticia said, with all the pride of a self-proclaimed oracle.

Jeremy looked at Jane, eyes wide. "Didja go out with him, after all, then?"

Jane gave him a quelling look. "You remember Mr. Stoner," she said to the class. "He's come back today because he's doing a film segment on the hundredth anniversary of St. Philomena's, and he's asked you to be a part of it.''

She thought they'd be thrilled. All the heads turned back to look at her. "You mean he didn't come for you?" Cathy Chang looked crushed.

"Of course he did," Leticia maintained stoutly.

"But she said—"

"It's just an excuse."

"Children!" Jane said sharply, trying her best to cut off the exchange. She determinedly did not look at Zack. He couldn't help but have heard. She just hoped he wouldn't comment. After all, she reminded herself, she had warned him.

He came in, followed by a woman with a clipboard, his assistant, no doubt, and a man with a camera. They stayed in the back of the room, but Zack strode to the front, leaned one hip on the edge of Jane's desk.

"Thank you, Ms. Kitto," he said. Then he turned to the class. "In just a minute, we're going to do some taping so you can go home tonight and tell your parents that you're all going to be television stars. But first, tell me about this class project you've got."

They looked at him blankly.

"The one to get your teacher married off."

Jane wanted to sink right through the floor.

The children looked at each other, embarrassed.

Finally Jeremy cleared his throat. "You interested?"

Jane sucked in her breath. "Jer—"

"I might be. If she loved me." He said it almost casually, as though he contemplated such things every day of the week. "But you have to realize that marriage is a very personal issue between two people. They have to love and respect and care about each other. They have to want to share their lives. And that's something no one else can make them do."

The kids looked at each other, then at the floor. Jane couldn't look at anyone at all.

"We only wanted to help," Cathy Chang said. "She deserves somebody good."

"She does," Zack agreed. He looked at Jane, and she lifted her eyes to meet his gaze. There was something in his, something she couldn't quite define, something urgent and compelling. Something that asked and waited for her answer.

He didn't say anything more.

IT WAS OVER.

Jane didn't know if they said "That's a wrap" or "It's in the can." But in less time than she'd thought possible, Zack's story was done.

And so was his reason to be a part of her life.

They were friends, of course. And she could look forward to seeing him on the tube just after the evening news most nights. Next autumn, on Sunday afternoons, she'd find him running downfield in some of the finest football stadiums in the country.

But he wouldn't be peeking in her classroom door anymore. And she wouldn't find him waiting for her in the principal's office. She wouldn't get to watch him scowling over photos or riding like the wind along the seashore. And he certainly wouldn't be telling anyone he'd consider marrying her! How ridiculous was that?

"—dinner with me?"

She blinked, jerked back to the present, astonished to find that the cameraman and production assistant had packed up and left, the last of the students had drifted away, and she and Zack were alone.

"Dinner?" she asked stupidly.

"A celebration."

"Because you're done?"

"If you like." His voice was quiet.

Dinner. Yes. She'd have dinner with him. It would be one last thing to hang on to. Another memory. Two friends sharing a meal, a little conversation, a few reminiscences, a promise, perhaps, to stay in touch.

"I'd like that."

"All finished?" Father Jack came into the room with Dan Capoletti.

He shook Zack's hand. "Great to see you again. Do you think you got good stuff?"

"I'm sure of it."

Dan slipped an arm around Jane's shoulders and gave her a quick squeeze. "Well, if you had Jane, you had the best."

Jane's fingers touched the charms on her bracelet. *Is Kelly right? Do you want me to throw myself at you? Would you come to me if I did?*

And she knew right then that she never would, and she wouldn't want him, anyway. If her Secret Admirer was Dan, she didn't want to know.

"She is the best," Zack agreed stiffly. "We were just going out to celebrate." He reached for Jane's hand and drew her from beneath Dan's arm.

Dan's brows went up. She felt Zack's fingers tighten on hers.

"Come on, Jane," he said. "Let's go."

He didn't offer to pick her up later. He followed her home.

He sat in her living room, drinking a scotch he'd poured himself, while Jane showered and changed. He stared at her in brooding silence when, at last, she appeared.

"All set."

Zack took her to a North Beach eatery just off Columbus, a diner called Fernie's. It was a regular, unpretentious neighborhood place with linoleum and Formica and paper napkins. There wasn't a fern in sight.

"I like it," Jane said when they were seated and had ordered.

"Good." Zack crumbled one of the bread sticks the waitress brought. He drank the beer he'd ordered, then asked for another.

He seemed oddly distracted. Jane did her best to draw him out, asking about what else he had to do on the St. Philomena segment.

He had some editing to do over the weekend. It would air on Monday. He lapsed into silence again. Everything else she tried to find out came like pulling teeth.

He asked for another beer halfway through the meal and grew increasingly quiet and moody as time wore on.

Maybe he was wishing he hadn't invited her tonight, Jane thought.

It had been a spur-of-the-moment thing. He probably regretted it. It had been interesting, fun even, to get to know her again, she thought. To show her how well he'd done, how much he'd grown, how successful a man he'd become. But now, undoubtedly, he was ready to move on.

He was staring out the window, into his beer, anywhere but at her. He shifted in his chair, flexed his shoulders.

He couldn't wait to leave.

She should be glad, Jane told herself. It was better this way. It would break her heart if she got involved with him and he left her.

It would?

The notion stopped her dead.

Silverware clattered. Glasses clinked. The baby in the next booth banged on his high chair. Outside, passersby talked and jostled each other. Inside, steaks sizzled on the grill and a tinny honky-tonk record played on.

Jane scarcely heard. She only heard herself asking the question again, then asking herself, why?

And knowing the answer the way she knew her own name.

She loved him.

Loved Zack Stoner?

Scant weeks ago it would have been laughable. Scant hours ago it had been unthinkable. And now?

She shut her eyes, tried to arrange her thoughts, steady her emotions, calm her suddenly unsteady heart.

She ventured another glance at Zack. His head was bent. He was looking at the bottom of yet another empty glass. He looked tense and worried and downright miserable.

"You finished?" Zack asked. His voice was gruff. His gaze lifted, locked just briefly with hers. She tried to guess what he was thinking, but couldn't. His eyes slid too quickly away.

"Yes," Jane said. "Thank you."

She felt almost as if she was speaking a foreign language, as if she had to say everything very carefully or she would commit some grievous error.

"Let's go."

He opened the door for her, then fell into step alongside her. He didn't take her hand. Instead he stuffed his own in his pockets, then hunched his shoulders and began trudging back up the hill.

Jane slanted him a glance. Zack Stoner. He wasn't the scary, tough, young boy she'd first met years ago. And he wasn't the hard-edged, hard-driving man she'd read about in the paper and saw on the news.

He was all those things . . . and more.

Strong. Thoughtful. Sensitive. Reliable. Funny. Good with children. Determined.

He was, Jane realized with a shock, all the things her Secret Admirer was.

But better than her Secret Admirer, he was here.

Was she going to spend her life in the hopes that someday Dan Capoletti, or whoever it was, would find the courage to approach her?

Or was she going to put her own courage to the test?

She'd decided on Paul because he'd seemed to fit all the outward signs of what she thought her perfect man should be. She knew now that she'd never been emotionally involved.

She was involved with Zack.

She didn't know how he felt about her.

She imagined he liked her. Sometimes she thought he might even desire her. She'd seen him looking at her with a kind of longing that had made her shiver and burn at the same time.

But did he love her?

They reached her doorstep without saying a word. Zack stopped on the steps, his hands still in his pockets, his expression remote, as if he were deliberately distancing himself from her.

As if he didn't care.

And Jane remembered the boy he had been.

She remembered the stoic indifference, the strong jaw, the stubborn chin, the firm, hard set of his mouth. As if he hadn't cared.

Then she remembered that she'd looked into his eyes.

She looked into them now. They were dark as night and deep as the sea, and they spoke to her of hopes and fears, wants and needs that she wasn't sure she saw or only imagined.

Nor was she sure if they were Zack's hopes and needs or simply a reflection of her own.

She knew, though, that to say good-night, would be to say goodbye. He would shake her hand, maybe even brush his lips across her cheek. But then he would turn and walk away. And she would see no more of Zachary Stoner.

But what would happen if she found the courage to ask him to stay?

Chapter Six

SO THIS WAS IT.

He should have left well enough alone instead of dragging things out. What had he thought would happen, for God's sake? That she would suddenly have a revelation over her barbecued ribs, realize she loved him and fall into his arms?

Get a life, Stoner, he told himself.

She didn't look any more comfortable with him now than she had in Father Jack's office that first day. All progress had been in the mind of the beholder.

He licked his lips. "Thanks, Jane. You were a big help. I'm glad we got to meet up again." He swallowed, took a step forward, brushed his lips against hers. He gave her a quick nod, turned on his heel and started down the steps.

"Zack!"

He stopped as if he'd been shot. Her voice was frantic, urgent. He turned slowly and looked at her.

Jane licked her lips. "Would you...like to come up and...see my horse?"

He stared at her. His jaw clenched so tightly a muscle twitched. What the hell was she playing at?

She gave him a tentative smile. "Zack?"

Wordlessly he turned. He went back up the steps, followed her to her apartment. He waited silently while she opened the door and led him in.

"I just thought you might," Jane said.

She knew she was babbling, her palms feeling suddenly as damp as her throat felt dry. He stood in the middle of the living room, watching her, his eyes hooded. "After last weekend, and—and you sharing your horses, I thought you might like to see mine. It's not real, of course. It's a print. I have it in . . . the bedroom."

One of Zack's brows lifted slightly. He didn't smile.

She turned toward the kitchen. "I'll make some coffee first."

"I don't need coffee."

It was the first full sentence he'd spoken in hours. It stopped her in her tracks.

She looked at him. He didn't move. His hands hung loosely at his sides, fingers lightly curled. He seemed balanced on the balls of his feet, anticipating, ready.

"What . . . do you need?"

He looked at her, and she thought that his eyes darkened even more.

"What do you think?" His voice was ragged. His fingers tightened into fists.

Jane rubbed her palms down the sides of her skirt, then took a step toward him.

The next thing she knew he was holding her in his arms.

In her dreams Jane had been held like this, with strength and need and, yes, almost desperation. She felt a tremor run through him, knew the heat of his hands against her back, the soft scrape of a day's stubble against her cheek.

And then his mouth touched hers.

This kiss was nothing like the one he'd given her on the porch just moments before.

That had been a duty kiss, a perfunctory brush of his lips on hers. This belonged to a different world, a different universe entirely. It was tender at first. Gentle. Seeking. And when she dared respond, opening her lips and tasting his in return, she felt him shudder, felt the kiss deepen, the urgency grow. And then it became hard, became passionate.

His tongue touched hers, traced her teeth, then plunged in again. And at the same time she felt the pressure of his hips against hers, knew the extent of his arousal, felt her own begin to uncurl somewhere deep inside.

The intensity of her feelings scared her. They were so strong, so sudden, so unplanned. So unlike what she'd ever imagined.

She took a deep, trembling breath, trying to get a grip on things, knowing she was losing it fast. But somehow she didn't care anymore. She'd tried to control her life, her goals, her emotions for too long.

She felt Zack's fingers come up and tangle in her hair, stroking through it, as his lips feathered light kisses across her cheeks and nose.

"Oh, God, Janey. Do you know what you're doing?" There was a tremor in his voice, too. It was harsh and hungry—a far cry from the easy, teasing Zack she'd grown to love, and even farther from the controlled Zack Stoner she'd shared dinner with this evening.

She slid her arms around his waist, tugged at his shirt, pulling it out of the waistband of his khakis, then pressing her hands against the warm, bare skin of his back. "I hope I do," she whispered against his shirtfront.

He stepped back, framed her face gently between his hands, not avoiding her gaze any longer, but staring intently into her eyes. She saw the questions in them, saw the need, the hunger. He dropped his hands to rest on her upper arms, then shut his eyes briefly. When he opened them again, he looked at her for another long moment, then bent his head. Their foreheads touched.

"I hope so, too," he said roughly.

He looked so worried that she smiled. She brought her hands around to his belly and pulled his shirt up and skimmed it over his head.

He drew a breath. His stomach was hard and flat, with an arrow of dark hair trailing from the thicker patch on his chest down into the waistband of his trousers. Jane licked her lips.

"Oh, Zack. You're beautiful."

"You're crazy."

Jane shook her head. "No. I don't think so. I think I just came to my senses."

Zack swallowed and touched her cheek. "You mean it? You're sure?"

She nodded.

The next thing she knew he had swung her up into his arms and was carrying her into her bedroom. "Let's see that horse," he muttered.

As she was trundled past, Jane flicked on the light. It was there, over the bed, a stunning black stallion, mane streaming as he galloped free and unfettered across a red rock canyon. She had bought it on impulse, with the money her grandmother had given her for Christmas. Right after she'd given the ring back to Paul.

She hadn't understood the impulse then. She was beginning to now.

Zack stood looking at it for a long moment, then looked down at her. He laid her on the bed, sat down beside her and began unbuttoning her blouse. His fingers were rough and callused, snagging on the silk. "Damn."

"Don't worry." Jane stroked her hands down his chest, insinuating them beneath the waistband. He held his breath, bit his lip, concentrated on the buttons and, at last, drew it open and slid it off her shoulders.

His fingers slid along her sides, cupping her breasts in the ivory lace of her bra. Jane lay trembling under his scrutiny, his fingers making her shiver with longing as they stroked the lace-covered flesh. He bent his head and kissed her shoulders and her neck.

Her fingers clenched around his belt. She fumbled with the fastening, released it, drew the zipper down. The backs of her fingers brushed against him once. Then again.

"Janey!"

She looked up into his hooded eyes, saw the tension in his face, the taut cords of his neck, the whiteness around his mouth.

She sat up, motioned him to stand, then hooked her fingers inside his shorts and pushed both them and his khakis down. He returned the favor, unfastening her skirt and sliding it slowly down her hips, taking with it her slip and panties. She kicked off her shoes, and he shed his.

They faced each other then, naked but for her bracelet and a thin silver chain and medallion he wore about his neck. They looked at each other, learned with their eyes the lines and curves, the planes and angles of each other's body. Jane's hands trembled, and to hide it, she clasped them, felt the bracelet on her right wrist with her other hand.

She hesitated, then bent her head, moving to undo it.

For Paul she couldn't have shed it, couldn't have turned her back on the man who had, for years, understood her better than any person on earth. But now she could.

For Zack she would.

It was a risk. A bigger risk than she had ever taken before. Paul she had let into her life. Zack she was letting into her heart.

And there were no guarantees. She could only hope.

"What are you doing?" Zack's voice was harsh, breaking into the stillness.

Jane looked up, startled at his tone. "I'm taking off my bracelet. I can't imagine you'll want it on me now."

"But it's special?"

"Yes."

"Yet you're taking it off."

"Yes, I am. Because you're far more special." She met his gaze unflinchingly, saw him swallow, then shut his eyes.

He sank down onto the bed, laced his fingers together, looked down at the floor between his feet.

Jane watched him, baffled, worried now, wondering what she'd said. "You are, Zack." She tried to reassure him. "I love that bracelet. I love what it means to me, how it's helped me become who I am. I love whoever it is who's given me the charms all these years. But what good does that love do if I can't show him?"

He lifted his gaze. "And you really don't know who it is?"

Jane shook her head. "How can I? He won't tell me. He won't even give me a hint. And I don't know why!"

Zack sat very quietly. He bent his head. "Maybe he's afraid," he said at last.

"That's stupid," Jane said crossly.

"Is it?" Zack looked right at her.

And suddenly, out of the blue, she remembered another conversation with almost the same words. One that had taken place in a classroom so many years ago.

But then their roles had been reversed.

She looked at him more closely. There was something in his eyes, something of the boy she'd known that first day. And she felt a stab of wonder, of astonishment.

She caught her breath. She could only say one word.

"Zack?" It was no more than a whisper. She didn't know what to ask.

He bent his head. His laced fingers clenched. Then he looked up at her again, and she saw everything in his eyes—all the despair, all the hope, all the fear. And she knew the answer. He didn't have to say a word.

She flung herself at him, toppled him backward on the bed, straddled him, looking down into his eyes.

And then she kissed him, long and hard and with every ounce of love and longing that was in her.

"Oh, Zack. I never knew."

He looked up at her, blinked, and smiled a bittersweet smile that twisted his mouth. He stroked her hair. "I know you didn't. I didn't want you to."

"But—but why?" She almost wailed the words.

"I told you—I was afraid. You think a twelve-year-old tough guy wants anyone to know he's giving charms to a prissy little girl?'' His tone was ragged as he looked into her eyes.

Jane smiled back. She laid her hand along his jaw, tracing the line of it, learning its strength, marveling in it. "No. I guess I can see that. But later...?''

"I couldn't. Outside I might've grown up and changed. Inside I was pretty much the same kid. Anyway, I didn't know how you'd feel about me being the one. It was better if it was a secret. I liked making you wonder. I liked watching you grow up.''

She felt her cheeks burn. "You were watching, weren't you?'' She was suddenly self-conscious at the memory of how much Zack must have known about her life for so many years.

He nodded. "As best I could. It wasn't that hard. You being such a sterling example of Catholic girl-hood.'' He grinned.

She shook her head. "I never knew,'' she said again, wonderingly. "But after college? Why didn't you tell me then?''

"You took off. London, remember?''

"But you still sent them.'' She reached down and touched the soaring eagle he'd sent the first year and the tiny replica of the Golden Gate Bridge that had come the second. "My wings and my roots,'' she said softly. She trailed her fingers across the chest of the man who had understood her well enough to choose them. "I cherished them. They were like the two halves of my life,'' she told him. "You'll never know how much they meant to me.''

"I'm glad.''

"But when I came home, why didn't you tell me then?''

"I was going to—last Valentine's Day. But by then you were otherwise engaged." His mouth twisted at the memory.

Jane touched the tragic face on the bracelet. "It wasn't what you intended to send?"

Zack shook his head. "No. Not until I heard about your engagement."

"It made me think," Jane told him quietly. "It made me begin to wonder if I'd gone wrong."

"Thank God for that. I thought I'd left it far too late. And when it didn't do the trick, when you stayed engaged all year, I really thought I had."

"Sometimes," Jane admitted, "it takes me a while. You could have come at any time, though," she told him. "You could have said."

Zack shook his head.

"But why not?"

He didn't speak for a long moment. "Maybe... if I had loved you less...."

And then she knew how much he'd cared, how much her rejection could have hurt him. "Oh, Zack," she whispered.

"I always did," he told her, his voice ragged. "From the first. I was like your stallion. Hard and tough and mean." His eyes drifted back for a moment to the picture above the bed. Then they came back to hers. "Soulless, I would have said, and Sister Gertrudis would have agreed with me. But you didn't. You saw something in me that nobody else ever saw."

But if she had seen Zack's potential, it was equally true that he had seen hers. And he'd taught her more than he would ever know. He had taught her what to look for in a man, had given her the hope that someday she would find the right one. He had taught her to risk.

He had taught her to love.

"I love you, too, Zack. I can't begin to tell you how much." She bent her head and kissed him, giving him all the love that she had stored for years.

And Zack, redeemed, kissed her back, rolled her over and loved her with an intensity that left her reeling. His hands trembled as they stroked her, learning her, worshiping her. His breath was hot as he kissed her, leaving her aching for more.

And when she drew him down to her, he came willingly, eagerly.

"I don't want to hurt you."

"No pain, no gain. Isn't that what Father Jack always says?" Jane teased.

"I thought he said, 'The Lord works in mysterious ways.'"

"That, too." And she lifted her hips to meet him, felt him touch, probe. And then she brought him home.

"I love you," she whispered against his neck, nipping him, tasting salt and sweat and something so essentially Zack.

He shuddered. His arms shook, his jaw tightened, his face became taut. "Oh, Janey. I can't—I need you now."

And then he moved, and Jane moved with him, savoring the feeling, the fullness, the friction that grew and grew. She writhed under him, cried out, felt Zack's body convulse even as her own contracted around him.

And then there was peace.

Love was a funny thing, Jane thought. It felt warm and heavy like the weight of Zack's body pressing into hers. It felt light and airy, like her heart, soaring over the world, as free as the stallion above the bed. It had anchors and it had wings. It made her want to laugh and cry at the same time. It was the most wonderful feeling in the world.

"Are you okay?" Zack asked her. He started to roll off. She held him fast right where he was.

"Never better." She smiled. "It's like all my dreams came true."

Zack smiled. "Mine, too." He rolled over then, and snuggled her body in the curve of his arm, holding her close. For a long while they simply lay quietly. Then Zack lifted his head and smiled down at her. "I suppose your students will think this was all their idea."

Jane groaned. "They'll be insufferable."

Zack hugged her. "Let them. We'll know the truth."

A while later Jane got up and shut off the light. There was no question of Zack leaving. No way she would let him go. She slid back into bed beside him, snuggling down against Zack's side again, curving one leg across his thighs, resting her head in the crook of his shoulder.

They lay wrapped together, cocooned in love, kissing softly, savoring the moment, cherishing the past, anticipating the future.

"My Secret Admirer," Jane murmured and touched her lips once more to his. "After all these years." She lifted her arm and jangled the bracelet lightly. "You have no idea how much this bracelet means to me."

"I'm glad."

"Going to give me another charm this year?" she teased. "Or is that all over now?"

"There's one left," Zack said. "It's always been yours. I've been saving it for you."

"What's that?"

He took her hand and wrapped her fingers around the tiny object that hung from the chain around his neck. "This."

But in the darkness Jane couldn't see. "What is it?"

He smiled as he drew her close once more. "My heart."

MS. SCROOGE
MEETS CUPID

Linda Randall Wisdom

A Note from Linda Randall Wisdom

Growing up, I always thought of Valentine's Day as a school party where our class brought in cute cards for everyone, and we shared heart-shaped cookies and pink punch. Sound familiar? For the past few years, I've thought of writing a Valentine variation on *A Christmas Carol*. What if a woman (normally the romantic one in a relationship) said, "Bah, humbug" when it came to Valentine's Day? What if everything to do with her love life turned into disaster on Valentine's Day and, even worse, what if she lived in a town that actively promoted Valentine's Day all year-round?

Naturally, she'd move to the other end of the earth and pretend February 14 isn't anything special. That's how Claire Madison was born in my mind. Valentine's Day is her Friday the thirteenth, and the least I could do was give her a man with romance in his soul to show her that curses, even Valentine ones, can be broken.

Happy Valentine's Day!

Linda

Chapter One

"TOM'S TAKING ME somewhere very romantic for Valentine's weekend."

"Steven made reservations at that new French restaurant that just opened up. To be honest, I hope he's thinking of proposing to me. Wouldn't that be romantic?"

"Last year, Joe sent me three dozen red roses. I'm hoping for four dozen this year."

"Godiva chocolates are more my style."

The women grouped around the coffeemaker giggled as each tried to outdo the others with their Valentine's Day expectations.

"The way they've been going on the past few days you'd think February 14 was equal to Christmas," Claire groaned, rolling her eyes in disgust as she passed the small kitchen en route to her office.

"Lighten up, Claire. At least they have a love life. You know what that is, don't you? Where a man wines and dines you, then expects a good time in bed as a thank you," Ellen Kendall, the art director, teased her. "Say, I'm having a Valentine costume party where everybody dresses up as their favorite romantic figure. Bring a date and have some fun for once."

Claire resisted the urge to pull out her hair. "No, thanks, I'd rather stay home and watch my lawn grow." Her swift ground-eating strides brought her to the large office she considered her home away from home. The art director was hot on her heels.

"You live in an eighteen-floor apartment, which means your so-called lawn is a balcony."

"I'm sure a few blades of grass will crop up sooner or later."

"Any word if you've made VP?" Ellen dropped into the soft turquoise chair opposite Claire's desk. The folds of her ankle-length skirt settled around the chair in a pastel rainbow. Ellen felt her position as art director allowed her to dress as she liked—which meant not one suit in her wardrobe.

Claire shook her head. "Not yet. I think they're going to wait until the next board meeting to make their decision." She adjusted the miniblinds, allowing more light into the room, before she sat behind her desk. "I don't think there'll be any problem. After all, I made St. Angelo's Pizza a household word when everyone else gave up on the account." She wasn't bragging; merely stating a fact.

"Careful, you might break your arm patting yourself on the back."

Claire smiled at her friend.

"You know, the way you stomp around the office this time of year, some of the staff have started calling you Ms. Scrooge." Ellen propped her elbows on the chair arms and rested her chin on her steepled fingertips. "What gives with your distaste for Valentine's Day, anyway? Besides Rob, the creep, that is?"

Claire shrugged, revealing none of her inner turmoil. "It's nothing more than advertising hype to sell more cards and chocolates. Christmas is barely over before there are pictures of a little, bald, naked guy flying around with a bow and arrow, for God's sake! Valentine's Day is hell!"

Ellen pushed herself up from the chair. "Well, sweetie, just because you don't have one romantic bone in your body doesn't mean you should ruin it for others. Besides, someone as gorgeous as you should have men falling all over her instead of running away."

Claire lifted her head just in time to see what suspiciously looked like pity in her friend's eyes. It only hardened her resolve. "I don't need one day of the year to allow me to grow all sentimental about hearts and flowers, Ellen. I can do that anytime I look at the artwork your department creates for some of our ads."

"Okay, so you haven't had the best of luck where Valentine's Day is concerned. It doesn't mean you should equate the day with Friday the thirteenth."

"Wrong. Friday the thirteenth has always been lucky for me," Claire insisted. "Believe me, Ellen, I have every right to hate that date. I would have been better off stepping on sidewalk cracks, walking under ladders and allowing black cats to cross my path than to ever think Valentine's Day is some kind of wonderful holiday for people to think about love and kisses." She picked up the phone when her intercom buzzed. "Yes, Pam?"

"Claire, your grandmother is on line two."

Claire stifled a groan. Right now, she couldn't handle speaking to the one person who knew just as much as she herself did about her feelings toward this time of year. "You couldn't tell her I'm in a meeting? Or that I'm out of the office for the next hour or so?"

Claire's assistant appeared in the doorway a few seconds later, looking regretful at having to interrupt. "I tried, Claire, I really did, but she said it's urgent, that she really needs to talk to you. Besides, she said she can tell when I'm lying to her and I should be ashamed of myself and—''

Claire waved off her explanation. "I know, I know. And if your grandmother knew you were lying to another grandmother she'd break down in tears. Gran is great with guilt trips." She picked up the phone and punched the button. "Hi, Gran." She made her voice falsely bright. "What a surprise to hear from you."

"Claire, darling, you sound tired. Are you getting enough sleep? Taking your vitamins? You know how you get when you don't take your vitamins in the morning." The clear musical voice didn't sound as if it belonged to a woman in her late seventies.

"I'm just fine," she said, waving as Ellen left the office. "I'm sorry I haven't called lately. It's been so busy here . . . ." her voice trailed off. *Big mistake,* her brain fairly screamed at her. *She'll catch you for sure on that one.*

"You know how I worry when I don't hear from you, but that isn't why I called. I'm calling to ask you to come out for a visit."

"Oh, Gran, I'd love to, but things are so busy right now and I'm in the middle of a killer of a campaign." She was babbling. She knew she was babbling. Her grandmother knew she was babbling. But somehow, she couldn't stop herself. "I know what! How about I fly you back here next month and we go shopping, take in a few shows, perhaps fly up to Boston or DC? Wouldn't that be wonderful?"

"That is exactly what we've done four times a year for the past five years."

"Not exactly. There was that fall we flew up to Canada and that time we took a cruise." Claire closed her eyes. She hated herself, really hated herself for sounding so defensive. She, the hotshot darling of the advertising world, couldn't put two words together in a sane sentence where her grandmother was concerned.

"I need you to come home, Claire."

Her ears pricked up. "Is something wrong? With you? With the inn?"

"I'm not getting any younger, dear, and I want you to come home, even if it's just for a short visit. I need you, Claire."

Claire automatically pressed her forefinger against the throbbing vein in her throat. It was racing a mile a minute. "Gran, tell me what's wrong. Is it something serious? What did the doctor say? You have seen the doctor, haven't you?"

"It's time I thought about passing the inn into stronger, more capable hands. You'll be pleased to know I found the perfect person. Remember, I told you I employed a very nice gentleman as manager a year and a half ago. He's interested in buying it. After all, I know you don't want it, but I would like you to come back for one last visit. After all, this was your home from early childhood. I realize you don't want to come back here at this time of year, but I hope you'll overlook that and come anyway."

Claire was known to be unflappable in a crisis. She never lost her temper, never got flustered and never uttered one wrong word. Unless her grandmother dropped one of the few bombs guaranteed to send Claire running. "Don't do anything until I get there. I'll see if I can get out on a flight tonight. I can get a rental car at the airport. You just rest and don't worry. I'll be there as soon as possible." During the entire conversation she scribbled notes on scrap paper and wildly gestured for her assistant to come in. "I love you, Gran."

She hung up and spun around, looking for anything that needed her immediate attention. "It's a family emergency. I'll talk to Hal before I leave, but you'd better reschedule my appointments for the next week or so. I'll be in touch daily by phone or fax." She wiped her damp palms on her skirt.

"Claire, she's fine," Pam assured her.

"No, she's not. Gran never asks for anything. I didn't find out she had her appendix out until she was in her third day of recovery and her friend, Stella, called me." She paused to pull in several deep breaths. "I think I'm going to hyperventilate."

Pam pushed her back into her chair. "No, you're not. You just think you are. Just as you thought you were breaking out in a rash before your meeting with Mr. Yakamoto." She pressed her hands against Claire's shoulders. "Now, think of lush green meadows, blue skies and white clouds," she crooned. "The sun is shining, the birds are singing and you're lying in the grass...."

"Sneezing my head off because of my hay fever," Claire finished for her. "This is crazy. I'm known for always remaining cool under fire. For standing up to CEOs of large corporations and not batting an eyelash. If they could see me now," she moaned, burying her face in her hands.

"Hey, everyone has their little foibles. Yours is getting yourself worked up ahead of time, so it's all out of your system when you march into those high-powered meetings. At least you're not throwing up like you usually do before a new presentation," Pam assured her. "So just relax, all right? Otherwise your face is going to turn blue. And boss, you know you won't even wear blue eye shadow.''

"Would you relax if you just got the news I did?" Claire glared at her. "Gran is not well. Knowing her, she called me because the doctor gave her only three days to live and she's probably known about this for the past year." She bit out the last few words, oblivious to the nonsense she was making; she, the woman who always knew what to say in short concise sentences. "I'll kill her if she's kept this from me."

Pam reached for the phone. Minutes later she advised Claire, "All right, you're booked on the seven p.m. flight into San Francisco and you're on the seven a.m. commuter flight the next morning. A rental car has been reserved for you, too. All you have to do is go home and pack."

"I wish I hadn't given up smoking," Claire muttered. "I really could use a cigarette."

Pam snatched a mint out of the crystal dish on the desk top and pushed it at her. "You'll have to settle for that instead."

Claire looked up at the woman who was more valuable than diamonds in her eyes. "You deserve a raise."

"I got that with my review two months ago."

She shook her head. "No one else makes me as crazy as Gran does." She stared at the work piled on her desk. She knew there were memos awaiting her signature, letters to dictate, artwork to approve. "Packing won't take me long. Cupid's Corners isn't exactly the fashion capital of the world."

Pam laughed. "I love the name of your hometown. They must treat Valentine's Day as a national holiday."

Claire's expression turned dark. "As far as they're concerned, they invented the damn day!"

BY THE TIME Claire landed at the small airfield she felt as if she'd gone through four lifetimes. She stumbled off the tiny plane, fumbled her way through paperwork for her rental car and was soon on the coastal highway leading to the town she'd left at the tender age of eighteen, vowing never to return.

So much for ten-year-old vows, she thought wryly, pushing down harder on the accelerator. The sooner she got there and settled everything, the sooner she'd be able to leave. And if Gran was selling the inn, she'd make sure she wasn't cheated on the deal. Then she'd hustle Gran back east with her.

Have a Romantic Dinner at St. Valentine's, the Restaurant with Candlelight, Violins and Your Favorite Person Sitting across the Table from You.

"I can't believe it," Claire muttered, taking her eyes off the road long enough to read the sign.

All Our Fudge comes in Varied Sizes of Hearts!

We Carry the Perfect Bread, Cheese and Wine for That Picnic for Two.

The closer Claire got to the Cupid's Corners turn-off, the more she felt as if she was heading for the city of Oz. The city limits sign was another shock.

Welcome to Cupid's Corners, the Town That Invented Romance!

"Naturally, it would be heart-shaped," she scoffed.

The sleepy village Claire remembered was no more. As she drove down the main street, aptly named Cherub Boulevard, she slowly scanned from right to left.

"Oh, my God," she breathed, not knowing what to stare at first. The bright red street signs with little cupids and cherubs painted on them? Or the bright red-and-white shop exteriors? Even the bakery kept with the theme with a sign outlined in old-fashioned script announcing that X-rated cakes and breads were available for every occasion. Just when she thought things couldn't be any worse she noticed the fancy streetlights—heart-shaped, of course.

Claire sped up, looking for the turnoff to her grandmother's inn.

"At least Madison's Motor Inn won't have changed to include all of this hearts-and-flowers nonsense," she murmured, flipping the turn signal. She almost drove off the road when she saw the huge, pink, heart-shaped sign up ahead.

Heart's Ease Inn. The Perfect Retreat for Lovers of all Ages. We're Here to Make Your Honeymoon or Anniversary Special, Whether It's Your First or Fiftieth.

Claire's foot slammed on the brakes, sending the car fishtailing all over the road before she could get it under control. She pushed open the door and hopped out, stomping around the car several times. It did nothing to dissipate the fury building up inside her. Finally she threw her head back and let loose a loud scream that startled several sea gulls circling overhead and sent them racing back to the open sea— where life was much calmer and red paper hearts weren't to be found.

Chapter Two

"SHE'S SUCH a lovely girl. And so talented. So creative," Hannah Madison chattered on as she bustled around the manager's office that had been given over to Pete Slattery more than a year ago. "The agency she works for has given her so many promotions because they don't want to lose her. She's turned some of her accounts into household words because she knows just what the consumers want." It was obvious she was parroting what she'd heard from others.

"Yes, lovely," Pete murmured, thinking of the photographs Hannah had been showing him since the day he'd begun work there. If he hadn't already seen pictures of the mysterious Claire, Pete would have replaced Hannah's description of *lovely* with "she has a nice personality even if she isn't conventionally pretty" and *talented* with "it may only be a clerk's job, but it's a beginning and she's sure to go far." Instead he'd mused off and on what it would be like to come face-to-face with Claire, and wondered if there was the slightest chance of sweeping the lady off her feet.

"Hannah, in case you've forgotten, we're fully booked this week and I'll have my hands full keeping the guests happy," he pointed out, wrapping his hands around the back of his head as he leaned back in his desk chair. "You'll have the pleasure of looking after your granddaughter during her visit. Of course," he added all too casually, "I promise to do my best to help out."

Hannah stared at him with just a hint of slyness in her rich brown eyes. "Thank you, Pete. I'm counting on you to help me persuade Claire to stay here permanently. I don't want her to go back to New York. Oh, I know they appreciate her and all, but that isn't her home and she's been gone a long time. I want her with me."

"I'll do what I can, Hannah." *And how!* "Just remember that she's a hotshot ad exec with a big-name agency. I can't imagine she'd be too happy in a small town where her talents can't be utilized," he said gently. He leaned forward to get a better look out the window as a sleek black convertible slowed in the driveway and stopped in front of the door. The driver climbed out, exposing first a nice length of leg, followed by a slender figure and a lovely face that was partially obscured by oversize sunglasses. *People usually arrive in pairs around here,* Pete thought, *just like the Ark. Too bad we're full up.*

"I can't believe it, she's already here!" Hannah cried out, looking over Pete's shoulder. "But she wasn't due until tomorrow!"

He felt a streak of heat race down his back. "She?"

"Claire." Hannah rushed out of the office.

Pete reached for his glasses lying on the desk and slipped them on so he could get a better look at the lady: short dark hair in a sleek, sophisticated cut; face still obscured by her sunglasses; slender figure clothed in those shorts that doubled as a skirt; and a matching jacket. He grinned at the look of horror on her face when she first saw the six-foot-tall statue of a winged cherub that doubled as a fountain, set in the middle of the circular drive.

"Well, Claire Madison," he murmured, swinging back around, "this should prove to be interesting."

"WHAT DO YOU MEAN our room isn't ready?" The strident voice was young, female and very unhappy.

"I'm sorry, Mrs. Hamilton, but one of our maids called in sick this morning and several guests didn't leave on time, so we hope you'll understand the delay. Please feel free to relax in our lounge with a complimentary cocktail." The reservations clerk's smile grew more strained by the minute.

Claire stood in the inn's doorway, watching the confrontation with amusement.

"No, you don't understand." Carroty red hair was teased to a halo around the young woman's pale face, but there was nothing angelic about the frustration etched in her features. "We were married this morning, this is our honeymoon and we need our room. And we need it *now*."

"Honey, it isn't their fault," the groom murmured, patting her hand. "Come on, sweetheart, we'll have it soon. You shouldn't get so upset, Alison."

The new Mrs. Hamilton practically crawled all over her husband of three hours. "I need to be alone with you, Chuck. We need this time alone." She breathed the last word in his ear. Chuck promptly turned as red as his bride's hair.

"Let me see if I can find you another bungalow." The reservations clerk swiftly turned back to her computer terminal.

"You never listen to me, Martin. If we'd taken the turnoff I told you to, we would have been here two hours ago."

"If we'd taken the turnoff you *screamed* at me to take, Jeanette, we would have ended up in Alaska."

Claire spun around to see a couple in their mid-forties walking past her. They were so involved in their argument, they walked past the reservation desk.

"They still took the wrong turnoff," she said chuckling to herself.

"Claire, darling, you look wonderful!" Hannah threw her arms around her granddaughter and enveloped her in a Chanel-scented hug. "I'm so glad you were able to get away."

"Considering you made it sound like life or death, I had no choice," she said dryly, stepping back and sharply eyeing her grandmother. Yes, she looked older, perhaps a bit more frail, but nothing like the ill, shell of a woman she'd expected to find. What was going on here? She gestured with her hand. "An inn for lovers?"

Hannah beamed with pride. "When Cupid's Corners decided to capitalize even more on its name, we all did our part. Pete suggested we advertise the inn in bridal magazines and travel magazines, and as a result we rarely have any vacancies." She tucked her arm through Claire's and led her down a side hallway to her private quarters.

The bickering couple's voices drifted after them. "This damn getting-away-from-it-all nonsense was your attorney's idea, not mine. *He* should have brought you. Considering what he charges for legal fees he could afford the prices they charge here better than I can."

"Oh, shut up, Martin."

"I only wish I had thought of that twenty-three years ago, when the minister asked if I would take you as my wife."

Hannah sighed as the conversation filtered down the hallway. "That must be the Bennetts. It seems they're filing for divorce, but her attorney suggested they go away to neutral territory first and see if they can work things out."

"Considering you call this an inn for lovers, your battling Bennetts could ruin your reputation." Claire looked down at the rich red carpeting. If she found even one cherub in her room she'd show good ol' Martin what a real scream was. "I need to get my luggage," she murmured.

"We'll have someone get it for you. You should have told the car rental agency where you were heading, dear." Hannah patted her hand. "They give out red cars for anyone coming here."

Claire's smile felt just a tiny bit strained as she recalled the conversation with the car rental agency clerk. "Yes. She tried, but I insisted on the black model instead."

Hannah stopped at the door leading to the suite of rooms that had always been Claire's.

"Why don't you freshen up and get some rest?" Hannah suggested. "You can meet Pete at dinner. We usually have wine and cheese in the lounge from five-thirty until seven. We'll see you then?"

Claire's hand on the doorknob stilled. "Pete?"

"Pete Slattery, my manager. The gentleman who wants to buy the inn. He's wonderful. Keeps up with all those nit-picky details I always hated dealing with." Hannah cupped Claire's cheek with her hand. The older woman's eyes were suspiciously bright. "I am so glad you're back here, Claire. Seeing you only a few times a year isn't enough. Now, go in and rest up. I'll have one of the boys bring your luggage in.'' She was gone before Claire could think to open her mouth and question Hannah's comment.

"It's jet lag,'' she murmured, turning the knob and pushing the door open. ''Jet lag, too much coffee and not enough sleep.''

She breathed her first sigh of relief when she found not one cherub in sight. Only tasteful pastel appointments. She pulled off her jacket and draped it over a chair back. Finding the phone, she went to call the office. ''I can't believe I came back here.''

"Hey, it's not so bad. There are even some people who found it peaceful.''

Claire turned around to gaze into a pair of drop-dead sexy blue eyes. Tiny white lines etched into tanned skin attested to the man's being well over the age of twenty-one, but most definitely not over the hill. She cataloged his bronzed features, shaggy, sunstreaked blond hair and dazzling white teeth.

She crossed her arms in front of her chest. ''Aren't you a little old to be a bellman around here? Wait, don't tell me. You're the activities director, right? Barbecues on the beach, a bit of sailing and maybe a few nature hikes. Although I wouldn't think a haven for lovers would bother with any outside activities.''

He dropped her two suitcases to the floor. ''Close, but no cigar. You're a snippy little thing, aren't you?'' Close up, he decided, the lady looked even better. He mentally thanked Hannah for asking him to persuade Claire to stay permanently. That was one task he'd take on very happily.

Claire's eyes narrowed. At five-nine, she couldn't remember the last time she'd been called little. But when the description came from a man who had to be at least six-three, it was apt. Her eyes swept over him, noting the scuffed toes of his leather deck shoes and traveling leisurely up his ragged denim cut-offs to a T-shirt—with sleeves hacked off—that might have been blue in another life.

"I should have guessed. You're Gran's manager."

He inclined his head in silent agreement at her clipped statement. "Pete Slattery. And you're Hannah's shy little Claire."

"I grew up."

He performed the same visual dissection she had a few minutes earlier. "Yes, I see you have. And you've done an admirable job, if I may say so."

Claire could feel her cheeks burning. To hide her agitation, she reached for her purse and opened it. After extracting a bill from her wallet, she held it out in the manner of a duchess bestowing a favor to one of her servants. "Thank you so much for bringing in my luggage, Mr. Slattery."

Flashing the kind of grin that turned a woman's insides to mush, he scissored two fingers around the money while giving a snappy salute with his other hand. "Yes, ma'am, thank you, ma'am." With a deep bow he backed out the door, closing it after him.

"The man should be under medical supervision," Claire muttered.

"THERE, NOW you look rested, more like yourself." Hannah greeted Claire as she stood in the lounge doorway warily, looking out for Pete Slattery.

"I had to wrap up a few things before I could leave the office, so I didn't feel quite like myself today," she murmured. "Gran, we need to talk. Privately."

"Later, dear." Hannah's smile didn't waver as she steered Claire through the room, pausing to greet guests by name—a feat Claire always envied her grandmother—and introduce Claire at the same time. "We'll have plenty of time to talk later."

Claire tamped down her frustration as she followed the older woman, snagging a glass of wine from a tray and downing half the contents in one gulp.

"My, my, I wouldn't have guessed the lady is a tippler." Warm breath brushed her ear. "You didn't look the type to overimbibe."

She turned her head and found herself speared by a familiar pair of twinkling blue eyes. With a discerning eye, she looked over his white dress shirt with the narrow blue stripes and charcoal slacks. "And I wouldn't have guessed that you knew how to dress like a grown-up."

"Yeah, well, nights can get pretty cool around here." Pete plucked the glass out of her hand.

"Yes, I know. I grew up here."

Pete watched several conflicting emotions flicker across her face. She hadn't been happy here, either. He wanted to say something to erase that frown creasing her forehead. Seeing her dressed in such a sexy outfit had been a surprise. Somehow he hadn't expected the very qualified Ms. Madison to show up wearing narrow-cut, soft, burgundy silk pants that clung to her legs, along with a matching bustier revealing bare skin he was certain was as soft as the silk covering it. He only regretted she wore a full, open jacket. Still, the evening was young; perhaps he could persuade her the air was too warm for a jacket. He could easily visualize her reaction. She would be subtly outraged and he'd love to see that sparkle flare up in her rich brown eyes. He opened his mouth to say something—anything—outrageous, in hopes of getting under her skin.

"Mr. Slattery, we need our bungalow changed tonight." Martin Bennett planted himself between them, uncaring how rude his gesture might look.

Pete's smile was as generous as it could be under the circumstances. "Mr. Bennett, as I explained to you earlier, I'm sorry we have no available rooms right now and no one checking out for several days. If you can be patient until then we'll do something the moment another bungalow is available."

"That's not good enough. You're not the one forced to stay next door to those sex fiends," he hissed in Pete's face. "At the rate they're going that boy will be dead in twenty-four hours from exhaustion."

"Frankly, Martin, I'm surprised you remember what hot-and-heavy honeymoon sex is," Jeanette drawled from behind. "Don't worry, Mr. Slattery. I'll just plug his ears the next time the young bride cries out in ecstasy. Although I doubt Martin would even recognize that sound." She led her husband away with a forceful tug of the hand.

Claire almost burst out laughing at the expression on Pete's face. She decided her stay here might not be so boring, after all.

"If those two are an example of how this place is a haven for lovers, I'm surprised the inn didn't close down long ago. But you could take it in the opposite direction and advertise it as a battleground for divorcing couples. Think how unique you'd be considered.'' Her face lit up at the idea. Her lips, colored in a softer shade than her outfit, curved upward. "At the rate things are going tonight, I can't wait to see what happens in Act Two."

Chapter Three

THERE IS MUSIC that gently wakes one up and there is music guaranteed to send one screaming from one's bed. Unfortunately, at six a.m., Claire was subjected to the latter.

"Death is too good for the fiend doing this," she muttered, rolling over onto her stomach and pulling her pillow over her head. The raucous music was only slightly muffled. She sat up and threw her pillow across the room. She uttered a few choice words, crawled out of bed and dragged her robe on.

Pete was whistling along with the haunting sounds of the Doors and on his thirtieth push-up when the pounding on his door first penetrated his early-morning muse.

"Hey, if Mr. Bennett's complaining again—" he began as he threw open his door. He grinned broadly as he rested his bare shoulder against the doorjamb. "Well, good morning, Madison Avenue. Didn't you sleep well? You look a little frazzled."

"No one can sleep well listening to *that*." Claire threw her arm out, pointing toward his stereo system.

He shrugged. "Rock music helps me get ready for the day. Sorry if it woke you up. I forgot you're staying next door."

"These used to be storage rooms."

"Yes, they did. Until I moved in." He cocked his head to one side. "You know, I think I like you better first thing in the morning when you're all mussed up and sleepy looking. You don't look like a yuppie clone now. In fact, you look very kissable." He started to lean over as if following through on his thoughts and almost lost his balance when Claire stepped back.

She dragged her hands through her hair. That she hadn't pulled the strands out by the roots was a major miracle. Pete leaned against the doorway, fascinated by the changing color in her face.

"We need to talk," she bit out.

He gestured with his hand. "Come on in."

For the first time, her agitated senses registered he was wearing nothing more than a pair of leopard-skin briefs that barely covered the essentials, his chest was sweaty and his damp hair slicked back from his forehead. Her hormones reminded her that this man's body was too good to be true, especially when this woman had gone without for far too long. How could she feel such an elemental attraction to a man who was rapidly driving her crazy?

"Breakfast, one hour." She turned on her heel and stalked back to her open bedroom door.

Pete leaned forward from the waist to watch her retreat. "You've got great taste in lingerie, Madison Avenue. Does your underwear look as good as that sheer excuse for a nightgown you're wearing?"

Her answering glare would have melted sheet metal.

"Boy, jet lag really makes her cranky," he murmured, going back into his suite.

CLAIRE HURRIEDLY dressed, muttering to herself the entire time. She dialed her grandmother's room, knowing she was always an early riser. No answer. A call to the front desk told her Hannah had gone for her usual sunrise walk and would probably return in about forty minutes. Her next call was to her office in hopes there was a crisis that needed her immediate attention. *Relaxation* wasn't a word in Claire's vocabulary.

"Everything is fine," Pam assured her. "Just take it easy, so you can handle things out there. How is your grandmother? Is it as bad as you feared?"

"Worse," she grimly replied. "Oh, not her health, but the situation here is a disaster. She's hired some aging beach bum to take over the inn for her, and the town has turned into some kind of living Valentine card. I saw so much red on my drive through town that I never want to see that color again! Now, are you really sure there's nothing I can't handle over the phone?"

"Be grateful things are quiet," Pam told her. "Don't worry, if anything critical comes up, I'll call you first thing. Just relax and have fun out there!"

Claire hung up, feeling even more depressed at the idea of not being needed. She was used to being in the middle of some sort of crisis that only she could handle.

"COFFEE, MS. MADISON?" The smiling waitress hovered over her with a coffeepot in one hand and a menu in the other.

"Yes, please."

"Why don't you just bring a carafe, Lisa," Pete suggested, sliding into the seat across from Claire. "Something tells me our favored guest here will need a lot of caffeine this morning."

"Sure thing, boss."

"My, we're so bright-eyed and bushy-tailed first thing in the morning," Claire drawled, after she had given the waitress her breakfast order and Pete merely requested his usual. "It must be something to do with Jim Morrison crooning 'People Are Strange' at the crack of dawn. What do you listen to at night?"

Pete slung one arm over the back of his chair, looking so relaxed it infuriated the usually frenetic Claire.

"I've learned that 'Light My Fire' works most of the time."

Her breath slammed its way out of her chest in one big rush. Claire was used to attention from handsome men whose charm was second nature, but Pete was blessed with something more fatal. Something more elemental, raw and sensual, that had a woman thinking about tousled sheets and an equally tousled man. Which was the last thing Claire wanted to think about; especially with a man in this particular town and at this particular time of year, which she considered her own personal kiss of death.

"My God, I can't believe it! Claire Madison, why look at you! When I agreed to meet Toni here I didn't know I'd be running into you."

Claire didn't have to look up to identify the chirpy voice. Only one person sounded so enthusiastic no matter what hour of the day or night. She forced her face into the warm expression she used at company functions when she would have preferred staying home with her paperwork.

"Hello, Melissa. It's been a long time," she greeted the woman standing over her.

Melissa Ryan dropped into the chair next to her. "I just can't believe you've come back to our tiny town," she gushed insincerely. "I mean, there you are working in New York as a secretary to important men. Well, maybe some people think secretaries aren't very important, but I know for a fact my Russ couldn't accomplish a thing without his Anna. He's going to be lost without her when she retires next year. Are you back here for good? I know Russ will be looking for a secretary," she trilled.

"I'm an account executive with an advertising agency, Melissa," Claire pointed out between gritted teeth. "And my personal assistant would come after me with an ax if I ever dared call her my secretary."

"I guess they have all sorts of different names back there, don't they?" Melissa was undaunted. "I heard you were married, too. That's right, it didn't happen after all, did it?" She tsked. "You poor dear, you just have the worst luck with men." She leaned forward, touching Claire's arm. "Have you seen Blake yet? I don't think we'll ever forget that Valentine's Dance our senior year! A bunch of us were talking about it at our last high school reunion. What a shame you weren't there." She turned to Pete. "You didn't live around here then, did you, Pete? Let me tell you, Claire has given us some times to laugh about over the years. I swear, she's like an institution in this town." Her laughter grated on her listeners' ears.

"Melissa, isn't that Toni over there?" Pete spoke up. "It's been nice seeing you and I hope you don't mind, but Claire and I have a lot of business to take care of this morning."

"Of course not." She jumped up. "We must get together for lunch, Claire. I'd love to hear all about the work you do in New York." She waggled her fingers as she bounced away.

"I'd rather eat dead rats," Claire muttered, picking up the carafe and refilling her coffee cup. She bit back a curse when the hot liquid burned her lip.

Pete observed her comments and actions with amusement. "Correct me if I'm wrong, but I get the feeling that Melissa isn't one of your favorite people."

Claire leaned back as the waitress set her breakfast in front of her. She flashed Pete one of her dazzling smiles that had charmed more than one prospective client over the years. "Melissa is untrustworthy, vindictive and self-centered. Those are just her good points. Of course, she might have changed since high school, but I doubt it. She considers irritating people her main aim in life." She dug into her breakfast, feeling hungrier than she had in a long time. "All right, I want the truth and nothing but. What exactly is wrong with Gran?"

"Wrong with Hannah? Other than she works too hard, tries to mother everyone and doesn't understand what the word relax means? Not a thing."

Claire carefully unclenched her jaw. "Blood pressure?"

"It was normal when she saw her doctor last week."

"Abnormal heartbeats?"

"I don't think so."

She looked down at her fingers which were systematically shredding her toast. "Arthritis?"

"She has some discomfort when the weather's cold and damp, but no more than usual and nothing she's really complained about." The light bulb went off over his head. "Ah, Hannah lured you back here with stories of pain and bad health and inferences she might not have long to live. The ultimate guilt trip."

She had to force the words out. "Something like that. Although, the way I feel right now, Gran could be suffering from bad health very soon."

"Claire, doesn't it say something that she went to such lengths to get you back here? She must miss you so much that she feels she has to lie," Pete said gently.

"We see each other several times a year."

"On your turf, not on hers."

"I take her to plays and concerts, we take side trips to wherever she wants to go." She felt obligated to defend herself.

"And not once have you come back here."

"There's no need to revisit the place you've grown up in if there are other more exciting places to visit," she argued. "After all, Gran never had a chance to travel years ago because she was raising me. The least I can do is repay her by taking her to places she's only read about."

Pete shook his head. "It seems you and Hannah have a differing opinion about this. She never thought she was giving up something for you, but she is hurt you've refused to return home in all these years."

Claire stood up so quickly the table wobbled. Pete's coffee mug danced dangerously close to the edge. "Do us both a favor and don't try to read people's minds. You're not very good at it. And do me an even greater favor. Don't play your music so loud tomorrow morning, because if you do you can expect to find that expensive stereo system of yours wrapped around your neck."

With open admiration Pete watched her stiff figure exiting the room. "Damn, I just bet she's something when she really loses her temper."

Claire marched through the lobby with the intention of finding Hannah. She headed for the paths that led to the beach, positive her grandmother would be out there communing with nature. Sure enough, she found the older woman seated in a beach chair set firmly in the sand.

"You lied to me," she began without preamble once she faced her grandmother.

Hannah was unfazed by Claire's verbal attack. "I didn't lie to you."

"You told me you were sick, maybe dying!"

"No, Claire, I never said that. Your imagination led you to believe that," Hannah said calmly. "I told you I'm seriously thinking of selling the inn and that you haven't been back here in a long time."

Claire breathed deeply. "Gran, you led me to believe you were very sick. Otherwise, I wouldn't have..."

Hannah's expression remained serene as she looked up at the woman she worried about so much. "Otherwise, you wouldn't have come back to Cupid's Corners, since this is the last place you want to be even though it is your home. You've been away from here too long, Claire. You need to settle the demons from your past before you can really go on in your life." She held up her hand to forestall any argument. "Don't pretend everything in your life is fine and dandy, because we both know better."

Claire pulled in a deep breath. "Gran, I am being considered for a very important promotion right now and I can't afford to have anything get in the way."

"Not even your grandmother's happiness? Her well-being?"

Hannah's soft-spoken questions hit their mark with painful accuracy. "I did come."

"It took you thinking I was dying though. Not because I just might want you back in your home."

"I'm also here to protect your interests. You're saying that Slattery wants to buy the inn. Where is the money coming from? You're not taking back a note from him, are you? How much are you paying him to play at being manager? How much are you selling the inn for?"

Hannah slowly pushed herself out of her chair. Even standing in the soft sand, she looked as self-assured as if she were standing in the middle of the inn's lounge. "The day you left for college you told me, very happily, I remind you, that you wanted nothing to do with the inn because you had no desire to come back here and run it. Pete fell in love with the inn at first sight." She held up her hand to stop any protest. "And no, that isn't something he said to me. It's what I saw in his face, in his eyes and heard in his voice. He's a natural-born innkeeper and he'll never look upon this as a job, but as a part of his soul."

Her eyes flashed fire. "I may be old, Claire, but I'm not senile. I know when someone is telling me the truth and when someone is trying to pull the wool over my eyes. Pete is one of the most honest men I've met in a long time. Perhaps you've taught yourself not to trust the opposite sex, but I'm not that cynical. I suggest you take your time here to look deep into yourself, Claire. New York has hardened you, turned you into a cold and cynical woman I don't know anymore. Oh, I still love you, but I'm not sure I like you very much." She turned away and took careful steps until she reached the path that wound its way up the cliff.

Stunned by her grandmother's words, Claire could only stand there and watch Hannah make her way up the path. She had no idea she was biting down hard on her lower lip until the pain registered in her brain.

"I don't know why she has to make it sound so bad," she muttered, turning away. She wandered along the beach, gesturing right and left as she talked to the swooping sea gulls. "She acts as if I shouldn't bother looking out for her best interests. She's never been out in the business world. She has no idea what kind of sharks are swimming around out there. Well I know all about them, and I intend to protect her whether she wants it or not."

PETE STOOD at the top of the cliff watching Claire's progress.

"She's not my little girl anymore," Hannah said sadly, stopping next to him and looking in the direction of his gaze. "I'm just glad I never told her about the arrangement you and I made last year. I hate to think what she'd do. She's turned so hard over the years. She's not my sweet little girl anymore."

"Big business tends to gobble up sweet little girls unless they can don some armor in time," he explained, his gaze lingering on Claire's legs. Used to the dark tan that many coastal women still preferred, he found Claire's pale, bare legs exciting. "Don't worry, Hannah, she's still of your blood. Just no matchmaking." He wagged his finger at her.

She smiled. "You didn't mind it when I introduced you to Dana."

Pete repressed a shudder. "Mind? Hannah, the woman made a black widow spider look friendly. I was never so grateful as when she turned her predatory sights on Jim Thatcher."

Hannah looked downward. "She refuses to admit she's unhappy," she murmured. "But I could see it in her eyes. Maybe I was wrong in getting her back here, but she needs to settle her feelings about this town.''

"Her Valentine jinx?" Pete asked. "Once it's known Claire's in town, all you'll hear about will be Claire's bad luck with Valentine's Day."

Hannah's lips tightened. "Only Melissa would be that spiteful. And to think I took care of that girl when she had the chicken pox." She shook her head as she walked away. "I should have allowed her to scratch all she wanted."

Pete divided his attention between grandmother and granddaughter. "Those two are more alike than they know. If they ever quit arguing and banded together, they'd be downright scary."

Chapter Four

"IT'S ENOUGH to make a person throw up," Claire said to herself as she looked at the twosomes clustered together near the driving range. She'd been told it had been set up six months ago under Pete's direction. Jerry, who was the unofficial golf pro and in charge of the range, was assisting one of the men with his swing. She stood there long enough to realize that Jerry already knew the names of the guests and the reasons why they were staying at the inn—whether they were honeymooners, celebrating an anniversary or just desiring a special getaway.

"I can't imagine it's the food that's causing your stomach problems," Pete commented, coming up to her from behind. "Our dining room is known for its excellent cuisine."

"No, it's looking at all the stupid smiles and kissy-face that's making me sick." She heartily wished Pete wasn't so good looking in those disreputable denim cut-offs and torn T-shirt. Somehow the clothing seemed to fit Pete's offbeat personality. It would be so much easier to dislike him if he didn't have such a killer smile. She reminded herself that her ex-fiancé had had a killer smile too. Except there was a quality in Pete her ex-fiancé never had. Which only made Pete that much more dangerous to her senses. "I understand there are fifteen newly married couples presently staying here. Within five years probably ten of them will be divorced. What does that say for a hotel that caters to lovers?"

"That those ten should have worked harder on making their marriage work if they truly wanted it to last," he promptly replied. "No one can ensure a perfect, long-lasting marriage. That's up to the participants, don't you think?"

"At least the Bennetts aren't pretending they're the lovebirds of the century," she muttered.

Pete chuckled. He laced his fingers through hers and led her away from the driving range. "The Bennetts are a law unto themselves."

Claire looked across the putting green at the inn. Its shell pink exterior shone softly under the afternoon sun. "He's threatening to sneak into the kitchen and pour saltpeter in the Hamiltons' food before room service delivers it."

"The Hamiltons are unique."

"Unique?" she repeated. "They've given a whole new meaning to the word insatiable and it's been barely twenty-four hours. I'll be surprised if they'll be able to leave here under their own power. It's a good thing they're young and in lust."

He gave her a telling look to indicate that he caught on to her choice of words. She was pointedly informing him she didn't believe in love. He'd already heard that from Hannah and from several others. "Oh, I don't know. I think we oldsters could give them a run for their money. A bit of seasoning does add something, don't you think?"

Claire couldn't remember the last time she'd blushed, but she could feel her cheeks burning red-hot under Pete's gaze. "That's something I wouldn't know about," she snapped before marching off.

"Hey, don't leave just when it was getting good," he called after her. "I'm enjoying our verbal foreplay. Let's see how far it can go." He was pleased to see her steps falter. So the lady wasn't as aloof as she liked to let people think.

"I have errands in town."

"I'll go with you."

She turned around but didn't stop her fast pace, although walking backward was hazardous. She was willing to chance it. "Oh, no. I wouldn't think of taking you away from your managerial duties. Besides, this is girl stuff. Nothing that would interest you." She spun back around and headed for the main building's front portico, where a valet brought her car from the parking lot.

From the short distance Pete watched Claire easily charm the valet with a warm smile as he handed her into her car. With a fatuous smile on his face, the young man watched Claire speed off.

"Close your mouth, son, before a fly thinks it's a new home," Pete advised, walking past him toward the lobby.

The valet reddened and snapped his mouth shut. "She's just so nice," he explained.

"Yeah, well, I wouldn't mind her being that nice to me," Pete muttered, heading for his office where he was certain he would find a pile of papers requiring his signature. It always seemed to be the price for his playing hooky on a beautiful morning like this.

CLAIRE LEFT HER CAR in a public parking lot near the middle of town so she could freely explore the new Cupid's Corners. She arranged for several pounds of heart-shaped fudge to be shipped back to her office, where she knew everyone would hate her for tempting them to forget their never-ending diets. She noticed the bookstore displayed colorfully bound editions of love poems in the front window. She tried not to sneer as she stared at postcards that cheerfully stated "I found love in Cupid's Corners."

"Why not have little naked cherubs running around town with their bow and arrows?" she murmured, stopping to inspect a clothing boutique where, naturally, all the clothing in the window was red. A hand-lettered sign suggested that the browsers come in and put a little love in their lives with a red lace nightgown. "They really need to get a little more original with their thinking." She quickly moved on before she succumbed to the invitation.

She decided she'd done enough sight-seeing and walked swiftly toward the drugstore. At least there she wouldn't be surrounded by all these happy, smiling faces that didn't cheer her up one little bit.

"Claire? Claire Madison, is that you?" The woman's squeal of delight assaulted Claire's ears.

Claire pasted a bright smile on her face as she turned to meet the owner of the chirpy voice. She should have known she would run into someone she knew. After all, the town wasn't all that large. "Guilty."

"I just knew it!" The blond woman Claire remembered as Toni Anderson threw her arms around Claire in a hug. Claire also remembered how Toni was best known as Olympic material for nonstop talking. "It's been so long. How long are you staying? You'll be here for all the festivities, won't you? Hasn't Hannah done a wonderful job with the inn? Of course, that darling of a manager she has is a big plus for her. Are you still working in New York? Are you married? Oh, that's right. It didn't work, did it?" She suddenly giggled. "I guess I haven't given you time to answer one of my questions, have I? Dan always says if I'd take the time to breathe, I'd give others a chance." She led Claire over to a quiet corner of the drugstore. "You look beautiful. Clothes like that you don't see around here except in fashion magazines." With frank envy she eyed Claire's bright outfit.

Claire was convinced her facial muscles hurt from her strained smile. "Yes, I'm staying with Gran. I really don't plan to stay long. I'm with an advertising firm in New York and you're right, the marriage didn't work."

Toni sighed. "Oh, Claire, that's terrible. I mean, Dan is my life. Not that our three kids aren't wonderful, but I can't imagine being without my husband. How lonely you must be."

"Far from it," Claire assured her a bit too brightly. Why didn't she think about driving an extra fifty miles to do her shopping, so she could have escaped this? "There's always so much going on—the theater, concerts, art showings along with business functions. I'm so busy I barely have time to take a breath."

Toni patted her shoulder. "It's not the same, is it? Oh, but you have to stay for the parties. Everyone will want to see you." She went on to give Claire details of their former classmates' lives. Claire wasn't surprised to hear a large percentage of the women had been married within a year out of high school.

"And I guess you've seen how much the town has changed," Toni prattled on. "Oh, we may seem a little too touristy at times but, people always seem to smile when they leave and that's what counts. And people come from all over for our Valentine dances." She shot her a slight embarrassed smile that didn't quite hit the mark. "Oh, Claire, I doubt anyone remembers what happened that night."

Even if you do, Claire said to herself, heartily wishing she was anywhere but there. She glanced down at her watch. "I need to get back to the inn. I promised Gran I wouldn't stay long."

"And here I've been chattering on," Toni said sighing. "I'm just so glad we had this chance to talk. We have to get together for lunch."

Claire's face tightened from the strain. "Yes, we must do lunch soon," she said insincerely, backing away. "It's good to see you, Toni." She quickly made her purchases and escaped to her car in hopes of getting out of town before anyone else recognized her.

"Terrific," she muttered, pressing down harder on the accelerator. "Once Toni, aka Western Union, gets on the phone, everyone in town will know that Claire Madison, February 14's jinx, is back. Which means this Valentine's Day will be a bust and something absolutely horrible is going to happen to ruin the day." She pounded the steering wheel with her fist. Mindful of the roads, she slowed the car down.

For a brief moment, a picture of Pete in those scandalous leopard-skin briefs entered her mind. Would a man like that allow a jinx to stop his pursuit? She doubted anything would stop someone as single-minded as him from anything he desired.

Claire groaned. Desire was the last word she should even think about. Especially where Pete was concerned.

Claire looked upward. "The gods hate me," she moaned. "They really hate me. I should have stayed in New York instead of coming to the Love Capital of the USA."

Chapter Five

"COME ON, Madison Avenue, we're going to party, my style."

Claire looked up from the cup of coffee she'd been toying with for the past half hour. There was nothing she hated more than drinking cold coffee. "You can party your style. I'm busy." She deliberately lifted the cup to her lips and sipped the cold brew. It took all of her willpower not to make a face.

Pete plucked the cup out of her hand. "Come on, Claire, you know you can't drink that stuff that way," he chided. "I sure know I can't watch you drink it. We're having a bonfire on the beach. We'll roast marshmallows, maybe make a few s'mores for the more daring and hoist a few beers. Come on down and see what we're all about." He curved his fingers over hers and pulled her out of her chair. "Now go put on something warm." He patted her on the rear as he gently pushed her on her way.

Claire's head snapped around so fast she was lucky she didn't get whiplash. "If you ever do that again, you will find yourself with a broken hand," she threatened in a low voice. She headed for the section housing the private quarters.

Claire quickly changed out of the dress she'd worn for dinner and into a pair of jeans and a pullover sweater.

"I'm only doing this to look nice for the others," she muttered as she ran a brush through her hair and added a touch of lipstick. "Pete Slattery doesn't deserve me looking my best, but the others do since they know I'm Hannah's granddaughter.''

She found Pete waiting for her by the reservations desk. His blond hair looked as if it hadn't been combed since that morning, but he was so devastating that it didn't matter. Claire gritted her teeth and tried to ignore the strong attraction she felt for the man.

''These evenings usually turn out to be a lot of fun,'' he told her as they walked outside. ''Tonight especially, since Jeanette Bennett expressed an interest in attending.''

''The Bickering Bennetts?'' she groaned. ''There goes any fun. Good ol' Martin is going to make everyone miserable.''

''Maybe not. I shoved a note under the Hamiltons' door in case they want to attend.'' He whistled a tune as he ambled along, his hands jammed into his pockets to prevent him from giving in to the temptation to touch her.

''I doubt they've even seen it. Ten to one they won't find it until the day they check out.''

Under the watchful eyes of two of the grounds keepers, a fire was already merrily burning when they reached the beach. Four couples were seated on blankets. Several groups were talking animatedly, with Hannah moving from one to the other.

''We wondered if you'd show up,'' a smiling woman with silver hair greeted Pete from her perch on a log. Seated next to her was a tall, lanky man who merely nodded his greeting. ''Hannah said you were bringing her granddaughter.'' She passed a smug look from one to the other.

"Now, May, everyone knows I don't miss any function when one of my favorite ladies is going to be attending," Pete playfully chided her. "Claire, this is May Webster and her husband, Ed. They've been coming here for their anniversary for the past ten years and this year they're celebrating their fiftieth in our tower suite complete with hot tub on the deck." He leaned down toward May. "So how many times have you and Ed made whoopee in that hot tub, May?"

She giggled and slapped his hand. "You are a devil, Pete. The one who should be using that sinful hot tub is you and this lovely girl, not two old fogies like Ed and me."

"Yeah, but we don't have anything special to celebrate," he confided in a mock whisper, slanting a wicked smile at a blushing Claire, "yet."

"Although our kids can't believe that we can still make the bedsprings squeak!" she chortled. "My granddaughter doesn't believe people our age would still be interested in sex, much less remember how to do it!"

Claire couldn't help smiling at the older woman's infectious mirth. "Just tell them you only hope they'll be as lucky as you are when they're your age," she advised.

Pete glanced at Claire. "I know I hope to be."

"You better keep a sharp eye on this one," May advised Claire. "He sure seems to be a handful."

"Oh, I'll keep something sharp on him all right."

Pete winced as he grabbed Claire's hand and led her over to the other side of the bonfire.

"Maybe I should frisk you for hidden weapons."

"Maybe you should dig out those marshmallows you talked about." She dropped onto an empty blanket and curled her legs beside her. "Actually a s'more would be even better as long as it doesn't come out heart-shaped."

"So it wasn't my charming company that tempted you to come down?" He dropped down beside her.

She shook her head. "Sorry."

The beginning of a grin curved his mouth. "No, you're not." He looked up. "Hey, Gary, how about throwing one of those bags of marshmallows over here?"

"Don't forget the chocolate and graham crackers!" Claire called out.

"Yeah, I've got a hungry woman here." Pete shot her a look that said loud and clear he was thinking of another kind of hunger.

"Come on, Jeanette, this is strictly summer camp crap," Martin grumbled, following his wife.

She spun on him. "Martin, just shut up, sit down and for once in your sorry life, pretend to have a good time!" she snapped.

Stunned by his wife's outburst, he did as she ordered.

Jeanette looked down, half surprised and half pleased at the outcome. "I should have done this a long time ago," she mumbled, sitting down beside him.

"Your settlement just got cut in half," he informed her. Claire watched them with equal parts exasperation and sorrow. "They would have been better battling it out in court than here," she murmured.

Pete followed her gaze. "No, there's still hope for them. Look at it this way, they're communicating. And they did come out here to see how they could work things out."

"By making life miserable for everyone else."

He shook his head. "Nope, more like providing an example for others to see what could happen to them if they don't bother to nurture what they have. Besides, seeing others in love might show Jeanette and Martin what they could have."

"Considering all your talk about the values of marriage, I'm surprised you don't have a wife and little ones running around." She was probing, and the smug expression on her grandmother's face as she sat down beside them told her the older woman knew what she was doing.

Pete settled back, wrapping his arms around his drawn up knees. "Oh, I found the right woman, but Hannah said I was too old for her. She figured at her age she should be allowed one wild and crazy time with a twenty-two-year-old stud." He winked at Hannah.

Claire's eyes almost popped out of their sockets. "Gran said that?" Her voice rose to a squeak. She turned to Hannah who merely kept smiling. "Gran, I can't believe it!"

"I may be old, Claire, but I'm certainly not dead," her grandmother said huffily.

Pete continued. "Hannah told me I'd get over my infatuation and the time would come when the right woman would enter my life and I'd have to be ready for her."

"But maybe she won't have an inn to offer for a dowry."

Instead of getting angry at her less-than-subtle dig, Pete broke into laughter. Hannah shook her head at her stubborn granddaughter and moved away murmuring that she was heading for people who would appreciate her.

Pete leaned over and draped an arm around Claire's shoulders. "Claire, you're about as subtle as a pipe wrench." She looked a bit wary and drew her head back as he lowered his. He paused, looking down at her face and smiled. "Don't worry, Claire, this won't hurt a bit."

His kiss might have started out teasing, but it soon escalated into something warmer. Before it flared out of control he drew back. His eyes reflected the orange flames of the bonfire. "Well, well, well," he murmured, studying her face. "Something new has been added."

Claire couldn't tear her eyes away from Pete. Her crook of an ex-fiancé might have been considered a champion of kissers, but his had been nothing compared to what they had just shared.

"Hey, boss, wanna cut down on the heavy-duty stuff?" Gary teased, dropping a bag of marshmallows and two long sticks in front of Pete. "We kids aren't allowed to view adult activities like that."

"Yeah, tell me that the next time I catch you and Lisa out behind one of the pool cabanas," Pete growled, glaring up at his grinning employee. "Why don't you make sure all the guests have plenty of marshmallows?"

"Yeah, but boss, you're the host. We're just here for the manual labor."

Pete looked torn, but he knew Gary was right. While cuddling up to Claire was so very tempting, his work did need to come first.

"I'll be back." It sounded like a very sexy promise. He made his way around the fiery circle, pausing to talk to each couple, exchange a joke or ask a question about their stay.

Claire sat there watching him at ease with each person, even the irascible Bennetts. She didn't see the face of what she privately dubbed an aging beach bum. His smile was not that of the opportunity seeker she feared he might be.

She made a mental note to ask him about his finances. After all, if this inn was as successful as it appeared to be, it would be worth a fair price. She didn't intend for her grandmother to be cheated just because the potential buyer had a winning smile and was a great kisser. She quickly crossed the latter off her list. It was much safer not to think about Pete's kisses or have wandering thoughts about any other areas in which he might be an expert.

The rest of the evening passed in a blur for Claire. Pete, who'd returned to her side as soon as he could, kept smiling at her. But it was Hannah's look that disturbed her the most. The older woman looked as if she was seeing her dreams come true.

"Running this kind of inn has gone to her head," Claire said under her breath as she watched Pete lean forward with a long fork to toast a marshmallow.

She accepted the rich s'mores with the melting chocolate and marshmallow wedged between two graham crackers. She didn't move away when Pete draped his arm around her shoulders and brought her closer to his side nor when his mouth found its way to her ear. She caught her breath when his teeth grazed the sensitive skin. She felt drowsy and content; a new feeling for the lady used to the fast track, and not an unwelcome one, either.

She had no idea of the time as the others began filtering away.

"Don't stay out too late," Hannah chirped, looking as if she hoped for the exact opposite. She walked up the path alongside May while Ed, still having not said a word, silently followed them.

"I've got to oversee the dousing of the fire," Pete murmured in her ear before getting to his feet.

She offered him a sleepy smile. "I'll wait."

A sharp breath hissed between his teeth. "I'll make it as fast as I can."

Cocooned in a haze as soft and gooey as the marshmallows she'd feasted on that evening, Claire watched Pete and the two boys poke and prod until they were satisfied the fire was completely out.

As the boys gathered up the blankets, Pete held out his hand. "Come on, let's take a walk."

Claire blinked in surprise. A walk? Somehow she'd expected something else. She allowed him to pull her to her feet. With his arm around her shoulders and hers around his waist, they walked along the beach, accompanied by teasing suggestions from the boys.

"They act as if this is something new for you," Claire said.

"It is."

She turned her head to look up at him. There was no devilish grin, nothing to indicate he was anything but serious. "Come on, Pete, I can't believe I'm the first woman you've taken to one of those affairs."

"But you are."

Her laughter was tinged with disbelief. "Try again, Pete. You don't kiss like a man who's gone without for a long time."

He stopped and swung her around, keeping his hands firmly on her shoulders, his thumbs caressing the hollow of her throat. "I believe in keeping my work and social life separate."

Now why did she feel disappointed by his flat statement? "So I'm just part of your work."

"Far from it. You're the bridge between the two. And no matter what you do or say, Claire Madison, I don't intend to let you go," he whispered, just before his mouth settled firmly on hers.

Claire's breath caught in her throat as Pete slid his tongue across her lower lip, bathing each corner with loving attention before dipping between her parted lips. She touched the tip of her tongue against his, feeling the satiny roughness.

His fingers tightened on her shoulders. "Touch me, Claire," he rasped.

"Pete," she said sighing, as she pushed her hands under his sweatshirt to find warm skin that prickled under her cold fingertips. "Yes."

He gathered her more fully against him, trapping her hands under his shirt as he feasted hungrily on her mouth, nipping and lapping. He roughly pulled her sweater away from her jeans so his hands could roam her bare back. He edged one finger under her bra strap, sliding back and forth.

"This is one time when I would wish for a clip in back instead of in front," he muttered against her mouth.

She tipped her head back. "Just shut up, Slattery, and kiss me again," she said, reveling in the sensual fog he wove around them.

"Finally the lady is getting the idea."

"Yes, darling, *yes!* Give it to me, baby!" The scream of ecstasy floated overhead.

Claire's and Pete's heads snapped up and whipped around in the direction of the feminine cry of rapture.

"I need it, Chuck. Make your Alison so hot she'll go up in flames!"

Pete looked down at Claire. She bit her lower lip to keep from laughing as the sounds of vigorous love-making reached their ears. His own shoulders shook as he forced the words out between chuckles.

"Well, I guess we can assume that the Hamiltons have decided to leave their room for some fresh air."

Chapter Six

WHILE THE NEWLY MARRIED Hamiltons' vocal display on the putting green hadn't exactly dampened Claire and Pete's enthusiasm, it had tempered the mood.

"Come on." He guided her back up the beach. "If we stay out here too much longer we might end up very embarrassed."

Claire shook her head as she chuckled. "I wouldn't have believed it if I hadn't heard it for myself. She sounded like something out of a bad novel."

"It's a good thing we don't have any adult channels available on the cable, or who knows what we might have heard." Pete kept his arm around her waist, so their hips bumped companionably as they walked along. "We'll take the roundabout way so we don't have to go anywhere near the putting green."

"True, we might see something that could upset our fragile natures," she said, choking.

"Can you imagine what good ol' Martin would have said if he'd been down there?"

"'Are they at it again?'" Claire managed a credible imitation of the older man's growl. "'Those two are worse than rabbits!'"

Pete steered them to the rear of the inn and made a stop at a small locked shed. He quickly unlocked the door and stepped inside for a moment.

"This might help. I set the timer so the sprinklers on the putting green will go off in about two minutes."

He held up a finger for silence until they heard two shrieks. "Yep, right on time."

"That was terrible." She didn't sound all that convincing.

"Can't have people think this is the kind of place where such shameful acts go on in public," he declared, as they walked through the rear door. When they reached Claire's room, he braced his arm against the door. "Going to invite me in?"

She turned around and leaned back against the door. "It's late," she murmured.

He mentally cursed the Hamiltons for ruining a beautiful thing. "You didn't think so five minutes ago."

"It wasn't late five minutes ago." The tip of her tongue appeared to wet her lips. "It was fun, Pete." She looked down, studying her shoes. "I saw the bulletin board out there. You seem to have a lot of activities to offer the guests. It's a lot more than what Gran used to have for them. From what I've heard, you're always on top of any problem before it blows up, and the staff adore you, even those who've been called on the carpet for one reason or another. That really says a lot."

"So you don't feel I'm so bad after all. Hey, aging beach bums tend to find jobs that keep them outside more than in."

She had the grace to flush. "Well, blond hair, blue eyes and a tan tend to make a person think only one thing."

Pete leaned down until their noses touched. "White sand, full moon, tropical breezes," he whispered, pressing feathery kisses around her face. "You in a sexy bikini bottom."

"What happened to the top?"

His teeth grazed her lower lip then gently pulled it down. "I took it off."

"No protest on my part?" Her breathing was becoming erratic.

"I didn't hear any. In fact, you helped."

"Then if you took off my top, what did I take off you?"

Pete froze then grinned. "Whatever you wanted to, darlin', whatever you wanted to."

This time his kiss wasn't rudely interrupted by amorous honeymooners. By the time Pete stepped back, Claire looked as if she'd turned to jelly, while inside she felt like a raging inferno.

"I have to go in," she said weakly.

"If you'd like, I could tuck you in." His voice wasn't any stronger.

She closed her eyes, visualizing Pete tucking her in, then climbing right in after her. "I . . . I think it would be better if I did it myself."

Disappointment flashed into his eyes and then quickly disappeared. "Then how about breakfast and a drive up the coast?"

"I really haven't spent much time with Gran, and I did come out here to be with her."

He straightened up. "There's a lot going on in town at this time of year." He pretended not to see her wince. "How about attending the Cupid's Cakefest with me?"

"I outgrew Cupid's Corners' idea of fun when I was in high school."

"Yeah, but I wasn't around to date you then. Trust me, you'll have a hell of a lot more fun than you did back then."

Her smile seemed stiff. "I'm sure I would," she murmured, pushing the door open. "Good night, Pete."

He stood there until her door closed and for some time after. He knew there was such a thing as love happening quickly. Now all he had to do was convince the lady.

CLAIRE NEVER INDULGED in anything as time wasting as daydreaming. So why had she been curled up in her bedroom window seat for the past two hours, watching the sun rise? And why was she thinking more about Pete than about calling her office? Suddenly that part of her world seemed very far away and maybe not all that important. The sun was just coming up when she began feeling sleepy. She took off her robe and slipped into bed, sensually aware of the cool sheets surrounding her and wondering how they would feel if she wasn't in this bed alone. On that thought her smile widened as she found herself drifting off to sleep and very pleasant dreams.

Steel guitars twanging, reverberating off the walls was her first warning. The equally loud woman's singing voice was next.

"No, he can't do this," she groaned, rolling over and pulling her pillow over her head, which only slightly muffled the ear-splitting sounds. But he did. More than that, the familiar song registered in her sleep-fogged brain. Gloria Estefan was right when she sang about bad boys. "He can."

The sound of her telephone ringing was a mere whisper compared to the noise booming from next door.

"Yes?" she shouted into the receiver. Thanks to the background vocals, there was no problem in guessing the identity of her caller.

"It was a toss-up, love," Pete cooed. "It was either this or 'Lay, Lady, Lay.' I figured you'd appreciate Estefan."

Claire fell back among the covers. "If there's a way to shut off the electricity to your room I will find it and make sure it's turned off for the rest of my stay." She breathed a sigh of relief when the music stopped.

"Ah darlin', I'm going to be so sweet to you you'll never want to leave me," he crooned.

"I gave up sugar years ago." With that she carefully replaced the receiver in the cradle. Funny, she found herself unable to stop smiling.

"OH, YES, my Jason and I were married for almost fifty years." Claire found Hannah seated in the lobby speaking to the Bennetts. "While I hated his dying, I was grateful he was taken quickly and with little pain. If it hadn't been for having Claire with me and having to run the inn, I'm sure I would have followed him soon after."

"Long marriages like yours just don't happen that much anymore," Jeanette commented.

"Why not?"

"Well, things are different now." Jeanette stumbled over the words, not expecting Hannah to question her statement. "More stress. More pressure."

"There wasn't any of that thirty years ago? My dear, marital problems have been the same down through the ages, they're just given different names," Hannah said gently. "But if you love someone enough, and each partner is willing to work hard to keep the marriage strong, there's no reason why you can't.''

"You sound like her idiotic divorce lawyer without all the fifty-dollar words,'' Martin growled, shifting uneasily under Hannah's serene smile.

"No, just a simple woman who knows if a body wants a divorce they'll do it without any talking ahead of time. Something tells me you two don't want to split up, you just forgot all the reasons you got married in the first place.''

"My father said I'd be sorry for marrying a bum like Martin.'' Jeanette's voice sounded strained, as if she was holding back tears. "He said that Martin would never come to anything.''

"I never believed there was a girl good enough for my son,'' Hannah said. "But when he brought his future wife home, I knew they were a perfect match. They loved each other until the day of their deaths.''

Claire stood back, unashamedly eavesdropping on the conversation. She heard the pain in her grandmother's voice at the revelation of old memories and the pain in the Bennetts' voices at the reminder of much more recent memories. She kept out of sight until the couple left Hannah.

"Hi, how about some breakfast with your favorite granddaughter?'' she asked brightly, walking up as if she had just arrived and hadn't overheard one word.

Hannah looked up and returned her smile. "You're my only granddaughter.''

"Details.'' She waved it off. "Come on, I'm starving.''

"How did you enjoy the bonfire last night?'' Hannah linked arms with her as they walked toward the dining room.

"It was very nice." What an understatement! a tiny gremlin shouted inside her brain.

"I understand the sprinklers on the putting green went off early last night." She slanted a sly glance in Claire's direction. "I hope you didn't get too wet."

Claire bent down and whispered in her grandmother's ear. "I think the ones who will worry about catching a cold are the Hamiltons. They ventured out for fresh air and couldn't keep their hands off each other for more than five seconds," Claire explained. "Pete thought a cold shower might help them remember where they were before someone stumbled over them. I think it did the trick."

Hannah led Claire to her corner table.

Claire picked up the heart-shaped menu and tried not to wince at the elegant red-and-gold lettering. "I didn't see this yesterday," she murmured, cringing as she read the proffered items—heart-shaped pancakes, Cupid's omelets, St. Valentine's pastries. She suddenly didn't feel very hungry.

"No, we don't bring these out until closer to Valentine's Day." Hannah reached across and covered Claire's hand with her own. "Dear, you can't keep feeling bitter about what happened in the past."

"Do you mean my Valentine wedding at which two police officers announced to the congregation that my groom had four other wives he'd neglected to divorce? And that he'd cleaned out their bank accounts before he disappeared?" Claire asked sardonically. "I was just lucky that the minister hadn't pronounced us man and wife yet."

"I told you the man would only give you grief."

Claire tried to smile but failed miserably. "Yes, but you didn't tell me that until afterward."

Hannah's hand tightened on hers. "You were so happy and I'd hoped I'd be wrong. And then you wouldn't talk about it."

"I didn't want to talk to anyone. Look at my track record, Gran. I was probably the only first-grader not to receive any Valentines from my class."

"You had been out with complications from the measles for three weeks."

"Then I broke my arm on Valentine's Day when I was ten."

"Which could have happened on any day."

"What about Sean standing me up for the sophomore Valentine's Dance?"

Hannah lifted her cup of tea before answering. "He should have called you to explain."

"Not to mention the St. Valentine's Ball, when Blake Foster spilled punch all over the dress I'd saved for eight months to buy?"

"I never liked Blake. I always considered him too wild." Hannah sounded pious.

"You never liked any of the boys I dated," Claire pointed out. "Even if you were ladylike enough to never say so."

"That's not true. But they were boys. Now, if we're talking *men,*" she stressed the last word, "there's only one I can name."

"Who?" Claire regretted her question the moment she asked it.

"Why, Pete, of course. He is a wonderful man and deserves a wonderful woman. And who better than my granddaughter." Hannah beamed.

Claire suddenly had the feeling that this Valentine's Day might turn out to be her worst yet.

Chapter Seven

"No."

"You said you would."

"I don't think I did. And if I did, I've changed my mind."

"Ah, come on, you know you want to."

"The last time I heard that male-oriented phrase I was sixteen. I didn't believe that male then. Why should I believe you now?"

"Because I'm more charming?"

Claire crossed her arms in front of her chest. Her willpower was rapidly dwindling, but she was determined to put up a good fight. "I've known charming men before. It's usually all on the surface, anyway."

Pete winced. "Madison Avenue, you're a tough nut to crack, you know that?"

"I just don't want to make it too easy for you."

He moved slowly toward Claire, forcing her to retreat until her back hit the wall. He planted his hands against the wall near her shoulders to prevent any idea of escape.

"Now, why don't you tell me your real reason for not wanting to attend the Cupid's Cakefest when you already said you'd go with me?" he murmured, inhaling her provocative perfume. "Of course, I did have to use a little bit of persuasion at the time. Maybe I should try it again." He slipped his hands to her shoulders.

She had no choice but to look up and into his startling blue eyes. The heat from his skin wrapped around her like a cocoon, although she felt far from safe in his arms. "There's no reason. I just feel I should be here with Gran. After all, you've successfully kidnapped me for a picnic on the beach and a drive up the coast for dinner. And don't forget that isolated little cove where you assured me there were submarine races, when we both know there was no such thing."

His lips curved in a toothy grin. "Yeah, but you went with me, didn't you? As for Hannah, I'd say you have a problem since she's helping out at the Cakefest. Of course, I'd be only too happy to drive you over there so you could spend time with her."

Claire's eyes narrowed. "You tricked me."

"You tricked yourself, sweetheart."

She pressed against his chest, hard. But he didn't budge. "All right, Slattery, you've made your point."

"I think I like you better when you're all soft and breathy," he murmured, dipping his head to nibble her ear. "Think if I work on it long enough I can coax you into that mood?"

She closed her eyes against the hot tide racing through her veins. "Not in this lifetime," she managed to mumble.

He tipped his hips forward. "Okay, so you don't want to go to the Cakefest. How about we stay around here and see what we can scare up?"

Claire had a pretty good idea about what was already up. "You know, maybe going to the fest would be a good idea." She had to get away before she collapsed in a quivering heap at his feet.

"I think we can wait another minute," he murmured, capturing her mouth with his own.

Claire was convinced Pete already knew every erogenous zone in her body. What would happen when he made love to her? That idea rapidly stiffened her spine and gave her the strength to resist. She quickly ducked under his arm and almost ran for her room. "I'll be ready in fifteen minutes," she muttered.

Pete collapsed against the wall, gasping for air as he mentally groped for his sanity. If Claire hadn't left when she had, he would have made love to her there in the hall. She had to know how she tempted him. He certainly had just given her plenty of signs! Taking another deep breath, he wondered if he had time for a quick cold shower before they left.

"YOU CAN DO IT. You are an adult. This is nothing more than an evening out." Claire's fingers tightened on the edge of the bathroom counter as she stared at herself in the mirror. She turned her head from one side to the other. It wouldn't take much to convince her red blotches were breaking out all over her face and throat. "You are the next executive vice president with Shaw and Associates," she reminded herself. "If you can deal with Billy Bob Wheezer and his sausages, you can deal with this. It should be a piece of cake! Oh, Claire, don't use that word!" She took several deep breaths then pushed herself away. After adding a brighter lipstick color than usual for courage, she felt ready. "Look on the bright side. You didn't throw up."

Feeling more capable she swept open the door of the bedroom to find Pete standing in front of her with his hand upraised to knock. He glanced down at his watch.

"Fifteen minutes exactly. I'm impressed."

"Time is money in the advertising game." She began to walk down the hall. "Shall we go?"

He loped along behind her. "You sound as if you're going to your execution."

Claire pushed open the glass door and breathed in the cool early-evening air.

"I don't like to be late," she explained. "I'm just grateful your car isn't red or I'd insist we take mine."

"Jeeps and bright red don't really go together in my mind." Pete took her hand. "Since I like to go horseback riding up in the hills, this is great for pulling the trailer."

"You have a horse?" She was surprised because he hadn't mentioned it before. Come to think of it, she couldn't remember exactly what they had talked about. Only that they laughed a lot. And kissed a lot. And touched a lot.

He nodded. "Two horses, actually. Do you ride?"

She shook her head. "I wouldn't have the time, anyway."

Pete swung himself into the driver's seat. "That's a shame. If you're not careful the day will come when you'll regret not stopping to take the time."

He ran the back of his fingers over her cheek, marveling at the silky feel of her skin. "But that's not a fit subject for tonight. Tonight is the night we pig out at the Cupid's Cakefest and you won't say one word about calories."

THE TOWN HALL was ablaze with lights and filled with laughter. Claire kept her head down, hoping and praying no one would recognize her.

Pete covered her nape with his palm as they walked inside.

"Every year this gets more crowded." He had to raise his voice to be heard as he nodded or lifted his hand several times in response to his name being called.

"Yes, I can see that." She looked around covertly, secretly relieved she hadn't seen anyone she knew. The last thing she wanted was for Pete to hear about her regrettable past. If he had to know then let her be the one to tell him, not someone else. She wished she'd stuck by her guns and refused to go. Of course, that was easier said than done when Pete was the one doing the persuading.

"Hey, Pete, how's the innkeeping going?" One man slapped him on the back and offered his hand. He looked at Claire quizzically.

"Just fine." Pete took his hand and asked a question, all the while pretending he didn't notice the man glancing curiously at Claire. Finally the man wandered off. "Forgive me for being rude, but I want you all to myself tonight," he whispered in her ear as he negotiated their way through the crowds. He stopped at one booth and chose two heart-shaped raspberry tarts. He handed one to Claire.

"I figured you'd prefer these tarts over the cherub cookies." He grinned.

"Why, Claire, I can't believe you actually came!"

She winced at the voice trilling in their direction.

"Hello, Melissa, Toni," she greeted the two women.

Melissa turned and stared at Pete with mock surprise. "My, my, Claire, your luck must be changing if you can show up with someone like Pete here. He's our most eligible bachelor, you know." She leaned forward. While her tone was confiding, the expression in her eyes mocked the idea. "Be careful tonight, Claire. You know you tend to do the most ridiculous things in public. Although I guess you have to be a lot more careful now because of your job. Hannah has been telling everyone how important you are at that advertising agency. It's amazing that you can hold down such an important position when you have such bad luck here."

Claire's smile didn't reach her eyes. "Perhaps it had something to do with the company I kept back then."

Melissa reared back. "You've grown claws since your senior year, Claire." She managed a stiff smile at Pete. "Claire has very bad luck around Valentine's Day, Pete. If I were you I'd make sure not to be in the fallout. Come on, Toni." With that parting shot, she sauntered off with her cohort.

"I'd like to see her boiled in acid," Claire muttered.

"Now, now, eat some more sweets," Pete suggested, pushing a chocolate-dipped cookie in her mouth. "The sugar will sweeten your disposition."

With her mouth stuffed full, she could only glare at him.

Pete kept a tight hold on her hand as they wandered through the huge hall.

"I'm so glad you came!" Hannah greeted them from her place in the booth that served strawberry-flavored funnel cakes, but her eyes remained on Claire. "I wanted you to see how much the Cakefest has grown." She beamed at Pete who stood behind Claire. "You two make such a lovely couple."

"Gran, you're pushing," Claire warned, feeling her cheeks turn a bright red.

She was undaunted. "Only because I care about you and want to see you happy."

Claire sneaked a glance at Pete who, she was convinced, had to be fidgeting with embarrassment under Hannah's grandmotherly gaze. Instead he smiled at Claire and rubbed his knuckles against the small of her back in a warm gesture.

"You're not helping," she reprimanded.

"Just doing my part."

Claire was afraid to ask his part in what.

"Claire Madison, look at you!" A tall beefy man ran up and gathered her up in his arms. "Talk about turning out pretty! With those braces gone and you filling out so nice, those lips of yours look good enough to eat."

"Excuse me." Pete tapped the man's shoulder. "But you're manhandling my date."

The man kept his arm wrapped around Claire's waist as he whipped around to face Pete. "Hey, buddy, I knew this girl long before you ever showed your pretty-boy face in this town. Those baby blue eyes of yours don't do one thing for me except make me want to rearrange that surfer-boy face of yours."

Pete's features tightened. "Hey, if you don't like me, just spit it out."

"Pete, that's not a good idea," Claire warned.

They went nose-to-nose. "You may be the hottest thing out at Hannah's hotel," the man continued, "but we all know you're nothing more than some fancy figurehead out there." He deliberately lowered his eyes. "Hell, you probably don't even have what it takes to get a woman into bed and keep her there."

Pete stood his ground. "Insults from ingrates don't bother me one bit."

"Oh no." Claire hid her face in her hands. "I don't think I can watch this."

"Oh yeah? Well, maybe this will bother you a hell of a lot." The man took his arm from Claire's waist so suddenly, she staggered into a group of people who were unashamedly eavesdropping on the encounter.

"Pete, watch out!" she screamed as the man swung his fist in Pete's direction. Claire covered her eyes, then peeked through slightly spread fingers. She didn't want to see the bloodshed that was sure to follow. And she prayed that the police wouldn't be called in. Either way, the onlookers would remember that the fight had something to do with Claire Madison. Once again she would be the talk of the town.

Chapter Eight

"Ow! HEY, that hurts! Ow!"

"You big baby." Claire dabbed the broken skin around Pete's eye with a damp cloth as he sat on the edge of his bed. "Did you honestly think you could take him in a fight?"

"How did I know he didn't have a glass jaw? Every big oaf like him usually does." Pete probed the inside of his mouth with his tongue and was grateful to discover none of his teeth were loosened. "His must have been made of bulletproof glass." He winced as he lifted his arms to pull off his shirt. Claire was rummaging through the medicine chest in the bathroom. Funny, all the times he thought of her in his bedroom, he hadn't imagined it would be for this!

"I knew I shouldn't have gone to that dumb fest," Claire muttered. "Things always go wrong for me around here this time of year."

"Only because you let them." Pete squinted through his good eye as he peered over her shoulder into the mirror. "Wow, he did a good job, didn't he? I'm going to have a black eye," he said almost proudly, turning his head.

"If you aren't careful you'll have another one," she threatened, as she walked back to the bed. She scanned the eye, already turning every color of the rainbow. His knuckles were skinned and looked equally painful.

"Ow!" he yelled when she began dabbing his cuts with antiseptic.

"Just be quiet, killer." To Pete's sorrow, she didn't show one ounce of sympathy for his painful condition. "And if you're a good boy and don't cry, I'll give you a lollipop," she crooned.

His reply to her offer was decidedly obscene.

"Temper, temper."

"If you want to make it better, try a kiss," he muttered.

Claire stepped back and viewed her warrior. His lower lip was rapidly turning a glorious shade of purple. "I don't think you want anything to touch that lip."

He lightly tapped his chin. "Maybe here?"

She bent down and brushed her lips across his chin. "Better?" she breathed against his skin.

"Some. Maybe you could try here, too." He tapped his cheek.

She complied.

"And here?" He looked at her hopefully as he touched his forehead.

Claire marked the exact spot with her tongue. She noticed his breathing turned rougher with each caress. "Now where else are you convinced it hurts?"

Because Pete's lower lip had puffed up so much, it looked as if he was pouting. "Well, I know where it hurts, but I don't think you'd believe me."

Claire's eyes lowered to his lap. "Oh, I think I'd believe you," she murmured, moving until she sat in his lap with her arms looped around his neck. "You should be proud of yourself. You've successfully undermined all of my defenses."

Pete's breath caught in his throat, not from pain, but from expectation. "Are you going to stay with me to make sure I don't have convulsions during the night?"

She tipped her head to one side. "I should be angry with you for dragging me to the fest and for getting into a fight and for a lot of other things. But right now, none of them seem to matter."

"Is that good?"

"The best you'll get for now."

He circled her waist with his arms and slowly drew her with him as he dropped backward onto the bed.

"Suddenly I feel better," he announced in a husky voice.

She wiggled her hips against him. "I'd agree with that."

Pete groaned. "Claire, you're killing me."

"Oh, if I wanted to, I could hurt you real bad," she crooned, running her fingers down his straining zipper. "Would you like me to do something about it? Such as this?" She fingered the zipper tab before slowly lowering it. "Do I hear a yes?" she cooed. His moan was a good enough reply. She sat up straight, looking him right in the eye, she tugged off his slacks. "Pete Slattery, be prepared for the night of your life."

Pete should have known Claire wasn't one to indulge in false advertising. She seduced him the same way he'd been seducing her. His eyes grew wider as she loosened each button of her dress, displaying an expanse of bare skin. His breath caught when he saw the demibra she wore along with matching string-bikini panties. Her skin was a darker gold from her days in the sun, her nipples straining against the lace.

"I do hope you've been taking your vitamins, because you're going to need every ounce of energy you have," she whispered, leaning forward and trailing wet kisses from his throat, down his chest, to the waist-band of his briefs.

Pete was lost from that moment on.

Claire wooed him with her lips, her teeth and her tongue, with erotic words guaranteed to excite even a dead man. She caressed his wounds with her healing touch then moved on to other areas that required a great deal of attention.

When her cool hands were replaced by her hot mouth, Pete was convinced he'd died and gone to heaven. Waves of hot fire raced through his body.

"Claire," he rasped, reaching for her. "Claire." It was all he could say as he grasped her shoulders and pulled her upward for his kiss. Their mouths slanted and mated as he rolled her onto her back and set himself between her parted legs. He wanted to bury himself into her heat, but first he wanted her just as crazy with desire as he was. He dipped his head and pulled one nipple into his mouth, rolling his tongue around it and finding joy in her ecstatic whimpers.

"Now, Pete, please." She circled him with her cool fingers and drew him down into her.

From that moment Pete knew there was no going back.

Their loving was furious, then slowed as they silently communicated to each other they wanted it to last as long as possible.

At last Pete arched his body against Claire and they cried out in pleasure.

"Well." He dampened his dry lips with his tongue. "I'd say that went rather well."

Claire looked up at him, stunned. "Rather well? We almost killed each other!"

His boyish grin found life again. "Yeah, but we didn't, did we? You know what that means, don't you?"

She arched an eyebrow in that imperious gesture that Pete found more endearing than intimidating. "That we did something wrong?"

His expression sobered. He fingered loose strands of her hair that lay against his arm. "That we did something very right." He raised himself up on one elbow. "I can't imagine too many people have experienced what we just did, Claire."

"If that was so, the world population would be a great deal smaller."

Frustration darkened his eyes for a fleeting second. "That isn't what I mean and you know it."

Fear showed briefly in her eyes. She swiftly covered his lips with her fingertips. "Don't say it, Pete."

He grasped her wrist and pulled her restraining hand away, pausing only long enough to drop a kiss on her fingertips. "Love can happen that fast, you know. And there's been that spark of awareness between us from the beginning."

Pete still had to convince her that saying the magic words wouldn't turn her into a pumpkin. But Claire was not about to discuss something so serious. Instead, she chose another tack, running her palms down his back, feeling the damp, cool skin that rapidly warmed under her touch.

"Don't talk, just show me," she invited.

Pete was only too happy to comply.

SECURE IN THE CIRCLE of Pete's arms, Claire lay on her side, watching the dawn light creep through the sheer curtains. While she wanted to lie there, warm and comfortable, she felt the need to sort out her erratic thoughts. As she carefully disentangled herself from his arms, Pete mumbled something unintelligible and rolled over.

She draped his shirt around her as she wandered into the kitchen of his suite, stopping long enough to set up the coffeepot. She explored a bit while the coffee brewed. She smiled at the desk piled high with papers, then stilled when a name caught her eye. Slowly she picked up the document and began to read. By the time she reached the middle, she had to sit down before her legs gave way.

"Why?" she asked herself under her breath. "Why?"

She had to get out of there, away from Pete. Grabbing her purse, she hurried to her own room. Just in time. Seconds later, tears flowed down her face as she stood in the shower almost violently washing Pete's scent from her body.

Within fifteen minutes a more composed Claire knocked on Hannah's door.

"My, dear, you're up early," the older woman greeted her. "After what happened last night I thought you'd sleep late."

Praying her grandmother didn't mean what happened after they returned to the inn, Claire thrust at her the paper she'd taken from Pete's desk. "Why didn't you come to me?"

Hannah's smile faltered as she saw the first words. She handed the paper back to Claire. "I had my reasons," she said quietly.

"Why?" Pain laced Claire's voice.

"When you left for college you vowed never to return. I needed to know the inn would go to someone who would take care of it as I have all these years. Pete is that person," she said simply. "I told you in the beginning that I was selling the inn to him and that's why I wanted you to come back. He's been more than a manager from almost the beginning and I'm grateful for his help."

"That's not what I mean and you know it!" Claire blinked rapidly to hold back her angry tears. Hurt tears. "I'm talking about the business arrangement the two of you came to six months after he began working for you. The one that's spelled out here so eloquently. Why couldn't you tell me? Come to me? I'm your granddaughter. Shouldn't I have known? I would have helped you, you know that."

"Yes, I know that, but this is between Pete and myself. It has nothing to do with you, dear."

"The man purchased a half interest in the inn with the option to buy the the other half! How do you know he hasn't taken advantage of you because you were having financial difficulties? How do you know there isn't some hidden clause that allows him to take the inn away from you without paying you another cent?"

"You, of all people, should know Pete better than that," Hannah argued. "I'm not senile yet and I can read and understand a straightforward contract." Her eyes flickered to a spot just beyond Claire's shoulder. "Dear, don't say anything you'll later regret."

"Better yet, Claire, why don't you just ask me all of those questions?" the subject of their argument said quietly from behind Claire's back.

She spun around, holding the now crumpled paper in her hand. "Why did you invest in the inn?"

"That's Hannah's and my business."

"Did you take advantage of her once you learned I wanted nothing to do with running the inn?"

Her question etched his features with pain. "Can you honestly ask that after what we shared last night?"

She stiffened her resolve even though she knew her reply would wipe out all that they had nurtured, fragile as it still was. "I have to know. I have to protect her interests." She ignored her grandmother's protesting cry.

He looked at her sadly. "No, Claire, I don't think you do." He turned and walked away, head bent and shoulders hunched. The proud lover of the previous night had been destroyed by just a few well-placed words.

Chapter Nine

"RIGHT NOW, I don't even want to think of you as my granddaughter," Hannah informed Claire in an icy tone that sent shivers down the younger woman's spine. "What you did was one of the coldest, cruelest things I have ever witnessed. Pete gave this inn a new life. If it hadn't been for him, I would have had to close it down a long time ago. I suggest you go away and think about what you've done." She turned around and closed her door with a soft click that sounded louder and more intimidating than if she had slammed the door behind her.

Claire couldn't remember the last time her grandmother had been this angry with her, if ever. But right now she was in no mood to mend fences. Right now all she wanted to do was get as far away as possible.

PETE WAS IN his office when he saw the black car race down the road.

"You look as if you just lost your best friend."

He turned from his post by the window. "I guess you could say I have."

Hannah stepped inside and closed the door behind her. "She hasn't had the best luck with men."

He shrugged. "It's the old story. You always hope you'll be considered contrary to the norm. I shouldn't have let my ego get in the way."

She peered at him closely. "You're in love with her."

"She's stubborn—mule-headed like her grand-mother—" he flashed a grin to soften his words "—but there's something about her that I can't resist."

"Then I suggest you find her and straighten things out between you."

"She doesn't want to stay here and I don't want to leave."

"All I can say is if things are meant to be, the two of you will work it out."

He felt a glimmer of hope. "Think so?"

"What will it cost you to find out?"

Pete sighed. "Just my heart."

CLAIRE HAD NO IDEA where she was going when she left the inn. It wasn't until she parked the car that she realized she was at Pete's cove. She pulled off her shoes and walked down the narrow pathway leading to the water. Once there, she sank to her knees and watched the waves flow gently against the sand. Time stood still as she stared at the rippling water and let the waves soothe her jumbled mind.

"Fancy meeting you here." Pete dropped to the sand. He followed her gaze. He doubted she was watching anything in particular and soon turned his attention to her profile.

"I don't believe you took advantage of Gran." Her words were hardly audible.

"I'm glad to hear that."

"I lashed out because I was hurt. She didn't come to me for help. Didn't even say anything about it," Claire murmured, pushing strands of hair away from her face.

"She didn't feel it was right. I'd expressed interest in the inn from the beginning. When she realized expenses were higher than income, she came to me with the offer of the partnership. No one else knows about it," he explained. "That was by mutual consent. People are accustomed to Hannah being the center of Heart's Ease Inn. And this is a place I've basically been looking for for a long time now." He went on to explain. "I used to manage a hotel in Florida. It was geared for guests on the fast track, and after a while, I realized it wasn't for me. I decided I'd look around for a small inn and after about six months of knocking around, I ended up here."

Claire bowed her head. "Even though Gran knew I didn't want anything to do with the inn, I still wish she'd felt she could have confided in me." Her voice wobbled. "I know it's because of all the horrible things I've said about this town."

Pete took a chance in touching her arm. "It might have something to do with what happened to you long ago," he murmured. "But curses are meant to be broken, you know?"

Her smile was filled with sorrow. "All of that seems so long ago. The thing is, it didn't stop back then." She turned her head to look at him fully. "I was to be married on Valentine's Day a couple of years ago. I deliberately chose that date because I felt it would break my so-called curse. Instead, my wedding was also attended by several uninvited guests. It appeared my husband-to-be had a few too many wives he hadn't bothered to divorce. He was wanted by the authorities all along the eastern seaboard." Her shoulders rose and fell. "After that, I decided February 14 wasn't meant for me."

"We could break the curse together. We're meant to be, Claire, if you'll just admit it."

Her smile held a wealth of meaning. She slowly got to her feet. "Oh, Pete, I don't think I'm meant to fall in love." She briefly caressed his cheek and walked away.

While all of Pete's senses ordered him to go after her, he knew now wasn't the time. He also knew he had a lot of thinking to do, because he wasn't about to let her get away.

WHOEVER SAID misery loves company didn't know Claire. The last thing she wanted was companionship, even that of her grandmother. She'd spent the last two days driving all over the countryside, trying not to think about Pete. Since their last time together, she hadn't seen him once. It was almost as if he was keeping out of her way, as well.

"You can't mean to sit around and pout all evening," Hannah scolded during dinner.

Claire didn't have to look around to know Pete wasn't in the dining room. Her body told of his absence.

"I am not pouting."

"Good, then you'll attend the Valentine's Ball with me tonight."

Claire groaned. "No. There is no way I'll go to that."

"Scared of showing all those twits you went to school with that you're above the past?"

Her head snapped up. If there was anything she disliked, it was being taunted.

"I'm just not in the mood for a party," she haughtily declared.

"There's a new dress in your closet that I know will fit you. Be ready in forty-five minutes. You know how I hate to be late." Hannah sailed out of the room.

As curiosity got the best of her, Claire hurried to peek in her closet. She didn't have to hunt for the dress. It stood out from the rest of her wardrobe—a bold, blazing red.

"EVERYONE IS STARING at me," Claire hissed as they entered the hall.

"It's just your imagination." Hannah shook off her words. "Just smile and be cordial to everyone."

"Claire, look at you!" A man Claire vaguely remembered from high school grasped her wrists, holding her arms out to her sides as he leered at her in the red silk strapless gown that fell in clinging folds. "You look really hot tonight. Save me a dance."

She smiled and nodded and the moment he was gone turned to a beaming Hannah. "Who was he?"

"Blake Foster. The boy you swore you'd never forget."

Claire looked at her grandmother in astonishment. "The cutest boy in my senior class lost most of his hair, looks ten months pregnant and has bad breath?"

"Makes Pete look pretty good, doesn't he?"

She stiffened. "Pete looked pretty good to begin with." She sneaked a few glances around the hall but couldn't find a man with dazzling blond good looks.

Claire felt as if Hannah had conspired to keep her granddaughter from becoming a wallflower. A never-ending line of men approached Claire for a dance. As the evening wore on, she was convinced her feet would fall off if she wasn't allowed to sit down.

"Quite the party girl, aren't you?" Melissa commented when Claire took a respite in the ladies room to refresh her lipstick and perfume. "I guess you were relieved Blake didn't get drunk again and spill punch on your dress."

Claire replaced the top to her lipstick with a decided snap and dropped it in her purse before turning to the other woman.

"Melissa, you were a bitch all through high school and you're still a bitch," she announced. "The thing is, a girl could get away with those antics. A woman can't." She ignored the woman's shocked gasp. "So, let's clear the air, shall we? I went parking with Russ after the homecoming game our junior year while you were home in bed with the flu. He tried to get me in the back seat by claiming that you put out. I told him you could do whatever you wanted. I didn't. And it was your so-called friend, Toni, who told everyone you went all the way with him after the Christmas dance. To think you married the man. I hope you don't come down with the flu anymore."

"You—you . . ." Words wouldn't come to Melissa.

"Yes, I'm sure," Claire said merrily. "Trust me, Melissa, you're nothing compared to the barracuda I've dealt with over the years." With a mental pat on her own back, Claire left the ladies room as Melissa began sputtering curses at a suddenly defensive Toni. "My, that felt good," she thought to herself, feeling lighter at heart than she had in a long time. Her smile dimmed when she thought of Pete.

"Come on, Claire," one of her former classmates urged her onto the dance floor.

Laughing freely, she followed. As they danced, a commotion began at the main door.

"I sure hope some drunks haven't shown up to spoil the evening," her partner told her.

She craned her head but couldn't see anything. "Whatever it is, it's stopped now."

She received her first warning something was wrong when her partner swung her around and stopped cold. Claire looked over her shoulder, then slowly completed her spin. Laughter rose around her.

"What are you doing?" she gasped, staring at the figure in front of her.

"Ladies and gentlemen, if we're here to celebrate Valentine's Day, we must observe it properly," Pete declared in a loud voice. "I am here to see that that happen."

Pete's near-naked body was clothed in what looked like an oversize diaper, and a gold strapped quiver of arrows was slung across his chest. He carried a gold bow in one hand and a red rose in the other, which he then presented to Claire with an elaborate bow.

"To the lady who deserves this day of love more than anyone else." His eyes bored into hers as he straightened up.

"Slattery, only a drunken idiot would come in here looking like that," one of the men yelled above a wave of laughter.

"If I'm drunk, I'm drunk on love. I'm here to promote love, and the best way to do that is to carry away the lady of my choice." He stepped forward and before anyone realized his intent, he grabbed Claire around the waist and slung her over his shoulder.

"What are you doing?" she squeaked, finally coming out of her shocked stupor.

"What I should have done in the beginning. Now be quiet so I can get out of here fast. I'm freezing." Dipping his head right and left, he walked out accompanied by a round of applause.

"I hope there's a wedding planned!" Hannah called out. "I want great-grandchildren!"

"I'll leave that to you," Pete called back.

"Put me down!" Claire demanded once they were outside.

"Are you kidding? You're the only thing keeping me from frostbite, although you're not wearing much more than I am." He crossed the parking lot to his Jeep and dumped her inside. He reached across her for a jacket, and then braced his hands on the seat. "Okay, here's the plan. We get married as soon as possible. And don't worry about any wives, ex or otherwise, running around, because you're the only woman I've ever proposed to. As for working, I see no problem in that. If the town wants to grow even more, who better to make it happen than a good advertising executive. So what do you say?" He looked a little apprehensive, not to mention endearing, as if wondering if he might have gone too far.

Claire bit the inside of her cheek to keep from smiling. She wasn't about to agree too soon. Slowly, she looped her arms around his neck. "How do you know we won't turn out like the Bennetts in thirty years—or even the Hamiltons?"

Pete grinned. "I wouldn't mind us turning out like the Hamiltons, although I'd probably have to double up on my vitamin E. I'll certainly try my best," he promised, "but I wouldn't worry about either couple. The Bennetts announced this evening that they're going to try to work harder at speaking to each other directly, instead of through their lawyers. And rumor has it Chuck Hamilton told his wife there's more to marriage than sex, so they'll be seen outside their room every now and then.''

Pete wrapped his arms around her. ''Put me out of my misery. What about us?''

Claire brushed her mouth against his. ''I guess I can't say no to such a tantalizing offer,'' she murmured, tracing his upper lip with her tongue. ''After all, how many women can say they were swept off their feet by Cupid?''

Harlequin is proud to present our best authors, their best books and the best for your reading pleasure!

Throughout 1993, Harlequin will bring you exciting books by some of the top names in contemporary romance!

In February,
look for
Twist of Fate by

Hannah Jessett had been content with her quiet life. Suddenly she was the center of a corporate battle with wealthy entrepreneur Gideon Cage. Now Hannah must choose between the fame and money an inheritance has brought or a love that may not be as it appears.

Don't miss **TWIST OF FATE** ...
wherever Harlequin books are sold.

HARLEQUIN®

I N T R I G U E®

43 Light St.

It looks like a charming old building near the Baltimore waterfront, but inside 43 Light Street lurks danger ... and romance.

Labeled a "true master of intrigue" by *Rave Reviews*, bestselling author Rebecca York continues her exciting series with #213 HOPSCOTCH, coming to you in February.

Paralegal Noel Emery meets an enigmatic man from her past and gets swept away on a thrilling international adventure— where illusion and reality shift like the images in a deadly kaleidoscope....

"Ms. York ruthlessly boggles the brain and then twists our jangled nerves beyond the breaking point in this electrifying foray into hi-tech skullduggery and sizzling romance!"
—Melinda Helfer, *Romantic Times*

Don't miss Harlequin Intrigue #213 HOPSCOTCH!

LS93-1

Harlequin®
Historical

FLASH: ROMANCE MAKES HISTORY!

History the Harlequin way, that is. Our books invite you to experience a past you never read about in grammar school!

Travel back in time with us, and pirates will sweep you off your feet, cowboys will capture your heart, and noblemen will lead you to intrigue and romance, *always* romance—because that's what makes each Harlequin Historical title a thrilling escape for you, four times every month. Just think of the adventures you'll have!

So pick up a Harlequin Historical novel today, and relive history in your wildest dreams....

Where do you find hot Texas nights, smooth Texas charm and dangerously sexy cowboys?

Crystal Creek

DEEP IN THE HEART

Wedding Bells—Texas Style!

Even a Boston blue blood needs a Texas education. Ranch owner J. T. McKinney is handsome, strong, opinionated and totally charming. And he is determined to marry beautiful Bostonian Cynthia Page. However, the couple soon discovers a Texas cattleman's idea of marriage differs greatly from a New England career woman's!

CRYSTAL CREEK reverberates with the exciting rhythm of Texas. Each story features the rugged individuals who live and love in the Lone Star State. And each one ends with the same invitation...

Y'ALL COME BACK...REAL SOON!

Don't miss *DEEP IN THE HEART* by Barbara Kaye. Available in March wherever Harlequin books are sold.